**TRAVEL BACK THROUGH TIME TO THE
STORIES THAT BEGAN SOME OF SCIENCE
FICTION'S MOST IMPORTANT CAREERS. . . .**

From Murray Leinster and Arthur C. Clarke to Anne Mc-
Caffrey and Lois McMaster Bujold and their many talented
companions who have over the years taken us on such memorable expeditions to distant stars and times, here are seventeen maiden voyages for you to share. Some of them will
bring back fond memories, others may be new discoveries.
But all of these stories — and the authors' own introductions
to them — will offer a wonderful reading experience for
anyone who treasures science fiction.

"The Runaway Skyscraper" — It was a landmark building,
the kind of structure that gave you a sense of permanence
and stability . . . or did it?

"The Isolinguals" — Would civilization be destroyed by a
mysterious plague that seemed to randomly turn normal
people into their own ancestors?

"Barter" — Her life was totally out of control — until a strange
little man turned up at her door asking for ammonia. . . .

WONDROUS
BEGINNINGS

WONDROUS BEGINNINGS

Edited by
Steven H. Silver
and Martin H. Greenberg

DAW BOOKS, INC.
DONALD A. WOLLHEIM, FOUNDER
375 Hudson Street, New York, NY 10014
ELIZABETH R. WOLLHEIM
SHEILA E. GILBERT
PUBLISHERS
www.dawbooks.com

First Printing, January 2003
1 2 3 4 5 6 7 8 9

To Elaine

CONTENTS

INTRODUCTION

by Steven H. Silver

ON August 10, 1628, the *Vasa* was launched in Stockholm. The pride of the Swedish navy, this ship was going to usher in a new class of warship with its maiden voyage. Shortly after firing a salute, however, the ship overbalanced, capsized, and sank beneath the waves.

On April 12, 1981, the space shuttle *Columbia* lifted off from Cape Canaveral. The first of America's shuttle fleet, its maiden voyage led to more than twenty-five missions over the next twenty years with more to come, and a fleet of shuttles built, more or less, in *Columbia*'s image.

On May 11, 1820, the *H.M.S. Beagle* was launched from Woolwich Naval Yard on its maiden voyage. It wouldn't achieve fame for more than a decade, until Charles Darwin joined the *Beagle*'s crew during its circumnavigatory cruise. The *Beagle*'s maiden voyage is now all but forgotten.

This last type of first voyage, the type that occurs not with a shout but with a whimper, is the most typical announcement of a new entity plying the seas. It is also typical of science fiction authors, whose initial publications are frequently lost amidst the mildewing pages of vintage pulp magazines. These stories have the same effect as smashing a bottle against the prow of a ship. They announce that there is a new vessel in the world.

Surprisingly, it is not always easy to determine which story qualifies as an author's first story. In some cases, the author will sell one story, but his second sale is published first. In other cases, an author's first story will be a collaboration with another, more experienced author. In the science fiction field, many of the authors began publishing in fanzines before their first professional sale.

Although science fiction is known for exploring the future, it also has a strong tradition of remembering its roots. Authors write stories and books in response to what has been published before. Readers seem to consistently rediscover the authors who defined the genre, from H. G. Wells to Robert Heinlein. It isn't just the "big names" who are rediscovered. Recently, publishers have been reprinting the works of Eric Frank Russell, James H. Schmitz, and others whose names don't necessarily spring to mind when somebody mentions science fiction.

Some of the stories included in *Wondrous Beginnings* are quite rare. L. Sprague de Camp's first story, "The Isolinguals," was first published in 1937. Until now, it has only been reprinted once. Although many of de Camp's fans may be aware of the title, actually reading the story, in which may be seen glimmerings of many of de Camp's later stories, has been practically impossible. The story, however, contains many of the themes which de Camp would later examine in such major works as *Lest Darkness Fall*, "A Gun for Aristotle," and other novels and stories.

Another author who managed to work several themes into his first story is Orson Scott Card. Card, of course, expanded his premiere story "Ender's Game" into a Hugo and Nebula Award-winning novel. He has not only followed many of the themes of "Ender's Game" throughout the books that make up that series, he has also examined them in a number of his other science fiction, fantasy, and mainstream novels.

Not all authors make careers as novelists. Although Howard Waldrop has written a couple of novels, he has made his name as the author of wonderful, offbeat short stories. "Lunchbox," a story about a maiden space voyage, was only a starting indication of the unusual point of view Waldrop was capable of achieving.

The authors included in *Wondrous Beginnings* comprise a group whose careers range from several decades in which they have proved themselves grand masters to authors who are only now coming onto the scene and making a name for themselves. They are authors whose imaginative ships have only recently been launched, but who give every indication of becoming a *Columbia* of the genre.

INTRODUCTION TO
"THE RUNAWAY SKYSCRAPER"

by Betty Dehardit,
Murray Leinster's daughter

William Fitzgerald Jenkins was born on June 16, 1896, in Norfolk, Virginia, the son of George Briggs and Mary Murry Jenkins. As a sixth grade student in Mrs. Clay's room at the Charlotte Street School in Norfolk, he had his first works published. He was required to write a composition on Robert E. Lee in honor of Lee's 102nd birthday. School superintendent R. A. Doble saw the composition and had it printed in the *Virginian Pilot* on January 28, 1909. Mr. Doble said that "he considered (it) a very remarkable school work . . . a notable fact about it being that the lad, who is only twelve years of age, wrote it offhand, in the presence of his teacher without any opportunity for outside coaching or study." A Confederate veteran read the story and sent young Will five dollars, making the piece his first "paid" publication. He used the money to build a glider and flew it successfully at Sandstorm Hill, Cape Henry, Virginia. Then he submitted an article on the glider to *Fly*, the first aeronautical magazine, and they gave him a prize for his achievement. Because of these accomplishments, many years later he turned to writing.

Will's education terminated after only three month of the eighth grade, ending his dream of becoming a physicist. He moved with his mother and older brother to Newark, New Jersey. To help with finances, he took a job as an office boy and then as a bookkeeper for the Prudential Insurance Company in Newark and wrote at night. Every day he would write 1,000 words and tear them up. At seventeen he began selling epigrams and fillers to *Smart Set*. Finally, he began selling stories to the pulps. When this happened, George Jean Nathan, editor of *Smart Set* suggested that he not use his real name in these inferior magazines, but save it for his magazine. Thus "Murray Leinster" was concocted from Jenkins' mother's maiden name and an ancestor, the Duke of Leinster, of Leinster County, Ireland. He went back to using his real name when he began to write westerns and to sell to the "slick" magazines.

He resigned his position with Prudential on his twenty-first birthday when he began to sell regularly to the pulps, never to work for anyone else again except the Office of War Information during World War II.

In 1919, Jenkins wrote "The Runaway Skyscraper." Sam Moskowitz, in *Seekers of Tomorrow*, writes, " 'The whole thing began when the clock on the Metropolitan Tower began to run backward.' That was the opening sentence of 'The Runaway Skyscraper' in the February 22, 1919, issue of *Argosy*." And with those words Murray Leinster began his science-fiction career. Already a veteran with two years of steady magazine sales behind him, young Leinster had sold *Argosy* a series of Happy Village stories and was fed up with predigested pablum. There would be no more in that series for a while, he wrote editor Mathew White, Jr., since he was working on a story opening with the lines, "The whole thing began when the clock on the Metropolitan Tower began to run backward."

"By return mail," recalled Leinster, "I got a letter telling me to let him see it when I finished. So I had to write it or admit I was lying.

"At the time the story was written, the home office of the Metropolitan Insurance Company was one of the tallest and most distinctive skyscrapers in New York, topped by a clock that was a city landmark. Readers of *Argosy* were enthralled to read of the building's remarkable journey in time back to a period hundreds of years before white men appeared on this continent. Some two thousand workers in the skyscraper thus find themselves confronted with the task of obtaining enough food to eat and suitable fuel to run the building's mammoth generators."

THE RUNAWAY SKYSCRAPER

by Murray Leinster

THE whole thing started when the clock on the Metropolitan Tower began to run backward. It was not a graceful proceeding. The hands had been moving onward in their customary deliberate fashion, slowly and thoughtfully, but suddenly the people in the offices near the clock's face heard an ominous creaking and groaning. There was a slight, hardly discernible shiver through the tower, and then something gave with a crash. The big hands on the clock began to move backward.

Immediately after the crash all the creaking and groaning ceased, and instead the usual quiet again hung over everything. One or two occupants of the upper offices put their heads out into the halls, but the elevators were running as usual, the lights were burning, and all seemed calm and peaceful. The clerks and stenographers went back to their ledgers and typewriters, the business callers returned to the discussion of their errands, and the ordinary course of business was resumed.

Arthur Chamberlain was dictating a letter to Estelle Woodward, his sole stenographer. When the crash came, he paused, listened, and then resumed his task.

It was not a difficult one. Talking to Estelle Woodward was at no time an onerous duty, but it must be admitted that Arthur Chamberlain found it difficult to keep his conversation strictly upon his business.

He was at this time engaged in dictating a letter to his principal creditors, the Gary & Milton Company, explaining that their demand for the immediate payment of the installment then due upon his office furniture was untimely and unjust. A young and budding engineer in New York never has too much money, and when he is young as Arthur Chamberlain was, and as fond of pleasant company, and not too fond of economizing, he is liable to find all demands for payment untimely and he usually considers them unjust as well. Arthur finished dictating the letter and sighed.

"Miss Woodward," he said regretfully, "I am afraid I shall never make a successful man."

Miss Woodward shook her head vaguely. She did not seem to take his remark very seriously, but then she had learned never to take any of his remarks seriously. She had been puzzled at first by his manner of treating everything with a half-joking pessimism, but now ignored it.

She was interested in her own problems. She had suddenly decided that she was going to be an old maid, and it bothered her. She had discovered that she did not like any one well enough to marry, and she was in her twenty-second year.

She was not a native of New York, and the few young men she had met there she did not care for. She had regretfully decided she was too finicky, too fastidious, but could not seem to help herself. She could not understand their absorption in boxing and baseball, and she did not like the way they danced.

She had considered the matter and decided that she would have to reconsider her former opinion of women who did not marry. Heretofore she had thought there must be something the matter with them. Now she believed that she would come to their own estate, and probably for the same reason. She could not fall in love and she wanted to.

She read all the popular novels and thrilled at the love scenes contained in them, but when any of the young men she knew became in the slightest degree sentimental, she found herself bored, and disgusted with herself for being bored. Still, she could not help it, and was struggling to reconcile herself to a life without romance.

She was far too pretty for that, of course, and Arthur Chamberlain often longed to tell her how pretty she really was, but her abstracted air held him at arm's length.

He lay back at ease in his swivel-chair and considered, looking at her with unfeigned pleasure. She did not notice it, for she was so much absorbed in her own thoughts that she rarely noticed anything he said or did when they were not in the line of her duties.

"Miss Woodward," he repeated, "I said I think I'll never make a successful man. Do you know what that means?"

She looked at him mutely, polite inquiry in her eyes.

"It means," he said gravely, "that I am going broke. Unless

something turns up in the next three weeks, or a month at the latest, I'll have to get a job."

"And that means—" she asked.

"All this will go to pot," he explained with a sweeping gesture. "I thought I'd better tell you as much in advance as I could."

"You mean you're going to give up your office—and me?" she asked, a little alarmed.

"Giving up you will be the harder of the two," he said with a smile, "but that's what it means. You'll have no difficulty finding a new place, with three weeks in which to look for one, but I'm sorry."

"I'm sorry, too, Mr. Chamberlain," she said, her brow puckered.

She was not really frightened, because she knew she could get another position, but she became aware of rather more regret than she had expected.

"Jove!" said Arthur suddenly. "It's getting dark, isn't it?"

It was. It was growing dark with unusual rapidity. Arthur went to his window and looked out.

"Funny," he remarked in a moment or two. "Things don't look just right, down there, somehow. There are very few people about."

He watched in growing amazement. Lights came on in the streets below, but none of the buildings lighted up. It grew darker and darker.

"It shouldn't be dark at this hour!" Arthur exclaimed.

Estelle went to the window by his side.

"It looks awfully queer," she agreed. "It must be an eclipse or something."

They heard doors open in the hall outside, and Arthur ran out. The halls were beginning to fill with excited people.

"What on Earth's the matter?" asked a worried stenographer.

"Probably an eclipse," replied Arthur. "Only it's odd we didn't read about it in the papers."

He glanced along the corridor. No one else seemed better informed than he, and he went back into his office.

Estelle turned from the window as he appeared.

"The streets are deserted," she said in a puzzled tone. "What's the matter? Did you hear?"

Arthur shook his head and reached for the telephone.

"I'll call up and find out," he said confidently. He held the receiver to his ear. "What the—" he exclaimed. "Listen to this!"

A small-sized roar was coming from the receiver. Arthur hung up and turned a blank face upon Estelle.

"Look!" she said suddenly, and pointed out of the window.

All the city was now lighted up, and such of the signs as they could see were brilliantly illumined. They watched in silence. The streets once more seemed filled with vehicles. They darted along, their headlamps lighting up the roadway brilliantly. There was, however, something strange even about their motion. Arthur and Estelle watched in growing amazement and perplexity.

"Are—are you seeing what I am seeing?" asked Estelle breathlessly. "I see them going backward!"

Arthur watched and collapsed into a chair.

"For the love of Mike!" he exclaimed softly.

He was roused by another exclamation from Estelle.

"It's getting light again," she said.

Arthur rose and went eagerly to the window. The darkness was becoming less intense, but in a way Arthur could hardly credit.

Far to the west, over beyond the Jersey hills—easily visible from the height at which Arthur's office was located—a faint light appeared in the sky, grew stronger and then took on a reddish tint. That, in turn, grew deeper, and at last the sun appeared, rising unconcernedly in the west.

Arthur gasped. The streets below continued to be thronged with people and motorcars. The sun was traveling with extraordinary rapidity. It rose overhead, and as if by magic the streets were thronged with people. Everyone seemed to be running at top speed. The few teams they saw moved at a breakneck pace—backward! In spite of the suddenly topsy-turvy state of affairs, there seemed to be no accidents.

Arthur put his hand to his head.

"Miss Woodward," he said pathetically. "I'm afraid I've gone crazy. Do you see things I do?"

Estelle nodded. Her eyes were wide open.

"What is the matter?" she asked helplessly.

She turned again to the window. The square was almost empty once more. The motor cars still traveling about the streets were going so swiftly they were hardly visible. Their speed seemed to increase steadily. Soon it was almost impossible to distinguish them, and only a grayish blur marked their paths along Fifth Avenue and Twenty-third Street.

It grew dusk, and then rapidly dark. As their office was on the western side of the building, they could not see the sun had sunk in the east, but subconsciously they realized that this must be the case.

In silence they watched the panorama grow black except for the streetlamps, remain thus for a time, and then suddenly spring into brilliantly illuminated activity.

Again this lasted for a little while, and the west once more began to glow. The sun rose somewhat more hastily from the Jersey hills and began to soar overhead, but very soon darkness fell again. With hardly an interval the city became illuminated, and the west grew red once more.

"Apparently," said Arthur, steadying his voice with a conscious effort, "there's been a cataclysm somewhere, the direction of the Earth's rotation has been reversed, and its speed immensely increased. It seems to take only about five minutes for a rotation now."

As he spoke, darkness fell for the third time. Estelle turned from the window with a white face.

"What's going to happen?" she cried.

"I don't know," answered Arthur. "The scientific fellows tell us if the Earth were to spin fast enough, the centrifugal force would throw us all off into space. Perhaps that's what's going to happen."

Estelle sank into a chair and stared at him, appalled. There was a sudden explosion behind them. With a start, Estelle jumped to her feet and turned. A little gilt clock over her typewriter desk lay in fragments. Arthur hastily glanced at his own watch.

"Great bombs and little cannon balls!" he shouted. "Look at this!"

His watch trembled and quivered in his hand. The hands were going around so swiftly it was impossible to watch the minute-hand, and the hour-hand traveled like the wind.

While they looked, it made two complete revolutions. In one of them the glory of daylight had waxed, waned, and vanished. In the other, darkness reigned except for the glow from the electric light overhead.

There was a sudden tension and catch in the watch. Arthur dropped it instantly. It flew to pieces before it reached the floor.

"If you've got a watch," Arthur ordered swiftly, "stop it this instant!"

Estelle fumbled at her wrist. Arthur tore the watch from her hand and threw open the case. The machinery inside was going so swiftly it was hardly visible. Relentlessly, Arthur jabbed a penholder in the works. There was a sharp click, and the watch was still.

Arthur ran to the window. As he reached it, the sun rushed up, day lasted a moment, there was darkness, and then the sun appeared again.

"Miss Woodward!" Arthur ordered suddenly. "Look at the ground!"

Estelle glanced down. The next time the sun flashed into view she gasped.

The ground was white with snow.

"What has happened?" she demanded, terrified. "Oh, what has happened?"

Arthur fumbled at his chin awkwardly, watching the astonishing panorama outside. There was hardly any distinguishing between the times the sun was up and the times it was below now, as the darkness and light followed each other so swiftly the effect was the same as one of the old flickering motion pictures.

As Arthur watched, this effect became more pronounced. The tall Fifth Avenue Building across the way began to disintegrate. In a moment, it seemed, there was only a skeleton there. Then that vanished, story by story. A great cavity in the earth appeared, and then another building became visible, a smaller, brown-stone unimpressive structure.

With bulging eyes Arthur stared across the city. Except for the flickering, he could see almost clearly now.

He no longer saw the sun rise and set. There was merely a streak of unpleasantly brilliant light across the sky. Bit by bit, building by building, the city began to disintegrate and become replaced by smaller, dingier buildings. In a little while those began to disappear and leave gaps where they vanished.

Arthur strained his eyes and looked far downtown. He saw a forest of masts and spars along the waterfront for a moment, and when he turned his eyes again to the scenery near him it was almost barren of houses, and what few showed were mean, small residences, apparently set in the midst of farms and plantations.

Estelle was sobbing.

"Oh, Mr. Chamberlain," she cried. "What is the matter? What has happened?"

Arthur had lost his fear of what their fate would be in his absorbing interest in what he saw. He was staring out of the window, wide-eyed, lost in the sight before him. At Estelle's cry, however, he reluctantly left the window and patted her shoulder awkwardly.

"I don't know how to explain it," he said uncomfortably, "but it's obvious that my first surmise was all wrong. The speed of the Earth's rotation can't have been increased, because if it had to the extent we see, we'd have been thrown off into space long ago. But—have you read anything about the Fourth Dimension?"

Estelle shook her head hopelessly.

"Well, then, have you ever read anything by Wells? *The Time Machine*, for instance?"

Again she shook her head.

"I don't know how I'm going to say it so you'll understand, but time is just as much a dimension as length and breadth. From what I can judge, I'd say there has been an earthquake, and the ground has settled a little with our building on it, only instead of settling down toward the center of the Earth, or sidewise, it's settled in this Fourth Dimension."

"But what does that mean?" asked Estelle uncomprehendingly.

"If the Earth had settled down, we'd have been lower. If it had settled to one side we'd have been moved one way or another, but as it's settled back in the Fourth Dimension, we're going back in time."

"Then—"

"We're in a runaway skyscraper, bound for some time back before the discovery of America—"

It was very still in the office. Except for the flickering outside everything seemed very much as usual. The electric light burned steadily, but Estelle was sobbing with fright, and Arthur was trying vainly to console her.

"Have I gone crazy?" she demanded between her sobs.

"Not unless I've gone mad, too," said Arthur soothingly.

The excitement had quite a soothing effect upon him. He had ceased to feel afraid, but was simply waiting to see what had happened. "We're way back before the founding of New York now, and still going strong."

"Are you sure that's what has happened?"

"If you look outside," he suggested, "you'll see the seasons following each other in reverse order. One moment the snow covers all the ground, then you catch a glimpse of autumn foliage, then summer follows, and next spring."

Estelle glanced out of the window and covered her eyes.

"Not a house," she said despairingly. "Not a building. Nothing, nothing, nothing!"

Arthur slipped his arm about her and patted hers comfortingly.

"It's all right," he reassured her. "We'll bring up presently, and there'll be. There's nothing to be afraid of."

She rested her head on his shoulder and sobbed hopelessly for a little while longer, but presently quieted. Then, suddenly, realizing that Arthur's arm was about her and that she was crying on his shoulder, she sprang away, blushing crimson.

Arthur walked to the window.

"Look there!" he exclaimed, but it was too late. "I'll swear to it I saw the *Half-Moon*, Hudson's ship," he declared excitedly. "We're way back now, and don't seem to be slackening up, either."

Estelle came to the window by his side. The rapidly changing scene before her made her gasp. It was no longer possible to distinguish night from day.

A wavering streak, moving first to the right and then to the left, showed where the sun flashed across the sky.

"What makes the sun wobble so?" she asked.

"Moving north and south of the equator," Arthur explained casually. "When it's farthest south—to the left—there's always snow on the ground. When it's farthest right it's summer. See how green it is?"

A few moments' observation corroborated his statement.

"I'd say," Arthur remarked reflectively, "that it takes about fifteen seconds for the sun to make the round trip from farthest north to farthest south." He felt his pulse. "Do you know the normal rate of the heartbeat? We can judge time that way. A clock will go all to pieces, of course."

"Why did your watch explode—and the clock?"

"Running forward in time unwinds a clock, doesn't it?" asked Arthur. "It follows, of course, that when you move it backward in time it winds up. When you move it too far back, you wind it so tightly that the spring just breaks to pieces."

He paused a moment, his fingers on his pulse.

"Yes, it takes about fifteen seconds for all the four seasons to pass. That means we're going backward in time about four years a minute. If we go on at this rate in another hour we'll be back in the time of the Northmen, and will be able to tell if they did discover America, after all."

"Funny we don't hear any noises," Estelle observed. She had caught some of Arthur's calmness.

"It passes so quickly that though our ears hear it, we don't separate the sounds. If you'll notice, you do hear a sort of humming. It's very high-pitched, though."

Estelle listened, but could hear nothing.

"No matter," said Arthur. "It's probably a little higher than your ears can catch. Lots of people can't hear a bat squeak."

"I never could," said Estelle. "Out in the country, where I come from, other people could hear them, but I couldn't."

They stood a while in silence, watching.

"When are we going to stop?" asked Estelle uneasily. "It seems as if we're going to keep on indefinitely."

"I guess we'll stop all right," Arthur reassured her. "It's obvious that whatever it was, it only affected our own building, or we'd see some other one with us. It looks like a fault or a flaw in the rock the building rests on. And that can only give so far."

Estelle was silent for a moment.

"Oh, I can't be sane!" she burst out semi-hysterically. "This can't be happening!"

"You aren't crazy," said Arthur sharply. "You're as sane as I am. Just something queer is happening. Buck up. Say something sensible, and you'll know you're all right. But don't get frightened now. There'll be plenty to get frightened about later."

The grimness in his tone alarmed Estelle. "What are you afraid of?" she asked quickly.

"Time enough to worry when it happens," Arthur retorted briefly.

"You—you aren't afraid we'll go back before the beginning of the world, are you?" asked Estelle in a sudden excess of fright.

Arthur shook his head.

"Tell me," said Estelle more quietly, getting a grip on herself. "I won't mind. But please tell me."

Arthur glanced at her. Her face was pale, but there was more resolution in it than he had expected to find.

"I'll tell you, then," he said reluctantly. "We're going back a little faster than we were, and the flaw seems to be a deeper one than I thought. At the roughest kind of an estimate, we're all of a thousand years before the discovery of America now, and I think nearer three or four. And we're gaining speed all the time. So, though I am as sure as I can be of anything that we'll stop this cave-in eventually, I don't know where. It's like a crevasse in the earth opened by an earthquake which may be only a few feet deep, or it may be hundreds of yards, or even a mile or two. We started off smoothly. We're going at a terrific rate. What will happen when we stop?"

Estelle caught her breath.

"What?" she asked quietly.

"I don't know," said Arthur in an irritated tone, to cover his apprehension. "How could I know?"

Estelle turned from him to the window again.

"Look!" she said, pointing.

The flickering had begun again. While they stared, hope springing up once more in their hearts; it became more pronounced. Soon they could distinctly see the difference between day and night.

They were slowing up! The white snow on the ground remained there for an appreciable time; autumn lasted quite a while. They could catch the flashes of the sun as it made its revolutions now, instead of seeming like a ribbon of fire. At last day lasted all of fifteen or twenty minutes.

It grew longer and longer. Then half an hour, then an hour. The sun wavered in mid-heaven and was still.

Far below them, the watchers in the tower of the skyscraper saw trees swaying and a bending in the wind. Though there was not a house or a habitation to be seen and a dense forest covered all of Manhattan Island, such of the world as they could see looked normal. Whatever, or rather in whatever epoch of time they were, they had arrived.

Arthur caught at Estelle's arm, and the two made a dash for the elevators. Fortunately one was standing still, the door opened, on their floor. The elevator-boy had deserted his post and was looking with all the rest, at the strange landscape that surrounded them.

No sooner had the pair reached the car, however, than the boy came hurrying along the corridor, three or four other people following him also at a run. Without a word the boy rushed inside, the others crowded after him, and the car shot downward, all of the newcomers panting from their sprint.

Theirs was the first car to reach bottom. They rushed out and to the western door. Here, where they had been accustomed to see Madison Square spread out before them, a clearing of perhaps half an acre in extent showed itself. Where their eyes instinctively looked for the dark bronze fountain, near which soap-box orators aforetime held sway, they saw a tent, a wigwam of hides and bark gaily painted. And before the wigwam were two or three brown-skinned Indians, utterly petrified with astonishment.

Behind the first wigwam were others, painted like the first with daubs of brightly colored clay. From them, too, Indians issued, and stared in incredulous amazement, their eyes growing wider and wider. When the group of white people confronted the Indians, there was a moment's deathlike silence. Then, with a wild yell, the redskins broke and ran, not stopping to gather together their belongings, nor pausing for even a second glance at the weird strangers who invaded their domain.

Arthur took two or three deep breaths of the fresh air and found himself even then comparing its quality with that of the city. Estelle stared about her with unbelieving eyes. She turned and saw the great bulk of the office building behind her, then faced this small clearing with a virgin forest on its farther side.

She found herself trembling from some undefined cause. Arthur glanced at her. He saw the trembling and knew she would have a fit of nerves in a moment if something did not come up demanding instant attention.

"We'd better take a look at this village," he said in an offhand voice. "We can probably find out how long ago it is from the weapons and so on."

He grasped her arm firmly and led her in the direction of the tents. The other people, left behind, displayed their emotions in different ways. Two or three of them—women—sat frankly down on the steps and indulged in tears of bewilderment, fright, and relief in a peculiar combination defying analysis. Two or three of the men swore, in shaken voices.

Meantime, the elevators inside the building were rushing and clanging, and the hall filled with a white-faced mob, desperately anxious to find out what had happened and why. The people poured out of the door and stared about blankly. There was a peculiar expression of doubt on every one of their faces. Each one was asking himself if he were awake, and having proved that by pinches, openly administered, the next query was whether they had gone mad.

Arthur led Estelle cautiously among the tents.

The village contained about a dozen wigwams. Most of them were made of strips of birchbark, cleverly overlapping each other, the seams cemented with gum. All had hide flaps for doors, and one or two were built almost entirely of hides, sewed together with strips of sinew.

Arthur made only a cursory examination of the village. His principal motive in taking Estelle there was to give her some mental occupation to ward off the reaction from the excitement of the cataclysm.

He looked into one or two of the tents and found merely couches of hides, with minor domestic utensils scattered about. He brought from one tent a bow and a quiver of arrows. The workmanship was good, but very evidently the maker had no knowledge of metal tools.

Arthur's acquaintance with archaeological subjects was very slight, but he observed that the arrowheads were chipped, and not rubbed smooth. They were attached to the shafts with strips of gut or tendon.

Arthur was still pursuing his investigation when a sob from Estelle made him look at her.

"Oh, what are we going to do?" she asked tearfully. "What are we going to do? Where are we?"

"You mean, when are we," Arthur corrected with a grim smile. "I don't know. Way back before the discovery of America, though. You can see in everything in the village that there isn't a trace of European civilization. I suspect that we are several thousand years back. I can't tell, of course, but this pottery makes me think so. See this bowl?"

He pointed to a bowl of red clay lying on the ground before one of the wigwams.

"If you'll look, you'll see that it isn't really pottery at all. It's a basket that was woven of reeds and then smeared with clay to make it fire-resisting. The people who made that didn't know about baiting clay to make it stay put. When America was discovered, nearly all the tribes knew something about pottery."

"But what are we going to do?" Estelle tearfully insisted.

"We're going to muddle along as well as we can," answered Arthur cheerfully, "until we can get back to where we started from. Maybe the people back in the twentieth century can send a relief party after us. When the skyscraper vanished, it must have left a hole of some sort, and it may be possible for them to follow us down."

"If that's so," said Estelle quickly, "why can't we climb up it without waiting for them to come after us?"

Arthur scratched his head. He looked across the clearing at the skyscraper. It seemed to rest very solidly on the ground. He looked up. The sky seemed normal.

"To tell the truth," he admitted, "there doesn't seem to be any hole. I said that more to cheer you up than anything else."

Estelle clenched her hands tightly and took a grip on herself.

"Just tell me the truth," she said quietly. "I was rather foolish, but tell me what you honestly think."

Arthur eyed her keenly.

"In that case," he said reluctantly, "I'll admit we're in a pretty bad fix. I don't know what has happened, how it happened, or anything about it. I'm just going to keep on going until I see a way clear to get out of this mess. There are two thousand of us people, more or less, and among all of us we must be able to find a way out."

Estelle had turned very pale.

"We're in no great danger from Indians," went on Arthur thoughtfully, "or from anything else that I know of except one thing."

"What is that?" asked Estelle quickly.

Arthur shook his head and led her back toward the skyscraper, which was now thronged with the people from all the floors who had come down to the ground and were standing excitedly about the concourse asking each other what had happened.

Arthur led Estelle to one of the corners.

"Wait for me here," he ordered. "I'm going to talk to this crowd."

He pushed his way through until he could reach the confec-

tionery and newsstand in the main hallway. Here he climbed up
on the counter and shouted:

"People, listen to me! I'm going to tell you what's happened!"

In an instant there was dead silence. He found himself the
center of a sea of white faces, every one contorted with fear and
anxiety.

"To begin with," he said confidently, "there's nothing to be
afraid of. We're going to get back where we started from! I
don't know how, yet, but we'll do it. Don't get frightened. Now
I'll tell you what's happened."

He rapidly sketched out for them, in words as simple as he
could make them, his theory that a flaw in the rock on which
the foundations rested had developed and let the skyscraper
sink, not downward, but into the Fourth Dimension.

"I'm an engineer," he finished. "What nature can do, we can
imitate. Nature let us into this hole. We'll climb out. In the
meantime, matters are serious. We needn't be afraid of not getting back. We'll do that. What we've got to fight is — starvation!"

"We've got to fight starvation, and beat it," Arthur continued
doggedly. "I'm telling you this now because I want you to
begin right at the beginning and pitch in and help. We have very
little food and a lot of us to eat it. First, I want some volunteers
to help with rationing. Next, I want every ounce of food in this
place put under guard where it can be served to those who need
it most. Who will help?"

The swift succession of shocks had paralyzed the faculties
of most of the people there, but half a dozen moved forward.
Among them was a single gray-haired man with an air of accustomed authority. Arthur recognized him as the president of
the bank on the ground floor.

"I don't know who you are or if you're right in saying what
has happened," said the gray-haired man. "But I see something's got to be done, and — well, for the time being I'll take
your word for what that is. Later on, we'll thrash this matter
out."

Arthur nodded. He bent over and spoke in a low voice to the
gray-haired man, who moved away.

"Grayson, Walters, Terhune, Simpson and Forsythe, come
here," the gray-haired man called at the doorway. A number of

men began to press dazedly toward him. Arthur resumed his harangue.

"You people—those of you who aren't too dazed to think—are remembering there's a restaurant in the building and no need to starve. You're wrong. There are nearly two thousand of us here. That means six thousand meals a day. We've got to have nearly ten tons of food a day, and we've got to have it at once."

"Hunt," someone suggested.

"I saw Indians," someone else shouted. "Can we trade with them?"

"We can hunt and we can trade with the Indians," Arthur admitted, "but we need food by the ton—by the ton, people! The Indians don't store up supplies, and, besides, they're much too scattered to have a surplus for us. But we've got to have food. Now, how many of you know anything about hunting, fishing, trapping, or any possible way of getting food?"

There were a few hands raised—pitifully few. Arthur saw Estelle's hand up.

"Very well," he said. "Those of you who raised your hands then, come with me up on the second floor, and we'll talk it over. The rest of you try to conquer your fright, and don't go outside for a while. We've got some things to attend to before it will be quite safe for you to venture out. And keep away from the restaurant. There are armed guards over the food. Before we pass it out indiscriminately, we'll see to it there's more for tomorrow and the next day."

He stepped down from the counter and moved toward the stairway. It was not worthwhile to use the elevator for the ride of only one floor. Estelle managed to join him, and they mounted the steps together.

"Do you think we'll pull through all right?" she asked quietly.

"We've got to!" Arthur told her, setting his chin firmly. "We've simply got to."

The gray-haired president of the bank was waiting for them at the top of the stairs. "My name is Van Deventer," he said, shaking hands with Arthur, who gave his own name.

"Where shall our emergency council sit?" he asked.

"The bank has a boardroom right over the safety vault. I daresay we can accommodate everybody there—everybody in the council, anyway."

Arthur followed into the boardroom, and the others trooped in after him.

"I'm just assuming temporary leadership," Arthur explained, "because it's imperative some things be done at once. Later on we can talk about electing officials to direct our activities. Right now we need food. How many of you can shoot?"

About a quarter of the hands were raised. Estelle's was among the number.

"How many are fishermen?"

A few more went up.

"What do the rest of you do?"

There was a chorus of "gardener." "I have a garden in my yard," "I grow peaches in New Jersey," and three men confessed that they raised chickens as a hobby.

"We'll want you gardeners in a little while. Don't go yet. But the most important are huntsmen and fishermen. Have any of you weapons in your offices?"

A number had revolvers, but only one man had a shotgun and shells.

"I was going on my vacation this afternoon straight from the office," he explained, "and have all my vacation tackle."

"Good man!" Arthur exclaimed. "You'll go after the heavy game."

"With a shotgun?" the sportsman asked, aghast.

"If you get close to them, a shotgun will do as well as anything, and we can't waste a shell on every bird or rabbit. Those shells of yours are precious. You other fellows will have to turn fishermen for a while. Your pistols are no good for hunting."

"The watchmen at the bank have riot guns," said Van Deventer, "and there are one or two repeating rifles there. I don't know about ammunition."

"Good! I don't mean about the ammunition, but about the guns. We'll hope for the ammunition. You fishermen get to work to improvise tackle out of anything you can get hold of. Will you do that?"

A series of nods answered his question.

"Now for the gardeners. You people will have to roam through the woods in company with the hunters and locate anything in the way of edibles that grows. Do all of you know what wild plants look like? I mean wild fruits and vegetables that are good to eat?"

A few of them nodded, but the majority looked dubious. The

consensus seemed to be that they would try. Arthur seemed a little discouraged.

"I guess you're the man to tell about the restaurant," Van Deventer said quietly. "And as this is the food commission, or something of that sort, everybody here will be better for hearing it. Anyway, everybody will have to know it before night. I took over the restaurant as you suggested, and posted some of the men from the bank that I knew I could trust about the doors. But there was hardly any use in doing it.

"The restaurant stocks up in the afternoon, as most of its business is in the morning and at noon. It only carries a day's stock of foodstuffs, and the—cataclysm, or whatever it was, came at three o'clock. There is practically nothing in the place. We couldn't make sandwiches for half the women that are caught with us, let alone the men. Everybody will go hungry tonight. There will be no breakfast tomorrow, nor anything to eat until we either make arrangements with the Indians for some supplies or else get food for ourselves."

Arthur leaned his jaw on his hand and considered. A slow flush crept over his cheek. He was getting his fighting blood up. At school, when he began to flush slowly, his schoolmates had known the symptom and avoided his wrath. Now he was growing angry with mere circumstances, but it would be nonetheless unfortunate for those circumstances.

"Well," he said at last deliberately, "we've got to—What's that?"

There was a great creaking and groaning. Suddenly a sort of vibration was felt underfoot. The floor began to take on a slight slant.

"Great heaven!" someone cried. "The building's turning over and we'll be buried in the ruins!"

The tilt of the floor became more pronounced. An empty chair slid to one end of the room. There was a crash.

Arthur woke to find someone tugging at his shoulders, trying to drag him from beneath the heavy table, which had wedged itself across his feet and pinned him fast, while a flying chair had struck him on the head.

"Oh, come and help," Estelle's voice was calling desperately. "Somebody come and help! He's caught in here!"

She was sobbing in a combination of panic and some unknown emotion. "Help me, please!" she gasped; then her voice broke despondently, but she never ceased to tug ineffectually at Chamberlain, trying to drag him out of the mass of crumpled wreckage.

Arthur moved a little, dazedly.

"Are you alive?" she called anxiously. "Are you alive? Hurry, oh, hurry and wiggle out. The building's falling to pieces."

"I'm all right," Arthur said weakly. "You get out before it all comes down."

"I won't leave you," she declared. "Where are you caught? Are you badly hurt? Hurry, please hurry!"

Arthur stirred, but could not loosen his feet. He half-rolled over, and the table moved as if it had been precariously balanced, and slid heavily to one side. With Estelle still tugging at him, he managed to get to his feet on the slanting floor and stared about him.

Arthur continued to stare about.

"No danger," he said weakly. "Just the floor of the one room gave way. The aftermath of the rock-flaw."

He made his way across the splintered flooring and piled-up chairs.

"We're on top of the safe-deposit vault," he said. "That's why we didn't fall all the way to the floor below. I wonder how we're going to get down."

Estelle followed him, still frightened for fear of the building falling upon them. Some of the long floorboards stretched over the edge of the vault and rested on a tall, bronze grating that protected the approach to the massive strong-box. Arthur tested them with his foot.

"They seem to be pretty solid," he said tentatively.

His strength was coming back to him every moment. He had been no more than stunned. He walked out on the planking to the bronze grating and turned.

"If you don't get dizzy, you might come on," he said. "We can swing down the grille from here to the floor."

Estelle followed gingerly and in a moment they were safely below. The corridor was quite empty.

"When the crash came," Estelle explained, her voice shaking with the reaction from her fear of a moment ago, "everyone thought the building was coming to pieces, and ran out. I'm afraid they've all run away."

"They'll be back in a little while," Arthur said quietly.

They went along the big marble corridor to the same western door, out of which they had first gone to see the Indian village. As they emerged into the sunlight, they met a few of the people who had already recovered from their panic and were returning.

A crowd of respectable size gathered in a few moments, all still pale and shaken, but coming back to the building which was their refuge. Arthur leaned wearily against the cold stone. It seemed to vibrate under his touch. He turned quickly to Estelle.

"Feel this!" he exclaimed.

She did so.

"I've been wondering what that rumble was," she said. "I've been hearing it ever since we landed here, but didn't understand where it came from."

"You hear a rumble?" Arthur asked, puzzled. "I can't hear anything."

"It isn't as loud as it was, but I hear it," Estelle insisted. "It's very deep, like the lowest possible bass note of an organ."

"You couldn't hear the shrill whistle when we were coming here," Arthur exclaimed suddenly, "and you can't hear the squeak of a bat. Of course, your ears are pitched lower than usual, and you can hear sounds that are lower than I can hear. Listen carefully. Does it sound in the least like a liquid rushing through somewhere?"

"Y–yes," said Estelle hesitatingly. "Somehow, I don't quite understand how, it gives me the impression of a tidal flow or something of that sort."

Arthur rushed indoors. When Estelle followed him, she found him excitedly examining the marble floor about the base of the vault.

"It's cracked," he said excitedly. "It's cracked — The vault rose all of an inch!"

Estelle looked and saw the cracks.

"What does that crack in the floor mean?"

"It means we're going to get back where we belong," Arthur cried jubilantly. "It means I'm on the track of the whole trouble. It means everything is going to be all right."

He prowled about the vault exultantly, noting exactly how the cracks in the floor ran and seeing in each a corroboration of his theory.

"I'll have to make some inspections in the cellar," he went

on happily, "but I'm nearly sure I'm on the right track and can figure out a corrective."

"How soon can we hope to start back?" asked Estelle eagerly.

Arthur hesitated; then a great deal of the excitement ebbed from his face, leaving it rather worried and stern.

"It may be a month, or two months, or a year," he answered gravely. "I don't know. If the first thing I try will work, it won't be long. If we have to experiment, I daren't guess how long we may be. But"—his chin set firmly—"we're going to get back."

Estelle looked at him speculatively. Her own expression grew a little worried, too. "But in a month," she said dubiously, "we—there is hardly any hope of our finding food for two thousand people for a month, is there?"

"We've got to," Arthur declared. "We can't hope to get that much food from the Indians. It will be days before they'll dare to come back to their village, if they ever come. It will be weeks before we can hope to have them earnestly at work to feed us, and that's leaving aside the question of how we'll communicate with them, and how we'll manage to trade with them. Frankly, I think everybody is going to have to draw his belt tight before we get through—if we do. Some of us will get along, anyway."

Estelle's eyes opened wide as the meaning of his last sentence penetrated her mind.

"You mean—that all of us won't—"

"I'm going to take care of you," Arthur said gravely, "but there are liable to be lively doings around here when people begin to realize they're really in a tight fix for food. I'm going to get Van Deventer to help me organize a police band to enforce martial law. We mustn't have any disorder, that's certain, and I don't trust a city-bred man in a pinch unless I know him."

He stooped and picked up a revolver from the floor, left there by one of the bank watchmen when he fled, in the belief that the building was falling.

Arthur stood at the window of his office and stared out toward the west. The sun was setting, but upon what a scene!

Where, from this same window, Arthur had seen the sun setting behind the Jersey hills, all edged with the angular roofs of factories, with their chimneys emitting columns of smoke, he now saw the same sun sinking redly behind a mass of luxuriant foliage. And where he was accustomed to look upon the tops of high buildings—each entitled to the name of "skyscraper"—he now saw miles and miles of waving green branches.

The wide Hudson flowed on placidly, all unruffled by the arrival of this strange monument upon its shores—the same Hudson Arthur knew as a busy thoroughfare of puffing steamers and chugging launches. Two or three small streams wandered unconcernedly across the land that Arthur had known as the most closely built-up territory on Earth. And far, far below him—Arthur had to lean well out of his window to see it—stood a collection of tiny wigwams. Those small bark structures represented the original metropolis of New York.

His telephone rang. Van Deventer was on the wire. The exchange in the building was still working. Van Deventer wanted Arthur to come down to his private office. There were still a great many things to be settled—the arrangements for commandeering offices for sleeping quarters for the women, and numberless other details. The men who seemed to have best kept their heads were gathering there to settle upon a course of action.

Arthur glanced out of the window again. He saw a curiously compact dark cloud moving swiftly across the sky to the west.

"Miss Woodward," he said sharply. "What is that?"

Estelle came to the window and looked.

"They are birds," she told him. "Birds flying in a group. I've often seen them in the country, though never as many as that."

"How do you catch birds?" Arthur asked her. "I know about shooting them, and so on, but we haven't guns enough to count. Could we catch them in traps, do you think?"

"I wouldn't be surprised," said Estelle thoughtfully. "But it would be hard to catch very many."

"Come downstairs," directed Arthur. "You know as much as any of the men here, and more than most, apparently. We're going to make you show us how to catch things."

Estelle smiled, a trifle wanly. Arthur led the way to the elevator. In the car he noticed that she looked distressed.

"What's the matter?" he asked. "You aren't really frightened, are you?"

"No," she answered shakily, "but—I'm rather upset about this thing. It's so—so terrible, somehow, to be back here, thousands of miles, or years, away from all one's friends and everybody."

"Please"—Arthur smiled encouragingly at her—"please count me your friend, won't you?"

She nodded, but blinked back some tears. Arthur would have tried to hearten her further, but the elevator stopped at their floor. They walked into the room where the meeting of cool heads was to take place.

Not more than a dozen men were in there talking earnestly but dispiritedly. When Arthur and Estelle entered, Van Deventer came over to greet them.

"We've got to do something," he said in a low voice. "A wave of homesickness has swept over the whole place. Look at those men. Everyone is thinking about his family and contrasting his cozy fireside with all that wilderness outside."

"You don't seem to be worried," Arthur observed with a smile.

Van Deventer's eyes twinkled.

"I'm a bachelor," he said cheerfully, "and I live in a hotel. I've been longing for a chance to see some real excitement for thirty years. Business has kept me from it up to now, but I'm enjoying myself hugely."

Estelle looked at the group of dispirited men.

"We'll simply have to do something," she said with a shaky smile. "I feel just as they do. This morning I hated the thought of having to go back to my boarding house tonight, but right now I feel as if the odor of cabbage in the hallway would seem like heaven."

Arthur led the way to the flat-topped desk in the middle of the room.

"Let's settle a few of the more important matters," he said in a businesslike tone. "None of us has any authority to act for the rest of the people in the tower, but so many of us are in a state of blue funk that those who are here must have charge for a while. Anybody have any suggestions?"

"Housing," answered Van Deventer promptly. "I suggest that we draft a gang of men to haul all the upholstered settees and rugs that are to be found to one floor, for the women to sleep on."

"M-m. Yes. That's a good idea. Anybody have a better plan?"

No one spoke. They all still looked much too homesick to take any great interest in anything, but they began to listen more or less halfheartedly.

"I've been thinking about coal," said Arthur. "There's undoubtedly a supply in the basement, but I wonder if it wouldn't be well to cut the lights off most of the floors, only lighting up the ones we're using."

"That might be a good idea later," Estelle said quietly, "but light is cheering, somehow, and everyone feels so blue that I wouldn't do it tonight. Tomorrow they'll begin to get up their resolution again, and you can ask them to do things."

"If we're going to starve to death," one of the other men said gloomily, "we might as well have plenty of light to do it by."

"We aren't going to starve to death," retorted Arthur sharply. "Just before I came down, I saw a great cloud of birds, greater than I had ever seen before. When we get at those birds—"

"When," echoed the gloomy one.

"They were pigeons," Estelle explained. "They shouldn't be hard to snare or trap."

"I usually have my dinner before now," the gloomy one protested, "and I'm told I won't get anything tonight."

The other men began to straighten their shoulders. The peevishness of one of their number seemed to bring out their latent courage.

"Well, we've got to stand it for the present," one of them said almost philosophically.

"What I'm most anxious about is getting back. Have we any chance?"

Arthur nodded emphatically.

"I think so. I have a sort of idea as to the cause of our sinking into the Fourth Dimension, and when that is verified, a corrective can be looked for and applied."

"How long will that take?"

"Can't say," Arthur replied frankly. "I don't know what tools, what materials, or what workmen we have, and that's rather more to the point. I don't even know what work will have to be done. The pressing problem is food."

"Oh, bother the food," someone protested impatiently. "I don't care about myself. I can go hungry tonight. I want to get back to my family."

"That's all that really matters," a chorus of voices echoed.

"We'd better not bother about anything else unless we find we can't get back. Concentrate on getting back," one man stated more explicitly.

"Look here," said Arthur incisively. "You've a family, and

so have a great many of the others in the tower, but your family and everybody else's family has got to wait. As an inside limit, we can hope to begin to work on the problem of getting back when we're sure there's nothing else going to happen. I tell you quite honestly that I think I know what is the direct cause of this catastrophe. And I'll tell you even more honestly that I think I'm the only man among us who can put this tower back where it started from. And I'll tell you most honestly of all that any attempt to meddle at this time with the forces that let us down here will result in a catastrophe considerably greater than the one that happened today."

"Well, if you're sure—" someone began reluctantly.

"I am so sure that I'm going to keep to myself the knowledge of what will start those forces to work again," Arthur said quietly. "I don't want any impatient meddling. If we start them too soon, God only knows what will happen."

Van Deventer was eyeing Arthur Chamberlain keenly.

"It isn't a question of your wanting pay in exchange for your services in putting us back, is it?" he asked coolly.

Arthur turned and faced him. His face began to flush slowly. Van Deventer put up one hand.

"I beg your pardon. I see."

"We aren't settling the things we came here for," Estelle interrupted.

She had noted the threat of friction and had hastened to put in a diversion. Arthur relaxed.

"I think that as a beginning," he suggested, "we'd better get sleeping arrangements completed. We can get everybody together somewhere, I daresay, and then secure volunteers for the work."

"Right." Van Deventer was anxious to make amends for his blunder of a moment before. "Shall I send the bank watchmen to go on each floor in turn and ask everyone to come downstairs?"

"You might start them," Arthur said. "It will take a long time for everyone to assemble."

Van Deventer spoke into the telephone on his desk. In a moment he hung up the receiver.

"They're on their way," he said.

Arthur was frowning to himself and scribbling in a notebook.

"Of course," he announced abstractedly, "the pressing problem is food. We've quite a number of fishermen, and a few hunters. We've got to have a lot of food at once, and everything considered, I think we'd better count on the fishermen. At sunrise we'd better have some people begin to dig bait and wake our anglers. They'd better make their tackle tonight, don't you think?"

There was a general nod.

"We'll announce that, then. The fishermen will go to the river under guard of the men we have who can shoot. I think what Indians there are will be much too frightened to try to ambush any of us, but we'd better be on the safe side. They'll keep together and fish at nearly the same spot, with our hunters patrolling the woods behind them, taking potshots at game, if they see any. The fishermen should make more or less of a success, I think. The Indians weren't extensive fishers that I ever heard of, and the river ought fairly to swarm with fish."

He closed his notebook.

"How many weapons can we count on altogether?" Arthur asked Van Deventer.

"In the bank, about a dozen riot guns and a half dozen repeating rifles. Elsewhere, I don't know. Forty or fifty men said they had revolvers, though."

"We'll give revolvers to the men who go with the fishermen. The Indians haven't heard firearms and will run at the report, even if they dare attack our men."

"We can send out the gun-armed men as hunters," someone suggested, "and send gardeners with them to look for vegetables and such things."

"We'll have to take a sort of census, really," Arthur suggested, "finding what everyone can do and getting him to do it."

"I never planned anything like this before," Van Deventer remarked, "and I never thought I should, but this is much more fun than running a bank."

Arthur smiled.

"Let's go and have our meeting," he said cheerfully.

But the meeting was a gloomy and despairing affair. Nearly everyone had watched the sun set upon the strange, wild landscape. Hardly an individual among the whole two thousand of them had ever been out of sight of a house before in his or her life. To look out at a vast, untouched wilderness where hitherto they had seen the most highly civilized city on the globe would

have been startling and depressing enough in itself, but to know
that they were alone in a whole continent of savages and that
there was not, indeed, in all the world a single community of
people they could greet as brothers was terrifying.

Few of them thought so far, but there was actually—if
Arthur's estimate of several thousand years' drop back through
time was correct—there was actually no other group of English-
speaking people in the world. The English language was yet to
be invented. Even Rome, the synonym for antiquity of culture,
might still be an obscure village inhabited by a band of tatter-
demalions under the leadership of an upstart Romulus.

Soft in the body as these people were, city-bred and unaccustomed to face other than the most conventionalized emer-
gencies of life, they were terrified. Hardly one of them had
even gone without a meal in all his life. To have the prospect of
having to earn their food, not by the manipulation of figures in
a book, or by expert juggling of profits and prices, but by literal
wresting of that food from its source in the earth or stream was
a really terrifying thing for them.

In addition, every one of them was bound to the life of modern times by a hundred ties. Many of them had families, a thousand years away. All had interests, engrossing interests, in
modern New York. One young man felt an anxiety that was really ludicrous because he had promised to take his sweetheart
to the theater that night, and if he did not come, she would be
very angry. Another was to be married in a week. Some of the
people were, like Van Deventer and Arthur, so situated they
could view the episode as an adventure, or, like Estelle, who
had no immediate fear because all her family was provided for
without her help and lived far from New York, so they would
not learn of the catastrophe for some time. Many, however, felt
instant and pressing fear for the families whose expenses ran always so close to their incomes that the disappearance of the
breadwinner for a week would mean actual want or debt. There
are very many such families in New York.

The people, therefore, that gathered hopelessly at the call of
Van Deventer's watchmen were dazed and spiritless. Their excitement after Arthur's first attempt to explain the situation to
them had evaporated. They were no longer keyed up to a high
pitch by the startling thing that had happened to them.

Nevertheless, although only half comprehending what had
actually occurred, they began to realize what that occurrence

meant. No matter where they might go over the whole face of the globe, they would always be aliens and strangers. If they had been carried away to some unknown shore, some wilderness far from their own land, they might have thought of building ships to return to their homes. They had seen New York vanish before their eyes, however. They had seen their civilization disappear while they watched.

They were in a barbarous world. There was not, for example, a single safety match on the whole Earth except those in the runaway skyscraper.

Arthur and Van Deventer, in turn with the others of the cooler heads, thundered at the apathetic people, trying to waken them to the necessity for work. They showered promises of inevitable return to modern times; they pledged their honor to the belief that a way would ultimately be found by which they would all yet find themselves safely back home again.

The people, however, had seen New York disintegrate, and Arthur's explanation sounded like some wild dream of an imaginative novelist. Not one person in all the gathering could actually realize that his home might yet be waiting for him, though at the same time he felt a pathetic anxiety for the welfare of its inmates.

Everyone was in a turmoil of contradictory beliefs. On the one hand they knew that all of New York could not be actually destroyed and replaced by a splendid forest in the space of a few hours, so the accident or catastrophe must have occurred to those in the tower, and on the other hand, they had seen all of New York vanish by bits and fragments, to be replaced by a smaller and dingier town, had beheld that replaced in turn, and at last had landed in the midst of this forest.

Everyone, too, began to feel an unusual and uncomfortable sensation of hunger. It was a mild discomfort as yet, but a few of them had experienced it before without an immediate prospect of assuaging the craving, and the knowledge that there was no food to be had somehow increased the desire for it. They were really in a pitiful state.

Van Deventer spoke encouragingly, and then asked for volunteers for immediate work. There was hardly any response. Everyone seemed sunk in despondency. Arthur then began to talk straight from the shoulder and succeeded in rousing them a little, but everyone was still rather too frightened to realize that work could help at all.

In desperation the dozen or so men who had gathered in Van Deventer's office went about among the gathering and simply selected men at random, ordering them to follow and begin work. This began to awaken the crowd, but they wakened to fear rather than resolution. They were city-bred, and unaccustomed to facing the unusual or the alarming.

Arthur noted the new restlessness, but attributed it to growing uneasiness rather than selfish panic. He was rather pleased that they were outgrowing their apathy. When the meeting had come to an end, he felt satisfied that by morning the latent resolution among the people would have crystalized, and they would be ready to work earnestly and intelligently on whatever tasks they were directed to undertake.

He returned to the ground floor of the building feeling much more hopeful than before. Two thousand people all earnestly working for one end are hard to down even when faced with such a task as confronted the inhabitants of the runaway skyscraper. Even if they were never able to return to modern times, they would still be able to form a community that might do much to hasten the development of civilization in other parts of the world.

His hope received a rude shock when he reached the great hallway on the lower floor. There was a fruit and confectionery stand here, and as Arthur arrived at the spot, he saw a surging mass of men about it. The keeper of the stand looked frightened, but was selling off his stock as fast as he could make change. Arthur forced his way to the counter.

"Here," he said sharply to the keeper of the stand, "stop selling this stuff. It's got to be held until we can dole it out where it's needed."

"I—I can't help myself," the keeper said. "They're takin' it anyway."

"Get back there," Arthur cried to the crowd. "Do you call this decent, trying to get more than your share of this stuff? You'll get your portion tomorrow. It is going to be divided up."

"Go to hell!" someone panted. "You c'n starve if you want to, but I'm going to look out f'r myself."

The men were not really starving, but had been put into a panic by the plain speeches of Arthur and his helpers, and were

seizing what edibles they could lay hands upon in preparation
for the hunger they had been warned to expect.

Arthur pushed against the mob, trying to thrust them away
from the counter, but his very effort intensified their panic.
There was a quick surge and a crash. The glass front of the
showcase broke in.

In a flash of rage Arthur struck out viciously. The crowd
paid not the slightest attention to him, however. Every man was
too panic-stricken, and too intent on getting some of this food
before it was all gone, to bother with him.

Arthur was simply crushed back by the bodies of the forty
or fifty men. In a moment he found himself alone amid the
wreckage of the stand, with the keeper wringing his hands over
the remnants of his goods.

Van Deventer ran down the stairs.

"What's the matter?" he demanded as he saw Arthur nursing
a bleeding hand cut on the broken glass of the showcase.

"Bolsheviki!" answered Arthur with a grim smile. "We
woke up some of the crowd too successfully. They got panic-
stricken and started to buy out this stuff here. I tried to stop
them, and you see what happened. We'd better look to the
restaurant, though I doubt if they'll try anything just now."

He followed Van Deventer up to the restaurant floor. There
were picked men before the door, but just as Arthur and the
bank president appeared two or three white-faced men went up
to the guards and started low-voiced conversations.

Arthur reached the spot in time to forestall bribery.

Arthur collared one man, Van Deventer another, and in a
moment the two were sent reeling down the hallway.

"Some fools have got panic-stricken!" Van Deventer explained to the men before the doors in a casual voice, though he
was breathing heavily from the unaccustomed exertion.
"They've smashed the fruit stand on the ground floor and stolen
the contents. It's nothing but blue funk! Only, if any of them
start to gather around here, hit them first and talk it over afterward. You'll do that?"

"We will!" the men said heartily.

"Shall we use our guns?" another asked hopefully.

Van Deventer grinned.

"No," he replied, "we haven't any excuse for that yet. But
you might shoot at the ceiling, if they get excited. They're just
frightened!"

He took Arthur's arm, and the two walked toward the stairway again.

"Chamberlain," he said happily, quickening his pace, "tell me why I've never had as much fun as this before!"

Arthur smiled a bit wearily.

"I'm glad you're enjoying yourself!" he said. "Because I'm not. I'm going outside and walk around a bit. I want to see if any cracks have appeared in the earth anywhere. It's dark, and I'll borrow a lantern down in the fire-room, but I want to find out if there are any more developments in the condition of the building."

Despite his preoccupation with his errand, which was to find if there were other signs of the continued activity of the strange forces that had lowered the tower through the Fourth Dimension into the dim and unrecorded years of aboriginal America, Arthur could not escape the fascination of the sight that met his eyes. A bright moon shone overhead and silvered the white sides of the tower, while the brightly-lighted windows of the offices within glittered like jewels set into the shining shaft.

From his position on the ground he looked into the dimness of the forest on all sides. Black obscurity had gathered beneath the dark masses of moonlit foliage. The tiny birch-bark teepees of the now deserted Indian village glowed palely. Above, the stars looked calmly down at the accusing finger of the tower— pointing upward, as if in reproach at their indifference to the savagery that reigned over the whole Earth.

Like a fairy tower of jewels the building rose. Alone among a wilderness of trees and streams it towered in a strange beauty; moonlit to silver, lighted from within to a mass of brilliant gems, it stood serenely still.

Arthur, carrying his futile lantern about its base, felt his own insignificance as never before. He wondered what the Indians must think. He knew there must be hundreds of eyes fixed upon the strange sight—fixed in awestricken terror or superstitious reverence upon this unearthly visitor to their hunting grounds.

A tiny figure, dwarfed by the building whose base he skirted, Arthur moved slowly about the vast pile. The earth seemed not to have been affected by the vast weight of the tower.

Arthur knew, however, that long concrete piles reached far

down to bedrock. It was these piles that had sunk into the Fourth Dimension, carrying the building with them.

Arthur had followed the plans with great interest when the Metropolitan was constructed. It was an engineering feat, and in the engineering periodicals, whose study was part of Arthur's business, great space had been given to the building and the methods of its construction.

While examining the earth carefully he went over his theory of the cause for the catastrophe. The whole structure must have sunk at the same time, or it, too, would have disintegrated, as the other buildings had appeared to disintegrate. Mentally, Arthur likened the submergence of the tower in the oceans of time to an elevator sinking past the different floors of an office building. All about the building the other skyscrapers of New York had seemed to vanish. In an elevator, the floors one passes seem to rise up.

Carrying out the analogy to its logical end, Arthur reasoned that the building itself had no more cause to disintegrate, as the buildings it passed seemed to disintegrate, than the elevator in the office building would have cause to rise because its surroundings seemed to rise.

Within the building, he knew, there were strange stirrings of emotions. Queer currents of panic were running about, throwing the people to and fro as leaves are thrown about by a current of wind. Yet, underneath all those undercurrents of fear was a rapidly growing resolution, strengthened by an increasing knowledge of the need to work.

Men were busy even then shifting all possible comfortable furniture to a single story for the women in the building to occupy. The men would sleep on the floor for the present. Beds of boughs could be improvised on the morrow. At sunrise on the following morning many men would go to the streams to fish, guarded by other men. All would be frightened, no doubt, but there would be a grim resolution underneath the fear. Other men would wander about to hunt.

There was little likelihood of Indians approaching for some days, at least, but when they did come Arthur meant to avoid hostilities by all possible means. The Indians would be fearful of their strange visitors, and it should not be difficult to convince them that friendliness was safest, even if they displayed unfriendly desires.

The pressing problem was food. There were two thousand

people in the building, soft-bodied and city-bred. They were unaccustomed to hardship, and could not endure what more primitive people would hardly have noticed.

They must be fed, but they must be taught to feed themselves. The fishermen would help, but Arthur could only hope that they would prove equal to the occasion. He did not know what to expect from them. From the hunters he expected but little. The Indians were wary hunters, and game would be shy if not scarce.

The great cloud of birds he had seen at sunset was a hopeful sign. Arthur vaguely remembered stories of great flocks of wood-pigeons which had been exterminated, as the buffalo was exterminated. As he considered, the remembrance became more clear.

They had flown in huge flocks which nearly darkened the sky. As late as the forties of the nineteenth century they had been an important article of food, and had glutted the market at certain seasons of the year.

Estelle had said the birds he had seen at sunset were pigeons. Perhaps this was one of the great flocks. If it were really so, the food problem would be much lessened, provided a way could be found to secure them. The ammunition in the tower was very limited, and a shell could not be found for every bird that was needed, nor even for every three or four. Great traps must be devised, or birdlime might possibly be produced. Arthur made a mental note to ask Estelle if she knew anything about birdlime.

A vague, humming roar, altering in pitch, came to his ears. He listened for some time before he identified it as the sound of the wind playing upon the irregular surfaces of the tower. In the city the sound was drowned by the multitude of other noises, but here Arthur could hear it plainly.

He listened a moment, and became surprised at the number of night noises he could hear. In New York he had closed his ears to incidental sounds from sheer self-protection. Somewhere he heard the ripple of a little spring. As the idea of a spring came into his mind, he remembered Estelle's description of the deep-toned roar she had heard.

He put his hand on the cold stone of the building. There was still a vibrant quivering of the rock. It was weaker than before, but was still noticeable. He drew back from the rock and looked up into the sky. It seemed to blaze with stars, more stars than

Arthur had ever seen in the city, and more than he had dreamed existed.

As he looked, however, a cloud seemed to film a portion of the heavens. The stars still showed through it, but they twinkled in a peculiar fashion that Arthur could not understand.

He watched in growing perplexity. The cloud moved very swiftly. Thin as it seemed to be, it should have been silvery from the moonlight, but the sky was noticeably darker where it moved. It advanced toward the tower and seemed to obscure the upper portion. A confused motion became visible among its parts. Wisps of it whirled away from the brilliantly lighted tower, and then returned swiftly toward it.

Arthur heard a faint tinkle, then a musical scraping, which became louder. A faint scream sounded, then another. The tinkle developed into the sound made by breaking glass, and the scraping sound became that of the broken fragments as they rubbed against the sides of the tower in their fall.

The scream came again. It was the frightened cry of a woman. A soft body struck the earth not ten feet from where Arthur stood, then another, and another.

Arthur urged the elevator-boy to greater speed. They were speeding up the shaft as rapidly as possible, but it was not fast enough. When they at last reached the height at which the excitement seemed to be centered, the car stopped with a jerk and Arthur dashed down the hall.

Half a dozen frightened stenographers stood there, huddled together.

"What's the matter?" Arthur demanded. Men were running from the other floors to see what the trouble was.

"The—the windows broke, and—something flew in at us!" one of them gasped: There was a crash inside the nearest office, and the women screamed again.

Arthur drew a revolver from his pocket and advanced to the door. He quickly threw it open, entered, and closed it behind him. Those left out in the hall waited tensely.

There was no sound. The women began to look even more frightened. The men shuffled their feet uneasily, and looked uncomfortably at one another. Van Deventer appeared on the scene, puffing a little from his haste.

The door opened again and Arthur came out. He was carrying something in his hand. He had put his revolver aside and looked somewhat foolish but very much delighted.

"The food question is settled," he said happily. "Look!"

He held out the object he carried. It was a bird, apparently a pigeon of some sort. It seemed to have been stunned, but as Arthur held it out it stirred, then struggled, and in a moment was flapping wildly in an attempt to escape.

"It's a wood-pigeon," said Arthur. "They must fly after dark sometimes. A big flock of them ran afoul of the tower and were dazed by the lights. They've broken a lot of windows, I daresay, but a great many of them ran into the stonework and were stunned. I was outside the tower, and when I came in, they were dropping to the ground by the hundreds. I didn't know what they were then, but if we wait twenty minutes or so *I* think we can go out and gather up our supper and breakfast and several other meals, all at once."

Estelle had appeared and now reached out her hands for the bird.

"I'll take care of this one," she said. "Wouldn't it be a good idea to see if there aren't some more stunned in the other offices?"

In half an hour the electric stoves of the restaurant were going at their full capacity. Men, cheerfully excited men now, were bringing in pigeons by armfuls, and other men were skinning them. There was no time to pluck them, though a great many of the women were busily engaged in that occupation.

As fast as the birds could be cooked they were served out to the impatient but much cheered castaways, and in a little while nearly every person in the place was walking casually about the halls with a roasted, broiled, or fried pigeon in his hands. The ovens were roasting pigeons, the frying pans were frying them, and the broilers were loaded down with the small but tender birds.

The unexpected solution of the most pressing question cheered everyone amazingly. Many people were still frightened, but less frightened than before. Worry for their families still oppressed a great many, but the removal of the fear of immediate hunger led them to believe that the other problems before them would be solved, too, and in as satisfactory a manner.

Arthur had returned to his office with four broiled pigeons in a sheet of wrapping paper. As he somehow expected, Estelle was waiting there.

"Thought I'd bring lunch up," he announced. "Are you hungry?"

"Starving!" Estelle replied, and laughed.

The whole catastrophe began to become an adventure. She bit eagerly into the bird. Arthur began as hungrily on another. For some time neither spoke a word. At last, however, Arthur waved the leg of his second pigeon toward his desk.

"Look what we've got here!" he said.

Estelle nodded. The stunned pigeon Arthur had first picked up was tied by one foot to a paperweight.

"I thought we might keep him for a souvenir," she suggested.

"You seem pretty confident we'll get back, all right," Arthur observed. "It was surely lucky those blessed birds came along. They've heartened up the people wonderfully!"

"Oh, I knew you'd manage somehow!" said Estelle confidently.

"I manage?" Arthur repeated, smiling. "What have I done?"

"Why, you've done everything," affirmed Estelle stoutly. "You've told the people what to do from the very first, and you're going to get us back."

Arthur grinned, then suddenly his face grew a little more serious.

"I wish I were as sure as you are," he said. "I think we'll be all right, though, sooner or later."

"I'm sure of it," Estelle declared with conviction. "Why, you—"

"Why I?" asked Arthur again. He bent forward in his chair and fixed his eyes on Estelle's. She looked up, met his gaze, and stammered:

"You—you do things," she finished lamely.

"I'm tempted to do something now," Arthur said. "Look here, Miss Woodward, you've been in my employ for three or four months. In all that time I've never had anything but the most impersonal comments from you. Why the sudden change?"

The twinkle in his eyes robbed his words of any impertinence.

"Why, I really—I really suppose I never noticed you before," said Estelle.

"Please notice me hereafter," said Arthur. "I have been noticing you. I've been doing practically nothing else."

Estelle flushed again. She tried to meet Arthur's eyes and failed. She bit desperately into her pigeon drumstick, trying to think of something to say.

"When we get back," went on Arthur meditatively, "I'll have nothing to do—no work or anything. I'll be broke and out of a job."

Estelle shook her head emphatically. Arthur paid no attention.

"Estelle," he said, smiling, "would you like to be out of a job with me?"

Estelle turned crimson.

"I'm not very successful," Arthur went on soberly. "I'm afraid I wouldn't make a very good husband; I'm rather worthless and lazy!"

"You aren't," broke in Estelle; "you're—you're—"

Arthur reached over and took her by the shoulders.

"What?" he demanded.

She would not look at him, but she did not draw away. He held her from him for a moment.

"What am I?" he demanded again. Somehow he found himself kissing the tips of her ears. Her face was buried against his shoulder.

"What am I?" he repeated sternly.

Her voice was muffled by his coat.

"You're—you're dear!" she said.

There was an interlude of about a minute and a half, then she pushed him away from her.

"Don't!" she said breathlessly. "Please don't!"

"Aren't you going to marry me?" he demanded.

Still crimson, she nodded shyly. He kissed her again.

"Please don't!" she protested.

She fondled the lapels of his coat, quite content to have his arms about her.

"Why mayn't I kiss you if you're going to marry me?" Arthur demanded.

She looked up at him with an air of demure primness.

"You—you've been eating pigeon," she told him in mock gravity, "and—and your mouth is greasy!"

It was two weeks later. Estelle looked out over the now familiar wild landscape. It was much the same when she looked far away but nearby there were great changes.

A cleared trail led through the woods to the waterfront, and a raft of logs extended out into the river for hundreds of feet. Both sides of the raft were lined with busy fishermen—men and women, too. A little to the north of the base of the building a huge mound of earth smoked sullenly. The coal in the cellar had given out and charcoal had been found to be the best substitute they could improvise. The mound was where the charcoal was made.

It was heartbreaking work to keep the fires going with charcoal, because it burned so rapidly in the powerful draft of the furnaces, but the original fire-room gang had been recruited to several times its original number from among the towerites, and the work was divided until it did not seem hard.

As Estelle looked down, two tiny figures sauntered across the clearing from the woods with a heavy animal slung between them. One was using a gun as a walking stick. Estelle saw the flash of the sun on its polished barrel.

There were a number of Indians in the clearing, watching with wide-open eyes the activities of the whites. Dozens of birch-bark canoes dotted the Hudson, each with its load of fishermen, industriously working for the white people. It had been hard to overcome the fear in the Indians, and they still paid superstitious reverence to the whites, but fair dealings coupled with a constant readiness to defend themselves had enabled Arthur to institute a system of trading for food that had so far proved satisfactory.

The whites had found spare electric lightbulbs valuable currency in dealing with the redskins. Picture wire, too, was highly prized. There was not a picture left hanging in any of the offices. Metal paper-knives bought huge quantifies of provisions from the eager Indian traders, and the story was current in the tower that Arthur had received eight canoe-loads of corn and vegetables in exchange for a broken-down typewriter. No one could guess what the savages wanted with the typewriter, but they had carted it away triumphantly.

Estelle smiled tenderly to herself as she remembered how Arthur had been the leading spirit in all the numberless enterprises in which the castaways had been forced to engage. He would come to her in a spare ten minutes, and tell her how everything was going. He seemed curiously boylike in those moments.

Sometimes he would come straight from the fire-room—he

insisted on taking part in all the more arduous duties—having hastily cleaned himself for her inspection, snatch a hurried kiss and then go off, laughing, to help chop down trees for the long fishing-raft. He had told them how to make charcoal, had taken a leading part in establishing and maintaining friendly relations with the Indians, and was now down in the deepest subbasement, working with a gang of volunteers to try to put the building back where it belonged.

Estelle had said, after the collapse of the flooring in the boardroom, that she heard a sound like the rushing of waters. Arthur, on examining the floor where the safe-deposit vault stood, found it had risen an inch. On these facts he had built up his theory. The building, like all modern skyscrapers, rested on concrete piles extending down to bedrock. In the center of one of those piles there was a hollow tube originally intended to serve as an artesian well. The flow had been insufficient and the well had been stopped up.

Arthur, of course, as an engineer, had studied the construction of the building with great care, and happened to remember that this partly hollow pile was the one nearest the safe-deposit vault. The collapse of the boardroom floor had suggested that some change had happened in the building itself, and that was found when he saw that the deposit vault had actually risen an inch.

He at once connected the rise in the flooring above the hollow pile with the pipe in the pile. Estelle had heard liquid sounds. Evidently water had been forced into the hollow artesian pipe under an unthinkable pressure when the catastrophe occurred.

From the rumbling and the suddenness of the whole catastrophe, a volcanic or seismic disturbance was evident. The connection of volcanic or seismic action with a flow of water suggested a geyser or a hot spring of some sort, probably a spring which had broken through its normal confines sometime before, but whose pressure had been sufficient to prevent the accident until the failure of its flow.

When the flow ceased, the building sank rapidly. For the fact that this "sinking" was in the fourth direction—the Fourth Dimension—Arthur had no explanation. He simply knew that in some mysterious way an outlet for the pressure had developed in that fashion, and that the tower had followed the spring in its fall through time.

The sole apparent change in the building had occurred above the one hollow concrete pile, which seemed to indicate that if access were to be had to the mysterious, and so far only assumed spring, it must be through that pile. While the vault retained its abnormal elevation, Arthur believed that there was still water at an immense and incalculable pressure in the pipe. He dared not attempt to tap the pipe until the pressure had abated.

At the end of the week he found the vault slowly settling back into place. When its return to normal was complete, he dared begin boring a hole to reach the hollow tube in the concrete pile.

As he suspected, he found water in the pile—water whose sulfurous and mineral nature confirmed his belief that a geyser reaching deep into the bosom of the Earth, as well as far back in the realms of time, was at the bottom of the extraordinary jaunt of the tower.

Geysers were still far from satisfactory things to explain. There are many of their vagaries which we cannot understand at all. We do know a few things which will affect them, and one thing is that "soaping" them will stimulate their flow in an extraordinary manner.

Arthur proposed to "soap" this mysterious geyser when the renewal of its flow should lift the runaway skyscraper back to the epoch from which the failure of the flow had caused it to fall.

He made his preparations with great care. He confidently expected his plan to work, and to see the skyscraper once more towering over midtown New York as was its wont, but he did not allow the fishermen and hunters to relax their efforts on that account. They labored as before, while deep down in the sub-basement of the colossal building Arthur and his volunteers toiled mightily.

They had to bore through the concrete pile until they reached the hollow within it. Then, when the evidence gained from the water in the pipe had confirmed his surmises, they had to prepare their "charge" of soapy liquids by which the geyser was to be stirred to renewed activity.

Great quantities of the soap used by the scrubwomen in scrubbing down the floors were boiled with water until a syrupy mess was evolved. Means had then to be provided by which this could be quickly introduced into the hollow pile, the

hole then closed, and then braced to withstand a pressure un-
paralleled in hydraulic science. Arthur believed that from the
hollow pile the soapy liquid would find its way to the geyser
proper, where it would take effect in stimulating the lessened
flow to its former proportions. When that took place he believed that the building would return to normal, modern times,
as swiftly and as surely as it had left them.

The telephone rang in his office, and Estelle answered it.
Arthur was on the wire. A signal was being hung out for all the
castaways to return to the building from their several occupa-
tions. They were about to soap the geyser.

Did Estelle want to come down and watch? She did! She
stood in the main hallway as the excited and hopeful people
trooped in. When the last was inside, the doors were firmly
closed. The few friendly Indians outside stared perplexedly at
the mysterious white strangers. The whites, laughing excitedly,
began to wave to the Indians. Their leave-taking was prema-
ture.

Estelle took her way down into the cellar. Arthur was await-
ing her arrival. Van Deventer stood near, with the grinning,
grimy members of Arthur's volunteer work gang. The massive
concrete pile stood in the center of the cellar. A big steam-boiler
was coupled to a tiny pipe that led into the heart of the mass of
concrete. Arthur was going to force the soapy liquid into the
hollow pile by steam.

At the signal steam began to hiss in the boiler. Live steam
from the fire-room forced the soapy syrup out of the boiler,
through the small iron pipe, into the hollow that led to the
geyser far underground. Six thousand gallons in all were forced
into the opening in a space of three minutes. Arthur's grimy
gang began to work with desperate haste. Quickly they withdrew the iron pipe and inserted a long steel plug, painfully
beaten from a bar of solid metal. Then, girding the colossal concrete pile, ring after ring of metal was slipped on, to hold the
plug in place.

The last of the safeguards was hardly fastened firmly when
Estelle listened intently. "I hear a rumbling!" she said quietly.

Arthur reached forward and put his hand on the mass of concrete

"It is quivering!" he reported as quietly. "I think we'll be on
our way in a very little while."

The group broke for the stairs, to watch the panorama as the runaway skyscraper made its way back through the thousands of years to the times that had built it for a monument to modern commerce. Arthur and Estelle went high up in the tower. From the window of Arthur's office they looked eagerly, and felt the slight quiver as the tower got underway. Estelle looked up at the sun, and saw it mend its pace toward the west. Night fell. The evening sounds became high-pitched and shrill, then seemed to cease altogether.

In a very little while there was light again, and the sun was speeding across the sky. It sank hastily, and returned almost immediately, via the east. Its pace became a breakneck rush. Down and up behind the hills and up in the east. Down in the west and up in the east. Down and up— The flickering began. The race back toward modern time had started.

Arthur and Estelle stood at the window and looked out as the sun rushed more and more rapidly across the sky until it became a streak of light, shifting first to the right and then to the left as the seasons passed in their turn.

With Arthur's arms about her shoulders, Estelle stared out across the unbelievable landscape, while the nights and days, the winters and summers, and the storms and calms of a thousand years swept past them into the irrevocable aeons.

Presently Arthur drew her to him and kissed her. While he kissed her, so swiftly did the days and years flee by, three generations were born, grew and begot children, and died again! Estelle, held fast in Arthur's arms, thought nothing of such trivial things. She put her arms about his neck and kissed him while the years passed them unheeded.

Of course you know that the building landed safely, in the exact hour, minute, and second from which it started, so that when the frightened and excited people poured out of it to stand in Madison Square and feel that the world was once more right side up, their hilarious and incomprehensible conduct made such of the world as was passing by to think a contagious madness had broken out.

Days passed before the story of the two thousand was believed, but at last it was accepted as truth, and eminent scientists studied the matter exhaustively.

There has been one rather queer result of the journey of the runaway skyscraper. A certain Isidore Eckstein, a dealer in jewelry novelties, whose office was in the tower when it disappeared into the past, has entered suit in the courts of the United

States against all holders of land on Manhattan Island. It seems that during the two weeks in which the tower rested in the wilderness he traded independently with one of the Indian chiefs, and in exchange for two near-pearly necklaces, sixteen finger-rings, and one dollar in money, received a title-deed to the entire island. He claims that his deed is a conveyance made previous to all other sales whatever.

Strictly speaking, he is undoubtedly right, as his deed was signed before the discovery of America. The courts, however, are deliberating the question with a great deal of perplexity. Eckstein is quite confident that in the end his claim will be allowed and he will be admitted as the sole owner of real estate on Manhattan Island, with all occupiers of buildings and territory paying his ground-rent at a rate he will fix himself. In the meantime, though the foundations are being reinforced so the catastrophe cannot occur again, his entire office is packed full of articles suitable for trading with the Indians. If the tower makes another trip back through time, Eckstein hopes to become a landholder of some importance.

No less than eighty-seven books have been written by members of the memorable two thousand in description of their trip to the hinterland of time, but Arthur, who could write more intelligently about the matter than anyone else, is too busy to bother with such things. He has two very important matters to look after. One is, of course, the reinforcement of the foundations of the building so that a repetition of the catastrophe cannot occur, and the other is to convince his wife—who is Estelle, naturally—that she is the most adorable person in the universe. He finds the latter task the more difficult because she insists that he is the most adorable person—

INTRODUCTION TO
"THE ISOLINGUALS"

by L. Sprague de Camp

When I moved to Scranton, John Clark, then job hunting in New York, resolved to try writing science fiction stories and turned to me for help. On my fortnightly visits to New York, I sat up late in his apartment over beer, helping to plot John's next story.

His first attempt, "Minus Planet," sold at once to F. Orlin Tremaine, editor of *Astounding Stories*. The story appeared in the issue of April 1937. John's next story, "Space Blister," came out in the issue of August 1937. Then followed some rejections, and he lost interest after he got a new job with the Wyeth Laboratories in Philadelphia and no longer felt the spur of penury.

Having seen what John could accomplish, I thought to do likewise. Having plenty of free time in Scranton, I ground out a little (3,000-word) story, "The Hairless Ones Come." It is a caveman tale, marginally science fiction, of a kind that many beginning writers undertake. H. G. Wells, Jack London, and Robert E. Howard all tried their hands at it.

The story dealt with the struggle between the Neanderthal men of the Fourth Glaciation and the supposedly superior Crô-Magnards who overran Europe when the ice retreated. My only distinction was that I took the viewpoint of the Neanderthalers, whom most writers on the theme had treated as ogres.

After four rejections by science fiction magazines, the story appeared in the January 1939 issue of *Golden Fleece*, a short-lived magazine of historical fiction. I plugged away and soon sold a more conventional SF story, "The Isolinguals," to Tremaine's *Astounding* (Sep. 1937). I followed it with "Hyperpilosity" (Apr. 1938). These early sales led me to think: Whee! Why hasn't someone told me about this before? It sure beats working! But then a string of rejections quickly brought me back to earth.

If you ask, what was my first published SF story? The answer depends on what you mean by "first." The first one I *began* was *Genus Homo*; the first one *completed* was "The Hairless Ones Come"; the first one *published* was "The Isolinguals." Take your pick.

THE ISOLINGUALS

by L. Sprague de Camp

NICK looked at the cop, and the cop looked at Nick. The fruit vendor's friendly smile suddenly froze. The cop didn't know it, but something had gone *ping* inside Nick's head. He wasn't Niccolo Franchetti any longer. He was Decimus Agricola, engineering officer of the good old XXXIInd Legion. He had been standing behind his ballista, laying it for the Parthians' next charge. Of the crew, only he and two privates had not been struck down by the Asiastics' terrible arrows.

Then something awful had happened: the vast red rock desert of Mesopotamia had vanished, and with it the swirling masses of hostile cavalry, the heaps of dead and wounded, and everything else. One of the ballista crew was gone likewise; the other had metamorphosed into this fat fellow in the tight clothes. His catapult had, in the same twinkling, become a little two-wheeled wagon piled with fruit. He was standing on a paved street, lined with buildings of fantastic height.

Decimus blinked incredulously. Sorcery! Those Parthians were said to be good at it. The man looking at him *must* be Cartoricus, the Gaulish replacement. "*Onere!*" he shouted. "Load!"

The man in dark blue just stared. Decimus lost his temper.

"What's the matter, don't you understand good Latin? They'll be at us again in a minute!" The man did nothing. Decimus felt for his sword. It wasn't there. He was wearing queer, uncomfortable clothes like the other. He snatched an apple; at the touch of it his mind reeled. It felt like a real apple, not a sorcerer's illusion. He bit into it. Then stark terror seized him. He threw the apple at the fat man and started to run.

Arthur Lindsley picked up the hand set. "Hello? . . . Oh, it's you, Pierre. How's the esteemed son-in-law this morning?"

"Fairish," replied the instrument. "I'm up at Rockefeller Med. Bill Jenkins has a case that might interest you. None of their high-powered psychiatrists have been able to do a thing with it. Want to come up?"

Lindsley looked at his watch. "Let's see—my elementary biology class lets out at two thirty. I can come up then."

"Fine. And could you round up a couple of good linguists and bring 'em along?"

"Huh? What for?"

"Take too long to explain over the phone. Can you bring them?"

"Well, there's Van Wyck over at Barnard, and Squier's office is down the hall. Say, are you and Elsa going to have Christmas dinner with us?"

"Sorry, but we promised my folks to have it with them this year. Yeah, we're taking the train for Quebec next Thursday. Thanks anyway. Now please bring some really good language sharks. It might be important."

Professor Lindsley sighed as he hung up. He didn't look forward with much pleasure to the undiluted company of his two sons all day Christmas. Hugh would talk interminably about the vacuum-cleaner business. Malcolm would drape himself over the furniture and make languid remarks in his newly acquired college voice about how art is all. What did Pierre mean by dragging Elsa off to spend Christmas with his Canuck parents? They were the only intelligent members of the family, besides himself—

Lindsley took the new Tenth Avenue Subway up to the Medical Center, with his two linguists in tow. Squier had been in, but not Van Wyck. A search of the language department had unearthed a Dr. Fedor Jevsky, who said he'd be ver-r-ry glad to come. Lindsley was a smallish man, very erect, with snapping

eyes and a diminutive white beard. He looked odd; leading the
rangy Squier and the obese Jevsky like a couple of puppies.

Dr. Jenkins' office was jammed. The thickset, shabby man
was speaking: "It's just like I told the guys down at the hospital, Doc; Mrs. Garfinkle and I been married ten years, and she
never showed no symptoms or nothin'. We're just poor woik-
ing people—"

Jenkins' bedside voice suddenly recovered its normal snap.
"Come in, Arthur; I take it these are your linguists. I've got a
queer job for them."

Pierre Lamarque's broad, coppery face grinned at his father-
in-law from across the room. Jenkins was explaining: "—and
all at once her normal personality went out like a light. She
began talking this gibberish, and didn't know her husband or
the city or anything else. That's just the trouble; we can't locate
a single physical paranoiac symptom, and aphasia won't work
either. Split personality, yes, but it doesn't explain her making
up what seems to be a whole new language of her own. But
that's not all. She's the third of these cases the hospital has received in twenty-four hours. Sure, naturally we gave 'em all the
routine tests."

The telephone rang. "Yes? Oh, Lord! . . . Yes. . . . No. . . .
Glad you let me know." Jenkins hung up. "Twelve more cases.
Seems to be an epidemic."

Jevsky had inclined his globular form—it was impossible
for him to bend—in front of the plain-looking woman on the
chair. She seemed to be so earnestly trying to tell him something with that rush of strange syllables. He suddenly seemed
to catch something, for he barked at her what sounded like
"Haybye-ded-yow?"

The rush of sound stopped, and the woman's face broke into
a grateful smile. Then the torrent began again.

Jevsky wasn't listening. He spoke to Jenkins. "What foreign
languages has Meesez Garfinkle studied?"

"None at all; she was born in New York City; both parents
spoke English, at least of a sort; she left school at the end of the
eighth grade. What do you think you've got, Dr. Jevsky?"

"I'm not sure, but it might be Gothic."

"What!"

The vast shoulders shrugged. "I know it sounds crazy, but
habai-dêdjau means "if I had" in Gothic. I don't really know

the language, except for a few fragments like that; nor, I theenk, will many of my colleagues. You, Dr. Squier?"

The other linguist shook his head. "The Celtic languages are my specialty. But I suppose there's at least one Gothic scholar in New York City. There's at least one of everything else."

Jenkins shook his head. "No, gentlemen, it's hardly worth trying to dig one up on such a fantastic hypothesis. Guess we have a new form of dementia here. Sorry I hauled you up; she acted so rational that I thought you might find something. By the way, what *is* Gothic?"

Squier answered: "The language of the ancient Goths; it's more or less the common ancestor of English, Dutch, and German. A complicated affair with about nine thousand useless inflections. We have only a partial knowledge of it."

The telephone rang again. When Jenkins had hung up, he swore. "More cases. They're coming in regularly now. They've got one who seems to be talking some kind of English dialect, and they're bringing him up here. Suppose you all stick around for a while."

They stood or sat on the floor. Lindsley argued with one of the Rockefeller psychiatrists about politics. The biologist thought Slidell and his so-called Union Party were a real menace, that they were aiming for a dictatorship and were pretty good shots. The psychiatrist didn't; he admitted that Slidell was a fanatical demagogue and all that, but said that if the other parties would stop trying to cut each other's throats they could squash the would-be dictator overnight.

At last the hospital men brought in a slim, blond youth with a harassed expression. Jenkins rose. "I understand you're—"

The young man interrupted. He spoke a peculiar English, rather like a strong Irish brogue. "If thou're going to ask me who I be, like the rest of these knaves, my name is Sergeant Ronald Blake, of the theerd company of Noll Croomle's foot, and a mor-r-tal enemy of ahl Papists! Now are ye satisfied?"

Squier said, "Whose foot? I mean, how do you spell him?"

The youth frowned. "I'm no clerk, but I bethink me 'tis C-r-o-m-w-e-l-l, Croomle."

Lindsley spoke up, "What year is it?"

"Certainly, 'tis the year of our Lord sixteen forty-eight."

The scientists looked at one another.

Jenkins said, "We seem to be getting somewhere, but I'm

not sure just where. Young man, suppose you tell us just what happened."

"Well, I had gone home on leave, and my wife asked me to go down to the butcher's, and I had just toorned on the main street o' the village when I spied my old friend Hawks. 'Hoy, Ronald,' he says, 'how's the brave soldyer lad? And is't true thou wert at Naseby?' So I began to tell him ahl about the great battle, and how at the end the Cavaliers fled like rabbits, with their long hair streamin' out behind—" The voice from the past, if such it was, rolled on and on. Sergeant Blake was evidently a man who believed in getting in all the details.

Later, Lindsley and his son-in-law sat in the former's office. Tobacco smoke crawled bluely up through the rays of the desk lamp.

"Something's gone haywire," said the professor. "I can't believe this is an ordinary form of insanity, or any extraordinary form, either. How can you explain how Mike Watrous, package dispatcher at a department store, a young man of little learning and few talents, not only gets the idea that he's a sergeant in the Parliamentary army in the English Civil War, but also acquires a complete biography, personality, and accent to go with it? How many literate people, let alone those of Mike's background and tastes, know that Oliver Cromwell pronounced his name 'Croomle'? In most cases of this kind the victim thinks he's Napoleon or Julius Caesar, but after the delusion has come on he doesn't know any more about Napoleon or Caesar, really, than he did before."

Lamarque shrugged. "Any other hypothesis I can think of seems equally crazy, unless you're going to admit the transmigration of souls, or some such nonsense. Suppose I caught this disease, or whatever it is, and thought I was the first Lamarque, who came over to Canada in 1746, or thereabouts. I wouldn't have the vaguest idea of how to go about talking eighteenth-century French."

Lindsley sighed. "And now they want us to drop everything we're doing and try to help them out. I wish they made these psychiatrists—and that includes our friend Jenkins—learn enough advanced biology so they wouldn't come running to us when they get stumped. But I suppose we'll have to go through

the motions, anyway. The worst of it is that I haven't the foggi-
est notion of where to start—"

Hans Rumpel was making a speech. He was in fine form.
His Yorktown audience drank in his flood of words, his piercing yells, his windmill gestures. "Red plot. . . . Jewish assas-
sins . . . Destruction of civilization—" he screeched.

Hans faltered; his oratory died away to a mumble. His audience was mildly surprised to see him going through the motions
of stroking an imaginary beard. Then his voice rose again, this
time not in English, but in mournful Hebrew. He was, in fact,
reciting a Hebrew service, just as he—not Hans Rumpel, but
Levi ben Eliezar, a respected rabbi of the Hasidim—had been
reciting it in a Krakow synagogue in the year 1784. The would-
be saviors of civilization from the horrors of democratic government looked at one another. Was he another of those cases
they had been reading about? Hans stopped his chant, gaped
at his audience, and fell on his knees. He was praying with
mountain-moving fervor—

Professor Lindsley emerged from behind the mountain of
books and papers and threw his eye shade in the corner. "Pierre!
Let's cut this damn nonsense and get some breakfast. It's seven
o'clock."

Lamarque appeared. "Any luck? None here, either, Can't
find anything definite, although Minakuchi's paper on ancestral
memory in rats might be worth following up."

Lindsley frowned. "Something you said the day before yesterday gave me an idea, but it popped out of my mind like a wa-
termelon seed, before I could grab it. I've been trying to think
of it ever since. Must be getting old."

Later, Lamarque made a face. "With all the advances in our
modern civilization, nobody has yet found how to make a drugstore serve good coffee. Oh, remind me to wire Quebec and tell
the folks the Christmas dinner is off. What's the latest from
Jenkins?"

"More of the same. At the present rate every hospital in New
York will be full in a couple of days, and all the medicos in
town are running around in circles, and the psychiatrists are just
dithering. Bill says they're fairly sure it isn't infectious, from
what case histories they've been able to trace. And *we* aren't
any further than when we started—"

*   *   *

Sunday, in the new church on Tremont Avenue, the Bronx, H. Perkins rolled his eyes around so that he could see the congregation. Pretty miserable showing. Why had the vestry wanted to build this church, anyway? He'd heard a lot about the "return to religion" since 1950, but they didn't seem to be returning to *his* denomination. Such a worried-looking lot, too! Between the threat of a dictatorship by that bellowing mounteback, Slidell, and the strange plague of insanity, he didn't wonder. What would happen if Slidell got in?

H. Perkins passed down the aisle with his most seraphic expression. The "plate"—a most unplatelike object, when you thought of it—was coming toward him again, giving forth a pleasant clink as each coin went into it. He reached over and took it from Mrs. Dinwiddie—and it was as though meek H. Perkins had never been. He, Joshua Hardy, had been standing on a heaving deck yelling to the verminous crew the commands from "Old Pegleg." They'd just sighted a Spaniard, and were cracking on sail to have a closer look. Might be the monthly treasure ship from Colon. And here he was, in the aisle of a church, surrounded by people in strange clothes, and holding a little velvet bag with two dark wood handles.

Josh was too impulsive to make a really top-notch pirate. He shook the bag; to his ears came that sweetest of sounds, the clink of coin. Better grab the loot and run, boys. "Avast, ye lubbers," he roared. "*Give* me that!" He snatched the other little bag. "Ho, you over there, stand and deliver! *Where* in fifteen thousand bloody hells is my cutlass?" He raced down the aisle to cut off the fellow with the remaining bag. Too late! The chase pounded out into the street—

Professor Lindsley slammed down his briefcase. "I'm about ready to give up and go in for the transmigration of souls after all," he said wrathfully to Lamarque, who was peering into a microscope. On the microscope slide was a bit of nerve tissue of one of the cases who had gotten himself killed by an automobile.

Lindsley continued: "They're going to start a concentration camp for new cases, as every institution for miles around is full. The roads leading out of New York are jammed; people are leaving. Glad we sent our womenfolks off to Quebec while you could still buy transportation. A driver of a Madison Avenue bus had a seizure and ran his bus into a hydrant between Fifty-third and Fifty-fourth Streets. What's new around here?"

"If you mean research, nothing. But the first case in the university faculty has happened."

"Huh? Tell me about it, quick!"

"It was in the lunchroom. You know Calderwood, the mathematician? As sane and sober a man as you'll find. Well, at lunch today he jumped up with a howl and began throwing things. Then he got into the kitchen and chased everybody out with a carving knife.

"But the best part happened next. Some of them watched him around a corner. He marched into the dining room, took off his pants, pulled a tablecloth off one of the tables, and wound it around his waist like a skirt. Then he stuck the knife through one of his garters.

"He must have been a sketch. Wish I'd been there to see. He strutted up and down for a while, apparently challenging the people, in his own lingo, to come back and fight.

"Well, our friend Squier heard the fuss and came up. Squier had a bright idea. He talked Gaelic to Calderwood, and he calmed down right away. Seems he wasn't Graham Calderwood any more, but the terrible Gavin MacTaggart, a wild Highlander looking for a MacDonald throat to cut. If he couldn't have a MacDonald, a Gordon would do. They got him rounded up eventually."

Lindsley took off his glasses and rubbed his red-rimmed eyes. "You're an unfeeling young devil. How'd you like to be a member of poor Graham's family? Did you see about my classes?"

"Yeah. One of your students in advanced biology is down too! Arne Holmgren. Know him? He thinks he's a Viking. When they took him away he was roaring some early Scandinavian battle-song; at least, that's what I suppose it was. Say, hadn't you better get some sleep? You can't work efficiently if you don't, you know."

Lindsley started to snap back an irritated reply, but checked himself. "Maybe you're right, Pierre. When my normally saintly disposition starts to go sour, there's something wrong. If anybody phones, tell 'em you don't know when I'll be back."

Chase Burge lay on his back with his eyes closed, enjoying the last moment of his doze. His conscience, which woke up a little more slowly than the rest of him, showed signs of stirring. He shouldn't have lost his temper yesterday in that argument. But, damn it, Hobart was so rabid on the subject.

Then he sat up suddenly, the last vapors of sleep gone from his brain. How had he gotten into this strange room? He'd gone to bed perfectly sober. He'd been snatched! He sprang from the bed.

The door opened and a man in a dressing gown walked into the room. Chase tensed himself to spring; but, no, the man might have a gun. Better find out what it was all about.

"Morning, son," said the kidnaper. "I think one of my shirts strayed into your bureau—"

"Where am I?" snarled Chase.

"Where—Oh, my Lord—" The gray-haired man looked at him with a horrified expression. "You've got it, too!"

"Got what? What did you kidnap me for? My folks haven't any dough to speak of!"

The other man composed himself with an effort. "Who do you think you are? No, I mean that as a serious question."

"I'm Chase Burge, of 351 West 55th Street, and I demonstrate automobiles for a living. Who are *you*?"

"I'm Chase Burge. Senior, that is. You're Chase Burge, Junior, and I'm your father."

"No, you're not. My father's dead, and he didn't look like you anyway. Is this a funny way of adopting me, or what?"

Chase Burge, Senior, sat down with a perplexed expression. "Let me explain. You just think you're me. But you're really me—no, I mean you're you. You're your own son, really; that is, you're the son of the man you think you are, but who is really me. Oh dear, I wish I could explain! It's this way: you're suffering a delusion that you're your own father—"

Chase interrupted. "You sound like something out of Gilbert and Sullivan. If anybody has delusions around here it's—uk!" His hand had touched his chin. In a flash he was at the mirror.

"Holy Moses, where did I get this D'Artagnan effect? Have I been unconscious long?"

"Why, you've been wearing that goatee for five years. Lots of the young men wear them."

Chase Burge, Junior, began to laugh hysterically. "Oh, Lord, I guess I am crazy! I know, this is a loony bin that I've been shut up in. I'm crazy, and so are you, unless you're one of the keepers."

Pierre Lamarque threw down *his* brief case. "I think I have something, but I'm not sure."

"Let's have it, quick!" barked Lindsley.

"Let me begin at the beginning. I was down at the hospital looking over the new cases. They had one who they said was an Englishman of about 1300. I couldn't understand him at all, never realized how fast the language changes. He told us we were a 'pock of foals,' which didn't make much sense, until a professor told me it meant 'pack of fools.'

"But the prize exhibit was one of the new cases from out of town—a Mrs. Rhodes of White Plains. They told me she was—or had been—one of the outstanding uplifters of her community; during the revival of prohibition agitation twelve years ago she was one of the leading lights in the movement.

"Well, you ought to see her now! She chatters in Renaissance Italian, and slinks around with a snaky glide you wouldn't believe possible for a lady prohibitionist in her forties. She's made a dead set for all the doctors in the place, until they're scared to be alone with her. Says she's Elena della Colleoni.

"That gave me an idea, so I stopped in at the library, and found that there really was such a person as Elena della Colleoni." Lamarque grinned wickedly. "She was a notorious strumpet at the court of Cesare Borgia."

Lindsley polished his glasses slowly. Lamarque knew that meant an idea coming, and kept still.

"I—think—I—begin—to see," said the older biologist. "First, the cases, when we catch them, all act scared to death, but otherwise perfectly sane, except that they've acquired the personality of someone, real or imaginary who lived before them.

"Secondly, the pseudopsyche is always an individual who might conceivably have been the case's direct ancestor, as in the case of the redcap over in the Jersey Heights Terminal who thought he was a Zulu warrior and tried to use a traveler's umbrella as an assagai. Sometimes the descent would be difficult to trace, as in the case of Mrs. Rhodes Colleoni, but you go back enough generations and you could be almost anybody's descendant. In one case—that of the young man who thought he was his own father—we know the phylogenic relationship of the case and its pseudopsyche for a fact.

"Thirdly, in at least some cases, and conceivably in all, the pseudopsyche corresponds to a person who really lived."

"But," objected Lamarque, "if they are real, how come the fact hasn't been noted before this?"

"Hm-m-m. Well, consider the ratio between the total number of people who've lived in the last couple of millennia and the number who were prominent enough to leave a historical record of their doings. You'll see how small the chances are of turning up any big shots.

"Fourthly, the average age of the pseudopsyche is around thirty. That doesn't prove anything by itself. Jerry Plotnik's revising the average to include the latest data now. But the age figures are much too closely grouped for a random distribution: no children, and hardly any elderly people.

"Now suppose—just suppose—that the pseudopsyche is a piece of ancestral memory that's gotten carried along in the germ cells, like a piece of ultra-microscopic motion-picture film, and suppose that something happens to substitute this carried-over memory for the case's real one. You'd think you're the ancestor whose memory you've been carrying around. For obvious reasons. It would end at a point before the time when the said ancestor's child from whom you're descended was conceived. Suppose we call the phenomenon genotropism. That's not a very good name, but it'll do until I think of a better one."

Lamarque whistled. "I hope if it happens to me that I'll be one of my French ancestors and not one of my aboriginal ones. I might be sort of unmanageable as an Ojibway Indian. But say, won't this knock Weismann's theory into a cocked hat?"

"If it's correct, it'll do worse than that. I'll have to eat what I've been saying for thirty years about Lamarkism's being a zombie among evolutionary theories. But remember, this idea of ours is still just an idea, and we haven't any *positive* evidence whatever yet. More than one scientist has been caught because he assumed that because a theory of his *might* account for certain facts, it therefore *was* the explanation."

"Uh-huh, I get you. But now that we have your theory, what are we going to do with it?"

"Damned if I know," said Lindsley, reaching for his pipe.

*   *   *

The manager of the "Venus" looked gloomily at his audience, if you could call it that. Everybody who could scrape up the price of a fare was trying to get out of town, and the rest weren't spending much on entertainment. You didn't feel safe on the streets any more. Still, burlesque was holding up better than any other form of entertainment: a lot of the movie places had closed. Then, too, a merciful providence had decreed that two of the "Venus'" biggest creditors should come down with the plague.

Betty Fiorelli was working up to the climax of her strip tease. A few more grinds and bumps, and more clothing had gone into the wings. He'd told her to give 'em the works. The cops weren't likely to send an inspector around at a time like this. A faint "Ah-h-h!" from the audience. But what was the girl up to? Instead of sidling coyly into the wings, she was standing squarely facing the audience, and her rich voice rolled out in verse after sonorous verse of classic Greek, which was just that to her hearers.

Three minutes later the few strollers on 42nd Street gaped incredulously at the sight of a tall and well-made young woman, clad—preciseiy in a pair of high-heeled shoes, speeding like an arrow along the sidewalk, while after her panted the manager of the "Venus" and three stage hands. They knew not that they pursued, not Betty Fiorelli, but Thea Tisimicles, the great poetess of Lemnos, whose contemporaries (of the Fifth Century BC) thought she surpassed even Sappho.

The fishy-eyed man was talking earnestly to Professor Lindsley: "O.K., but I think you scientific guys are nuts for not getting out while the getting's good. You can stay until we pull out the inner police cordon, and then out you go. There's no use keeping the cordon there when the gangs of iso—isolinguals have begun turning up all over New Joisey and Westchester. What does 'isolingual' mean, anyway?"

"It means they speak the same language. You can see how it is. A case speaks Anglo-Saxon, say. He wanders around until he runs into somebody else who speaks Anglo-Saxon, and they join up for purposes of offense and defense. Pretty soon you have a gang. Come in, Jerry. Dr. Plotnik, Detective Inspector Monahan. Dr. Plotnik's been helping us with the mathematical side of our research."

"You mean he's one of these lightning calculators?"

"Whoop! You'll insult him. He's a mathematical genius, which is something else."

The detective applied another match to his cigar, "Something's fishy about this whole business."

Plotnik gave a sort of gurgle. "You're telling us?"

"No, sonny, I didn't just mean the disease. The National Patriots have been showing all kinds of activity. We've been getting reports from the police all over the country. A lot of them have been filtering into New York, when everybody else is trying to get out. We've caught a few trying to get through the cordons. And the big bug who owns 'em, Slidell, has disappeared."

"What!" exclaimed Lindsley.

"Yeah. You ain't read about it in the papers, because they all been too busy with the plague. But it looks to me—it almost looks—as if there might be a human origin to it."

"But how?" Plotnik stopped.

"I dunno. Maybe they poisoned the water. Thought I'd take a little run down below the cordon and see if we couldn't catch one of these tough babies that Slidell's been sending around to beat up people he don't like. Maybe we could find out why they ain't afraid of the plague. Like to come along?"

Plotnik stood up, almost upsetting his chair. "You get Pierre Lamarque to go instead of me; I just had an idea that'll take a little time to work out."

Snowflakes glided slantwise out of a gray January sky. "Better park here," said the detective, as Lindsley swung his car off Broadway at 72nd Street. "Won't do to go too far downtown. Look, there's another!"

Lindsley and Lamarque peered through the windows, and saw a hurrying figure slip into a doorway. There was something odd about the figure.

Lamarque spoke: "He's wearing a football helmet!"

"Huh?" said the detective, blinking. "Well, anyways, we're gonna take a closer look at his fancy headpiece. Got your guns, you two?" He slid out of the car, skidded a little on the snow, and steadied himself.

"Town's sure gonna get buried in snow, with nobody to remove it. Keep your eyes peeled for the isos."

The three marched abreast along the deserted street. Professor Lindsley almost stumbled over a body, half buried in the snow. He recognized a State trooper's uniform. He looked about, squinting against the snowflakes, and realized that the half dozen other darkish humps in the snow were also corpses. "Say, Monahan—"

"Sh-h! Want our friend to hear you? Now, Professor Lamarque, you stand on this side of the doorway and tackle him in the legs when he comes out. I'll do the rest." Lamarque had given up trying to explain that he wasn't a full professor. Moreover, unless something was done about the plague soon, it looked as though he never *would* be a full professor. The university buildings were deserted save for a few dauntless scientists still trying to get at the cause and cure of the affliction.

"Remember," Monahan was whispering, "the foist guy that shows a sign of going nutty, one of the others taps him on the head, but gentlelike, see? We don't want no fractured skulls." He flipped his blackjack up and down to illustrate "gentlelike."

The black outline of a man, weaving slowly along the sidewalk, materialized out of the snowflakes. He came up to the ambuscade, saying something in a pleading whine.

"Naw, scram you!" hissed the detective, flipping his blackjack suggestively.

The man scrammed.

Lindsley looked nervously up and down the street, and at the two younger men beside the doorway, Damn it, he'd been a fool to come! Guerrilla warfare was no occupation for a sixty-year-old biology professor. He'd partly brought it on himself, by being the only man to present a plausible theory to the authorities—well, at least as plausible as any others. With New York City practically lost to civilized control they'd have listened to anybody. At the present rate, in another month New England and the Middle Atlantic States would be a wilderness, inhabited solely by roving bands of isolinguals who battled each other with clubs, rocks, and the loot of hardware stores.

Suppose some of them came along now? Thinking that they had been translated by magic into a strange and terrifying world, they were as dangerous as wild beasts. Lindsley wondered what it was like to shoot a man. And then the door opened and the man in the football helmet came out.

Lamarque tackled the fellow neatly below the knees. He got out one yell before the detective was all over him, kneeling on his ribs and stuffing snow in his mouth. Then Monahan yanked off the helmet and slapped the man's skull with his blackjack.

"Come on!" he snapped, getting up and dragging the body by the coat collar toward the car.

A cluster of figures loomed out of the semidarkness. Lindsley counted six—no, seven, and felt in his pocket for the pistol. The seven just stared. Monahan brought out *his* pistol. The seven gave back apprehensively. Evidently they'd had painful experience—perhaps in the Battle of Herald Square, when a National Guard detachment and a troop of State police had scattered a horde of embattled isolinguals, only to be seized themselves, many of them, and start killing each other.

One of the seven spoke up in what sounded like a Slavonic tongue. The detective tried to smile sweetly. "Can't understand you," he said, wagging his head. The leader's sigh was audible above the hiss of the falling flakes, and the seven trudged off.

The detectives stuffed their captive into the car. Lindsley let in the clutch slowly; the right rear wheel spun a few revolutions and then gripped the snow.

Monahan yelled in his ear, "Step on it, Doc!"

Lindsley jumped and tried to comply. In the mirror he had a glimpse of people swarming out of the doorway. A submachine gun crackled; a hole the diameter of a finger appeared in the windshield, surrounded by a spiderweb of cracks. Lindsley heard a gasp from the captive, and a stream of profanity from Monahan. "They got our prisoner, the—"

The car slithered around the corner of West End and 72nd. "Damn good thing this wasn't an old front-engined car," the rasping voice continued. "They'd have let daylight into us sure. Bet the rear end looks like a gravel sizer. Take it easy, Doc; they can't see to shoot more'n a block or two."

Later Monahan said, "Nope, the stiff didn't have no papers on him, but I still think he's a National Patriot. How you coming along with those helmets?"

"All finished," replied Lindsley. "I've been standing over the analysts with a club for twenty-four hours. The shielding inside the helmet was a lead-bismuth-antimony alloy, with traces of platinum and two of the rare metals. My son-in-law's gone out to wire the specifications to Albany and Washington."

"Hope it ain't too late. We better clear out tonight, before any more of us come down with the plague."

"There's still one telephone wire open," continued Lindsley. "And the man I was talking to told me the first case has been reported from San Francisco. A scrub lady started doing a hula.

Must be a Polynesian sailor in her family tree somewhere. I—ah—" The voice trailed off. Professor Arthur Lindsley was asleep.

A lurch and the clash of metal on metal awoke him. "Hey, what—"

The detective's heroic cursing left off. "You hurt? Guess we're all right. Hey, Joe, where the hell are we? Poughkeepsie? We're on our way to Albany, Professor, or rather we *was* on our way before the truck pushed us into this here lamppost. Guess it was a case driving, from the way he weaved. Maybe I should'a tried to hunt up a plane."

Lamarque's voice came out of the dark: "Looks as if there's been another battle, from the corpses scattered around. Will that left door still open? Say, Monahan, don't you ever sleep?"

"Yeah, I grab a little now and then. Come on."

The drugstore's shattered front gaped at them with a defeated air. Inside, the detective's flashlight dug a pallid clerk out from behind the soda fountain. "Don't shoot, please!" he quavered. "You're not isolinguals? A gang of 'em took over the town yesterday, and then this evening a bigger gang came along and drove 'em out. I thought they'd all gone and came down to open up shop, but some more came along just now. Look, quick, there they are again!"

"Stand back there!" roared Monahan. The figure in the doorway shouted something back, and the detective's pistol went off.

"Quick, you guys, pile the—" But the two scientists and the other cop were already furiously building a barricade of chairs and tables. A few stones sailed past their heads and made beautiful crashes among the glassware.

Lindsley peered over the top of the upturned table. A figure, wild in the moonlight, rose from the sidewalk and raised a length of pipe or something. Lindsley fumbled for his pistol. Where the devil was the safety catch on the thing? He pulled the trigger. As his senses cleared after the flash and report, he saw that the figure was still there. He gripped the gun in both hands and tried again. The figure doubled over and went *fthup!* in the slush.

Hours later Lamarque wiped his mouth on his sleeve. "If I drink another malted milk, I'll get indigestion. What else have you, Mr. Bloom?"

"Sorry, sir, but the isos cleaned out all the pies and bread and things. And the gas is shut off, so I can't make any coffee. It'll have to be sodas or nothing, unless you want to try some cough drops."

"Ugh! Any luck on the phone, Joe?"

"Nope. Unless somebody finds us by dark it'll be just tough. They're waiting for that to rush us."

Unless somebody found them— There wouldn't be any street lights to shoot by. And four pistols wouldn't stop the horde of isolinguals waiting out of sight around the corners.

Darkness—no moon this time. The voices of the isos wafted into the drugstore. The leaders were evidently haranguing their men. Then there was a full-throated yell, and the slopping of many feet in the slush. Bloom, the clerk, was carefully setting a row of bottles on the floor to use as missiles. If you didn't have a gun, you had to use something.

Lamarque's pistol cracked. "Got one!"

Then the fusillade. But they came on in a solid mass. Lindsley thought, "These are really good, honest citizens I'm shooting, except for their malady." He realized that he had been squeezing the trigger of an empty gun. How the devil did you load the things? He'd never get it figured out before they swarmed in and finished them off. They were almost in the drugstore now—

Monahan stopped his target practice to say, "Now why the hell are they all running one way? What's that noise? If it's a machine gun, boy, we're saved!"

Lindsley never imagined he'd find that implacable hammering the sweetest of sounds. The armored car skidded to a stop, and two football-helmeted soldiers jumped out.

Monahan turned to Lamarque. "What's that? Sorry, but I didn't get you. What? *Hey!*" He flung his arms around the young biologist in a bearlike hug. "Soldier! You got any more helmets?"

Lamarque's muttering rose to a frenzied shriek.

"Yeah, they're in the truck."

"*What* truck?"

"They were right behind us; ought to be along any—Yeah, here they come."

"Well, get one, quick! This guy's gone screwy like the others!"

When the helmet had been forced on Lamarque's unwilling

head, Monahan rubbed his shins. "Lord, Professor, I didn't know you was that strong. I guess the guy you toined into never loined no Queensbury rules or nothing. But you shouldn't have tried to bite me."

Lamarque was acutely embarrased. "I—I'm sorry. You know I haven't any recollection of the past few minutes at all, up to the time you put the helmet on me—"

"'S all right; it wasn't your fault. Now let's find some of the isos we winged and put helmets on them. . . ."

Forty-eight hours later, Lindsley rubbed his eyes. "What do you mean by waking me up at this time of day, you young scoundrel? Oh, the paper. What's the news, quick?"

Lamarque seated himself on the bed with his slightly satanic grin. "You guessed right. They sent the army down to surround the area we figured the radiations were coming from, or rather that Plotnik figured they were coming from by finding the mass center of the locations of the cases reported. They were all wearing our cute little helmets, so the radiations didn't affect them.

"When they closed in and started searching houses they rounded up several thousand National Patriots. There was a little shooting, but most of the N.P.s surrendered quietly enough when they saw what they were up against.

"The military located the cause of the whole works in an old house on Christopher Street. The place was full of radio apparatus from cellar to roof. They found Slidell himself, and his master mind, a Dr. Falk, whom nobody ever heard of, but who modestly describes himself as the greatest scientist of the age. Maybe he's right.

"This Falk got scared when he saw bayonets pointed at his stomach, and let out the whole story. Seems he found a complicated combination of harmonics on a long radio wave that would work this ancestral-memory switch, and he and Slidell figured to disorganize the whole country with it. And when his broadcasting set was turned off and everybody became himself again, we'd find Slidell installed as dictator and the N.P.s running everything. Of course, in the meantime they'd be wearing the helmets and would be shielded from the radiations.

"The army turned the thing off right away, and all our medieval knights and yeomen are now ordinary citizens, and busy picking up the pieces. Slidell, of course, made a speech. Too bad there wasn't a stenographer there to record it. I suppose he and Falk will be shot for murder, treason, and every other crime on the books, though I think they could plead insanity with some justice.

"Oh, yes, you're now the head of the department, and I'm a full professor. Also, we're famous, and are about to be intensively photographed and interviewed."

Lindsley scratched his diminutive beard. "Seems to me, Pierre, that we're getting away with murder. Plotnik really figured out the source of those radiations, and Monahan had the idea of suspecting the N.P.s and setting out to catch one."

"Don't worry about them. They're getting their share of the glory."

"I suppose so. But right now what I want is a vacation from all scientific thought."

INTRODUCTION TO
"FREEDOM OF THE RACE"

by Anne McCaffrey

I had started reading science fiction with an intense dedication and tried my hand at writing stories in the early 50s. At that point in time, I met one of the editors of *Fantastic Magazine* and she kindly read some of my earliest attempts at short stories. She also kindly told me just how far off telling a good one I was.

There was a lot of excitement over Civil Rights then—and I was trying to get pregnant. So it occurred to me that one of the most basic rights was having a child of your own species. So I sat me down and typed out "Freedom of the Race" ... rather grotesque since few alien species would be biologically compatible with us humanoids. (Unless you go with the Pan Spermia theory which I later did in "Nimisha's Ship.") I think what started me on that vein were all those elegant blondes in hubcap bras on the covers of *Amazing* and *Fantastic*.

Women certainly were provided as "decorative broads" with no role at all in the action of the story except to be stupid enough to have to have the "scientist" in the story explain what it was all about. (The upshot of that was eventually *Restoree*.)

All enthused with myself, I sent the story in to *Science Fiction Plus*, which Sam Moskowitz had just started—on the notion that he wouldn't have enough stories sent in yet. He did kindly pick mine, edited out the worst blunders, and since it was under 1000 words, whomped up some advertising that I had won a contest for a good story under 1000 words. A notice to that effect ran in the local *Montclair Times* and I got a whole $100 for the yarn.

My first published story! Well, there was cheering in my house and when I got the check, I waved it in all the doubters' faces, even my small son's. He was singularly unimpressed.

But I WAS a PUBLISHED AUTHOR, and I have never forgotten that thrill nor the smell of the finished magazine when my copy arrived. I still get a charge out of seeing my books on store shelves and practically purr audibly when there is a window featuring the novels. I don't think anyone ever forgets their First Published Story, even if later professional expertise makes you wince and cringe at how badly you expressed yourself.

Good wishes to all who want to be published! It's a great feeling.

FREEDOM OF THE RACE

by Anne McCaffrey

THE labor pains were increasing. The dainty Martian doctor arrived and examined her briefly. He chattered away at the Martian nurse in charge. Although she understood Martian, Jean's mind registered the conversation dimly, for the odd amnesia of birthing dulled her to everything.

The next spasm contracted her womb. She breathed deeply, slowly, as she'd been taught, expanding abdominal muscles to give the womb more freedom. All her energy was concentrated on breathing and relaxing, but slowly the doctor's words reached her mind.

"Such a healthy animal, an excellent breeder. I have high hopes that everything will go all right in this case. If so, I'll insist the commissioner use her again. It's against our policy, but we are desperate."

"So," thought Jean in her semistupor, "that's what happened to the girls who didn't come back to the Center. They died insuring life to these multiple monsters. They weren't set free.

Viny was right and we wouldn't believe her. She must be dead, too."

Again the Martian nurse ordered her to turn over, and Jean felt the cold metal of the fetuscope on her swollen abdomen. She tried unsuccessfully to breathe deeply as another contraction gripped her, and she wanted so to turn back to her side. It wouldn't matter what she wanted . . . she was just an animal incubator. There would be no narcotic ease to this birth. There was too much danger of asphyxiating the Martian get whose lungs at birth were curiously delicate.

"O ingenious conquerors," she thought. "You arrive on our good green Earth from your desiccated world. You end our petty national squabbles by enslaving us. All the indignities and offices of slavery are heaped on every head. And they all pale with banality against your crowning psychological coup. You make us bear, not half-breeds toward which we might conceivably grow attached, but your own spawn that your fragile wives could not carry on our oxygen-loaded Terra. Could there be a greater indignity?

How she and the other girls had prayed for failure in implantation, devised schemes for miscarriage, for some small way to abort the fetus successfully, even with the penalty of slow-burn! Jean vividly remembered the slow-burning she had had to witness two years ago when she was sixteen. It had taken agonizing, shrieking hours for that girl to be consumed by the creeping, crawling, crisping organism.

The pains crowded in on each other with so precious little time between for rest—rest that meant survival for her. She couldn't be far from the transition to second-stage labor, she thought with hope. Her fellow brood mares had said it was easy—that a Martian was so small it emerged easily.

That was before the vogue of multiple births.

The rare instances of multiple births to a Martian were always stillborn . . . until the experiment of transplanting twin placentae into a Terran womb, resulting in successful birth of twins. After that, the fad was on. With a little scientific help, twins, triplets, quintuplets, of whichever sex desired were reluctantly borne by Terran girls.

In the midst of this mirthless reminiscence, Jean felt an irresistible urge to bear down and she responded automatically. She heard around her sudden movements, excited brusque orders from the Martian nurse who had never left her side for four months.

She was conscious of several more Martian voices now, and very bright lights. She opened her eyes wearily and saw she was in the delivery room, her bed being pushed against a slab table. Beside her were the Martian parents of the get within her . . . their odd yellow wolf-eyes gleaming in the dark.

Then she felt the hands of the Terran nurses on her, moving her to the delivery table. The girl at her head fumbled to catch her under the arms and was severely reprimanded by the nervous Martian doctor.

"You'll burn slow if you harm her," he shouted in his high, whining voice.

"She'll be all right," the nurse replied, with unexpected firmness for a Terran answering a Martian.

The nurse bent low and said softly in Jean's ear: "Don't worry, baby, everything will be all right—another batch of dead, deformed offspring for our eager Martian 'liberators.'"

Jean snapped alert despite the excruciating pain.

The Terran nurse smiled. A grim, triumphant smile. "*German measles*," she whispered. "Eighty per cent of Earth women who catch the disease from their third to fifth month of pregnancy produce children with some defect or deformity, deaf mutes, mongolian idiots, and blind. In the case of fragile, Martian offspring, the total is one hundred percent. There hasn't been a normal Martian baby born in six months."

Jean remembered six months ago, when she had a slight fever and flushing of the skin! It was too mild for the Martians to notice and over so quickly that she hadn't complained. Pregnant women's greatest fear was now their savior! This was only the beginning. Terra would be free.

ABOUT "PROOF,"
OF COURSE

by Hal Clement

I'm rather surprised how little I seem to have changed in sixty years. My first story, published in 1942, shows pretty clearly the attitude I still have toward science and science fiction. Whether this means I matured early or never matured at all I can't, of course, say objectively.

I had realized by the age of nineteen that my personal viewpoint, like those of the rest of my species, was not the only possible correct one. This quickly became a conscious attitude, which soon caused me to react negatively to any sentence beginning with the words "of course," trying to decide why anyone would regard that particular attitude as obvious, and to set up situations in which some other "of course" would be more reasonable. This seems best accomplished by World Building, and pretty well describes the underlying basis of most of my work published since, though the detailed treatment (I hope) has improved as I learned more about the universe I, and presumably most of my readers, live in (Okay, there's another story seed. If it takes root in your mind, go ahead and write it; I'll probably never get around to it, and if I do the chances are strongly against the two stories' being alike enough to arouse suspicions of plagiarism. Some people say there's only one story, or only three, or only seventeen; I regard the number of ways a situation can be led to an outcome as one of the better illustrations of the concept of infinity).

So—of course matter doesn't have to be solid. Of

course a planet has nearly the same surface gravity all over.

Of course a planet has about the same atmosphere at sea level—if it has anything that serves as sea level; there's another story seed—all over its surface (see your file of back *Galileos*; it was a world-building article, not a story, in one of the very early issues. I lack the ambition to check which one. It justified a major difference in air composition between northern and southern hemispheres of a planet, and I think someone once did make use of it—again, in an issue of *Galileo*).

Of course the oxidizing part of a living organism's nutrient must be a gas.

Of course a planet's overall climate can't change seriously in one lifetime (all right, I'm philosophically a Republican even if I did write "Cycle of Fire." I don't have to be a Fundamentalist one).

Of course.

"Proof" may therefore be a youthful declaration of an initial basic attitude which hasn't changed much since. I *have* learned a lot of things which have let me discipline my imagination more effectively; but even in "Proof," my life-forms weren't gaseous. There are, of course, rules. One of them, of course, is that life needs a very complex physical structure, and I don't fight that.

PROOF

by Hal Clement

KRON held his huge freighter motionless, feeling forward for outside contact. The tremendous interplay of magnetic and electrostatic fields just beyond the city's edge was as clearly perceptible to his senses as the city itself—a mile-wide disk ringed with conical field towers, stretching away behind and to each side. The ship was poised between two of the towers; immediately behind it was the field from which Kron had just taken off. The area was covered with cradles of various forms—cup-shaped receptacles which held city craft like Kron's own; long, boat-shaped hollows wherein reposed the cigarlike vessels which plied between the cities; and towering skeleton frameworks which held upright the slender double cones that hurtled across the dark, lifeless regions between stars.

Beyond the landing field was the city proper; the surface of the disk was covered with geometrically shaped buildings— cones, cylinders, prisms, and hemispheres, jumbled together.

Kron could "see" all this as easily as a human being in an airplane can see New York; but no human eyes could have perceived this city, even if a man could have existed anywhere near it. The city, buildings and all, glowed with a savage, white heat; and about and beyond it—a part of it, to human eyes— raged the equally dazzling, incandescent gases of the solar photosphere.

The freighter was preparing to launch itself into that fiery ocean; Kron was watching the play of the artificial reaction fields that supported the city, preparatory to plunging through them at a safe moment.

There was considerable risk of being flattened against the edge of the disk if an inauspicious choice was made, but Kron was an experienced flier, and slipped past the barrier with a sudden, hurtling acceleration that would have pulped any body of flesh and bone. The outer fringe of the field flung the globe sharply downward; then it was free, and the city was dwindling above them.

Kron and four others remained at their posts; the rest of the crew of thirty relaxed, their spherical bodies lying passive in the cuplike rests distributed through the ship bathing in the fierce radiance on which those bodies fed, and which was continually streaming from a three-inch spheroid at the center of the craft. That an artificial source of energy should be needed in such an environment may seem strange, but to these creatures the outer layers of the Sun were far more inhospitable to life than is the stratosphere of Earth to human beings.

They had evolved far down near the solar core, where pressures and temperatures were such that matter existed in the "collapsed" state characteristic of the entire mass of white dwarf stars. Their bodies were simply constructed: a matrix of close-packed electrons—really an unimaginably dense electrostatic field, possessing quasi-solid properties—surrounded a core of neutrons, compacted to the ultimate degree. Radiation of sufficient energy, falling on the "skin," was stabilized, altered to the pattern and structure of neutrons; the tiny particles of neutronium which resulted were borne along a circulatory system—of magnetic fields, instead of blood—to the nucleus, where it was stored.

The race had evolved to the point where no material appendages were needed. Projected beams and fields of force were their limbs, powered by the annihilation of some of their own neutron substance. Their strange senses gave them awareness not only of electromagnetic radiation, permitting them to "see" in a more or less normal fashion, but also of energies still undreamed of by human scientists. Kron, now hundreds of miles below the city, was still dimly aware of its location, though radio waves, light, and gamma rays were all hopelessly fogged in the clouds of free electrons. At his goal, far down in the solar interior, "seeing" conditions would be worse—anything more than a few hundred yards distant would be quite indetectable even to him.

Poised beside Kron, near the center of the spheroidal Sunship, was another being. Its body was ovoid in shape, like that of the Solarian, but longer and narrower, while the ends were tipped with pyramidal structures of neutronium, which projected through the "skin." A second, fainter static aura outside the principal surface enveloped creature; and as the crew relaxed in their cups, a beam energy from this envelope impinged on Kron's body. It carried a meaning, transmitting a clear thought from one being to the other.

"I still find difficulty in believing my senses," stated the stranger. "My own worlds revolve about another which is somewhat similar to this; but such a vast and tenuous atmosphere is most unlike conditions at home. Have you ever been away from Sol?"

"Yes," replied Kron, "I was once on the crew of an interstellar projectile. I have never seen your star, however; my acquaintance with it is entirely through hearsay. I am told it consists almost entirely of collapsed matter, like the core of our own; but there is practically no atmosphere. Can this be so? I should think, at the temperature necessary for life, gases would break free of the core and form an envelope."

"They tend to do so, of course," returned the other, "but our surface gravity is immeasurably greater than anything you have here; even your core pull is less, since it is much less dense than our star. Only the fact that our worlds are small, thus causing a rapid diminution of gravity as one leaves them, makes it possible to get a ship away from them at all; atoms, with only their original velocities, remain within a few miles of the surface.

"But you remind me of my purpose on this world—to check certain points of a new theory concerning the possible behavior of aggregations of normal atoms. That was why I arranged a trip on your flier; I have to make density, pressure, temperature, and a dozen other kinds of measurements at a couple of thousand different levels, in your atmosphere. While I'm doing it, would you mind telling me why you make these regular trips—and why, for that matter, you live so far above your natural level? I should think you would find life easier below, since there would be no need to remain in sealed buildings or to expend such a terrific amount of power in supporting your cities?"

Kron's answer was slow.

"We make the journeys to obtain neutronium. It is impossible to convert enough power from the immediate neighborhood of the cities to support them; we must descend periodically for more, even though our converters take so much as to lower the solar temperature considerably for thousands of miles around each city.

"The trips are dangerous—you should have been told that. We carry a crew of thirty, when two would be enough to man this ship, for we must fight, as well as fly. You spoke truly when you said that the lower regions of Sol are our natural home; but for eons we have not dared to make more than fleeting visits, to steal the power which is life to us.

"Your little worlds have been almost completely subjugated by your people, Sirian; they never had life-forms sufficiently powerful to threaten seriously your domination. But Sol, whose core alone is far larger than the Sirius B pair, did develop such creatures. Some are vast, stupid, slow-moving, or immobile; others are semi-intelligent and rapid movers; all are more than willing to ingest the ready-compacted neutronium of another living being."

Kron's tale was interrupted for a moment, as the Sirian sent a ray probing out through the ship's wall, testing the physical state of the inferno beyond. A record was made, and the Solarian resumed.

"We, according to logical theory, were once just such a race—of small intelligence, seeking the needs of life among a horde of competing organisms. Our greatest enemy was a being much like ourselves in size and power—just slightly superior in both ways. We were somewhat ahead in intelligence, and I suppose we owe them some thanks—without the competition they provided, we should not have been forced to develop our minds to their present level. We learned to cooperate in fighting them, and from that came the discovery that many of us together could handle natural forces that a single individual could not even approach, and survive. The creation of force effects that had no counterpart in nature was the next step; and, with the understanding of them, our science grew.

"The first cities were of neutronium, like those of today, but it was necessary to stabilize the neutrons with fields of energy; at core temperature, as you know, neutronium is a gas. The cities were spherical and much smaller than our present ones. For a long time, we managed to defend them.

"But our enemies evolved, too; not in intelligence, but in power and fecundity. With overspecialization of their physical powers, their mentalities actually degenerated; they became little more than highly organized machines, driven, by an age-old enmity toward our race, to seek us out and destroy us. Their new powers at last enabled them neutralize, by brute force, the fields which held our cities in shape; and then it was that, from necessity, we fled to the wild, inhospitable upper regions of Sol's atmosphere. Many cities were destroyed by the enemy before a means of supporting them was devised; many more fell victims to forces which we generated, without being able to control, in the effort. The dangers of our present-day trips seem trivial beside those our ancestors braved, in spite of the fact that ships not infrequently fail to return from their flights. Does that answer your question?"

The Sirian's reply was hesitant. "I guess it does. You of Sol must have developed far more rapidly than we, under that drive; your science, I know, is superior to ours in certain ways, although it was my race which first developed space flight."

"You had greater opportunities in that line," returned Kron. "Two small stars, less than a diameter apart, circling a larger one at a distance incomparably smaller than the usual interstellar interval, provided perfect ground for experimental flights; between your world and mine, even radiation requires some hundred and thirty rotations to make the journey, and even the nearest other star is almost half as far.

"But enough of this—history is considered by too many to be a dry subject. What brings you on a trip with a power flier? You certainly have not learned anything yet which you could not have been told in the city."

During the conversation, the Sirian had periodically tested the atmosphere beyond the hull. He spoke rather absently, as though concentrating on something other than his words.

"I would not be too sure of that, Solarian. My measurements are of greater delicacy than we have ever before achieved. I am looking, for a very special effect, to substantiate or disprove a hypothesis which I have recently advanced—much to the detriment of my prestige. If you are interested, I might explain: laugh afterward if you care to—you will not be the first.

"The theory is simplicity itself. It has occurred to me that matter—ordinary substances like iron and calcium—might actually take on solid form, like neutronium, under the proper conditions. The normal gas, you know, consists of minute particles traveling with considerable speed in all directions. There seems to be no way of telling whether or not these atoms exert appreciable forces on one another; but it seems to me that if they were brought closely enough together, or slowed down sufficiently, some such effects might be detected."

"How, and why?" asked Kron. "If the forces are there, why should they not be detectable under ordinary conditions?"

"Tiny changes in velocity due to mutual attraction or repulsion would scarcely be noticed when the atomic speeds are of the order of hundreds of kilometers per second," returned the Sirian. "The effects I seek to detect are of a different nature. Consider, please. We know the sizes of the various atoms, from their radiations. We also know that under normal conditions, a given mass of any particular gas fills a certain volume. If, however, we surround this gas with an impenetrable container and exert pressure, that volume decreases. We would expect that decrease to be proportional to the pressure, except for an easily determined constant due to the size of the atoms, if no interatomic forces existed; to detect such forces, I am making a complete series of pressure-density tests, more delicate than any heretofore, from the level of your cities down to the neutron core of your world.

"If we could reduce the kinetic energy of the atoms—slow

down their motions of translation—the task would probably be simpler; but I see no way to accomplish that. Perhaps, if we could negate nearly all of that energy, the interatomic forces would actually hold the atoms in definite relative positions, approximating the solid state. It was that somewhat injudicious and perhaps too imaginative suggestion which caused my whole idea to be ridiculed on Sirius."

The ship dropped several hundred miles in the few seconds after Kron answered; since gaseous friction is independent of change in density, the high pressures of the regions being penetrated would be no bar to high speed of flight. Unfortunately, the viscosity of a gas does increase directly as the square root of its temperature; and at the lower levels of the Sun, travel would be slow.

"Whether or not our scientists will listen to you, I cannot say," said Kron finally. "Some of them are a rather imaginative crowd, I guess, and none of them will ignore any data you may produce.

"I do not laugh, either. My reason will certainly interest you, as your theory intrigues me. It is the first time anyone has accounted even partly for the things that happened to us on one of my flights."

The other members of the crew shifted slightly on their cradles; a ripple of interest passed through them, for all had heard rumors and vague tales of Kron's time in the space carrier fleets. The Sirian settled himself more comfortably; Kron dimmed the central globe of radiance a trifle, for the outside temperature was now considerably higher, and began the tale.

"This happened toward the end of my career in space. I had made many voyages with the merchant and passenger vessels, had been promoted from the lowest ranks, through many rotations, to the post of independent captain. I had my own cruiser—a special long-period explorer, by the Solarian government. She was shaped like our modern interstellar carriers, consisting of two cones, bases together, with the field ring just forward of their meeting point. She was larger than most, being designed to carry fuel for exceptionally long flights.

"Another cruiser, similar in every respect, was under the command of a comrade of mine, named Akro; and the two of us were commissioned to transport a party of scientists and explorers to the then newly discovered Fourth System, which lies, as you know, nearly in the plane of the solar equator, but about half again as distant as Sirius.

"We made good time, averaging nearly half the speed of radiation, and reached the star with a good portion of our hulls still unconsumed. We need not have worried about that, in any case; the star was denser even than the Sirius B twins, and neutronium was very plentiful. I restocked at once, plating my inner walls with the stuff until they had reached their original thickness, although experience indicated that the original supply was ample to carry us back to Sol, to Sirius, or to Procyon B.

"Akro, at the request of the scientists, did not refuel. Life was present on the star, as it seems to be on all stars where the atomic velocities and the density are high enough; and the biologists wanted to bring back specimens. That meant that room would be needed, and if Akro replated his walls to normal thickness, that room would be lacking—as I have mentioned, these were special long-range craft, and a large portion of their volume consisted of available neutronium.

"So it happened that the other ship left the Fourth System with a low, but theoretically sufficient, stock of fuel, and half a dozen compartments filled with specimens of alien life. I kept within detection distance at all times, in case of trouble, for some of those life-forms were as dangerous as those of Sol, and like them, all consumed neutronium. They had to be kept well under control to safeguard the very walls of the ship, and it is surprisingly difficult to make a wild beast, surrounded by food, stay on short rations.

"Some of the creatures proved absolutely unmanageable; they had to be destroyed. Others were calmed by lowering the atomic excitation of their compartments, sending them into a stupor; but the scientists were reluctant to try that in most cases, since not all of the beings could stand such treatment.

"So, for nearly four hundred solar rotations, Akro practically fought his vessel across space—fought successfully. He managed on his own power until we were within a few hundred diameters of Sol; but I had to help him with the landing—or try to, for the landing was never made.

"It may seem strange, but there is a large volume of space in the neighborhood of this Sun which is hardly ever traversed. The normal landing orbit arches high over one of the poles of rotation, enters atmosphere almost tangentially somewhere between that pole and the equator, and kills as much as remains of the ship's velocity in the outer atmospheric layers. There is a minimum of magnetic interference that way, since the flier practically coasts along the lines of force of the solar magnetic field.

"As a result, few ships pass through the space near the plane of the solar equator. One or two may have done so before us, and I know of several that searched the region later; but none encountered the thing which we found.

"About the time we would normally have started correcting our orbits for a tangential landing, Akro radiated me the information that he could not possibly control his ship any farther with the power still available to him. His walls were already so thin that radiation loss, ordinarily negligible, was becoming a definite menace to his vessel. All his remaining energy would have to be employed in keeping the interior of his ship habitable.

"The only thing I could do was to attach our ships together with an attractor beam, and make a nearly perpendicular drop to Sol. We would have to take our chances with magnetic and electrostatic disturbances in the city-supporting fields which cover so much of the near-equatorial zones, and try to graze the nucleus of the Sun instead of its outer atmosphere, so that Akro could replenish his rapidly failing power.

"Akro's hull was radiating quite perceptibly now; it made an easy target for an attractor. We connected without difficulty, and our slightly different linear velocities caused us to revolve slowly about each other, pivoting on the center of mass of our two ships. I cut off my driving fields, and we fell spinning toward Sol.

"I was becoming seriously worried about Akro's chances of survival. The now-alarming energy loss through his almost consumed hull threatened to exhaust his supply long before we reached the core; and we were still more than a hundred diameters out. I could not give him any power; we were revolving about each other at a distance of about one-tenth of a solar diameter. To lessen that distance materially would increase our speed of revolution to a point where the attractor could not overcome centrifugal force; and I had neither power nor time to perform the delicate job of exactly neutralizing our rotary momentum without throwing us entirely off course. All we could do was hope.

"We were somewhere between one hundred and one hundred and fifty diameters out when there occurred the most peculiar phenomenon I have ever encountered. The plane of revolution of our two ships passed near Sol, but was nearly perpendicular to the solar equator; at the time of which I speak, Akro's ship was almost directly between my flier and the Sun. Observations had just shown that we were accelerating Sunward at an unexpectedly high pace, when a call came from Akro.

"'Kron! I am being pulled away from your attractor! There is a large mass somewhere near, for the pull is gravitational, but it emits no radiation that I can detect. Increase your pull, if you can; I cannot possibly free myself alone.'

"I did what I could, which was very little. Since we did not know the location of the disturbing dark body, it was impossible to tell just what I should do to avoid bringing my own or Akro's vessel too close. I think now that if I had released him immediately he would have swung clear, for the body was not large, I believe. Unfortunately, I did the opposite, and nearly lost my own ship as well. Two of my crew were throwing as much power as they could convert and handle into the attractor, and trying to hold it on the still easily visible hull of Akro's ship; but the motions of the latter were so peculiar that aiming was a difficult task. They held the ship as long as we could see it; but quite suddenly the radiations by means of which we perceived the vessel faded out, and before we could find a band which would get through, the sudden cessation of our centripetal acceleration told us that the beam had slipped from its target.

"We found that electromagnetic radiations of wavelengths in the octave above H-alpha would penetrate the interference, and Akro's hull was leaking energy enough to radiate in that band. When we found him, however, we could scarcely believe our senses; his velocity was now nearly at right angles to his former course, and his hull radiation had become far weaker. What terrific force had caused this acceleration, and what strange field was blanketing the radiation, were questions none of us could answer.

"Strain as we might, not one of us could pick up an erg of radiant energy that might emanate from the thing that had trapped Akro. We could only watch, and endeavor to plot his course relative to our own, at first. Our ships were nearing each other rapidly, and we were attempting to determine the time and distance of closest approach, when we were startled by the impact of a communicator beam. Akro was alive! The beam was weak, very weak, showing what an infinitesimal amount of power he felt he could spare. His words were not encouraging.

"'Kron! You may as well cut your attractor, if you are still trying to catch me. No power that I dare supply seems to move me perceptibly in any direction from this course. We are badly shocked, for we hit something that felt almost solid. The walls, even, are strained, and may go at any time.'

"'Can you perceive anything around you?' I returned. 'You seem to us to be alone in space, though something is absorbing most of your radiated energy. There must be energies in the cosmos of which we have never dreamed, simply because they did not affect our senses. What do your scientists say?'

"'Very little,' was the answer. 'They have made a few tests, but they say that anything they project is absorbed without reradiating anything useful. We seem to be in a sort of energy vacuum—it takes everything and returns nothing.'

"This was the most alarming item yet. Even in free space, we had been doubtful of Akro's chances of survival; now they seemed reduced to the ultimate zero.

"Meanwhile, our ships were rapidly approaching each other. As nearly as my navigators could tell, both vessels were pursuing almost straight lines in space. The lines were nearly perpendicular but did not lie in a common plane; their minimum distance apart was about one one-thousandth of a solar diameter. His velocity seemed nearly constant, while I was accelerating Sunward. It seemed that we would reach the near-intersection point almost simultaneously, which meant that my ship was certain to approach the energy vacuum much too closely. I did not dare to try to pull Akro free with an attractor; it was only too obvious that such an attempt could only end in disaster for both vessels. If he could not free himself, he was lost.

"We could only watch helplessly as the point of light marking the position of Akro's flier swept closer and closer. At first, as I have said, it seemed perfectly free in space; but as we looked, the region around it began to radiate feebly. There was nothing recognizable about the vibrations, simply a continuous spectrum, cut off by some interference just below the H-alpha wavelength and, at the other end, some three octaves higher. As the emission grew stronger, the visible region around the stranded ship larger, fading into nothingness at the edges. Brighter and broader the patch of radiance grew, as we swept toward it."

That same radiance was seriously inconveniencing Gordon Aller, who was supposed to be surveying for a geological map of northern Australia. He was camped by the only water hole in many miles, and had stayed up long after dark preparing his cameras, barometer, soil kit, and other equipment for the morrow's work.

The arrangement of instruments completed, he did not at once retire to his blankets. With his back against a smooth rock, and a short, blackened pipe clenched in his teeth, he sat for some time, pondering. The object of his musing does not matter to us; though his eyes were directed heavenward, he was sufficiently accustomed to the southern sky to render it improbable that he was paying much attention to its beauties.

However that may be, his gaze was suddenly attracted to the zenith. He had often seen stars which appeared to move when near the edge of his field of vision—it is a common illusion; but this one continued to shift as he turned his eyes upward.

Not far from Achernar was a brilliant white point, which brightened as Aller watched it. It was moving slowly northward, it seemed; but only a moment was needed for the man to realize that the slowness was illusory. The thing was slashing almost vertically downward at an enormous speed, and must strike Earth not far from his camp.

Aller was not an astronomer and had no idea of astronomical distances or speeds. He may be forgiven for thinking of the object as traveling perhaps as fast as a modern fighting plane, and first appearing at a height of two or three miles. The natural conclusion from this belief was that the crash would occur within a few hundred feet of the camp. Aller paled; he had seen pictures of the Devil's Pit in Arizona.

Actually, of course, the meteor first presented itself to his gaze at a height of some eighty miles, and was then traveling at a rate of many miles per second relative to Earth. At that speed, the air presented a practically solid obstacle to its flight, and the object was forced to a fairly constant velocity of ten or twelve hundred yards a second while still nearly ten miles from Earth's surface. It was at that point that Aller's eyes caught up with, and succeeded in focusing upon, the celestial visitor.

That first burst of light had been radiated by the frightfully compressed and heated air in front of the thing; as the original velocity departed, so did the dazzling light. Aller got a clear view of the meteor at a range of less than five miles, for perhaps ten seconds before the impact. It was still incandescent, radiating a bright cherry-red; this must have been due to the loss from within, for so brief a contact even with such highly heated air could not have warmed the Sunship's neutronium walls a measurable fraction of a degree.

Aller felt the ground tremble as the vessel struck. A geyser of earth, barely visible in the reddish light of the hull, spouted skyward, to fall back seconds later with a long-drawn-out rumble. The man stared at the spot, two miles away, which was still giving off a faint glow. Were "shooting stars" as regularly shaped as that? He had seen a smooth, slender body, more than a hundred feet in length, apparently composed of two cones of unequal length, joined together at the bases. Around the longer cone, not far from the point of juncture, was a thick bulging ring; no further details were visible at the distance from which he had observed. Aller's vague recollections of meteorites, seen in various museums, brought images of irregular, clinkerlike objects before his mind's eye. What, then, could this thing be?

He was not imaginative enough to think for a moment of any possible extraterrestrial source for an aircraft; when it did occur to him that the object was of artificial origin, he thought more of some experimental machine produced by one of the more progressive Earth nations.

At the thought, Aller strapped a first-aid kit to his side and set out toward the crater, in the face of the obvious fact that nothing human could possibly have survived such a crash. He stumbled over the uneven terrain for a quarter of a mile and then stopped on a small rise of ground to examine more closely the site of the wreck.

The glow should have died by this time, for Aller had taken all of ten minutes to pick his way those few hundred yards; but the dull-red light ahead had changed to a brilliant orange radiance against which the serrated edges of the pit were clearly silhouetted. No flames were visible; whence came the increasing heat? Aller attempted to get closer, but a wave of frightfully hot

air blistered his face and hands and drove him back. He took up
a station near his former camp, and watched.

If the hull of the flier had been anywhere near its normal
thickness, the tremendous mass of neutronium would have
sunk through the hardest of rocks as though they were liquid.
There was, however, scarcely more than a paper thickness of
the substance at any part of the walls; and an upthrust of
adamantine volcanic rock not far beneath the surface of the
desert proved thick enough to absorb the Sunship's momentum
and to support its still enormous weight. Consequently, the ship
was covered only by a thin layer of powdered rock which had
fallen back into the crater. The disturbances arising from the
now extremely rapid loss of energy from Akro's ship were, as a
result, decidedly visible from the surface.

The hull, though thin, was still intact; but its temperature
was now far above the melting point of the surrounding rocks.
The thin layer of pulverized material above the ship melted and
flowed away almost instantly, permitting free radiation to the
air above; and so enormous is the specific heat of neutronium
that no perceptible lowering of hull temperature occurred.

Aller, from his point of observation, saw the brilliant fan of
light that sprang from the pit as the flier's hull was exposed—
the vessel itself was invisible to him, since he was only slightly
above the level of the crater's mouth. He wondered if the impact of the "meteor" had released some pent-up volcanic energy, and began to doubt, quite justifiably, if he was at a safe
distance. His doubts vanished and were replaced by certainty as
the edges of the crater began to glow dull red, then bright orange, and slowly subsided out of sight. He began packing the
most valuable items of his equipment, while a muted, continuous roaring and occasional heavy thuds from the direction of
the pit admonished him to hasten.

When he straightened up, with the seventy-pound pack settled on his shoulders, there was simply a lake of lava where the
crater had been. The fiery area spread even as he watched; and
without further delay he set off on his own back trail. He could
see easily by the light diffused from the inferno behind him;
and he made fairly good time, considering his burden and the
fact that he had not slept since the preceding night.

The rock beneath Akro's craft was, as we have said, extremely hard. Since there was relatively free escape upward for
the constantly liberated energy, this stratum melted very

slowly, gradually letting the vessel sink deeper into the earth. What would have happened if Akro's power supply had been greater is problematical; Aller can tell us only that some five hours after the landing, as he was resting for a few moments near the top of a rocky hillock, the phenomenon came to a cataclysmic end.

A quivering of the earth beneath him caused the surveyor to look back toward his erstwhile camp. The lake of lava, which by this time was the better part of a mile in breadth, seemed curiously agitated. Aller, from his rather poor vantage point, could see huge bubbles of pasty lava hump themselves up and burst, releasing brilliant clouds of vapor. Each cloud illuminated earth and sky before cooling to invisibility, so that the effect was somewhat similar to a series of lightning flashes.

For a short time—certainly no longer than a quarter of a minute—Aller was able to watch as the activity increased. Then a particularly violent shock almost flung him from the hilltop, and at nearly the same instant the entire volume of molten rock fountained skyward. For an instant it seemed to hang there, a white, raging pillar of liquid and gas; then it dissolved, giving way before the savage thrust of the suddenly released energy below. A tongue of radiance, of an intensity indescribable in mere words, stabbed upward, into and through the lava, volatilizing instantly. A dozen square miles of desert glowed white, then an almost invisible violet, and disappeared in superheated gas. Around the edges of this region, great gouts of lava and immense fragments of solid rock were hurled to all points of the compass.

Radiation exerts pressure; at the temperature found in the cores of stars, that pressure must be measured in thousands of tons per square inch. It was this thrust, rather than the by no means negligible gas pressure of the boiling lava, which wrought most of the destruction.

Aller saw little of what occurred. When the lava was hurled upward, he had flung an arm across his face to protect his eyes from the glare. That act unquestionably saved his eyesight as the real flash followed; as it was, his body was seared and blistered through his clothing. The second, heavier, shock knocked his feet from under him, and he half crawled, half rolled down to the comparative shelter of the little hill. Even here, gusts of hot air almost cooked him; only the speed with which the phenomenon ended saved his life.

Within minutes, both the temblors and hot winds had ceased; and he crawled painfully to the hilltop again to gaze wonderingly at the five-mile-wide crater, ringed by a pile of tumbled, still-glowing rock fragments.

Far beneath that pit, shards of neutronium, no more able to remain near the surface than the steel pieces of a wrecked ocean vessel can float on water, were sinking through rock and metal to a final resting place at Earth's heart.

"The glow spread as we watched, still giving no clue to the nature of the substance radiating it," continued Kron. "Most of it seemed to originate between us and Akro's ship; Akro himself said that but little energy was being lost on the far side. His messages, during that last brief period as we swept by our point of closest approach, were clear—so clear that we could almost see, as he did, the tenuous light beyond the ever-thinning walls of his ship; the light that represented but a tiny percentage of the energy being sucked from the hull surface.

"We saw, as though with his own senses, the tiny perforation appear near one end of the ship; saw it extend, with the speed of thought, from one end of the hull to the other, permitting the free escape of all the energy in a single instant; and, from our point of vantage, saw the glowing area where the ship had been suddenly brightened, blazing for a moment almost as brightly as a piece of Sun matter.

"In that moment, every one of us saw the identifying frequencies as the heat from Akro's disrupted ship raised the substance which had trapped him to an energy level which permitted atomic radiation. Every one of us recognized the spectra of iron, of calcium, of carbon, and of silicon and a score of the other elements—Sirian, I tell you that that 'trapping field' was *matter*—matter in such a state that it could not radiate, and could offer resistance to other bodies in exactly the fashion of a solid. I thought, and have always thought, that some strange field of force held the atoms in their 'solid' positions; you have convinced me that I was wrong. The 'field' was the sum of the interacting atomic forces which you are trying to detect. The energy level of that material body was so low that those forces were able to act without interference. The condition you could not conceive of reaching artificially actually exists in nature!"

"You go too fast, Kron," responded the Sirian. "Your first

idea is far more likely to be the true one. The idea of unknown radiant or static force fields is easy to grasp; the one you propose in its place defies common sense. My theories called for some such conditions as you described, granted the one premise of a sufficiently low energy level; but a place in the real Universe so devoid of energy as to absorb that of a well-insulated interstellar flier is utterly inconceivable. I have assumed your tale to be true as to details, though you offer neither witnesses nor records to support it; but I seem to have heard that you have somewhat of a reputation as an entertainer, and you seem quick-witted enough to have woven such a tale on the spot, purely from the ideas I suggested. I compliment you on the tale, Kron; it was entrancing; but I seriously advise you not to make anything more out of it. Shall we leave at that, my friend?"

"As you will," replied Kron.

INTRODUCTION TO "LOOPHOLE"

by Arthur C. Clarke

I have a soft spot for this story as it marked my first appearance in *Astounding Stories* (April 1946). Actually, it was my second sale to John Campbell—the much longer "Rescue Party," which appeared in the May issue, had been sold a few days earlier. I can still remember the excitement of receiving those checks, and hope that Flight Lieutenant Clarke brought drinks all around in the Officer's Mess.

Looking at it again for the first time in decades, I realize—alas!—that "Loophole" is now even more topical than when I wrote it in September 1945, a month after the dropping of the first atomic bomb.

A couple of statistics: I see that "Loophole" was Opus 16—and *this* introduction to it is Opus 1071 . . . And John paid me $36—quite a useful sum in those far-off days.

LOOPHOLE

by Arthur C. Clarke

FROM: President
To: Secretary, Council of Scientists.
  I have been informed that the inhabitants of Earth have succeeded in releasing atomic energy and have been making ex-

periments with rocket propulsion. This is most serious. Let me have a full report immediately. And make it *brief* this time.

K.K. IV.

From: Secretary, Council of Scientists
To: President

The facts are as follows. Some months ago our instruments detected intense neutron emission from Earth, but an analysis of radio programs gave no explanation at the time. Three days ago a second emission occurred and soon afterward all radio transmissions from Earth announced that atomic bombs were in use in the current war. The translators have not completed their interpretation, but it appears that the bombs are of considerable power. Two have so far been used. Some details of their construction have been released, but the elements concerned have not yet been identified. A fuller report will be forwarded as soon as possible. For the moment all that is certain is the inhabitants of Earth *have* liberated atomic power, so far only explosively.

Very little is known concerning rocket research on Earth. Our astronomers have been observing the planet carefully ever since radio emissions were detected a generation ago. It is certain that long-range rockets of some kind are in existence on Earth, for there have been numerous references to them in recent military broadcasts. However, no serious attempt has been made to reach interplanetary space. When the war ends, it is expected that the inhabitants of the planet may carry out research in this direction. We will pay very careful attention to their broadcasts and the astronomical watch will be rigorously enforced.

From what we have inferred of the planet's technology, it should require about twenty years before Earth develops atomic rockets capable of crossing space. In view of this, it would seem that the time has come to set up a base on the Moon, so that a close scrutiny can be kept on such experiments when they commence.

Trescon.

(Added in manuscript.)

The war on Earth has now ended, apparently owing to the intervention of the atomic bomb. This will not affect the above arguments but it may mean that the inhabitants of Earth can devote themselves to pure research again more quickly than expected. Some broadcasts have already pointed out the application of atomic power in rocket propulsion.

T.

Arthur C. Clarke   103

From: President.
To: Chief of Bureau of Extra-Planetary Security. (C.B.E.P.S.)
 You have seen Trescon's minute.

 Equip an expedition to the satellite of Earth immediately. It is to keep a close watch on the planet and to report at once if rocket experiments are in progress.

 The greatest care must be taken to keep our presence on the Moon a secret. You are personally responsible for this. Report to me at yearly intervals, or more often if necessary.
 K.K. IV.

From: President.
To: C.B.E.P.S.
 Where is the report on Earth?!!
 K.K. IV.

From: C.B.E.P.S.
To: President.
 The delay is regretted. It was caused by the breakdown of the ship carrying the report.

 There have been no signs of rocket experimenting during the past year, and no reference to it in broadcasts from the planet.
 Ranthe.

From: C.B.E.P.S.
To: President.
 You will have seen my yearly reports to your respected father on this subject. There have been no developments of interest for the past seven years, but the following message has just been received from our base on the Moon:

 Rocket projectile, apparently atomically propelled, left Earth's atmosphere today from Northern land-mass, traveling into space for one quarter diameter of planet before returning under control.
 Ranthe.

From: President.
To: Chief of State.
 Your comments, please.
 K.K. V.

From: Chief of State.
To: President.

This means the end of our traditional policy.

The only hope of security lies in preventing the Terrestrials from making further advances in this direction. From what we know of them, this will require some overwhelming threat.

Since its high gravity makes it impossible to land on the planet, our sphere of action is restricted. The problem was discussed nearly a century ago by Anvar, and I agree with his conclusions. We must act *immediately* along those lines.

F.K.S.

From: President.
To: Secretary of State.

Inform the Council that an emergency meeting is convened for noon tomorrow.

K.K. V.

From: President.
To: C.B.E.P.S.

Twenty battleships should be sufficient to put Anvar's plan into operation. Fortunately there is no need to arm them—yet. Report progress of construction to me weekly.

K.K. V.

From: C.B.E.P.S.
To: President.

Nineteen ships are now completed. The twentieth is still delayed owing to hull failure and will not be ready for at least a month.

Ranthe.

From: President.
To: C.B.E.P.S.

Nineteen will be sufficient. I will check the operational plan with you tomorrow. Is the draft of our broadcast ready yet?

K.K. V.

From: C.B.E.P.S.
To: President.

Draft herewith:

People on Earth!

We, the inhabitants of the planet you call Mars, have for

many years observed your experiments toward achieving interplanetary travel. *These experiments must cease.* Our study of your race has convinced us that you are not fit to leave your planet in the present state of your civilization. The ships you now see floating above your cities are capable of destroying them utterly, and will do so unless you discontinue your attempts to cross space.

We have set up an observatory on your Moon and can immediately detect any violation of these orders. If you obey them, we will not interfere with you again. Otherwise, one of your cities will be destroyed every time we observe a rocket leaving the Earth's atmosphere.

By order of the President and Council of Mars.

Ranthe.

From: President.
To: C.B.E.P.S.

I approve. The translation can go ahead.

I shall not be sailing with the fleet, after all. You will report to me in detail immediately on your return.

K.K. V.

From: C.B.E.P.S.
To: President.

I have the honor to report the successful completion of our mission. The voyage to Earth was uneventful; radio messages from the planet indicated that we were detected at a considerable distance and great excitement had been aroused before our arrival. The fleet was dispersed according to plan and I broadcast the ultimatum. We left immediately and no hostile weapons were brought to bear against us.

I shall report in detail within two days.

Ranthe.

From: Secretary, Council of Scientists.
To: President.

The psychologists have completed their report, which is attached herewith.

As might be expected, our demands at first infuriated this stubborn and high-spirited race. The shock to their pride must have been considerable, for they believed themselves to be the only intelligent beings in the Universe.

However, within a few weeks there was a rather unexpected change in the tone of their statements. They had begun to realize that we were intercepting all their radio transmissions, and some messages have been broadcast directly to us. They state that they have agreed to ban all rocket experiments, in accordance with our wishes. This is as unexpected as it is welcome. Even if they are trying to deceive us, we are perfectly safe now that we have established the second station just outside the atmosphere. They cannot possibly develop spaceships without our seeing them or detecting their tube radiation.

The watch on Earth will be continued rigorously, as instructed.

Trescon.

From: C.B.E.P.S.
To: President.

Yes, it is quite true that there have been no further rocket experiments in the last ten years. We certainly did not expect Earth to capitulate so easily!

I agree that the existence of this race now constitutes a permanent threat to our civilization and we are making experiments along the lines you suggest. The problem is a difficult one, owing to the great size of the planet. Explosives would be out of the question, and a radioactive poison of some kind appears to offer the greatest hope of success.

Fortunately, we now have an indefinite time in which to complete this research, and I will report regularly.

Ranthe.

End of Document

From: Lieutenant Commander Henry Forbes, Intelligence Branch, Special Space Corps.
To: Professor S. Maxton, Philological Department, University of Oxford.
Route: Transender II (via Schenectady.)

The above papers, with others, were found in the ruins of what is believed to be the capital Martian city. (Mars Grid KL302895.) The frequent use of the ideograph for "Earth" suggests that they may be of special interest and it is hoped that they can be translated. Other papers will be following shortly.

H. Forbes, Lt/Cdr.

(Added in manuscript.)
Dear Max,

Sorry I've had no time to contact you before, I'll be seeing you as soon as I get back to Earth.

Gosh! Mars *is* in a mess! Our coordinates were dead accurate and the bombs materialized right over their cities, just as the Mount Wilson boys predicted.

We're sending a lot of stuff back through the two small machines, but until the big transmitter is materialized we're rather restricted, and, of course, none of us can return. So hurry up with it!

I'm glad we can get to work on rockets again. I may be old-fashioned, but being squirted through space at the speed of light doesn't appeal to me!

Yours in haste,
Henry.

DEADEYE WRITING
"THE DEAD MAN"

by Gene Wolfe

The little black card file that holds the index to my library
has ten cards headed *Biography*. There are perhaps thirty titles to a card, so you see. Furthermore, I have actually read
many of those books; and though I hate to admit it, most
are flawed. Nearly always it is the same flaw—between
page and page the part we most want to read is missing.

Let us say that the subject is an actress. There will be a
chapter on her antecedents and several chapters on her
girlhood. The last will end something like this: "In spite
of that C- in Theater, Emma resolved to go to New York
and try her luck."

And the next will begin like this: "Well before the year
drew to a close, Emma was starring on Broadway." The
part we really wanted to read, the part we bought the
book to read, isn't there.

For me, this is it.

In May of 1954 I rotated out of Korea. I was discharged
a month after that, and was able to enroll at the University
of Houston thanks to the GI Bill. In 1956 I graduated, and
Rosemary and I were married. She was working as a secretary, I as an engineer; we had no money beyond our
salaries. I had written for a college magazine before I went
into the Army, and I decided to try to write a book and sell
it so that we could escape from our furnished attic.

By January of 1965 Rosemary was no longer working,
and we had three children. We were renting a lovely little
house on an unpaved street by then, but money remained

very tight. I had written an unpublishable mystery novel and a number of short stories, including "Trip Trap," which would eventually be my third sale; but I had sold exactly nothing. For reasons that I have forgotten utterly now, I had to go downtown and meet someone for lunch—I no longer know who. I phoned him from the lobby of his building; he said he would be along in a minute or two, and I sat down in one of the chairs the building provided for people like me and picked up a copy of *Reader's Digest*.

It contained a fascinating article about crocodiles. In it, I learned that they could not chew, and that they dug dens in the soft banks of rivers, dark and muddy caves in which they stored their prey until it had decayed enough for them to tear away the putrid flesh and gulp it down. When I was still a child, the fear of death had been laid upon me by Rudyard Kipling's "The Undertakers," and as I read this article, the memory of that sinister tale returned with a vengeance. When I returned home, I wrote the story you are about to read.

Six magazines rejected it; the seventh took it and paid me eighty dollars. Eighty dollars was a great deal to us in those days, but the mere fact that "The Dead Man" had sold meant far more. For close to ten years I had been trying to sell what I wrote before going to work, in the evenings, and on weekends to augment an income frequently stretched to the breaking point. My little story is only words on paper now, one of millions of short stories published almost anonymously in thousands of magazines; but I ask you to treat it gently just the same.

In the darkness of 1965, it sang of hope.

THE DEAD MAN

by Gene Wolfe

WHEN the peasant came out of his house in the morning, the Brahman was sitting cross-legged in the sunshine before his own door. The Brahman was old, emaciated by fasting in the way often seen in wandering fakirs but seldom in settled members of the highest caste. And although the peasant was early abroad to escape the banter of the women (water-carrying being unfit for a man), the Brahman had been about before him, for when he neared the ford he could see floating in the slack water the marigold wreaths the Brahman had cast in to propitiate the river and the magar and the other powers of the waters.

The magar was a crocodile. Nine days ago it had taken the wife of the peasant's half brother as she waded across the ford, so notifying the villagers that the crossing was unsafe again, as it was said to have been in their grandfathers' time but had not been within living memory.

That same day, his own wife had been bitten on the foot when she kicked a jackal snuffing too near the spot where their son was playing. She had cursed, then laughed at the bloody scratch left by the frightened jackal's teeth; but next morning her foot was hot to the touch and twice its healthy size. Now, after prayers and poultices of dung, it was better. She could hobble on it, though not far, and cook and care for the child; but it would be long yet before she could bring water, and his mother—who had cried, and shrieked that the gods intended the destruction of the wives of all her sons—was too old.

With a pad on his shoulder, he could carry their largest jar easily, for he was a strong man, brown and lean from hard work in the fields of millet and upland rice. Stepping with care so as not to stir the mud, he bent slowly; and where the depth was great enough to take the jar, he filled it with the morning-cool, nearly stagnant water. There was nothing at the ford to disturb the peace of daybreak, though a hundred feet away, where the village stood just above the flood mark, many were stirring into wakefulness.

The magar was not to be seen. The peasant knew well how cleverly a crocodile assumes the very angle and position most natural to a stranded log on a sandbar, and how softly shadow-like it slips through still water without rippling the surface; but it was not there. He shouldered the jar again and began the walk uphill.

He and his fellow villagers, ignorant of the comparative religion of the schools, would cheerfully have killed the magar if they could. Indeed, one of the boatmen had been fishing for it with an iron hook as thick as a man's thumb hidden in the well-rotted haunch of a goat. Still, until the boatman caught it or they found it far enough from water to be slain with axes and spears, they would have been fools not to try to persuade it to be content with homage from their village and, especially, to move on up or downstream. Possibly in the dry season, when the river would dwindle to a trickle, something might be done. The peasant set down the water jar carefully so as not to waken his family. He heard his mother's rasping breath; as the jar made a soft *chunk* on the earthen floor, his wife moaned and moved her arm.

The second jar was smaller and older than the first, with a chipped place at the lip. He took it up and left the dimness of his home again for the brilliance of the street. The house had smelled of smoke; outside a breeze brought the rank, indescribable early-morning smell of second growth jungle, a jungle cut fifty years before for timber, now growing up again in hardwoods. By the water, the river-odor of rotten vegetation returned, and the gray warmth of dust under his bare feet changed once more to the cold slipperiness of mud.

This time he was not quite so careful, and one of his feet slid a trifle, sending out a slow cloud of fine black sediment. He took two more steps in the direction of the barely perceptible current before bending to fill his jar.

Without warning, his left calf was struck by steel bars, simultaneously from front and rear. A hip-dislocating wrench sent him sprawling in the shallows while the half-filled jar rocked in the waves of his struggle. Because he was a strong man, taller and bigger of bone than most of his people, he had time for one full-throated scream, and time to draw the breath for another, before the water closed over his nose and mouth.

For a few seconds he resisted before instinct, or reason, or the passivity of India and the East made him swallow, hug his chest with his arms, and submit, feeling the dark, cold fingers of the river loose his rag of turban and tangle his long, black hair. Then, as his heart pounded and his ears swelled and the trapped breath tried to burst past his closed throat and locked lips, he fought again, ignoring the pain already creeping into his numbed leg.

When next he came to know our world—*maya*, that which is not God—it was as a small circle of pale blue far above his eyes. He tried to blink and discovered that he could not, and that his mouth was filled with water and mud (or perhaps with blood) which he could not expel. Even the muscles that con-

trolled the motions of his eyes had forgotten their function, so
that he could not direct his gaze to right or left; but he found, in
the absence of this ability, that he could treat his field of vision
as a window and shift his attention to one side or the other, so
as to peer slantwise across his own eyes and examine the edges,
where the ghosts of the newly dead and the more material
demons flutter away from a man's view.

He was lying in a dark abscess in the earth, on mud, as his
shoulders told him. Toward his feet was the carcass of a young
blackbuck, its belly stretched by the rapid decomposition that
attacks dead ruminants.

To his left (he strained to see, and in straining felt the verte-
brae of his neck more ever so slightly, grating one upon another) nearly hidden in shadow, rose the familiar, undulating
curves of a young and not unslender woman lying on her
side—the roundness of the head, the concavity of the neck, the
rise of the shoulder declining to the waist, and the strong domination of the childbearing hips tapering to thighs and knees
lost in darkness. A drugged and whirling concourse of surmises
rushed through his mind, until simultaneously and without consciousness of contradiction he felt that he lay in the palace of a
scaled river-spirit and asleep beside his wife.

His attention was drawn from the woman by an alteration in
the light, the passage of some dark object across the disk of
blue. It came again, hesitated, and returned by the path it had
come. This it did three times in what could have been a hundred
breaths; and while he watched it, he became aware of a stench
indescribably fetid in the air that stirred sluggishly through his
nostrils.

The dark object crossed the light for the fourth time, and he
saw it to be a leaf at the tip of a twig. Then he understood that
his shadowy vault was the den of the magar, hollowed in the
mud of the river bank, where he lay with his face beneath the
"chimney" providing the minute ventilation necessary to prevent the den from filling with the gases of putrefaction. When
the sun rose higher, it would become an oven in which decay
would luxuriate and dead flesh rise like dough until the bodies
were soft enough to be dismembered easily. He did not connect
this with the crocodile's teeth, which were of piercing shape
only, unable to grind or cut; nor with its short front legs, which
were unable to reach what its jaws held, although he knew these
things.

He knew all these things and the habits of the magar—the rotting-den and the sudden grab at the ford or the rush up from the water—but he was unafraid, though he knew without looking a second time the identity of the woman beside him. After a long while he rose and began working his way out through the chimney, uncertain even as he did whether he laboriously pushed the earth aside to enlarge the hole or merely drifted through, and up like smoke.

The village was quiet now with the emptiness of noon, when the men were in the fields. He heard sobbing from his house as he dragged his injured leg along the village street, and the softer sound of chanted prayers. Sunlight shone brighter than he could recall having seen it ever before, the dazzle from the dust and the sides of the mud houses so great that he scarcely cast a shadow as he stood in the doorway of his home; neither the young woman, nor the old, nor the Brahman saw him until he entered the gloom of the interior where they sat, though his son ceased his gurgling and stared with wide brown eyes.

When they saw him at last, he could not speak, but looked from face to face, beginning and ending with his wife, conscious of having come to the close of something. After a moment the Brahman muttered, "Do not address it. It is seldom good to hear what they will say." He took up a handful of saffron powder from the brass bowl beside him and flung it into the air, calling upon a Name that brought dissolution and release.

WE'RE COMING THROUGH
THE WINDOW

by Barry N. Malzberg

"We're Coming Through The Window" is my first published science fiction story but not the first science fiction
story I had written. That was "Final War" (*Fantasy & Science Fiction*, April, 1968) which had been written almost
two years earlier but had not been intended as science fiction and indeed sold to *Fantasy & Science Fiction* only after
a series of failures at the so-called literary markets and
after a title change. (All of this rather mystifying data is
recorded in more numbing detail in the prologue to
"Final War" in an early Ace collection of which it is the
title story and in the headnote to the story in Robert
Hoskins's mid-seventies anthology, *The Liberated Future*.)
As much as I owe to Edward Ferman for accepting "Final
War" and as much as I owe to that story, its intent was
never science fiction and the sale to *Fantasy & Science Fiction* occurred in a kind of disguise. "We're Coming
Through the Window" is the real thing, the true quill: a
science fiction story intended for the science fiction mar-
ketplace and its sale on January 11, 1967 for all of $36.00
changed my life. I had sold in the genre. I could be a science fiction writer after all, maybe. I certainly hadn't had
any luck as a literary writer.

The story is only 1200 words (when I called my practical father to announce the sale, he said, "Well, that's
good; next time you have to sell something for 12,000
words and get $360.") and an overbearing introduction
would be misguided, would topple that fragile balance

of introduction and story which is necessary in an anthology. So only a few comments: I was involuntarily unemployed, job search not going well, my wife was at work, Stephanie Jill, nine months in December, 1966 was scooting in the living room with the help of her walker chair and I felt on Stephanie Jill's behalf that I had reached an early professional bottom. How would this helpless child who looked at me so tenderly ever thrive with an unemployed father? In that despair but with a certain low cunning which I later came to understand was one definition of "professionalism," I drafted this story in half an hour and sent it to Fred Pohl at *Galaxy*. If he had rejected it, I would have changed the address to "Mr. Campbell" and then "Mr. Ferman" or even "Mr. Knight" or "Mr. Ross" but that was happily unnecessary. I was so delighted to sell this story—I took it as an utter vindication and waved the check at Stephanie Jill, who shrugged—that I wrote a sequel the day that check arrived. It sold (also to *Galaxy*) but that took almost eight years and many changes in the name of the addressee who appeared in print as "Mr. Baen." I was at what I laughingly called "a different stage of my career" then and that sale of "I'm Going Through the Door" meant very little. Paid better, though . . . $75.00 if I recall for approximately the same length.

The editor's solicitation asks how I feel about this story now and how it might relate to my later work: the answer is I feel for it the greatest affection. It did exactly what I wanted, gave me what I needed. I don't think it relates to my later work at all. I don't think that anyone— me, neither—reading this could have in any way predicted the quantity and kind of work I would be publishing as science fiction over the next thirty-three years. That is not necessarily a good thing: all of us, even the indifferent Stephanie Jill, might have felt better if I had gone where and how this sour but pleasant little story had wanted to go.

WE'RE COMING THROUGH THE WINDOW

by Barry N. Malzberg

DEAR Mr. Pohl:
     Unfortunately I, William Coyne, cannot send you a manuscript for consideration due to reasons very much beyond my control which you will soon understand. All that I can do in the very limited time and with the limited opportunities available is to write things down as best I can in the form of this letter and hope that you will he patient and understanding enough to see the great story possibilities in my problem. Perhaps after you see how important and unusual the situation is here you will consent to write a story out of it yourself and keep 50% (fifty percent) of the proceeds which seems fair enough because you don't have to think up any ideas. Or, if you find yourself too busy to write it, you might turn it over to one of your regular authors in which case he will do the same thing and I will allow him only 40% (forty percent) of the sale price. But since this is a million-dollar idea as you will see, there should be plenty of money in it for everyone if you'll only *work fast*.

     Last week I, William Coyne, invented a time machine. That is correct, *I* created from my own notes the first time machine. I, William Coyne, twenty-nine years old, unemployed and presently living in very cramped quarters. I built it by myself in these three furnished rooms on the West Side of Manhattan, running back and forth between the hall sink and my bedroom because, like my own body, the mechanism is 85% undistilled water. The machine worked out very well, considering that I know next to nothing about electronics and the only science courses I have ever taken were for my high school equivalency diploma. I am not very advanced, as they say. Instead, I just kind of fiddle around and I guess I fiddled myself into the machine.

     It is a very simple device, Mr. Pohl, and a very successful one; the only trouble is that its range is extremely limited. At the present time it will take me back only four months into time or forward seventeen minutes, it is poorly calibrated and at no time can I leave the actual time field which embraces only five square feet. It is an early model and it will have to be refined then on part of the proceeds from the story you will write about me.

In spite of the problems, though, it definitely works. Just last Tuesday I shot myself back three months in time, found the newspaper of that date lying on my desk and my own humble form, the form of William Coyne, tossing fitfully upon the bed. It was an eerie experience, meeting myself for the first time and it shook me up considerable. But when I came back to the present time with the help of the machine and before I could even look around, I was interrupted by the dashing appearance of my double who motioned me urgently and requested in a whisper that four minutes hence I would please go backward four minutes in time. Then he—me—vanished.

It was very frightening, let me tell you, talking to myself, William Coyne, in my own rooms. But I counted off the four minutes and used the machine to go backwards; then I met *my* earlier self and told him—me, that is—to go back four minutes in four minutes. Like that.

All right, Mr. Pohl, I know what you're thinking right now. You're saying that this is all old stuff for you and your writers (even though in my case, the case of William Coyne, it happens to be one hundred percent [100%] absolute true fact) and that you've seen it a thousand (1,000) ways. I read science fiction too or I used to read it before I got into this mess. But stay with me, Mr. Pohl. There are a couple of things I haven't explained to you yet which will make clear why this situation is 100% sockaroo for a good man like yourself.

You can imagine how I got the plans for the time machine, of course. That's right, a few months ago I woke up in the morning to find all of them written out for me in my own hand-writing on my dresser table (that was what I did when I shot myself back the first time). I just used them. So I guess I didn't really invent it—or, that all of us invented it. But that is of little importance, Mr. Pohl, except to point out that I am not a creative genius and that is why I need help in my situation very, very fast.

You see the trouble is this: I told you that the machine didn't calibrate exactly and every time I go back to the present I don't get to the *exact* present but instead a few seconds or minutes off in either direction. So now, every time I jump around, I always come back to meet myself and if I jump back and try to come in exactly on time I just make more difficulties. The same thing happens every time I go back in time; I'm always meeting myself on the way.

Well, what it comes down to is this: I'm always coming across myself now and the more I try to straighten things out the worse it gets. As a matter of fact, Mr. Pohl, I'm afraid to make any more jumps because the more I've tried to straighten out this situation, the worse it's become.

Well, the truth is that there are now about three hundred (300) of us in these rooms, Mr. Pohl, all of us fooling around with these small time machines and none of us getting along very well. I mean, *I've* stopped trying to straighten myself out but most of the others haven't yet . . . they have to learn the hard way and in the meantime there are just more and more of us. Right now there are about 310 (three hundred and ten) for instance, just in the few short minutes I've been able to borrow the typewriter from the other fifty-three of us who are all trying to write letters for help.

As a matter of fact, we're about to be evicted for overcrowding, Mr. Pohl, and in the bargain there's just no food or space left here any more. And any time one of us goes out for food he seems never to come back with it . . . not that it would do us any good because I had two cents (2¢) in my pocket when this all began and we would need several thousand of us to get enough food to feed ten of us if you see what I mean.

This is my situation, the situation of William Coyne. What can I (we) do? We need to make big money from the machine real fast, that's the point, but we can't get out of the field so how are we going to make it? And then we just keep on meeting up with ourselves and having to explain things all over again and we're all dead broke. Please, please: would you have one of your writers if not yourself write a story about me (about us) and send the money just as soon as you can? We're all kind of desperate, here.

Hopefully,
WILLIAM COYNE
William Coyne
William coyne & . . .

INTRODUCTION TO
"THE HERO"

by George R. R. Martin

Aspiring writers often ask me if I had to suffer through years of rejection before finally making my first professional sale. Many of them seem almost disappointed when I tell them, "No." Every successful writer is supposed to have at least one room of his house papered with old yellowing rejection slips.

But my first sale came pretty quickly once I began to submit to professional markets. "The Hero" sold its third time out. Prior to sending it to *Galaxy*, the story had been bounced by *Playboy* and *Analog* . . . although the *Analog* rejection came with a personal letter from the legendary editor John W. Campbell Jr., which took much of the sting out of the rejection. Before "The Hero," I had tried three earlier stories (only one of them SF) on a variety of professional markets without success, so for me the fourth time was the charm.

Sounds relatively painless, doesn't it? Ah, but it had taken me long years to get the point. Before the first sale must come the first rejection, and for me that was actually the bigger hurdle in many ways.

I had always made up stories, and even as a kid I sometimes wrote them down and sold them to friends in the projects, complete with dramatic readings, but it was not until high school that I began to say, "a writer," when people asked, "What are you going to be when you grow up?" (Before that I used to say, "an astronaut," and everyone would laugh. They still laughed when I said, "a writer," but not as loudly).

I might even have said "a science fiction writer." I had been reading SF, fantasy, and horror indiscriminately ever since one of my mother's friends gave me Robert A. Heinlein's *Have Spacesuit, Will Travel* for Christmas one year. It was the first hardcover I ever owned, and for years the only one, but I found paperbacks of the other Heinlein juveniles and then moved on to *Starship Troopers* and *The Puppet Masters*. I began to mainline Ace Doubles, gulped down Andre Norton, John Taine, Eric Frank Russell, enthused over Jerry Sohl and puzzled at A.E. van Vogt. I found Robert E. Howard and his Conan stories, and Cthulhu found me. A mention in a fanzine led me to pick up the paperback edition of an obscure British fantasy called *The Fellowship of the Ring* . . . although the beginning, which seemed to be all about smoking pipe weed and some odd little people with hairy feet, almost made me put it down again. Thankfully I persisted, and worlds opened before me.

Even before my love affair with SF began, though, I had been hooked on comic books. I was actually on the verge of giving them up in high school, when along came Stan Lee, Jack Kirby, and Steve Ditko to reinvent the superhero genre with the *Fantastic Four* and *The Amazing Spider-Man*. Not only did I resume reading funny books, but I started mailing my comments to their letter columns . . . and to my delight, my letters began to be published. Thus the first words of mine ever to see print were actually "Dear Stan and Jack."

Comics fandom was in its infancy then, just beginning to spin off from SF fandom, which is much older in both senses of the word. When my name and address started appearing fairly regularly in the Marvel letter columns, I began to receive fanzines, and before long I was mailing off my sticky quarters to buy more. The early comics fanzines were labors of love, many edited by high school kids no older than myself. The classy ones were published on old drum mimeographs, the others by a process known as ditto, which produced pages of faint purple type that seemed to fade even as you turned them. Mixed in among the articles about Golden Age comics and discussions of the current offerings from Marvel, DC, and Gold Key was a variety of amateur fiction—superhero stories chiefly (Howard Waldrop was an exception), some illustrated, the rest told in prose by aspiring writers who couldn't draw. "Text stories," they were called in the fannish parlance of that era, to distinguish them from the illustrated comic strips.

I had once won a prize for drawing a horse in kindergarten, but that was about the limit of my artistic talents. On the other hand, I had an old Underwood typewriter that I had salvaged from my Aunt Gladys' attic. Aside from cutting the interior out of every o and e (which might have had something to do with how hard I pounded the keys, I must confess), it worked fine, and even had this nifty two-color ribbon which allowed me to type in red whenever I wanted to (I used it a lot in those early days).

Thus I decided to try and write some text stories, on the theory that mine couldn't be much worse than some of the ones I was reading.

Comics fandom was where I wrote all those early, awful stories that other writers use to build up their impressive collection of rejection slips. I didn't get any rejection slips, however; the fanzines were so hungry for material, they were only too glad to publish anything I sent them.

My earliest fiction appeared in the pages of *Batwing* and *Star-Studded Comics*, in *Ymir* and *In-Depth*. I became, in fact, quite a well-known writer of text stories in the small frog pond of infant comics fandom; I even won something called an "Alley Award" one year for "best fan fiction," although the people giving it to me couldn't afford a trophy, so you'll have to take my word for it.

By the time I graduated from high school, I had checked L. Sprague de Camp's *Science Fiction Handbook* out of the Bayonne Public Library so often I had it half memorized; there was no better resource for an aspiring SF author. I even picked up a few issues of the Cele Goldsmith *Amazing* and *Fantastic*, the only SF magazines they carried in the Bayonne candy store when I got my funny books and Ace Doubles, so I knew about the magazine markets.

But I never sent them a story. I wasn't good enough. I wasn't old enough. Rather than face the specter of possible rejection, it was easier to write another text story about Powerman or Dr. Weird, knowing that it was sure to be published and gets me lots of nice egoboo. I was

going to be a writer, sure . . . one of these days. I was
going to have a girlfriend, too, one of these days. But just
then the notion of actually sending a real story to a real
editor was almost (though not quite) as terrifying as the
notion of asking a girl for a date. There is no scorn quite
so withering as imagined scorn.

Then came college. I chose Northwestern University at
least in part because the Medill School of Journalism offered a course in commercial short-story writing—which,
alas, was dropped from the curriculum just about the same
time I arrived on campus. As a journalism major, I was at
the typewriter constantly, honing my prose . . . but I needed
to work on my storytelling as well, so I looked for any opportunity I could find to write short stories for credit.

I found one my sophomore year, while taking a course in
Scandinavian history. In place of the required term paper, I
convinced my professor to let me submit a piece of historical fiction about the siege of the great Helsinki fortress of
Sveaborg during the Russo-Swedish War of 1808. "The
Fortress" not only netted me an A for the term paper, but
also got me my first professional rejection. Professor Scott
liked it so well that he submitted the story with a letter of
recommendation to *American Scandinavian Review*. Their editor promptly returned it . . . with a personal note that said
the story was "very good," but too long for their purposes.

I had been rejected . . . and discovered that it hardly
hurt at all.

That realization turned a corner for me. Come my junior year, I signed up for a course in Creative Writing,
turned out a number of short stories, and started sending
them to professional markets as soon as they came back
from the prof.

"The Hero" was the third story I wrote for that course.
I don't recall that it much impressed my instructor, who
neither understood nor liked SF, but I persisted in sending it out anyway.

The rejections from *Playboy* and *Analog* both came in
the spring of 1969, after which I fired the story off to Fred
Pohl at *Galaxy*. Whereupon it vanished. No one had told
me that *Galaxy* and *If* had been sold, and that Fred Pohl
was no longer their editor. By the time I found out, I was
a senior. My original manuscript was lost and magazines

would not read carbon copies, so I had to retype the whole damn story before I could send it out again. I almost decided it wasn't worth the effort. Almost . . .

Fortunately, I did retype the story, and sent it off to *Galaxy* again, this time to the new editor (Eljer Jakobsson) at the new address, where another aspiring writer was reading the slush. His name was Gardner Dozois, and he was the one who fished "The Hero" out of the slush pile and passed it on to Jakobsson. Only then somehow the manuscript slipped behind a filing cabinet and was lost again.

I was too busy graduating to notice, but in the summer of 1970, home in New Jersey for a few months before starting grad school, I remembered my long-lost story and actually summoned up the nerve to phone the *Galaxy* offices (long distance! from New Jersey to New York!) and ask what had become of it.

That was when I heard the tale of the filing cabinet . . . and how someone had finally moved the files, thereby unearthing my story and the purchase order.

They were buying it.

THEY WERE BUYING IT!

I was back at Northwestern when *Galaxy* published "The Hero" in its February, 1971, issue. A friend of mine drove me all around Evanston, Skokie, Wilmette, and the north side of Chicago that day, so I could buy every issue I could find. Thirty years later, that still remains one of the most magical days of my life.

THE HERO

by George R. R. Martin

THE city was dead and the flames of its passing spread a red stain across the green-gray sky.

It had been a long time dying. Resistance had lasted almost

a week and the fighting had been bitter for a while. But in the end the invaders had broken the defenders, as they had broken so many others in the past. The alien sky with its double sun did not bother them. They had fought and won under skies of azure blue and speckled gold and inky black.

The Weather Control boys had hit first, while the main force was still hundreds of miles to the east. Storm after storm had flailed at the streets of the city, to slow defensive preparations and smash the spirit of resistance.

When they were closer the invaders had sent up howlers. Unending high-pitched shrieks had echoed back and forth both day and night and before long most of the populace had fled in demoralized panic. By then the attackers' main force was in range and launched plague bombs on a steady westward wind.

Even then the natives had tried to fight back. From their defensive emplacements ringing the city the survivors had sent up a hail of atomics, managing to vaporize one whole company whose defensive screens were overloaded by the sudden assault. But the gesture was a feeble one at best. By that time incendiary bombs were raining down steadily upon the city and great clouds of acid gas were blowing across the plains.

And behind the gas, the dreaded assault squads of the Terran Expeditionary Force moved on the last defenses.

Kagen scowled at the dented plastoid helmet at his feet and cursed his luck. A routine mopping-up detail, he thought. A perfectly routine operation—and some damned automatic interceptor emplacement somewhere had lobbed a low-grade atomic at him.

It had been only a near miss but the shock waves had damaged his hip rockets and knocked him out of the sky, landing him in this godforsaken little ravine east of the city. His light plastoid battle armor had protected him from the impact but his helmet had taken a good whack.

Kagen squatted and picked up the dented helmet to examine it. His long-range com and all of his sensory equipment were out. With his rockets gone, too, he was crippled, deaf, dumb, and half-blind. He swore.

A flicker of movement along the top of the shallow ravine caught his attention. Five natives came suddenly into view, each carrying a hair-trigger submachine gun. They carried them at the ready, trained on Kagen. They were fanned out in line, covering him from both right and left. One began to speak.

He never finished. One instant, Kagen's screech gun lay on the rocks at his feet. Quite suddenly it was in his hand.

Five men will hesitate where one alone will not. During the brief flickering instant before the natives' fingers began to tighten on their triggers. Kagen did not pause, Kagen did not hesitate, Kagen did not think.

Kagen killed.

The screech gun emitted a loud, ear-piercing shriek. The enemy squad leader shuddered as the invisible beam of concentrated high-frequency sound ripped into him. Then his flesh began to liquefy. By then Kagen's gun had found two more targets.

The guns of the two remaining natives finally began to chatter. A rain of bullets enveloped Kagen as he whirled to his right and he grunted under the impact as the shots caromed off his battle armor. His screech gun leveled—and a random shot sent it spinning from his grasp.

Kagen did not hesitate or pause as the gun was wrenched from his grip. He bounded to the top of the shallow ravine with one leap, directly toward one of the soldiers.

The man wavered briefly and brought up his gun. The instant was all Kagen needed. With all the momentum of his leap behind it, his right hand smashed the gun butt into the enemy's face and his left, backed by fifteen hundred pounds of force, hammered into the native's body right under the breastbone.

Kagen seized the corpse and heaved it toward the second native, who had ceased fire briefly as his comrade came between himself and Kagen. Now his bullets tore into the airborne body. He took a quick step back, his gun level and firing.

And then Kagen was on him. Kagen knew a searing flash of pain as a shot bruised his temple. He ignored it, drove the edge of his hand into the native's throat. The man toppled, lay still.

Kagen spun, still reacting, searching for the next foe.

He was alone.

Kagen bent and wiped the blood from his hand with a piece of the native's uniform. He frowned in disgust. It was going to be a long trek back to camp, he thought, tossing the blood-soaked rag casually to the ground.

Today was definitely not his lucky day.

He grunted dismally, then scrambled back down into the ravine to recover his screech gun and helmet for the hike.

On the horizon, the city was still burning.

Ragelli's voice was loud and cheerful as it came crackling over the short-range communicator nestled in Kagen's fist. "So it's you, Kagen," he said laughing. "You signaled just in time. My sensors were starting to pick up something. Little closer and I would've screeched you down."

"My helmet's busted and the sensors are out," Kagen replied. "Damn hard to judge distance. Long-range com is busted, too."

"The brass was wondering what happened to you," Ragelli cut in. "Made 'em sweat a little. But I figured you'd turn up sooner or later."

"Right," Kagen said. "One of these mudworms zapped the hell out of my rockets and it took me a while to get back. But I'm coming in now."

He emerged slowly from the crater he had crouched in, coming in sight of the guard in the distance. He took it slow and easy.

Outlined against the outpost barrier, Ragelli lifted a ponderous silver-gray arm in greeting. He was armored completely in a full durralloy battlesuit that made Kagen's plastoid armor look like tissue paper, and sat in the trigger-seat of a swiveling screech-gun battery. A bubble of defensive screens enveloped him, turning his massive figure into an indistinct blur.

Kagen waved back and began to eat up the distance between them with long, loping strides. He stopped just in front of the barrier, at the foot of Ragelli's emplacement.

"You look damned battered," said Ragelli, appraising him from behind a plastoid visor, aided by his sensory devices. "That light armor doesn't buy you a nickel's worth of protection. Any farm boy with a pea shooter can plug you."

Kagen laughed. "At least I can move. You may be able to stand off an Assault Squad in that durralloy monkey suit, but I'd like to see you do anything on offense, chum. And defense doesn't win wars."

"Your pot," Ragelli said. "This sentry duty is boring as hell." He flicked a switch on his control panel and a section of the barrier winked out. Kagen was through it at once. A split second later it came back on again.

Kagen strode quickly to his squad barracks. The door slid open automatically as he approached it and he stepped inside gratefully. It felt good to be home again and back at his normal weight. These light-gravity mudholes made him queasy after a while. The barracks were artificially maintained at Wellington-normal gravity, twice Earth-normal. It was expensive but the brass kept saying that nothing was too good for the comfort of our fighting men.

Kagen stripped off his plastoid armor in the squad ready room and tossed it into the replacement bin. He headed straight for his cubicle and sprawled across the bed.

Reaching over to the plain metal table alongside his bed, he yanked open a drawer and took out a fat greenish capsule. He swallowed it hastily, and lay back to relax as it took hold throughout his system. The regulations prohibited taking syn-thastim between meals, he knew, but the rule was never enforced. Like most troopers, Kagen took it almost continuously to maintain his speed and endurance at maximum.

He was dozing comfortably a few minutes later when the com box mounted on the wall above his bed came to sudden life.

"Kagen."

Kagen sat up instantly, wide awake.

"Acknowledged," he said.

"Report to Major Grady at once."

Kagen grinned broadly. His request was being acted on quickly, he thought. And by a high officer, no less. Dressing quickly in loose-fitting brown fatigues, he set off across the base.

The high officers' quarters were at the center of the outpost. They consisted of a brightly lit, three-story building, blanketed overhead by defensive screens and ringed by guardsmen in light battle armor. One of the guards recognized Kagen and he was admitted on orders.

Immediately beyond the door he halted briefly as a bank of sensors scanned him for weapons. Troopers, of course, were not allowed to bear arms in the presence of high officers. Had he been carrying a screech gun, alarms would have gone off all over the building while the tractor beams hidden in the walls and ceilings immobilized him completely.

But he passed the inspection and continued down the long corridor toward Major Grady's office. A third of the way down, the first set of tractor beams locked firmly onto his wrists. He struggled the instant he felt the invisible touch against his skin—but the tractors held him steady. Others, triggered automatically by his passing, came on as he continued down the corridor.

Kagen cursed under his breath and fought with his impulse to resist. He hated being pinned by tractor beams, but those were the rules if you wanted to see a high officer.

The door opened before him and he stepped through. A full bank of tractor beams seized him instantly and immobilized him. A few adjusted slightly and he was snapped to rigid attention, although his muscles screamed resistance.

Major Carl Grady was working at a cluttered wooden desk a few feet away, scribbling something on a sheet of paper. A large stack of papers rested at his elbow, an old-fashioned laser pistol sitting on top of them as a paperweight.

Kagen recognized the laser. It was some sort of heirloom, passed down in Grady's family for generations. The story was that some ancestor of his had used it back on Earth, in the Fire Wars of the early twenty-first century. Despite its age, the thing was still supposed to be in working order.

After several minutes of silence Grady finally set down his pen and looked up at Kagen. He was unusually young for a high officer but his unruly gray hair made him look older than he was. Like all high officers, he was Earth-born; frail and slow before the assault squad troopers from the dense, heavy-gravity War Worlds of Wellington and Rommel.

"Report your presence," Grady said curtly. As always, his lean, pale face mirrored immense boredom.

"Field Officer John Kagen, assault squads, Terran Expeditionary Force."

Grady nodded, not really listening. He opened one of his desk drawers and extracted a sheet of paper.

"Kagen," he said, fiddling with the paper. "I think you know why you're here." He tapped the paper with his finger. "What's the meaning of this?"

"Just what it says, Major," Kagen replied. He tried to shift his weight but the tractor beams held him rigid.

Grady noticed and gestured impatiently. "At rest," he said. Most of the tractor beams snapped off, leaving Kagen free to move, if only at half his normal speed. He flexed in relief and grinned.

"My term of enlistment is up within two weeks, Major. I don't plan to reenlist. So I've requested transportation to Earth. That's all there is to it."

Grady's eyebrows arched a fraction of an inch but the dark eyes beneath them remained bored.

"Really?" he asked. "You've been a soldier for almost twenty years now, Kagen. Why retire? I'm afraid I don't understand."

Kagen shrugged. "I don't know. I'm getting old. Maybe I'm just getting tired of camp life. It's all starting to get boring, taking one damn mudhole after another. I want something different. Some excitement."

Grady nodded. "I see. But I don't think I agree with you, Kagen." His voice was soft and persuasive. "I think you're underselling the T.E.F. There is excitement ahead, if you'll only give us a chance." He leaned back in his chair, toying with a pencil he had picked up. "I'll tell you something, Kagen. You know, we've been at war with the Hrangan Empire for nearly three decades now. Direct clashes between us and the enemy have been few and far between up to now. Do you know why?"

"Sure," Kagen said.

Grady ignored him. "I'll tell you why," he continued. "So far each of us has been struggling to consolidate his position by grabbing these little worlds in the border regions. These mudholes, as you call them. But they're very important mudholes. We need them for bases, for their raw materials, for their industrial capacity and for the conscript labor they provide. "That's why we try to minimize damage in our campaigns. And that's why we use psych war tactics like the howlers. To frighten away as many natives as possible before each attack. To preserve labor."

"I know all that," Kagen interrupted with typical Wellington bluntness. "What of it? I didn't come here for a lecture."

Grady looked up from the pencil. "No," he said. "No, you didn't. So I'll tell you, Kagen. The prelims are over. It's time for the main event. There are only a handful of unclaimed worlds left. Soon now, we'll be coming into direct conflict with the Hrangan Conquest Corps. Within a year we'll be attacking their bases."

The major stared at Kagen expectantly, waiting for a reply.

When none came, a puzzled look flickered across his face. He leaned forward again.

"Don't you understand, Kagen?" he asked. "What more excitement could you want? No more fighting these piddling civilians in uniform, with their dirty little atomics and their primitive projectile guns. The Hrangans are a real enemy. Like us, they've had a professional army for generations upon generations. They're soldiers, born and bred. Good ones, too. They've got screens and modern weapons. They'll be foes to give our assault squads a real test."

"Maybe," Kagen said doubtfully. "But that kind of excitement isn't what I had in mind. I'm getting old. I've noticed that I'm definitely slower lately—even Synthastim isn't keeping up my speed."

Grady shook his head. "You've got one of the best records in the whole T.E.F., Kagen. You've received the Stellar Cross twice and the World Congress Decoration three times. Every com station on Earth carried the story when you saved the landing party on Torego. Why should you doubt your effectiveness now? We're going to need men like you against the Hrangans. Reenlist."

"No," said Kagen emphatically. "The regs say you're entitled to your pension after twenty years and those medals have earned me a nice bunch of retirement bonuses. Now I want to enjoy them." He grinned broadly. "As you say, everyone on Earth must know me. I'm a hero. With that reputation, I figure I can have a real screech-out."

Grady frowned and drummed on the desk impatiently. "I know what the regulations say, Kagen. But no one ever really retires—you must know that. Most troopers prefer to stay with the front. That's their job. That's what the War Worlds are all about."

"I don't really care, Major," Kagen replied. "I know the regs and I know I have a right to retire on full pension. You can't stop me."

Grady considered the statement calmly, his eyes dark with thought.

"All right," he said after a long pause. "Let's be reasonable about this. You'll retire with full pension and bonuses. We'll set you down on Wellington in a place of your own. Or Rommel if you like. We'll make you a youth barracks director—any age group you like. Or a training camp director. With your record you can start right at the top."

"Uh-uh," Kagen said firmly. "Not Wellington. Not Rommel. Earth."

"But why? You were born and raised on Wellington—in one of the hill barracks, I believe. You've never seen Earth."

"True," said Kagen. "But I've seen it in camp telecasts and flicks. I like what I've seen. I've been reading about Earth a lot lately, too. So now I want to see what it's like." He paused, then grinned again. "Let's just say I want to see what I've been fighting for."

Grady's frown reflected his displeasure. "I'm from Earth, Kagen," he said. "I tell you, you won't like it. You won't fit in. The gravity is too low—and there are no artificial heavy gravity barracks to take shelter in. Synthastim is illegal, strictly prohibited. But War Worlders need it, so you'll have to pay exorbitant prices to get the stuff. Earthers aren't reaction trained, either. They're a different kind of people. Go back to Wellington. You'll be among your own kind."

"Maybe that's one of the reasons I want Earth," Kagen said stubbornly. "On Wellington I'm just one of hundreds of old vets. Hell, every one of the troopers who *does* retire heads back to his old barracks. But on Earth I'll be a celebrity. Why, I'll be the fastest, strongest guy on the whole damn planet. That's got to have some advantages."

Grady was starting to look agitated. "What about the gravity?" he demanded. "The Synthastim?"

"I'll get used to light gravity after a while, that's no problem. And I won't be needing that much speed and endurance, so I figure I can kick the Synthastim habit."

Grady ran his fingers through his unkempt hair and shook his head doubtfully. There was a long, awkward silence. He leaned across the desk.

And, suddenly, his hand darted toward the laser pistol.

Kagen reacted. He dove forward, delayed only slightly by the few tractor beams that still held him. His hand flashed toward Grady's wrist in a crippling arc.

And suddenly wrenched to a halt as the tractor beams seized Kagen roughly, held him rigid and then smashed him to the floor.

Grady, his hand frozen halfway to the pistol, leaned back in the chair. His face was white and shaken. He raised his hand

and the tractor beams let up a bit. Kagen climbed slowly to his feet.

"You see, Kagen," said Grady. "That little test proves you're as fit as ever. You'd have gotten me if I hadn't kept a few tractors on you to slow you down. I tell you, we need men with your training and experience. We need you against the Hrangans. Reenlist."

Kagen's cold blue eyes still seethed with anger. "Damn the Hrangans," he said. "I'm not reenlisting and no goddamn little tricks of yours are going to make me change my mind. I'm going to Earth. You can't stop me."

Grady buried his face in his hands and sighed.

"All right, Kagen," he said at last. "You win. I'll put through your request."

He looked up one more time, and his dark eyes looked strangely troubled.

"You've been a great soldier, Kagen. We'll miss you. I tell you that you'll regret this decision. Are you sure you won't reconsider?"

"Absolutely sure," Kagen snapped.

The strange look suddenly vanished from Grady's eyes. His face once more took on the mask of bored indifference.

"Very well," he said curtly. "You are dismissed."

The tractors stayed on Kagen as he turned. They guided him—very firmly—from the building.

"You ready, Kagen?" Ragelli asked, leaning casually against the door of the cubicle.

Kagen picked up his small travel bag and threw one last glance around to make sure he hadn't forgotten anything. He hadn't. The room was quite bare.

"Guess so," he said, stepping through the door.

Ragelli slipped on the plastoid helmet that had been cradled under his arm and hurried to catch up as Kagen strode down the corridor.

"I guess this is it," he said as he matched strides.

"Yeah," Kagen replied. "A week from now I'll be taking it easy back on Earth while you're getting blisters on your tail sitting around in that damned duralloy tuxedo of yours."

Ragelli laughed. "Maybe," he said. "But I still say you're nuts to go to Earth of all places, when you could command a whole damned training camp on Wellington. Assuming you wanted to quit at all, which is also crazy—"

The barracks door slid open before them and they stepped through, Ragelli still talking. A second guard flanked Kagen on the other side. Like Ragelli, he was wearing light battle armor.

Kagen himself was in full dress whites, trimmed with gold braid. A ceremonial laser, deactivated, was slung in a black leather holster at his side. Matching leather boots and a polished steel helmet set off the uniform. Azure blue bars on his shoulder signified field officer rank. His medals jangled against his chest as he walked.

Kagen's entire third assault squad was drawn up at attention on the spacefield behind the barracks in honor of his retirement. Alongside the ramp to the shuttlecraft, a group of high officers stood by, cordoned off by defensive screens. Major Grady was in the front row, his bored expression blurred somewhat by the screens.

Flanked by the two guards, Kagen walked across the concrete slowly, grinning under his helmet. Piped music welled out over the field, and Kagen recognized the T.E.F. battle hymn and the Wellington anthem.

At the foot of the ramp he turned and looked back. The company spread out before him saluted in unison on a command from the high officers and held the position until Kagen returned the salute. Then one of the squad's other field officers stepped forward, and presented him with his discharge papers.

Jamming them into his belt, Kagen threw a quick, casual wave to Ragelli, then hurried up the ramp. It lifted slowly behind him.

Inside the ship, a crewman greeted him with a curt nod. "Got special quarters prepared for you," he said. "Follow me. Trip should only take about fifteen minutes. Then we'll transfer you to a starship for the Earth trip."

Kagen nodded and followed the man to his quarters. They turned out to be a plain, empty room, reinforced with duralloy plates. A viewscreen covered one wall. An acceleration couch faced it.

Alone, Kagen sprawled out on the acceleration couch, clipping his helmet to a holder on the side. Tractor beams pressed down gently, holding him firmly in place for the liftoff.

A few minutes later a dull roar came from deep within the ship and Kagen felt several gravities press down upon him as the shuttlecraft took off. The viewscreen, suddenly coming to life, showed the planet dwindling below.

The viewer blinked off when they reached orbit. Kagen started to sit up but found he still could not move. The tractor beams held him pinned to the couch.

He frowned. There was no need for him to stay in the couch once the craft was in orbit. Some idiot had forgotten to release him.

"Hey," he shouted, figuring there would be a com box somewhere in the room. "These tractors are still on. Loosen the damned things so I can move a little."

No one answered.

He strained against the beams. Their pressure seemed to increase. The blasted things were starting to pinch a little, he thought. Now those morons were turning the knob the wrong way.

He cursed under his breath. "No," he shouted. "Now the tractors are getting heavier. You're adjusting them the wrong way."

But the pressure continued to climb and he felt more beam's locking on him, until they covered his body like an invisible blanket. The damn things were really starting to hurt now.

"You idiots," he yelled. "You morons. Cut it out, you bastards." With a surge of anger he strained against the beams, cursing. But even Wellington-bred muscle was no match for tractors. He was held tightly to the couch.

One of the beams was trained on his chest pocket. Its pressure was driving his Stellar Cross painfully into his skin. The sharp edge of the polished metal had already sliced through the uniform and he could see a red stain spreading slowly through the white.

The pressure continued to mount and Kagen writhed in pain, squirming against his invisible shackles. It did no good. The pressure still went higher and more and more beams came on.

"Cut it out!" he screeched. "You bastards, I'll rip you apart when I get out of here. You're killing me, dammit!"

He heard the sharp snap of a bone suddenly breaking under the strain. Kagen felt a stab of intense pain in his right wrist. An instant later there was another snap.

"Cut it out!" he cried, his voice shrill with pain. "You're killing me. Damn you, you're killing me!"

And suddenly he realized he was right.

*   *   *

Grady looked up with a scowl at the aide who entered the office.

"Yes? What is it?"

The aide, a young Earther in training for high officer rank, saluted briskly. "We just got the report from the shuttlecraft, sir. It's all over. They want to know what to do with the body."

"Space it," Grady replied. "Good as anything." A thin smile flickered across his face and he shook his head. "Too bad. Kagen was a good man in combat but his psych training must have slipped somewhere. We should send a strong note back to his barracks conditioner. Though it's funny it didn't show up until now."

He shook his head again. "Earth," he said. "For a moment he even had me wondering if it was possible. But when I tested him with my laser, I knew. No way, no way." He shuddered a little. "As if we'd ever let a War Worlder loose on Earth." Then he turned back to his paperwork.

As the aide turned to leave, Grady looked up again.

"One more thing," he said. "Don't forget to send that PR release back to Earth. Make it War-Hero-Dies-When-Hrangans-Blast-Ship. Jazz it up good. Some of the big com networks should pick it up and it'll make good publicity. And forward his medals to Wellington. They'll want them for his barracks museum."

The aise nodded and Grady returned to his work. He still looked quite bored.

MY (OTHER) WORLD AND WELCOME TO IT: WRITING "LUNCHBOX"

by Howard Waldrop

Like, in Jean Shepherd's phrase, getting ready for deep-sea diving, or a trip to the subject planet, I gird myself and suit up for a trip back in time—back past 2000, past 1990, way past 1980, back . . . back . . . inexorably borne against the current, to the year 1970.

My parents were divorced in 1967. My father died in 1968. I have been married since August of that year to my first, and only, ex-wife. The marriage will last until 1973; there will be one child, whom I will see penultimately when she is eighteen months old, and the last time on the day she is married at age twenty-two. I have already the last dog I will own, who I will have to put to sleep in 1977.

I'm living in Arlington, Texas, where I have grown up. I am in my fifth year in college, not having enough money (and working thirty-six hours a week in three twelve-hour shifts at night) for full-time tuition the first two semesters.

I will receive my draft notice for The Late Unpleasantness in Southeast Asia on my birthday in 1970. (It wasn't even delivered to me, but to a lady over on the next block. She drives over, hands it to me, and says "I think this is *important*.")

Right, lady.

I read it—report date's late in October—sigh, hug the dog and drive over to the theater at college to tell my wife.

You think I've got troubles? Over in England, the Beatles are breaking up.

My literary career to this point:

In 1966 I sold a joke to *Playboy Party Jokes*. (Being twenty at the time, and in California on a visit when the issue it was in came out, I had to wait till I got back to Texas, where you could buy *Playboy* at eighteen, instead of California's twenty-one.)

I had sold an article on Charles Ives, and the possibility of the "rock novel" (as it was then called, pre-*Tommy*) in 1969, to *Crawdaddy*. It was to appear in issue #33. Issue #32 stayed on the stands for three months. Then I got word third-hand: the mag's *dead*. A year later (1970) I got a 4th-class package—inside are two issues of the *all-new* ownership *Crawdaddy*, one with my article in it, and a check for $60. (I would write four or five articles that year for *Crawdaddy*[2], *all* of them accepted, *all* of which came back the next year when *that* incarnation of *Crawdaddy* died.)

I had sold a comic-book script to Warren Publishing Company (for a big $25) that had appeared in *Eerie* #33 in 1969.

I had, besides working as a linotype operator, or putting in fifty or sixty hours at the college theater, and being married and having a dog, been writing and writing and writing for the last three years, with the above to show for it. I had a pile of rejection slips—or, in some cases with the rock magazines, still in their infancy, rejections written *across* the first page of the manuscript—*that high*. And still I wrote.

One of the things I wrote, in August of the year in question, before the draft notice, was "Lunchbox."

Bear with me.

Originally, the probes which we were sending to Mars were to be called *Voyagers*, which was the name later used for the deep-space probes, and the name *Viking* was to be substituted for those headed for Mars. In the draft of the story I sent out, the lander was called *Voyager*. We'd already sent two hard-landing vehicles there in the *Mariner* series (which had first told us how *hot* Venus was, instead of the Devonian sea-world we'd always imagined; and which had sent back the first photos of Mars, before impact, which showed it to be more like the Moon than like the Mars of our dreams; there was nary a canal. The 1965 series of twenty-something black-and-white photos beamed back changed our views of the planet *overnight*.)

So I sat down on a 110-degree August day and wrote about what I thought *might* happen when the first (then-*Voyager*) landed on a changed Mars, one with no threats, no dead sea-bottom, no Dejah Thoris laying eggs, no Tweels, no *It's—The Terrors From Beyond Space*.

One of the things that had *always* bothered me about first contact stories, of any kind, is the assumption that they'll *see* like we do. That is, visible light, which is about an inch in the mile that is the electromagnetic spectrum. We evolved seeing in those emissions from Ol' Sol; life in other places, maybe even in this solar system might spring up in which there are advantages to seeing in infrared, X-ray, even shortwave. I posited a Mars where the Kind used ultraviolet and infrared ("the Haze eyes") which, to anybody watching them from Mission Control would be like watching the Id Monster coming toward the house "from the north-northeast, Morbius."

I had a probe, I had beings that used another part of the spectrum, a cold-loving food source (responsible for the seasonal color changes noted for centuries on Mars.) And, as per the title, I was using some of the feelings elucidated by Tom Lehrer in the introduction to one of his songs about American know-how "allowing us to spend $60 billion to put some clown on the Moon" (which we had done the year before).

So with a light head and a heavy heart (the same knowledge that—wonderfully—let us put a couple of clowns on the Moon was helping us daily dump a couple of hundred tons of ordance on every man, woman, and child in both Vietnams), I sent the story, all 1400 words of it, to *F&SF*.

In those days, Ed Ferman took *exactly* sixty days to say no, so the story returned early in October of 1970, after I'd gotten my draft notice. (It would be twenty-eight years before I would sell to *The Magazine of Fantasy and Science Fiction*—it was by then to Gordon Van Gelder as editor, but with the *check* still sent by Ed Ferman—and he sent a note with it, saying he was glad I *finally sold something* to the magazine, which is one of the nicest things anyone has done in the erratic, jagged nightmare that is my career.)

So, getting my affairs in order, I sent "Lunchbox" off to *Analog.*

Late in October, I went to the AFEES in Dallas, was neglected, detected, and inspected, raised my hand, found myself on a plane to California with a dozen other morons, and met Uncle Sugar in Fort Ord.

The fourth day of basic training, after Drill Sergeant Scott "in charge of the Rs through Zs and all that shit" had taught us the finer points of push-ups, we had mail call. There was a letter from my wife Linda Lou, enclosing the xerox of the check from *Analog* for "Lunchbox."

I got to enjoy *that* for about two minutes before I got to knock out a couple of hundred more push-ups.

I've killed plenty of magazines and anthologies in my time (the list of publications that have had a Waldrop story in its last issue or volume is a roll of honor I wear like a shiny badge.)

I've only killed one editor, and that was John W. Campbell, Jr.

(Everybody who sold a story to *Analog* between late 1970 and the middle of 1971 *could* make that claim.) The man had sat at the same desk since late 1937, blithely changing the field for good and bad for more than thirty years; he buys a story from me; seven months later, he dies. Coincidence, or what?

Meanwhile I am at Fort Ord; by and by I am at Fort Gordon, Georgia; I will finish my illustrious military career ("that catapulted me to the rank of corporal"— Woody Allen) at Fort Bragg, North Carolina, one of the two non-jump-qualified soldiers in the 18th Airborne Corps ("When you can type nineteen words a minute, you go where they need you.")

Somewhere, in all this, Ben Bova, Campbell's successor at *Analog* wrote me and asked if he could change *Voyager* to *Viking* to keep up with the changed terminology.

("No, Ben. Keep it the same and make me look like an idiot.") "Of course you might, Mr. Bova, sir," I said.

I got out of the Army in May 1972. On the stands was the May 1972 *Analog*, with "Lunchbox" in it, with an illustration by Kelly Freas. The story went into the Army with me, and came out with me. (I had sold my second story the month before.)

There's a postscript I only heard about, from the man himself, later.

Lester del Rey was then editing the Dutton *Best Science Fiction Stories of the Year* (the first series, that Gardner Dozois would later take over, before starting his own.) For some reason del Rey wanted "Lunchbox" for the 1973 book.

He wrote me at my last Army address: they forwarded it to my Home of Record (from which I'd *already* moved *twice* since leaving the Army). Anyway, I never got the contract; time ran out; the *Best SF* that year didn't have "Lunchbox" in it.

I'm glad, in many ways. To have my *first* story in a *Best of the Year* would have been *wrong*; to have "Lunchbox" in *any Best of the Year* would have been *especially wrong*. I doubt that that early in my career I would have had the character to turn down the contract: I *sure as hell* wouldn't have had the character to turn down the *money*. ("If adversity and bad luck are character-building," said my friend George R. R. Martin a couple of years ago, "yours is as tall as the Malay Towers.")

So.

My first published story, in all its ragged glory; the product of a bad year at the end of an even-stranger decade. Like most of the stories that have followed, it's got funny stuff; there's also a nougat of bitterness about the disparity between our abilities, technologies, and dreams, and the uses to which they were being put (and to which they *could* be put by creatures who didn't *see* things the way we did.)

I was truly proud to sell this story; as I said. I got to enjoy it somewhere between doing deep knee-bends and digging a latrine.

Which, when you think about it, was what Kubrick was saying in *2001* (the year I'm writing *this*):

HAL 9000 = an entrenching tool.

LUNCHBOX

by Howard Waldrop

IT came down on a flame toward the gray and red landscape, hissing through the thin air, lower and lower as the dim sun rose up the edge of the planet. The ground below was turning from shadow to sunlight, and the metal eye of the craft reflected the eye and heart of the sun.

It dropped more slowly still, and the pillar under it changed from bright orange to nothingness and shimmer as the propellants burned away and the nitrogen pressure tanks were emptied in the last twenty feet of the drop. It settled with a small thump, and the legs made the machine plumb level inside their hydraulic casings.

The planet was quiet and still.

The sun beaded the horizon in the deathstill frosty calm of dawn.

Man's first claim to daybreak on Mars.

The noise rose from stillness to roar to pandemonium inside the Mission Control Room. Cigars were passed around, papers were thrown into the air, the unloosed tension went from desk to desk. Checklists fell like snow in the cyclone of the room.

Then the men resettled at their consoles, ready for the Big Broadcast of 1977. Above them, television commentators were telling the public that what they had just seen was a celebration by the men at the consoles because the first of the Viking series had landed on the red planet, Mars.

Krvl, resting in their den, heard the scream of a ruined xr. Parts of Krvl roused, other parts remained dormant, others were reproducing in a random manner, ready for the formation of a motherbud later in the day.

Krvl shifted himself sluggishly, aware that something was amiss. Xrs roamed at night, and by the slight pulsing in its head, Krvl knew it was dawnlight—when xrs should be dying. They did not scream when they died. And what but an xr went about at night?

And what, except the Kind, destroyed xrs?

Krvl paused/moved to the chute-tube of the den. It availed themself of an xr pouch and slid out, leaving its reproducing self behind.

Outside, it was a wonderfully murky morning.

The first photographs from Mars showed a hummocked landscape of powdered sand and clay/grit-sized particles. The scanning lens mounted atop the module showed the hummocks. The close-up lens in the bottom of the Viking showed the clay-sized particles.

The scanning camera on top turned completely every two minutes. It recorded a scene each twenty degrees of arc and sent them back after two minutes of rumination within the devices that made up the innards of the Viking.

The pictures were marvelously sharp and clear, and showed a rolled landscape of dunes. Readings gave back a temperature of −27°F but the temperature was slowly rising in the fairly bright morning sunlight.

Krvl seeped across warm dunes. He would have to hurry to gather xrs before they died completely in the hot burning sunlight that would come in an hour. Krvl liked to hunt in the morning better than the evening, though chances of getting a near-live xr were much less. This morning, Krvl also wanted to find the thing that had made the xr scream. He had heard a small sound like it often when he retrieved a half-live xr for his meal from the ice vein that ran through his den. But never from above, in the open, at night, that loud.

He suggled down a dune. Already it was warmer. In thirty minutes the heat would become unbearable. He *would* have to hurry. Krvl liked the summer least of all the times.

He came into view of the xr crawl.

The close-up lens of the Viking began to turn slowly, photographing then relaying pictures back to Earth. First was a photograph showing the third leg of the Viking which showed a discoloration, a darker smudge protruding from beneath the landing leg. When the photograph was relayed a matter of minutes later, the interpreters became tense for the first time. They immediately sent signals to the machine to take a much closer series of pictures of the third leg of the craft.

The scanning camera, meanwhile, showed a patch of darker smudges in a dip between two dunes.

Excitement ran high. The bottom of the Viking opened and a long sticky string uncurled on the ground. The interpreting people got down to work.

They tried to get the long string as near as possible to the third leg of the craft. They tried, but got no closer than four inches.

The string withdrew up into the craft like a long tongue.

The xrs had shifted a lot during the night. Krvl came over the dunes and saw the thick webbing of them strewn over miles and miles of desert.

He opened his pouch and began gathering them up, putting them inside with the small ends up. He would look back every so often, and those that had not moved their large ends up, he took out and dropped back to the desert. The sun was very very warm now.

He would have to hurry, or they would lose the rebirth fluid into the air through evaporation.

The instruments in the craft showed a temperature at minus eleven degrees Farenheit as the first of the sample gatherers was fired toward the darker smudge between the two dunes. The small rocket was propelled by liquid nitrogen pressure, and as it left, the nitrogen compressor, powered by the same nuclear generator which ran everything on the craft, sucked in more air from outside, to compress and liquefy.

The small rocket arced out, between the dunes, and landed amidst the darker tones of the camera lens. It sat a few moments, the last of the nitrogen bubbling off, and then a small grapple and net affair slid out, scooped, opened and closed. An activator signaled for the craft to start the winch that would draw the collector back.

Krvl straightened at the sound. A high thin pop, and then a thud quite near. He looked in the direction of the sound.

There was a slight hiss. He saw deepfrost form around a depression in the midst of the xr crawl. As he watched, xrs began crawling toward the depression, first a few, then more and more, then a virtual riot of them. And with the sun blazing.

All thoughts of xr gathering were forgotten. This was a new and strange thing. As mysterious as the xr scream early this day.

He/she/it walked toward the moving xrs. Krvl scanned the horizon for other signs of strangeness. Out a ways, between the nearest dunes, he saw a much larger depression, and a solitary, curiously flattened xr. More newness.

He stopped. A group of xrs was being gathered, folded, compacted, crushed into a tight mass before him. The folding stopped. Then the mass moved, without walking, toward the edge of the xr crawl.

Krvl looked and watched and followed, but could not decide what or how this thing happened.

An invisibility. He reasoned.

Krvl pulled out his twelfth and thirteenth Haze eyes.

He stopped at what he saw. His Haze eyes were good only when the air cleared and the Hazelight came down. Using them now, though, he could barely make out the countryside, but was taken aback at the other thing he saw.

A creature sat far off between the two dunes. With one of its feet it was standing atop the crushed xr, and had extended a claw from itself into the xr patch, where the claw had scooped up some of the things and was pulling them back toward itself.

Carefully, Krvl followed the claw as it was pulled back into the Haze creature. It had no business bothering his crawl.

The scanning camera showed the collection rocket being pulled back into the Viking. Then the series of landscapes as the camera rotated. Then the rocket, winched closer, and behind it the drag path where the grapple had slid through the sand.

Then more landscape. Then the rocket, still closer. One of the interpreters asked that the camera be frozen on the winching process next time around; he thought he had seen some interesting phenomena. The camera came around. The rocket was close, closer. There were marks behind the dragging grapple which did not seem to be made by its passage. Then the rocket was pulled within the innards of the craft. Then there were more markings on the ground.

The interpreter leaped up.

Some of the monitors showed activity within the spacecraft.
The last picture was sideways.
All was black.

Krvl had followed the claw until the creature pulled inside
itself. Then he looked at the Haze creature, sitting very high on
its four appendages. It looked at him through its single eye.

Krvl gave it a universal greeting, while he assumed a warning stance. It did not move.

Krvl touched it. Nothing happened. Perhaps it was dormant
while digesting its food.

Krvl pulled at its leg, lifting it from the ground.

Immediately the creature hissed, and sent its leg forward to
the sand. A shower of dust flew up, and the creature rocked and
settled on its legs again in the same relative position.

Krvl was very wary now. He asked it why it had entered his
domain without respect. It did not answer. He pulled at its leg
again. This time it moved violently, rocked toward him and
back, sending up a great geyser of sand.

It would not do, Krvl decided, to have a mindless creature
threaten one's food supply.

Krvl took action. The eye was always a good place to start.

On Earth, consternation.

That afternoon, a Kind called Mrgk stood respectfully at the
edge of Krvl's crawlpatch and asked to come visit.

Krvl was happy to see them again. Mrgk came in and
smelled the xr smell, cold and delicate, on his sensors.

"To devour the xr," said Mrgk.

"To devour the xr," answered Krvl. "I have a new thing to
show."

"What is it?" asked Mrgk.

"You will have to use your Haze eyes," said Krvl.

They went into the den, to the back, near Krvl's xr bin.

"Here," said Krvl.

It lay on its back, legs up.

"This is most strange," Mrgk said. "What can it be?"

"I think it some sort of creature of the Haze," answered
Krvl. "I found it raiding my crawl this morninghunt."

As they watched, the creature let out a hissing scream. Its
legs thrashed in and out, moving up and down, trying to find
footing in the air. Just as suddenly, it quit.

"Can it hurt us?" asked Mrgk.

"I think not," said Krvl. "I blinded it before I brought it back to my humble denning. Or I thought I did. It struggled fiercely much as you just saw, on the way back. I later found a smaller eye on its nether side, which I also removed."

"It has no other appendages?" asked Mrgk. "Four seem such a small number."

"It had," answered Krvl. "Six more clawlike devices tightly wound inside. I discarded those also, fearing they could be harmful." He indicated a tangled pile of loops and grapples. "I believe it to be fully incapacitated now, though seemingly able to live somewhat, like the xr. It moves from time to time."

"This is a most wondrous creature. We shall have to tell the other Kind."

"I will take it to the next Meet," said Krvl.

"Very strange indeed."

"I have not yet shown the best part," said Krvl modestly. "After rendering it helpless, I cracked its shell. Inside I found a wonderful newness. Note its stomach is very cold?"

Mrgk bent close, saw the deepfrost forming on its insides.

Krvl dropped a stiff xr into the body. In a few seconds, it swelled, grew, moved, began running about, trying to climb out the slick sides.

"Simply marvelous," said Mrgk.

"I think this Haze creature was able to make its stomach very cold, so that it could ingest fully live xrs. Imagine," said Krvl.

"But will it not lose this ability?" asked Mrgk.

"I think not. It remains the same as this morninghunt. It has lost none of its coldness," answered Krvl.

"Then it is a wondrous find. Wondrous. We shall be able to place xrs in it and then ingest them fully live ourselves. Oh, I can imagine the taste already!"

Mrgk paused. "Do you realize every Kind will try to find one of these Haze creatures, so they will be able to rejuvenate their xrs? You'll start a craze, Krvl, a positive craze."

Krvl was pleased. Buds formed quickly on his back.

In front of them, between the four legs, the nuclear generator hummed and the compressor pockpocked, making more liquid nitrogen. The legs suddenly hissed and moved, searching back and forth for footing in the air of the den.

THE ORIGIN OF
"ENDER'S GAME"

by Orson Scott Card

"Ender's Game" began with the battle room, a null-gravity space where children play a combat "game" that prepares them to command soldiers and ships in three-dimensional space warfare. I thought of it when I was sixteen years old.

My older brother, while home on leave from the Army in 1967, had broken his leg in a bicycle accident and was reassigned to Fort Douglas in Salt Lake City. This allowed him to come down to our home in Orem on weekends to attend church in one of the many congregations on the Brigham Young University campus. There he met Laura Dene Low, a voracious reader and talented writer, whom he would eventually marry.

During their courtship, Laura learned that I loved reading, and she and Bill thrust upon me a copy of Isaac Asimov's *Foundation* trilogy. I had not been a steady reader of science fiction. I had had two previous excursions into the field. When I was eight years old, having blown through all the books in the children's section of the Santa Clara, California public library that seemed remotely interesting to me, I crept surreptitiously into the forbidden main stacks and found, mostly because of their position in a low shelf unit that happened to be the first I came upon, the tiny collection of science fiction books that the library had—mostly science fiction compilations edited by Dikty or Conklin. In those books many of the stories were incomprehensible to me at my age, but a few had set me to dreaming. I have found a few of them in the years since and realized that I was reading classics of a literature just beginning to grow up: Poul Anderson's "Call Me Joe," for instance, Robert Heinlein's "All You Zombies," and Lloyd Biggle, Jr.'s, "Tunesmith."

Once I had read all the science fiction I could understand, though, I went on to other reading and didn't look back—until, when I was in junior high school in Mesa, Arizona, my brother Bill handed me a paperback called *Catseye* by Andre Norton. As I read it, I returned to that dreamstate of being somewhere strange and marvelous, inaccessible through any other door, and again I found myself in a library—this time the one at the old East Mesa Junior High—where I read everything by Andre Norton (including her Viking novel, of all things) and then went on to the Heinlein juveniles. I still carry the best of these books around in my head and doubtless inadvertently echo them in all that I write: *Galactic Derelict, Tunnel in the Sky. The Time Traders, Citizen of the Galaxy, Starborn, The Stars Are Ours, Starman's Son.*

Again, however, I had soon exhausted the supply of science fiction in that library and simply moved on to other books that captured my heart in other ways. I did not become a science fiction fanatic, one of those readers who become so addicted to the imaginative leaps of the genre that they are impatient with reading anything else. On the contrary, I relished science fiction as one food group among many in my literary diet. While living in Santa Clara I had read T.H.White's *Sword in the Stone*, for instance, and a series of historical novels by William Altsheler dealing with the French and Indian Wars and the American Civil War, not to mention my mother's favorite series of novels, the Williamsburg books by Elswyth Thane. If you had asked me to name my favorite kind of fiction in those years, I would certainly have told you "historical novels," and perhaps the most important to me was Mark Twain's *The Prince and the Pauper*, which started me on a lifelong fascination with English history (and yes, I can still name all the kings and ruling queens pretty much in order, right down to the usurper Stephen of Blois and the nine days' queen, Lady Jane Grey).

The books that had the most powerful effect on me

were not fiction, however. During my childhood years in California I was building up my picture of how the world works, and seminal reading during that time consisted of three works: William L. Shirer's *The Rise and Fall of the Third Reich*, Bruce Catton's trilogy *The Army of the Potomac*, and the Book of Mormon. The Shirer I read because my older sister was assigned it in high school and passed it along to me, understanding, as I did, how important it was to understand World War II as the fulcrum of modern history. I wept, both waking and sleeping, over some of the things that I learned about human nature while reading that book; but I also acquired the indelible understanding of what war is for and why even the most peaceful nation is forced to engage in bloody struggles from time to time— indeed, it was having *Rise and Fall of the Third Reich* in my memory that made it impossible for me to regard the "antiwar" movement of the sixties as anything other than the childish, shortsighted, self-indulgent don't-draft-*me*-but-don't-call-me-a-coward-either movement that it mainly was (as proved by its complete disappearance with the abolition of the draft and the gung-ho way most of its one-time practitioners embraced or at least ignored the criminal military ventures of Bill "Don't Think About The Dress While I'm Bombing Foreigners" Clinton).

The Army of the Potomac taught me a different kind of lesson. With its concentration on the daily life of the soldiers and the way they paid a bitter price for the failures and successes of their generals and yet still went on, year after year, until the war was won, I gained what I think of as the true perspective on the nature of war. A general succeeds, not just because he knows where to put his troops, but because he has trained his troops and won their trust and loyalty so that they will perform unexpected and impossible feats of arms for him. With such an army, the commander must also not be a fool (as witness the failures of George McClellan), but given the limited talents of Robert E. Lee as a tactician and strategist (what, really, did he think he was doing at Gettysburg, where if anything he emulated the less-than-brilliant tactics of Ambrose Burnside at Fredericksburg?), his success in sustaining the war for four years can only be ascribed to the adoration his soldiers had for Marse Bob and his willingness to tolerate better commanders than himself in high position under him. Grant, on the other hand, understood strategy far better, but it took him a while to win the hearts of his men. Even at that, it was not so much that they loved him as that they trusted that he would not waste their lives the way so many previous commanders had. They might die by the thousands, but in the end, they knew that those who survived would not retreat ignominiously but rather would move relentlessly on against the enemy until they won. Trust and love were at the root of military survival, and only then was genius able to play a role in bringing victory.

The Book of Mormon, with its compelling history of the rise and fall, rise and fall of nations over a great span of time, shaped my view of history, keeping in my mind through all my study of history the fact that however high a civilization might rise, its fall is inevitable, because supremacy carries with it the ever-germinating seeds of corruption, decay, and crumbling collapse. History does not repeat itself, per se, but rather, because history consists of the deeds of people acting in, for, and through communities, history shows over and over again what the rules of community formation and dissolution are and how human nature does not change regardless of the technologies and cultures and self-stories they develop. My first version of the Book of Mormon was an illustrated children's version by Emma Man Petersen, which gave a hero-centered view of the stories in the book, but I have returned to the Book of Mormon again and again until, having reread it more than any other book, I have found lessons about human nature that served me well at every stage of my study of history. (Indeed, if you couple the Book of Mormon with the essay on leadership in Section 121 of the Doctrine and Covenants, I can say that I got my complete conceptual framework of human history from Joseph Smith.)

Those who have read *Ender's Game* (or the original novelet "Ender's Game" that is included with this book) will recognize that these accounts of my childhood reading are not digressions at all, but rather give the source of the story. Having laid the general groundwork, though,

let me now account for the particular motifs that domi-
nate "Ender' s Game."

Let me return to Asimov's *Foundation* trilogy. When
Laura Dene and Bill gave me those books to read, I
plunged back into science fiction for the third time in my
life, reading everything I could get my hands on. Where
in the late fifties, sci-fi had been little more than a handful of anthologies, and in the early sixties what was available was mostly "juveniles"—books for preadolescent
readers—now in the late sixties science fiction was a pros-
perous and growing category of book publishing, and I
haunted the science fiction section of the BYU Bookstore,
where I found all the other novels and stories of Asimov
(who, despite his huge numbers of books, in fact wrote
only a smallish corpus of fiction), *The Moon Is a Harsh
Mistress* and *Glory Road* by Heinlein; *The Left Hand of
Darkness* and the other Hainish novels of LeGuin, not to
mention her *Earthsea* books; Larry Niven alone (*Ring-
world*, *Protector*, and many other powerful stories) and in
collaboration (*The Mote in God's Eye* with Jerry Pournelle);
Harlan Ellison as writer and editor (*Dangerous Visions* and
Partners in Wonder); the fantasists J. R. R. Tolkien (the
Middle Earth books, of course, but also "Leaf by Niggle"
and "Smith of Wootton Major") and C. S. Lewis (I didn't
care for the *Perelandra* books, but still love *Narnia* and,
above all, *Till We Have Faces*); and, above all, the incanta-
tory prose, which must be read aloud, of Ray Bradbury,
especially in the collections *Dandelion Wine*, *The Martian
Chronicles*, and *I Sing the Body Electric*.

But it was right at the beginning of this third "wave"
of science fiction in my life that I decided that I was going
to write in this genre. Upon finishing *Second Foundation*,
the third volume of the original *Foundation* trilogy, I knew
that it was science fiction that provided the tools a writer
could use to tell stories with enough size and scope to create, not just hero-tales, but histories—stories of community rather than mere stories of individuals. I did not
think in those terms yet, of course, but that was the im-
petus behind my decision to attempt to write fiction—the
hunger to write stories that were larger than the lives of
the people in them, stories about people acting together
in common cause, and those who gathered, unified, and

led them. While on the surface much of my work might seem to be about extraordinary heroes, in fact the stories are invariably about how human and ordinary these "geniuses" are, and how their true genius was not in the obvious talents that others saw, but in their ability to create powerful communities out of weak individuals.

With that as-yet-unarticulated goal in mind, I set out to think up my own sci-fi story idea, which to my mind involved "coming up with something in the future that would be different from today." Since my brother Bill was at that time the most interesting person in the family—the one who had volunteered for the Army while a war raged in Vietnam, the one who had been so outstanding in basic training that he was flagged for Officers Candidate School, which he dropped out of after only a few weeks because he rejected the whole dehumanizing and counterproductive system of officer training—it is no surprise that I came up with the question of how you train commanders for war in space.

And now I must backtrack one last time to one of the books I read after my second "wave" of sci-fi reading. In the same junior high library where I found Norton's and Heinlein's juveniles, I also found Nordhoff & Hall's *Bounty* trilogy, *Mutiny on the Bounty*, *Men Against the Sea* and *Pitcairn's Island* (with their own brilliantly clear exposition of community formation and breakdown). Following up on these books, I read the same authors' book on World War I fighter pilots, and while the book as a whole was nowhere near as important to me as the *Bounty* trilogy, there was one key moment that stuck with me. In this fictionalized account, the young pilots are warned that the thing most likely to kill them in combat was their habit of thinking flat—of looking for danger to the left and right, and even behind them, while forgetting that danger was far more likely to come from above or below. Land-based thinking would kill them in the sky.

So as I rode along in my father's car, being driven to high school at Brigham Young High, I knew that one of the biggest challenges in training commanders for war in space would be getting rid of gravity-based thinking. For even the best pilots still think of "up" and "down" in gravity-centered ways—indeed, up and down are far more important to pilots than to tank commanders! But in space, thinking of "up" and "down" will force you into patterns that make you both predictable and vulnerable to surprise. Those old patterns would have to be expunged and new ones brought into play. Simulators couldn't do it. You'd have to get the soldiers' bodies moving through neutral-gravity space until thinking in a truly thee-dimensional way was second nature to them.

I realized at once, however, that it would be too expensive and impractical simply to take soldiers out into space and start them flying around in the equivalent of the obstacle course and shooting range and war games of contemporary military training. Individual air supplies and protective suits for each trainee and the attrition of accidentally losing soldiers who hurtle off into space were simply not necessary to accomplish the mind-reshaping purpose of the training. Instead, the training would have to be accomplished within walls: A hollow cube in space, a football field's length in every direction, in which trainees could learn to hurl themselves bodily through space without fear of flying off into oblivion.

My brothers and I had played combat games ever since our cowboy-and-Indian days, and in the era when I was coming up with the battle room we had taken to using squirt guns and spray bottles so that there would be no "I got you!" "No you didn't!" arguments—either you were soaked with water on some vulnerable place or you weren't. Naturally, the battle room (as I now thought of it) would need a system for marking and enforcing successful "hits," and laserizing the system used in fencing seemed the obvious solution. Instead of pressure suits, the trainees would wear suits that sensed when a laser struck them for a sufficient amount of time or with sufficient intensity to cause damage. Then that portion of the suit would go rigid, forcing the trainee to limp along; if a hit was in a vital place, the whole suit would go rigid and the trainee's weapon would cease to fire.

Essentially, the battle room was now complete in my mind. I was sixteen years old and I had come up with a futuristic setting for . . . some story or other. Even at that age I had sense enough to know that I still didn't have a tale to tell, or even the germ of one. And when, the next year, I actually started writing science fiction stories, they weren't about the battle room at all. They were about a family with hereditary psionic powers like the telepaths in Norton's novels or in Zenna Henderson's stories of The People. These tales, which grew into *The Worthing Saga*, were the ones I sent off for publication and for which I received rejection letters—encouraging ones, but rejections all the same. And when I worked on science fiction during my missionary service in Brazil, it was to the Worthing stories I returned again and again. I remembered the battle room idea, but I also knew that whatever the story was going to be, I wasn't ready to write it. Besides, it was just about military training, and had nothing like the scope and emotional power of the stories I was writing about blue-eyed miracle workers in the Forest of Waters.

It was not until I got a rejection letter from Ben Bova for my story "The Tinker" that I returned to the battle room, and that was for a very practical reason. Ben wrote to me that he liked the way I wrote and wanted a story from me, but *Analog* magazine did not publish fantasy.

Well, I was appalled at that comment. "The Tinker" was well within the range of science fiction stories, I thought, dealing as it did with people with psionic powers. But by then I was working as an editor myself (at BYU Press in 1975), and I understood that Ben was not responding to what the story actually was, but rather what it seemed to be—and that he was right to do so. "The Tinker" did not include the framing information needed to be able to identify it as science fiction. Instead, it had people doing powerful things in a magical way, surrounded by trees and in a medieval-like setting. It was then that I learned the practical difference between sci-fi and fantasy: Fantasy has trees, and science fiction has rivets. That really is the entire difference, despite the elaborate definitions drawn up by theorists in the field. There is no sci-fi story that cannot be told as fantasy, and no fantasy story that cannot be told as sci-fi. The differences are merely cosmetic—is the magic done with a machine or an amulet? And ultimately it boils down to this: If it happens in a rural, medieval setting, it *feels* like fantasy, while if it happens in a plate-metal future, it *feels* like science fiction.

Since at that time I was up to my eyeballs in the artistic success and financial failure of my repertory theater company in Provo, Utah, I desperately needed to make more money than I was getting as an editor. Since selling Amway was not among my options (I am a gifted anti-salesman, able to convince anyone never to buy the thing I'm selling even if it's necessary to save their lives), I knew that my only hope of earning money above my salary was by writing. Playwriting wouldn't do it—it took too much time and brought too little return. Only fiction offered the possibility of earning money quickly, and only science fiction had a short story market lucrative enough to be worth writing but low-paid enough that the top professionals didn't waste their time on it, leaving the field open to newcomers like me. So even though by preference I would probably still have preferred writing historical fiction, science fiction was the more practical choice, and I soon learned that it was the best choice for me, since I can do, within sci-fi, almost everything that historical fiction can accomplish, while having the absolute freedom provided by the science fiction audience, which is the most open-minded and intelligent set of readers available to any writer, period. (Just try writing something truly innovative for the supposedly experiment-loving literary audience and see how receptive and open-minded or even perceptive *they* are, in the main.)

I needed a story that had the feel of science fiction and that I could sell to Ben Bova at *Analog*, the editor who was most encouraging to me. I was twenty-four years old, and for eight years I had harbored that battle room idea. It was time to write "Ender's Game."

Only one piece remained to fall in place. Determined to write the story, and with the experience of writing a couple of dozen plays and a handful of short stories behind me, I knew that I needed a compelling character. The obvious choice was to tell about someone who either did not fit in to the training regimen of the battle room or someone who was surpassingly brilliant at it—or both. But still nothing fell into place for me until it dawned on me that the orientation toward gravity is so ingrained in us—so built into the genes of primates whose survival depended on babies knowing better than to fall out of trees in their sleep—that the best time to break that gravity-centered mind-set is in childhood, the earlier the better.

This led to a whole series of obvious extrapolations: Children with military potential would have to be identified at a very early age through accurate and reliable testing; there had to be an enemy so dangerous that parents would allow their little children to be drafted and governments would pay the enormous cost of constructing battle rooms in space. I also recognized that the role of foot soldiers in space would be fairly limited, so that the battle room would really be needed to train pilots and, perhaps more important, the commanders who would deploy them, a far smaller and therefore more practical number of trainees than if you tried to train enough soldiers for regiments and brigades, let alone divisions and corps.

My hero would be the best and yet the least willing of trainees, and he would be a young child. Because at the moment I was reading a book on chess (it didn't help—I still get bored too quickly to be a good chess player) and because I was reading absurdist plays at the time, including Beckett's "Endgame," I thought I should name my hero "Ender" so I could call it "Ender's Game." I tagged on the last name "Wiggin" because it had a vaguely hobbity, "small" feeling that did not sound at all heroic. Ender Wiggin. Why not? It was as good as any other name. (I was just as whimsical in naming Mazer Rackham—Rackham for the fairy-book illustrator who was in vogue just then, and Mazer—then spelled Maeser—for Karl G. Maeser, the first head of Brigham Young University, the one-volume history of which I was indexing at the time.)

Of course far more went into the story than the sources I've mentioned here—events in my own life gave shape and meaning to the story in ways that I probably still don't understand—and, in the end, the story took the form it did because it felt right—felt important and true—to the author at the time he was writing it, a statement which is true of most stories and of all the honest ones. Wherever the ideas came from, I wrote it essentially in two sittings, beginning in longhand as I sat on the lawn outside the Salt Palace in Salt Lake City while a girlfriend took her boss' children to the circus, and then at the office on one of BYU's typewriters. One draft, which my mother retyped for me and mailed off to *Analog*. Ben Bova asked me to cut it in half, but I knew enough from directors' comments about my plays that all that meant was that it felt long to him. So I cut out a couple of extraneous battle scenes, my mother retyped it again (you had to do that in the days before word processors, and she typed a hundred words a minute with perfect accuracy), and I sent back a manuscript that was essentially my first draft minus six pages. Ben bought it and, after I declined to retitle it "Professional Soldier," he published it in the form you are about to read now.

ENDER'S GAME

by Orson Scott Card

"WHATEVER your gravity is when you get to the door, remember—the enemy's gate is *down*. If you step through your own door like you're out for a stroll, you're a big target and you deserve to get hit. With more than a flasher." Ender Wiggins paused and looked over the group. Most were just watching him nervously. A few understanding. A few sullen and resisting.

First day with this army, all fresh from the teacher squads, and Ender had forgotten how young new kids could be. He'd been in it for three years, they'd had six months—nobody over nine years old in the whole bunch. But they were his. At eleven, he was half a year early to be a commander. He'd had a toon of his own and knew a few tricks, but there were forty in his new army. Green. All marksmen with a flasher, all in top shape, or they wouldn't be here—but they were all just as likely as not to get wiped out first time into battle.

"Remember," he went on, "they can't see you till you get through that door. But the second you're out, they'll be on you.

So hit that door the way you want to be when they shoot at you. Legs go under you, going straight down." He pointed at a sullen kid who looked like he was only seven, the smallest of them all. "Which way is down, greenoh!"

"Toward the enemy door." The answer was quick. It was also surly, as if to say, Yeah, yeah, now get on with the important stuff.

"Name, kid?"

"Bean."

"Get that for size or for brains?"

Bean didn't answer. The rest laughed a little. Ender had chosen right. The kid was younger than the rest, must have been advanced because he was sharp. The others didn't like him much, they were happy to see him taken down a little. Like Ender's first commander had taken him down.

"Well, Bean, you're right onto things. Now I tell you this, nobody's gonna get through that door without a good chance of getting hit. A lot of you are going to be turned into cement somewhere. Make sure it's your legs. Right? If only your legs get hit, then only your legs get frozen, and in nullo that's no sweat." Ender turned to one of the dazed ones. "What're legs for? Hmmm?"

Blank stare. Confusion. Stammer.

"Forget it. Guess I'll have to ask Bean here."

"Legs are for pushing off walls." Still bored.

"Thanks, Bean. Get that, everybody?" They all got it, and didn't like getting it from Bean. "Right. You can't *see* with legs, you can't *shoot* with legs, and most of the time they just get in the way. If they get frozen sticking straight out you've turned yourself into a blimp. No way to hide. So how do legs go?"

A few answered this time, to prove that Bean wasn't the only one who knew anything. "Under you. Tucked up under."

"Right. A shield. You're kneeling on a shield, and the shield is your own legs. And there's a trick to the suits. Even when your legs are flashed you can *still* kick off. I've never seen anybody do it but me—but you're all gonna learn it."

Ender Wiggins turned on his flasher. It glowed faintly green in his hand. Then he let himself rise in the weightless workout room, pulled his legs under him as though he were kneeling, and flashed both of them. Immediately his suit stiffened at the knees and ankles, so that he couldn't bend at all.

"Okay, I'm frozen, see?"

He was floating a meter above them. They all looked up at him, puzzled. He leaned back and caught one of the handholds on the wall behind him, and pulled himself flush against the wall.

"I'm stuck at a wall. If I had legs, I'd use legs, and string myself out like a string *bean*, right?"

They laughed.

"But I don't have legs, and that's *better*, got it? Because of this." Ender jackknifed at the waist, then straightened out violently. He was across the workout room in only a moment. From the other side he called to theim "Got that? I didn't use hands, so I still had use of my flasher. *And* I didn't have my legs floating five feet behind me. Now watch it again."

He repeated the jackknife, and caught a handhold on the wall near them. "Now, I don't just want you to do that when they've flashed your legs. I want you to do that when you've still got legs, because it's better. And because they'll never be expecting it. All right now, everybody up in the air and kneeling."

Most were up in a few seconds. Ender flashed the stragglers, and they dangled, helplessly frozen, while the others laughed. "When I give an order, you move. Got it? When we're at a door and they clear it, I'll be giving you orders in two seconds, as soon as I see the setup. And when I give the order you better be out there, because whoever's out there first is going to win, unless he's a fool. I'm not. And you better not be, or I'll have you back in the teacher squads." He saw more than a few of them gulp, and the frozen ones looked at him with fear. "You guys who are hanging there. You watch. You'll thaw out in about fifteen minutes, and let's see if you can catch up to the others."

For the next half hour Ender had them jackknifing off walls. He called a stop when he saw that they all had the basic idea. They were a good group, maybe. They'd get better.

"Now you're warmed up," he said to them, "we'll start working."

Ender was the last one out after practice, since he stayed to help some of the slower ones improve on technique. They'd had good teachers, but like all armies they were uneven, and some of them could be a real drawback in battle. Their first battle might be weeks away. It might be tomorrow. A schedule was never printed. The commander just woke up and found a note by his bunk, giving him the time of his battle and the name of his opponent. So for the first while he was going to drive his boys until they were in top shape—all of them. Ready for anything, at any time. Strategy was nice, but it was worth nothing if the soldiers couldn't hold up under the strain.

He turned the corner into the residence wing and found himself face to face with Bean, the seven-year-old he had picked on all through practice that day. Problems. Ender didn't want problems right now.

"Ho, Bean."

"Ho, Ender."

Pause.

"Sir," Ender said softly.

"We're not on duty."

"In my army, Bean, we're always on duty." Ender brushed past him.

Bean's high voice piped up behind him. "I know what you're doing, Ender, sir, and I'm warning you."

Ender turned slowly and looked at him. "Warning me?"

"I'm the best man you've got. But I'd better be treated like it."

"Or what?" Ender smiled menacingly.

"Or I'll be the worst man you've got. One or the other."

"And what do you want? Love and kisses?" Ender was getting angry now.

Bean was unworried. "I want a toon."

Ender walked back to him and stood looking down into his eyes. "I'll give a toon," he said, "to the boys who prove they're worth something. They've got to be good soldiers, they've got to know how to take orders, they've got to be able to think for themselves in a pinch, and they've got to be able to keep respect. That's how I got to be a commander. That's how you'll get to be a toon leader. Got it?"

Bean smiled. "That's fair. *If* you actually work that way, I'll be a toon leader in a month."

Ender reached down and grabbed the front of his uniform and shoved him into the wall. "When I say I work a certain way, Bean, then that's the way I work."

Bean just smiled. Ender let go of him and walked away, and didn't look back. He was sure, without looking, that Bean was still watching, still smiling, still just a little contemptuous. He might make a good toon leader at that. Ender would keep an eye on him.

Captain Graff, six foot two and a little chubby, stroked his belly as he leaned back in his chair. Across his desk sat Lieutenant Anderson, who was earnestly pointing out high points on a chart.

"Here it is, Captain," Anderson said. "Ender's already got them doing a tactic that's going to throw off everyone who meets it. Doubled their speed."

Graff nodded.

"And you know his test scores. He thinks well, too."

Graff smiled. "All true, all true, Anderson, he's a fine student, shows real promise."

They waited.

Graff sighed. "So what do you want me to do?"

"Ender's the one. He's got to be."

"He'll never be ready in time, Lieutenant. He's eleven, for heaven's sake, man, what do you want, a miracle?"

"I want him into battles, every day starting tomorrow. I want him to have a year's worth of battles in a month."

Graff shook his head. "That would have his army in the hospital."

"No, sir. He's getting them into form. And we need Ender."

"Correction, Lieutenant. We need somebody. You think it's Ender."

"All right, I think it's Ender. Which of the commanders if it isn't him?"

"I don't know, Lieutenant." Graff ran his hands over his slightly fuzzy bald head. "These are children, Anderson. Do you realize that? Ender's army is nine years old. Are we going to put them against the older kids? Are we going to put them through hell for a month like that?"

Lieutenant Anderson leaned even farther over Graff's desk.

"Ender's test scores, Captain!"

"I've seen his bloody test scores! I've watched him in battle, I've listened to tapes of his training sessions. I've watched his sleep patterns, I've heard tapes of his conversations in the corridors and in the bathrooms, I'm more aware of Ender Wiggins than you could possibly imagine! And against all the arguments, against his obvious qualities, I'm weighing one thing. I have this picture of Ender a year from now, if you have your way. I see him completely useless, worn down, a failure, because he was pushed farther than he or any living person could go. But it doesn't weigh enough, does it, Lieutenant, because there's a war on, and our best talent is gone, and the biggest battles are ahead. So give Ender a battle every day this week. And then bring me a report."

Anderson stood and saluted. "Thank you, sir."

He had almost reached the door when Graff called his name. He turned and faced the captain.

"Anderson," Captain Graff said. "Have you been outside, lately I mean?"

"Not since last leave, six months ago."

"I didn't think so. Not that it makes any difference. But have you ever been to Beaman Park, there in the city? Hmm? Beautiful park. Trees. Grass. No nullo, no battles, no worries. Do you know what else there is in Beaman Park?"

"What, sir?" Lieutenant Anderson asked.

"Children," Graff answered.

"Of course, children," said Anderson.

"I mean children. I mean kids who get up in the morning when their mothers call them and they go to school and then in the afternoons they go to Beaman Park and play. They're happy, they smile a lot, they laugh, they have fun. Hmmm?"

"I'm sure they do, sir."

"Is that all you can say, Anderson?"

Anderson cleared his throat. "It's good for children to have fun, I think, sir. I know I did when I was a boy. But right now the world needs soldiers. And this is the way to get them."

Graff nodded and closed his eyes. "Oh, indeed, you're right, by statistical proof and by all the important theories, and dammit they work and the system is right but all the same Ender's older than I am. He's not a child. He's barely a person."

"If that's true, sir, then at least we all know that Ender is making it possible for the others of his age to be playing in the park."

"And Jesus died to save all men, of course." Graff sat up and looked at Anderson almost sadly. "But we're the ones," Graff said, "we're the ones who are driving in the nails."

Ender Wiggins lay on his bed staring at the ceiling. He never slept more than five hours a night—but the lights went off at

2200 and didn't come on again until 0600. So he stared at the ceiling and thought.

He'd had his army for three and a half weeks. Dragon Army. The name was assigned, and it wasn't a lucky one. Oh, the charts said that about nine years ago a Dragon Army had done fairly well. But for the next six years the name had been attached to inferior armies, and finally, because of the superstition that was beginning to play about the name, Dragon Army was retired. Until now. And now, Ender thought, smiling, Dragon Army was going to take them by surprise.

The door opened quietly. Ender did not turn his head. Someone stepped softly into his room, then left with the sound of the door shutting. When soft steps died away Ender rolled over and saw a white slip of paper lying on the floor. He reached down and picked it up.

"Dragon Army against Rabbit Army, Ender Wiggins and Carn Carby, 0700."

The first battle. Ender got out of bed and quickly dressed. He went rapidly to the rooms of each of his toon leaders and told them to rouse their boys. In five minutes they were all gathered in the corridor, sleepy and slow. Ender spoke softly.

"First battle, 0700 against Rabbit Army. I've fought them twice before but they've got a new commander. Never heard of him. They're an older group, though, and I know a few of their old tricks. Now wake up. Run, doublefast, warm-up in workroom three."

For an hour and a half they worked out, with three mock battles and calisthenics in the corridor out of the nullo. Then for fifteen minutes they all lay up in the air, totally relaxing in the weightlessness. At 0650 Ender roused them and they hurried into the corridor. Ender led them down the corridor, running again, and occasionally leaping to touch a light panel on the ceiling. The boys all touched the same light panel. And at 0658 they reached their gate to the battleroom.

The members of toons C and D grabbed the first eight handholds in the ceiling of the corridor. Toons A, B, and E crouched on the floor. Ender hooked his feet into two handholds in the middle of the ceiling, so he was out of everyone's way.

"Which way is the enemy's door?" he hissed.

"Down!" they whispered back, and laughed.

"Flashers on." The boxes in their hands glowed green. They

waited for a few seconds more, and then the gray wall in front
of them disappeared and the battleroom was visible.

Ender sized it up immediately. The familiar open grid of
most early games, like the monkey bars at the park, with seven
or eight boxes scattered through the grid. They called the boxes
stars. There were enough of them, and in forward enough positions, that they were worth going for. Ender decided this in a
second, and he hissed, "Spread to near stars. E hold!"

The four groups in the corners plunged through the force
field at the doorway and fell down into the battleroom. Before
the enemy even appeared through the opposite gate Ender's
army had spread from the door to the nearest stars.

Then the enemy soldiers came through the door. From their
stance Ender knew they had been in a different gravity, and
didn't know enough to disorient themselves from it. They came
through standing up, their entire bodies spread and defenseless.

"Kill 'em, E!" Ender hissed, and threw himself out the door
knees first, with his flasher between his legs and firing. While
Ender's group flew across the room the rest of Dragon Army
lay down a protecting fire, so that E group reached a forward
position with only one boy frozen completely, though they had
all lost the use of their legs—which didn't impair them in the
least. There was a lull as Ender and his opponent, Carn Carby,
assessed their positions. Aside from Rabbit Army's losses at the
gate, there had been few casualties, and both armies were near
full strength. But Carn had no originality—he was in a four-
corner spread that any five-year-old in the teacher squads might
have thought of. And Ender knew how to defeat it.

He called out, loudly, "E covers A, C down. B, D angle east
wall." Under E toon's cover, B and D toons lunged away from
their stars. While they were still exposed, A and C toons left
their stars and drifted toward the near wall. They reached it together, and together jackknifed off the wall. At double the normal speed they appeared behind the enemy's stars, and opened
fire. In a few seconds the battle was over, with the enemy almost entirely frozen, including the commander, and the rest
scattered to the corners. For the next five minutes, in squads of
four, Dragon Army cleaned out the dark corners of the battleroom and shepherded the enemy into the center, where their
bodies, frozen at impossible angles, jostled each other. Then
Ender took three of his boys to the enemy gate and went
through the formality of reversing the one-way field by simul-

taneously touching a Dragon Army helmet at each corner. Then Ender assembled his army in vertical files near the knot of frozen Rabbit Army soldiers.

Only three of Dragon Army's soldiers were immobile. Their victory margin—38 to 0—was ridiculously high, and Ender began to laugh. Dragon Army joined him, laughing long and loud. They were still laughing when Lieutenant Anderson and Lieutenant Morris came in from the teachergate at the south end of the battleroom.

Lieutenant Anderson kept his face stiff and unsmiling, but Ender saw him wink as he held out his hand and offered the stiff, formal congratulations that were ritually given to the victor in the game.

Morris found Carn Carby and unfroze him, and the thirteen-year-old came and presented himself to Ender, who laughed without malice and held out his hand. Carn graciously took Ender's hand and bowed his head over it. It was that or be flashed again.

Lieutenant Anderson dismissed Dragon Army, and they silently left the battleroom through the enemy's door—again part of the ritual. A light was blinking on the north side of the square door, indicating where the gravity was in that corridor. Ender, leading his soldiers, changed his orientation and went through the force field and into gravity on his feet. His army followed him at a brisk run back to the workroom. When they got there they formed up into squads, and Ender hung in the air, watching them.

"Good first battle," he said, which was excuse enough for a cheer, which he quieted. "Dragon Army did all right against Rabbits. But the enemy isn't always going to be that bad. And if that had been a good army we would have been smashed. We still would have won, but we would have been smashed. Now let me see B and D toons out here. Your takeoff from the stars was way too slow. If Rabbit Army knew how to aim a flasher, you all would have been frozen solid before A and C even got to the wall."

They worked out for the rest of the day.

That night Ender went for the first time to the commanders' mess hall. No one was allowed there until he had won at least one battle, and Ender was the youngest commander ever to make it. There was no great stir when he came in. But when some of the other boys saw the Dragon on his breast pocket,

they stared at him openly, and by the time he got his tray and
sat at an empty table, the entire room was silent, with the other
commanders watching him. Intensely self-conscious, Ender
wondered how they all knew, and why they all looked so hostile.

Then he looked above the door he had just come through.
There was a huge scoreboard across the entire wall. It showed
the win/loss record for the commander of every army; that
day's battles were lit in red. Only four of them. The other three
winners had barely made it—the best of them had only two
men whole and eleven mobile at the end of the game. Dragon
Army's score of thirty-eight mobile was embarrassingly better.

Other new commanders had been admitted to the commanders' mess hall with cheers and congratulations. Other new
commanders hadn't won thirty-eight to zero.

Ender looked for Rabbit Army on the scoreboard. He was
surprised to find that Carn Carby's score to date was eight wins
and three losses. Was he that good? Or had he only fought
against inferior armies? Whichever, there was still a zero in
Carn's mobile and whole columns, and Ender looked down
from the scoreboard grinning. No one smiled back, and Ender
knew that they were afraid of him, which meant that they would
hate him, which meant that anyone who went into battle against
Dragon Army would be scared and angry and less competent.
Ender looked for Carn Carby in the crowd, and found him not
too far away. He stared at Carby until one of the other boys
nudged the Rabbit commander and pointed to Ender. Ender
smiled again and waved slightly. Carby turned red, and Ender,
satisfied, leaned over his dinner and began to eat.

At the end of the week Dragon Army had fought seven battles in seven days. The score stood 7 wins and 0 losses. Ender
had never had more than five boys frozen in any game. It was
no longer possible for the other commanders to ignore Ender. A
few of them sat with him and quietly conversed about game
strategies that Ender's opponents had used. Other much larger
groups were talking with the commanders that Ender had defeated, trying to find out what Ender had done to beat them.

In the middle of the meal the teacher door opened and the
groups fell silent as Lieutenant Anderson stepped in and looked
over the group. When he located Ender he strode quickly across
the room and whispered in Ender's ear. Ender nodded, finished

his glass of water, and left with the lieutenant. On the way out, Anderson handed a slip of paper to one of the older boys. The room became very noisy with conversation as Anderson and Ender left.

Ender was escorted down corridors he had never seen before. They didn't have the blue glow of the soldier corridors. Most were wood paneled, and the floors were carpeted. The doors were wood, with nameplates on them, and they stopped at one that said "Captain Graff, supervisor." Anderson knocked softly, and a low voice said, "Come in."

They went in. Captain Graff was seated behind a desk, his hands folded across his pot belly. He nodded, and Anderson sat. Ender also sat down. Graff cleared his throat and spoke.

"Seven days since your first battle, Ender."

Ender did not reply.

"Won seven battles, one every day."

Ender nodded.

"Scores unusually high, too."

Ender blinked.

"Why?" Graff asked him.

Ender glanced at Anderson, and then spoke to the captain behind the desk. "Two new tactics, sir. Legs doubled up as a shield, so that a flash doesn't immobilize. Jackknife takeoffs from the walls. Superior strategy, as Lieutenant Anderson taught, think places, not spaces. Five toons of eight instead of four of ten. Incompetent opponents. Excellent toon leaders, good soldiers."

Graff looked at Ender without expression. Waiting for what, Ender wondered. Lieutenant Anderson spoke up.

"Ender, what's the condition of your army?"

Do they want me to ask for relief? Not a chance, he decided. "A little tired, in peak condition, morale high, learning fast. Anxious for the next battle."

Anderson looked at Graff. Graff shrugged slightly and turned to Ender.

"Is there anything you want to know?"

Ender held his hands loosely in his lap. "When are you going to put us up against a good army?"

Graff's laughter rang in the room, and when it stopped, Graff handed a piece of paper to Ender.

"Now," the captain said, and Ender read the paper: "Dragon

Army against Leopard Army, Ender Wiggins and Pol Slattery, 2000."

Ender looked up at Captain Craff. "That's ten minutes from now, sir."

Graff smiled. "Better hurry, then, boy."

As Ender left he realized Pol Slattery was the boy who had been handed his orders as Ender left the mess hall.

He got to his army five minutes later. Three toon leaders were already undressed and lying naked on their beds. He sent them all flying down the corridors to rouse their toons, and gathered up their suits himself. When all his boys were assembled in the corridor, most of them still getting dressed, Ender spoke to them.

"This one's hot and there's no time. We'll be late to the door, and the enemy'll be deployed right outside our gate. Ambush, and I've never heard of it happening before. So we'll take our time at the door. A and B toons, keep your belts loose, and give your flashers to the leaders and seconds of the other toons."

Puzzled, his soldiers complied. By then all were dressed, and Ender led them at a trot to the gate. When they reached it the force field was already on one-way, and some of his soldiers were panting. They had bad one battle that day and a full workout. They were tired.

Ender stopped at the entrance and looked at the placement of the enemy soldiers. Some of them were grouped not more than twenty feet out from the gate. There was no grid, there were no stars. A big empty space. Where were most of the enemy soldiers? There should have been thirty more.

"They're flat against this wall," Ender said, "where we can't see them."

He took A and B toons and made them kneel, their hands on their hips. Then he flashed them, so that their bodies were frozen rigid.

"You're shields," Ender said, and then had boys from C and D kneel on their legs and hook both arms under the frozen boys' belts. Each boy was holding two flashers. Then Ender and the members of E toon picked up the duos, three at a time, and threw them out the door.

Of course, the enemy opened fire immediately. But they mainly hit the boys who were already flashed, and in a few moments pandemonium broke out in the battleroom. All the soldiers of Leopard Army were easy targets as they lay pressed flat against the wall or floated, unprotected, in the middle of the battleroom; and Ender's soldiers, armed with two flashers each, carved them up easily. Pol Slattery reacted quickly, ordering his men away from the wall, but not quickly enough—only a few were able to move, and they were flashed before they could get a quarter of the way across the battleroom.

When the battle was over Dragon Army had only twelve boys whole, the lowest score they had ever had. But Ender was satisfied. And during the ritual of surrender Pol Slattery broke form by shaking hands and asking, "Why did you wait so long getting out of the gate?"

Ender glanced at Anderson, who was floating nearby. "I was informed late," he said. "It was an ambush."

Slattery grinned, and gripped Ender's hand again. "Good game."

Ender didn't smile at Anderson this time. He knew that now the games would be arranged against him, to even up the odds. He didn't like it.

It was 2150, nearly time for lights out, when Ender knocked at the door of the room shared by Bean and three other soldiers. One of the others opened the door, then stepped back and held it wide. Ender stood for a moment, then asked if he could come in. They answered, of course, of course, come in, and he walked to the upper bunk, where Bean had set down his book and was leaning on one elbow to look at Ender.

"Bean, can you give me twenty minutes?"

"Near lights out," Bean answered.

"My room," Ender answered. "I'll cover for you."

Bean sat up and slid off his bed. Together he and Ender padded silently down the corridor to Ender's room. Bean entered first, and Ender closed the door behind them.

"Sit down," Ender said, and they both sat on the edge of the bed, looking at each other.

"Remember four weeks ago, Bean? When you told me to make you a toon leader?"

"Yeah."

"I've made five toon leaders since then, haven't I? And none of them was you."

Bean looked at him calmly.

"Was I right?" Ender asked.

"Yes, sir," Bean answered.

Ender nodded. "How have you done in these battles?"

Bean cocked his head to one side. "I've never been immobilized, sir, and I've immobilized forty-three of the enemy. I've
obeyed orders quickly, and I've commanded a squad in mop-up
and never lost a soldier."

"Then you'll understand this." Ender paused, then decided
to back up and say something else first.

"You know you're early, Bean, by a good half year. I was,
too, and I've been made a commander six months early. Now
they've put me into battles after only three weeks of training
with my army. They've given me eight battles in seven days.
I've already had more battles than boys who were made commander four months ago. I've won more battles than many
who've been commanders for a year. And then tonight. You
know what happened tonight."

Bean nodded. "They told you late."

"I don't know what the teachers are doing. But my army is
getting tired, and I'm getting tired, and now they're changing
the rules of the game. You see, Bean, I've looked in the old
charts. No one has ever destroyed so many enemies and kept so
many of his own soldiers whole in the history of the game. I'm
unique—and I'm getting unique treatment."

Bean smiled. "You're the best, Ender."

Ender shook his head. "Maybe. But it was no accident that I
got the soldiers I got. My worst soldier could be a toon leader
in another army. I've got the best. They've loaded things my
way—but now they're loading it all against me. I don't know
why. But I know I have to be ready for it. I need your help."

"Why mine?"

"Because even though there are some better soldiers than
you in Dragon Army—not many, but some—there's nobody
who can think better and faster than you." Bean said nothing.
They both knew it was true.

Ender continued, "I need to be ready, but I can't retrain the
whole army. So I'm going to cut every toon down by one, including you. With four others you'll be a special squad under
me. And you'll learn to do some new things. Most of the time
you'll be in the regular toons just like you are now. But when I
need you. See?"

Bean smiled and nodded. "That's right, that's good, can I
pick them myself?"

"One from each toon except your own, and you can't take any toon leaders."

"What do you want us to do?"

"Bean, I don't know. I don't know what they'll throw at us. What would you do if suddenly our flashers didn't work, and the enemy's did? What would you do if we had to face two armies at once? The only thing I know is—there may be a game where we don't even try for score. Where we just go for the enemy's gate. That's when the battle is technically won—four helmets at the corners of the gate. I want you ready to do that any time I call for it. Got it? You take them for two hours a day during regular workout. Then you and I and your soldiers, we'll work at night after dinner."

"We'll get tired."

"I have a feeling we don't know what tired is." Ender reached out and took Bean's hand, and gripped it. "Even when it's rigged against us, Bean. We'll win."

Bean left in silence and padded down the corridor.

Dragon Army wasn't the only army working out after hours now. The other commanders had finally realized they had some catching up to do. From early morning to lights out soldiers all over Training and Command Center, none of them over fourteen years old, were learning to jackknife off walls and use each other as living shields.

But while other commanders mastered the techniques that Ender had used to defeat them, Ender and Bean worked on solutions to problems that had never come up.

There were still battles every day, but for a while they were normal, with grids and stars and sudden plunges through the gate. And after the battles, Ender and Bean and four other soldiers would leave the main group and practice strange maneuvers. Attacks without flashers, using feet to physically disarm or disorient an enemy. Using four frozen soldiers to reverse the enemy's gate in less than two seconds. And one day Bean came to workout with a 300-meter cord.

"What's that for?"

"I don't know yet." Absently Bean spun one end of the cord. It wasn't more than an eighth of an inch thick, but it could have lifted ten adults without breaking.

"Where did you get it?"

"Commissary. They asked what for. I said to practice tying knots."

Bean tied a loop in the end of the rope and slid it over his shoulders.

"Here, you two, hang on to the wall here. Now don't let go of the rope. Give me about fifty yards of slack." They complied, and Bean moved about ten feet from them along the wall. As soon as he was sure they were ready, he jackknifed off the wall and flew straight out, fifty yards. Then the rope snapped taut. It was so fine that it was virtually invisible, but it was strong enough to force Bean to veer off at almost a right angle. It happened so suddenly that he had inscribed a perfect arc and hit the wall hard before most of the other soldiers knew what had happened. Bean did a perfect rebound and drifted quickly back to where Ender and the others waited for him.

Many of the soldiers in the five regular squads hadn't noticed the rope, and were demanding to know how it was done. It was impossible to change direction that abruptly in nullo. Bean just laughed.

"Wait till the next game without a grid! They'll never know what hit them."

They never did. The next game was only two hours later, but Bean and two others had become pretty good at aiming and shooting while they flew at ridiculous speeds at the end of the rope. The slip of paper was delivered, and Dragon Army trotted off to the gate, to battle with Griffin Army. Bean coiled the rope all the way.

When the gate opened, all they could see was a large brown star only fifteen feet away, completely blocking their view of the enemy's gate.

Ender didn't pause. "Bean, give yourself fifty feet of rope and go around the star." Bean and his four soldiers dropped through the gate and in a moment Bean was launched sideways away from the star. The rope snapped taut, and Bean flew forward. As the rope was stopped by each edge of the star in turn, his arc became tighter and his speed greater, until when he hit the wall only a few feet away from the gate, he was barely able to control his rebound to end up behind the star. But he immediately moved all his arms and legs so that those waiting inside the gate would know that the enemy hadn't flashed him anywhere.

Ender dropped through the gate, and Bean quickly told him

how Griffin Army was situated. "They've got two squares of stars, all the way around the gate. All their soldiers are under cover, and there's no way to hit any of them until we're clear to the bottom wall. Even with shields, we'd get there at half strength and we wouldn't have a chance."

"They moving?" Ender asked.

"Do they need to?"

"I would." Ender thought for a moment. "This one's tough. We'll go for the gate, Bean."

Griffin Army began to call out to them.

"Hey, is anybody there!"

"Wake up, there's a war on!"

"We wanna join the picnic!"

They were still calling when Ender's army came out from behind their star with a shield of fourteen frozen soldiers. William Bee, Griffin Army's commander, waited patiently as the screen approached, his men waiting at the fringes of their stars for the moment when whatever was behind the screen became visible. About ten yards away the screen suddenly exploded as the soldiers behind it shoved the screen north. The momentum carried them south twice as fast, and at the same moment the rest of Dragon Army burst from behind their star at the opposite end of the room, firing rapidly.

William Bee's boys joined battle immediately, of course, but William Bee was far more interested in what had been left behind when the shield disappeared. A formation of four frozen Dragon Army soldiers was moving headfirst toward the Griffin Army gate, held together by another frozen soldier whose feet and hands were hooked through their belts. A sixth soldier hung to his waist and trailed like the tail of a kite. Griffin Army was winning the battle easily, and William Bee concentrated on the formation as it approached the gate. Suddenly the soldier trailing in back moved—he wasn't frozen at all! And even though William Bee flashed him immediately, the damage was done. The formation drifted to the Griffin Army gate, and their helmets touched all four corners simultaneously. A buzzer sounded, the gate reversed, and the frozen soldier in the middle was carried by momentum right through the gate. All the flashers stopped working, and the game was over.

The teachergate opened and Lieutenant Anderson came in. Anderson stopped himself with a slight movement of his hands when he reached the center of the battleroom. "Ender," he called, breaking protocol. One of the frozen Dragon soldiers near the south wall tried to call through jaws that were clamped shut by the suit. Anderson drifted to him and unfroze him.

Ender was smiling.

"I beat you again, sir," Ender said.

Anderson didn't smile. "That's nonsense, Ender," Anderson said softly. "Your battle was with William Bee of Griffin Army."

Ender raised an eyebrow.

"After that maneuver," Anderson said, "the rules are being revised to require that all of the enemy's soldiers must be immobilized before the gate can be reversed."

"That's all right," Ender said. "It could only work once, anyway." Anderson nodded, and was turning away when Ender added, "Is there going to be a new rule that armies be given equal positions to fight from?"

Anderson turned back around. "If you're in one of the positions, Ender, you can hardly call them equal, whatever they are."

William Bee counted carefully and wondered how in the world he had lost when not one of his soldiers had been flashed and only four of Ender's soldiers were even mobile.

And that night as Ender came into the commanders' mess hall, he was greeted with applause and cheers, and his table was crowded with respectful commanders, many of them two or three years older than he was. He was friendly, but while he ate he wondered what the teachers would do to him in his next battle. He didn't need to worry. His next two battles were easy victories, and after that he never saw the battle-room again.

It was 2100 and Ender was a little irritated to hear someone knock at his door. His army was exhausted, and he had ordered them all to be in bed after 2030. The last two days had been regular battles, and Ender was expecting the worst in the morning.

It was Bean. He came in sheepishly, and saluted.

Ender returned his salute and snapped, "Bean, I wanted everybody in bed."

Bean nodded but didn't leave. Ender considered ordering him out. But as he looked at Bean it occurred to him for the first time in weeks just how young Bean was. He had turned eight a week before, and he was still small and—no, Ender thought, he wasn't young. Nobody was young. Bean had been in battle, and with a whole army depending on him he had come through and won. And even though he was small, Ender could never think of him as young again.

Ender shrugged and Bean came over and sat on the edge of the bed. The younger boy looked at his hands for a while, and finally Ender grew impatient and asked, "Well, what is it?"

"I'm transferred. Got orders just a few minutes ago."

Ender closed his eyes for a moment. "I knew they'd pull something new. Now they're taking—where are you going?"

"Rabbit Army."

"How can they put you under an idiot like Carn Carby!"

"Carn was graduated. Support squads."

Ender looked up. "Well, who's commanding Rabbit then?"

Bean held his hands out helplessly.

"Me," he said.

Ender nodded, and then smiled. "Of course. After all, you're only four years younger than the regular age."

"It isn't funny," Bean said. "I don't know what's going on here. First all the changes in the game. And now this. I wasn't the only one transferred, either, Ender. Ren, Peder, Brian, Wins, Younger. All commanders now."

Ender stood up angrily and strode to the wall. "Every damn toon leader I've got!" he said, and whirled to face Bean. "If they're going to break up my army, Bean, why did they bother making me a commander at all?"

Bean shook his head. "I don't know. You're the best, Ender. Nobody's ever done what you've done. Nineteen battles in fifteen days, sir, and you won every one of them, no matter what they did to you."

"And now you and the others are commanders. You know every trick I've got, I trained you, and who am I supposed to replace you with? Are they going to stick me with six greenohs?"

"It stinks, Ender, but you know that if they gave you five crippled midgets and armed you with a roll of toilet paper you'd win."

They both laughed, and then they noticed that the door was open.

Lieutenant Anderson stepped in. He was followed by Captain Graff.

"Ender Wiggins," Graff said, holding his hands across his stomach.

"Yes, sir," Ender answered.

"Orders."

Anderson extended a slip of paper. Ender read it quickly, then crumpled it, still looking at the air where the paper had been. After a few moments he asked, "Can I tell my army?"

"They'll find out," Graff answered. "It's better not to talk to them after orders. It makes it easier."

"For you or for me?" Ender asked. He didn't wait for an answer. He turned quickly to Bean, took his hand for a moment, and then headed for the door.

"Wait," Bean said. "Where are you going? Tactical or Support School?"

"Command School," Ender answered, and then he was gone and Anderson closed the door.

Command School, Bean thought. Nobody went to Command School until they had gone through three years of Tactical. But then, nobody went to Tactical until they had been through at least five years of Battle School. Ender had only had three.

The system was breaking up. No doubt about it, Bean thought. Either somebody at the top was going crazy, or something was going wrong with the war—the real war, the one they were training to fight in. Why else would they break down the training system, advance somebody—even somebody as good as Ender—straight to Command School? Why else would they ever have an eight-year-old greenoh like Bean command an army?

Bean wondered about it for a long time, and then he finally lay down on Ender's bed and realized that he'd never see Ender again, probably. For some reason that made him want to cry. But he didn't cry, of course. Training in the preschools had taught him how to force down emotions like that. He remembered how his first teacher, when he was three, would have been upset to see his lip quivering and his eyes full of tears.

Bean went through the relaxing routine until he didn't feel like crying anymore. Then he drifted off to sleep. His hand was near his mouth. It lay on his pillow hesitantly, as if Bean couldn't decide whether to bite his nails or suck on his fingertips. His forehead was creased and furrowed.

His breathing was quick and light. He was a soldier, and if

anyone had asked him what he wanted to be when he grew up, he wouldn't have known what they meant.

There's a war on, they said, and that was excuse enough for all the hurry in the world. They said it like a password and flashed a little card at every ticket counter and customs check and guard station. It got them to the head of every line.

Ender Wiggins was rushed from place to place so quickly he had no time to examine anything. But he did see trees for the first time. He saw men who were not in uniform. He saw women. He saw strange animals that didn't speak, but that followed docilely behind women and small children. He saw suitcases and conveyor belts and signs that said words he had never heard of. He would have asked someone what the words meant, except that purpose and authority surrounded him in the persons of four very high officers who never spoke to each other and never spoke to him.

Ender Wiggins was a stranger to the world he was being trained to save. He did not remember ever leaving Battle School before. His earliest memories were of childish war games under the direction of a teacher, of meals with other boys in the gray and green uniforms of the armed forces of his world. He did not know that the gray represented the sky and the green represented the great forests of his planet. All he knew of the world was from vague references to "outside."

And before he could make any sense of the strange world he was seeing for the first time, they enclosed him again within the shell of the military, where nobody had to say "There's a war on" anymore because no one within the shell of the military forgot it for a single instant of a single day.

They put him in a spaceship and launched him to a large artificial satellite that circled the world.

This space station was called Command School. It held the ansible.

On his first day Ender Wiggins was taught about the ansible and what it meant to warfare. It meant that even though the starships of today's battles were launched a hundred years ago, the commanders of the starships were men of today, who used the ansible to send messages to the computers and the few men on each ship. The ansible sent words as they were spoken, orders as they were made. Battleplans as they were fought. Light was a pedestrian.

For two months Ender Wiggins didn't meet a single person. They came to him namelessly, taught him what they knew, and left him to other teachers. He had no time to miss his friends at Battle School. He only had time to learn how to operate the simulator, which flashed battle patterns around him as if he were in a starship at the center of the battle. How to command mock ships in mock battle by manipulating the keys on the simulator and speaking words into the ansible. How to recognize instantly every enemy ship and the weapons it carried by the pattern that the simulator showed. How to transfer all that he learned in the nullo battles at Battle School to the starship battles at Command School.

He had thought the game was taken seriously before. Here they hurried him through every step, were angry and worried beyond reason every time he forgot something or made a mistake. But he worked as he had always worked, and learned as he had always learned. After a while he didn't make any more mistakes. He used the simulator as if it were a part of himself. Then they stopped being worried and gave him a teacher.

Maezr Rackham was sitting cross-legged on the floor when Ender awoke. He said nothing as Ender got up and showered and dressed, and Ender did not bother to ask him anything. He had long since learned that when something unusual was going on, he would often find out more information faster by waiting than by asking.

Maezr still hadn't spoken when Ender was ready and went to the door to leave the room. The door didn't open. Ender turned to face the man sitting on the floor. Maezr was at least forty, which made him the oldest man Ender had ever seen close up. He had a day's growth of black and white whiskers that grizzled his face only slightly less than his close-cut hair. His face sagged a little and his eyes were surrounded by creases and lines. He looked at Ender without interest.

Ender turned back to the door and tried again to open it.

"All right," he said, giving up. "Why's the door locked?"

Maezr continued to look at him blankly.

Ender became impatient. "I'm going to be late. If I'm not supposed to be there until later, then tell me so I can go back to bed." No answer. "Is it a guessing game?" Ender asked. No answer. Ender decided that maybe the man was trying to make him angry, so he went through relaxing exercise as he leaned on the door, and soon he was calm again. Maezr didn't take his eyes off Ender.

For the next two hours the silence endured, Maezr watching Ender constantly, Ender trying to pretend he didn't notice the old man. The boy became more and more nervous, and finally ended up walking from one end of the room to the other in a sporadic pattern.

He walked by Maezr as he had several times before, and Maezr's hand shot out and pushed Ender's left leg into his right in the middle of a step. Ender fell flat on the floor.

He leaped to his feet immediately, furious. He found Maezr sitting calmly, cross-legged, as if he had never moved. Ender stood poised to fight. But the other's immobility made it impossible for Ender to attack, and he found himself wondering if he had only imagined the old man's hand tripping him up.

The pacing continued for another hour, with Ender Wiggins trying the door every now and then. At last he gave up and took off his uniform and walked to his bed.

As he leaned over to pull the covers back, he felt a hand jab roughly between his thighs and another hand grab his hair. In a moment he had been turned upside down. His face and shoulders were being pressed into the floor by the old man's knee, while his back was excruciatingly bent and his legs were pinioned by Maezr's arm. Ender was helpless to use his arms, and he couldn't bend his back to gain slack so he could use his legs. In less than two seconds the old man had completely defeated Ender Wiggins.

"All right," Ender gasped. "You win."

Maezr's knee thrust painfully downward.

"Since when," Maezr asked in a soft, rasping voice, "do you have to tell the enemy when he has won?"

Ender remained silent.

"I surprised you once, Ender Wiggins. Why didn't you destroy me immediately afterward? Just because I looked peaceful? You turned your back on me. Stupid. You have learned nothing. You have never had a teacher."

Ender was angry now. "I've had too many damned teachers, how was I supposed to know you'd turn out to be a—" Ender hunted for a word. Maezr supplied one.

"An enemy, Ender Wiggins," Maezr whispered. "I am your enemy, the first one you've ever had who was smarter than you. There is no teacher but the enemy, Ender Wiggins. No one but the enemy will ever tell you what the enemy is going to do. No one but the enemy will ever teach you how to destroy and conquer. I am your enemy, from now on. From now on I am your teacher."

Then Maezr let Ender's legs fall to the floor. Because the old man still held Ender's head to the floor, the boy couldn't use his arms to compensate, and his legs hit the plastic surface with a loud crack and a sickening pain that made Ender wince. Then Maezr stood and let Ender rise.

Slowly the boy pulled his legs under him, with a faint groan of pain, and he knelt on all fours for a moment, recovering. Then his right arm flashed out. Maezr quickly danced back and Ender's hand closed on air as his teacher's foot shot forward to catch Ender on the chin.

Ender's chin wasn't there. He was lying flat on his back, spinning on the floor, and during the moment that Maezr was off-balance from his kick Ender's feet smashed into Maezr's other leg. The old man fell on the ground in a heap.

What seemed to be a heap was really a hornet's nest. Ender couldn't find an arm or a leg that held still long enough to be grabbed, and in the meantime blows were landing on his back and arms. Ender was smaller—he couldn't reach past the old man's flailing limbs.

So he leaped back out of the way and stood poised near the door.

The old man stopped thrashing about and sat up, cross-legged again, laughing. "Better, this time, boy. But slow. You will have to be better with a fleet than you are with your body or no one will be safe with you in command. Lesson learned?"

Ender nodded slowly.

Maezr smiled. "Good. Then we'll never have such a battle again. All the rest with the simulator. I will program your battles, I will devise the strategy of your enemy, and you will learn to be quick and discover what tricks the enemy has for you. Remember, boy. From now on the enemy is more clever than you. From now on the enemy is stronger than you. From now on you are always about to lose."

Then Maezr's face became serious again. "You will be about to lose, Ender, but you will win. You will learn to defeat the enemy. He will teach you how."

Maezr got up and walked toward the door. Ender stepped back out of the way. As the old man touched the handle of the

door, Ender leaped into the air and kicked Maezr in the small of
the back with both feet. He hit hard enough that he rebounded
onto his feet, as Maezr cried out and collapsed on the floor.

Maezr got up slowly, holding on to the door handle, his face
contorted with pain. He seemed disabled, but Ender didn't trust
him. He waited warily. And yet in spite of his suspicion he was
caught off guard by Maezr's speed. In a moment he found himself on the floor near the opposite wall, his nose and lip bleeding where his face had hit the bed. He was able to turn enough
to see Maezr open the door and leave. The old man was limp-
ing and walking slowly.

Ender smiled in spite of the pain, then rolled over onto his
back and laughed until his mouth filled with blood and he
started to gag. Then he got up and painfully made his way to the
bed. He lay down and in a few minutes a medic came and took
care of his injuries.

As the drug had its effect and Ender drifted off to sleep he
remembered the way Maezr limped out of his room and
laughed again. He was still laughing softly as his mind went
blank and the medic pulled the blanket over him and snapped
off the light. He slept until the pain woke him in the morning.
He dreamed of defeating Maezr.

The next day Ender went to the simulator room with his
nose bandaged and his lip still puffy. Maezr was not there. Instead, a captain who had worked with him before showed him
an addition that had been made. The captain pointed to a tube
with a loop at one end. "Radio. Primitive, I know, but it loops
over your ear and we tuck the other end into your mouth like
this."

"Watch it," Ender said as the captain pushed the end of the
tube into his swollen lip.

"Sorry. Now you just talk."

"Good. Who to?"

The captain smiled. "Ask and see."

Ender shrugged and turned to the simulator. As he did a
voice reverberated through his skull. It was too loud for him to
understand, and he ripped the radio off his ear.

"What are you trying to do, make me deaf?"

The captain shook his head and turned a dial on a small box
on a nearby table. Ender put the radio back on.

"Commander," the radio said in a familiar voice.

Ender answered, "Yes."

"Instructions, sir?"

The voice was definitely familiar. "Bean?" Ender asked.

"Yes, sir."

"Bean, this is Ender."

Silence. And then a burst of laughter from the other side. Then six or seven more voices laughing, and Ender waited for silence to return. When it did, he asked, "Who else?"

A few voices spoke at once, but Bean drowned them out. "Me, I'm Bean, and Peder, Wins, Younger, Lee, and Vlad."

Ender thought for a moment. Then he asked what the hell was going on. They laughed again.

"They can't break up the group," Bean said. "We were commanders for maybe two weeks, and here we are at Command School, training with the simulator, and all of a sudden they told us we were going to form a fleet with a new commander. And that's you."

Ender smiled. "Are you boys any good?"

"If we aren't, you'll let us know."

Ender chuckled a little. "Might work out. A fleet."

For the next ten days Ender trained his toon leaders until they could maneuver their ships like precision dancers. It was like being back in the battleroom again, except that now Ender could always see everything, and could speak to his toon leaders and change their orders at any time.

One day as Ender sat down at the control board and switched on the simulator, harsh green lights appeared in the space—the enemy.

"This is it," Ender said. "X, Y, bullet, C, D, reserve screen, E, south loop, Bean, angle north."

The enemy was grouped in a globe, and outnumbered Ender two to one. Half of Ender's force was grouped in a tight, bulletlike formation, with the rest in a flat circular screen—except for a tiny force under Bean that moved off the simulator, heading behind the enemy's formation.

Ender quickly learned the enemy's strategy: whenever Ender's bullet formation came close, the enemy would give way, hoping to draw Ender inside the globe where he would be surrounded. So Ender obligingly fell into the trap, bringing his bullet to the center of the globe.

The enemy began to contract slowly, not wanting to come within range until all their weapons could be brought to bear at once. Then Ender began to work in earnest. His reserve screen approached the outside of the globe, and the enemy began to concentrate his forces there. Then Bean's force appeared on the opposite side, and the enemy again deployed ships on that side.

Which left most of the globe only thinly defended. Ender's bullet attacked, and since at the point of attack it outnumbered the enemy overwhelmingly, he tore a hole in the formation. The enemy reacted to try to plug the gap, but in the confusion the reserve force and Bean's small force attacked simultaneously, with the bullet moved to another part of the globe. In a few more minutes the formation was shattered, most of the enemy ships destroyed, and the few survivors rushing away as fast as they could go.

Ender switched the simulator off. All the lights faded. Maezr was standing beside Ender, his hands in his pockets, his body tense. Ender looked up at him.

"I thought you said the enemy would be smart," Ender said.

Maezr's face remained expressionless. "What did you learn?"

"I learned that a sphere only works if your enemy's a fool. He had his forces so spread out that I outnumbered him whenever I engaged him."

"And?"

"And," Ender said, "you can't stay committed to one pattern. It makes you too easy to predict."

"Is that all?" Maezr asked quietly.

Ender took off his radio. "The enemy could have defeated me by breaking the sphere earlier."

Maezr nodded. "You had an unfair advantage."

Ender looked up at him coldly. "I was outnumbered two to one."

Maezr shook his head. "You have the ansible. The enemy doesn't. We include that in the mock battles. Their messages travel at the speed of light."

Ender glanced toward the simulator. "Is there enough space to make a difference?"

"Don't you know?" Maezr asked. "None of the ships was ever closer than thirty thousand kilometers to any other."

Ender tried to figure the size of the enemy's sphere. Astronomy was beyond him. But now his curiosity was stirred.

"What kind of weapons are on those ships? To be able to strike so fast?"

Maezr shook his head. "The science is too much for you. You'd have to study many more years than you've lived to understand even the basics. All you need to know is that the weapons work."

"Why do we have to come so close to be in range?"

"The ships are all protected by force fields. A certain distance away the weapons are weaker and can't get through. Closer in the weapons are stronger than the shields. But the computers take care of all that. They're constantly firing in any direction that won't hurt one of our ships. The computers pick targets, aim; they do all the detail work. You just tell them when and get them in a position to win. All right?"

"No." Ender twisted the tube of the radio around his fingers. "I have to know how the weapons work."

"I told you, it would take—"

"I can't command a fleet—not even on the simulator—unless I know." Ender waited a moment, then added, "Just the rough idea."

Maezr stood up and walked a few steps away. "All right, Ender. It won't make any sense, but I'll try. As simply as I can." He shoved his hands into his pockets. "It's this way, Ender. Everything is made up of atoms, little particles so small you can't see them with your eyes. These atoms, there are only a few different types, and they're all made up of even smaller particles that are pretty much the same. These atoms can be broken, so that they stop being atoms. So that this metal doesn't hold together anymore. Or the plastic floor. Or your body. Or even the air. They just seem to disappear, if you break the atoms. All that's left is the pieces. And they fly around and break more atoms. The weapons on the ships set up an area where it's impossible for atoms of anything to stay together. They all break down. So things in that area—they disappear."

Ender nodded. "You're right, I don't understand it. Can it be blocked?"

"No. But it gets wider and weaker the farther it goes from the ship, so that after a while a force field will block it. OK? And to make it strong at all, it has to be focused, so that a ship can only fire effectively in maybe three or four directions at once."

Ender nodded again, but he didn't really understand, not well enough. "If the pieces of the broken atoms go breaking more atoms, why doesn't it just make everything disappear?"

"Space. Those thousands of kilometers between the ships, they're empty. Almost no atoms. The pieces don't hit anything, and when they finally do hit something, they're so spread out they can't do any harm." Maezr cocked his head quizzically. "Anything else you need to know?"

"Do the weapons on the ships—do they work against anything besides ships?"

Maezr moved in close to Ender and said firmly, "We only use them against ships. Never anything else. If we used them against anything else, the enemy would use them against us. Got it?"

Maezr walked away, and was nearly out the door when Ender called to him.

"I don't know your name yet," Ender said blandly.

"Maezr Rackham."

"Maezr Rackham," Ender said, "I defeated you."

Maezr laughed.

"Ender, you weren't fighting me today," he said. "You were fighting the stupidest computer in the Command School, set on a ten-year-old program. You don't think I'd use a sphere, do you?" He shook his head. "Ender, my dear little fellow, when you fight me, you'll know it. Because you'll lose." And Maezr left the room.

Ender practiced ten hours a day with his toon leaders. He never saw them, though, only heard their voices on the radio. Battles came every two or three days. The enemy had something new every time, something harder—but Ender coped with it. And won every time. And after every battle Maezr would point out mistakes and show Ender that he had really lost. Maezr only let Ender finish so that he would learn to handle the end of the game.

Until finally Maezr came in and solemnly shook Ender's hand and said, "That, boy, was a good battle."

Because the praise was so long in coming, it pleased Ender more than praise had ever pleased him before. And because it was so condescending, he resented it.

"So from now on," Maezr said, "we can give you hard ones."

From then on Ender's life was a slow nervous breakdown.

He began fighting two battles a day, with problems that steadily grew more difficult. He had been trained in nothing but the game all his life, but now the game began to consume him. He woke in the morning with new strategies for the simulator and went fitfully to sleep at night with the mistakes of the day preying on him. Sometimes he would wake up in the middle of the night crying for a reason he didn't remember. Sometimes he woke with his knuckles bloody from biting them. But every day he went impassively to the simulator and drilled his toon leaders until the battles, and drilled his toon leaders after the battles, and endured and studied the harsh criticism that Maezr Rackham piled on him. He noted that Rackham perversely criticized him more after his hardest battles. He noted that every time he thought of a new strategy the enemy was using it within a few days. And he noted that while his fleet always stayed the same size, the enemy increased in numbers every day.

He asked his teacher.

"We are showing you what it will be like when you really command. The ratios of enemy to us."

"Why does the enemy always outnumber us?"

Maezr bowed his gray head for a moment, as if deciding whether to answer. Finally he looked up and reached out his hand and touched Ender on the shoulder. "I will tell you, even though the information is secret. You see, the enemy attacked us first. He had good reason to attack us, but that is a matter for politicians, and whether the fault was ours or his, we could not let him win. So when the enemy came to our worlds, we fought back, hard, and spent the finest of our young men in the fleets. But we won, and the enemy retreated."

Maezr smiled ruefully. "But the enemy was not through, boy. The enemy would never be through. They came again, with more numbers, and it was harder to beat them. And another generation of young men was spent. Only a few survived. So we came up with a plan—the big men came up with the plan. We knew that we had to destroy the enemy once and for all, totally, eliminate his ability to make war against us. To do that we had to go to his home worlds—his home world, really, since the enemy's empire is all tied to his capital world."

"And so?" Ender asked.

"And so we made a fleet. We made more ships than the enemy ever had. We made a hundred ships for every ship he had sent against us. And we launched them against his twenty-eight worlds. They started leaving a hundred years ago. And they carried on them the ansible, and only a few men. So that someday a commander could sit on a planet somewhere far from the battle and command the fleet. So that our best minds would not be destroyed by the enemy."

Ender's question had still not been answered. "Why do they outnumber us?"

Maezr laughed. "Because it took a hundred years for our ships to get there. They've had a hundred years to prepare for us. They'd be fools, don't you think, boy, if they waited in old tugboats to defend their harbors. They have new ships, great ships, hundreds of ships. All we have is the ansible, that and the fact that they have to put a commander with every fleet, and when they lose—and they will lose—they lose one of their best minds every time."

Ender started to ask another question.

"No more, Ender Wiggins. I've told you more than you ought to know as it is."

Ender stood angrily and turned away. "I have a right to know. Do you think this can go on forever, pushing me through one school and another and never telling me what my life is for? You use me and the others as a tool, someday we'll command your ships, someday maybe we'll save your lives, but I'm not a computer, and I have to *know*!"

"Ask me a question, then, boy," Maezr said, "and if I can answer, I will."

"If you use your best minds to command the fleets, and you never lose any, then what do you need me for? Who am I replacing, if they're all still there?"

Maezr shook his head. "I can't tell you the answer to that, Ender. Be content that we will need you, soon. It's late. Go to bed. You have a battle in the morning."

Ender walked out of the simulator room. But when Maezr left by the same door a few moments later, the boy was waiting in the hall.

"All right, boy," Maezr said impatiently, "what is it? I don't have all night and you need to sleep."

Ender wasn't sure what his question was, but Maezr waited. Finally Ender asked softly, "Do they live?"

"Does who live?"

"The other commanders. The ones now. And before me."

Maezr snorted. "Live. Of course they live. He wonders if they live." Still chuckling, the old man walked off down the hall. Ender stood in the corridor for a while, but at last he was tired and he went off to bed. They live, he thought. They live, but he can't tell me what happens to them.

That night Ender didn't wake up crying. But he did wake up with blood on his hands.

Months wore on with battles every day, until at last Ender settled into the routine of the destruction of himself. He slept less every night, dreamed more, and he began to have terrible pains in his stomach. They put him on a very bland diet, but soon he didn't even have an appetite for that. "Eat," Maezr said, and Ender would mechanically put food in his mouth. But if nobody told him to eat he didn't eat.

One day as he was drilling his toon leaders the room went black and he woke up on the floor with his face bloody where he had hit the controls.

They put him to bed then, and for three days he was very ill. He remembered seeing faces in his dreams, but they weren't real faces, and he knew it even while he thought he saw them. He thought he saw Bean sometimes, and sometimes he thought he saw Lieutenant Anderson and Captain Graff. And then he woke up and it was only his enemy Maezr Rackham.

"I'm awake," he said to Maezr.

"So I see," Maezr answered. "Took you long enough. You have a battle today."

So Ender got up and fought the battle and he won it. But there was no second battle that day, and they let him go to bed earlier. His hands were shaking as he undressed.

During the night he thought he felt hands touching him gently, and he dreamed he heard voices saying, "How long can he go on?"

"Long enough."

"So soon?"

"In a few days, then he's through."

"How will he do?"

"Fine. Even today, he was better than ever."

Ender recognized the last voice as Maezr Rackham's. He resented Rackham's intruding even in his sleep.

He woke up and fought another battle and won.

Then he went to bed.

He woke up and won again.

And the next day was his last day in Command School,

though he didn't know it. He got up and went to the simulator for the battle.

Maezr was waiting for him. Ender walked slowly into the simulator room. His step was slightly shuffling, and he seemed tired and dull. Maezr frowned.

"Are you awake, boy?" If Ender had been alert, he would have cared more about the concern in his teacher's voice. Instead, he simply went to the controls and sat down. Maezr spoke to him.

"Today's game needs a little explanation, Ender Wiggins. Please turn around and pay strict attention."

Ender turned around, and for the first time he noticed that there were people at the back of the room. He recognized Graff and Anderson from Battle School, and vaguely remembered a few of the men from Command School—teachers for a few hours at some time or another. But most of the people he didn't know at all.

"Who are they?"

Maezr shook his head and answered, "Observers. Every now and then we let observers come in to watch the battle. If you don't want them, we'll send them out."

Ender shrugged. Maezr began his explanation. "Today's game, boy, has a new element. We're staging this battle around a planet. This will complicate things in two ways. The planet isn't large, on the scale we're using, but the ansible can't detect anything on the other side of it—so there's a blind spot. Also, it's against the rules to use weapons against the planet itself. All right?"

"Why, don't the weapons work against planets?"

Maezr answered coldly, "There are rules of war, Ender, that apply even in training games."

Ender shook his head slowly. "Can the planet attack?"

Maezr looked nonplussed for a moment, then smiled. "I guess you'll have to find that one out, boy. And one more thing. Today, Ender, your opponent isn't the computer. I am your enemy today, and today I won't be letting you off so easily. Today is a battle to the end. And I'll use any means I can to defeat you."

Then Maezr was gone, and Ender expressionlessly led his toon leaders through maneuvers. Ender was doing well, of course, but several of the observers shook their heads, and

Graff kept clasping and unclasping his hands, crossing and uncrossing his legs. Ender would be slow today, and today Ender couldn't afford to be slow.

A warning buzzer sounded, and Ender cleared the simulator board, waiting for today's game to appear. He felt muddled today, and wondered why people were there watching. Were they going to judge him today? Decide if he was good enough for something else? For another two years of grueling training, another two years of struggling to exceed his best? Ender was twelve. He felt very old. And as he waited for the game to appear, he wished he could simply lose it, lose the battle badly and completely so that they would remove him from the program, punish him however they wanted, he didn't care, just so he could sleep.

Then the enemy formation appeared, and Ender's weariness turned to desperation.

The enemy outnumbered him a thousand to one, the simulator glowed green with them, and Ender knew that he couldn't win.

And the enemy was not stupid. There was no formation that Ender could study and attack. Instead the vast swarms of ships were constantly moving, constantly shifting from one momentary formation to another, so that a space that for one moment was empty was immediately filled with formidable enemy force. And even though Ender's fleet was the largest he had ever had, there was no place he could deploy it where he would outnumber the enemy long enough to accomplish anything.

And behind the enemy was the planet. The planet, which Maezr had warned him about. What difference did a planet make, when Ender couldn't hope to get near it? Ender waited, waited for the flash of insight that would tell him what to do, how to destroy the enemy. And as he waited, he heard the observers behind him begin to shift in their seats, wondering what Ender was doing, what plan he would follow. And finally it was obvious to everyone that Ender didn't know what to do, that there was nothing to do, and a few of the men at the back of the room made quiet little sounds in their throats.

Then Ender heard Bean's voice in his ear. Bean chuckled and said, "Remember, the enemy's gate is *down*." A few of the other toon leaders laughed and Ender thought back to the simple games he had played and won in Battle School. They had put him against hopeless odds there, too. And he had beaten them. And he'd be damned if he'd let Maezr Rackham beat him with a cheap trick like outnumbering him a thousand to one. He had won a game in Battle School by going for something against the rules—he had won by going against the enemy's gate.

And the enemy's gate was down.

Ender smiled, and realized that if he broke this rule they'd probably kick him out of school, and that way he'd win for sure: He would never have to play a game again.

He whispered into the microphone. His six commanders each took a part of the fleet and launched themselves against the enemy. They pursued erratic courses, darting off in one direction and then another. The enemy immediately stopped his aimless maneuvering and began to group around Ender's six fleets.

Ender took off his microphone, leaned back in his chair, and watched. The observers murmured out loud now. Ender was doing nothing—he had thrown the game away.

But a pattern began to emerge from the quick confrontations with the enemy. Ender's six groups lost ships constantly as they brushed with each enemy force—but they never stopped for a fight, even when for a moment they could have won a small tactical victory. Instead they continued on their erratic course that led, eventually, down. Toward the enemy planet.

And because of their seemingly random course the enemy didn't realize it until the same time that the observers did. By then it was too late, just as it had been too late for William Bee to stop Ender's soldiers from activating the gate. More of Ender's ships could be hit and destroyed, so that of the six fleets only two were able to get to the planet, and those were decimated. But those tiny groups *did* get through, and they opened fire on the planet.

Ender leaned forward now, anxious to see if his guess would pay off. He half expected a buzzer to sound and the game to be stopped, because he had broken the rule. But he was betting on the accuracy of the simulator. If it could simulate a planet, it could simulate what would happen to a planet under attack.

It did.

The weapons that blew up little ships didn't blow up the entire planet at first. But they did cause terrible explosions. And on the planet there was no space to dissipate the chain reaction.

On the planet the chain reaction found more and more fuel to feed it.

The planet's surface seemed to be moving back and forth, but soon the surface gave way in an immense explosion that sent light flashing in all directions. It swallowed up Ender's entire fleet. And then it reached the enemy ships.

The first simply vanished in the explosion. Then, as the explosion spread and became less bright, it was clear what happened to each ship. As the light reached them they flashed brightly for a moment and disappeared. They were all fuel for the fire of the planet.

It took more than three minutes for the explosion to reach the limits of the simulator, and by then it was much fainter. All the ships were gone, and if any had escaped before the explosion reached them, they were few and not worth worrying about. Where the planet had been there was nothing. The simulator was empty.

Ender had destroyed the enemy by sacrificing his entire fleet and breaking the rule against destroying the enemy planet. He wasn't sure whether to feel triumphant at his victory or defiant at the rebuke he was certain would come. So instead he felt nothing. He was tired. He wanted to go to bed and sleep.

He switched off the simulator, and finally heard the noise behind him.

There were no longer two rows of dignified military observers. Instead there was chaos. Some of them were slapping each other on the back; some of them were bowed, head in hands; others were openly weeping. Captain Graff detached himself from the group and came to Ender. Tears streamed down his face, but he was smiling. He reached out his arms, and to Ender's surprise he embraced the boy, held him tightly, and whispered, "Thank you, thank you, thank you, Ender."

Soon all the observers were gathered around the bewildered child, thanking him and cheering him and patting him on the shoulder and shaking his hand. Ender tried to make sense of what they were saying. Had he passed the test after all? Why did it matter so much to them?

Then the crowd parted and Maezr Rackham walked through. He came straight up to Ender Wiggins and held out his hand.

"You made the hard choice, boy. But heaven knows there was no other way you could have done it. Congratulations. You beat them, and it's all over."

All over. Beat them. "I beat *you*, Maezr Rackham."

Maezr laughed, a loud laugh that filled the room. "Ender Wiggins, you never played me. You never played a *game* since I was your teacher."

Ender didn't get the joke. He had played a great many games, at a terrible cost to himself. He began to get angry.

Maezr reached out and touched his shoulder. Ender shrugged him off. Maezr then grew serious and said, "Ender Wiggins, for the last months you have been the commander of our fleets. There were no games. The battles were real. Your only enemy was *the* enemy. You won every battle. And finally today you fought them at their home world, and you destroyed their world, their fleet, you destroyed them completely, and they'll never come against us again. You did it. You."

Real. Not a game. Ender's mind was too tired to cope with it all. He walked away from Maezr, walked silently through the crowd that still whispered thanks and congratulations to the boy, walked out of the simulator room and finally arrived in his bedroom and closed the door.

He was asleep when Graff and Maezr Rackham found him. They came in quietly and roused him. He awoke slowly, and when he recognized them he turned away to go back to sleep.

"Ender," Graff said. "We need to talk to you."

Ender rolled back to face them. He said nothing.

Graff smiled. "It was a shock to you yesterday, I know. But it must make you feel good to know you won the war."

Ender nodded slowly.

"Maezr Rackham here, he never played against you. He only analyzed your battles to find out your weak spots, to help you improve. It worked, didn't it?"

Ender closed his eyes tightly. They waited. He said, "Why didn't you tell me?"

Maezr smiled. "A hundred years ago, Ender, we found out some things. That when a commander's life is in danger he becomes afraid, and fear slows down his thinking. When a commander knows that he's killing people, he becomes cautious or insane, and neither of those help him do well. And when he's mature, when he has responsibilities and an understanding of the world, he becomes cautious and sluggish and can't do his job. So we trained children, who didn't know anything but the game, and never knew when it would become real. That was the theory, and you proved that the theory worked."

Graff reached out and touched Ender's shoulder. "We launched the ships so that they would all arrive at their destination during these few months. We knew that we'd probably have only one good commander if we were lucky. In history it's been very rare to have more than one genius in a war. So we planned on having a genius. We were gambling. And you came along and we won."

Ender opened his eyes again and then realized that he was angry. "Yes, you won."

Graff and Maezr Rackham looked at each other. "He doesn't understand," Graff whispered.

"I understand," Ender said. "You needed a weapon, and you got it, and it was me."

"That's right," Maezr answered.

"So tell me," Ender went on, "how many people lived on that planet that I destroyed."

They didn't answer him. They waited a while in silence, and then Graff spoke. "Weapons don't need to understand what they're pointed at, Ender. We did the pointing, and so we're responsible. You just did your job."

Maezr smiled. "Of course, Ender, you'll be taken care of. The government will never forget you. You served us all very well."

Ender rolled over and faced the wall, and even though they tried to talk to him, he didn't answer them. Finally they left.

Ender lay in his bed for a long time before anyone disturbed him again. The door opened softly. Ender didn't turn to see who it was. Then a hand touched him softly.

"Ender, it's me, Bean." Ender turned over and looked at the little boy who was standing by his bed.

"Sit down," Ender said.

Bean sat. "That last battle, Ender. I didn't know how you'd get us out of it."

Ender smiled. "I didn't. I cheated. I thought they'd kick me out."

"Can you believe it! We won the war. The whole war's over, and we thought we'd have to wait till we grew up to fight in it, and it was us fighting it all the time. I mean, Ender, we're little kids. I'm a little kid, anyway." Bean laughed and Ender smiled.

Then they were silent for a little while, Bean sitting on the edge of the bed, Ender watching him out of half-closed eyes.

Finally Bean thought of something else to say.

"What will we do now that the war's over?" he said.

Ender closed his eyes and said, "I need some sleep, Bean."

Bean got up and left and Ender slept.

Graff and Anderson walked through the gates into the park. There was a breeze, but the sun was hot on their shoulders.

"Abba Technics? In the capital?" Graff asked.

"No, in Biggock County. Training division," Anderson replied. "They think my work with children is good preparation. And you?"

Graff smiled and shook his head. "No plans. I'll be here for a few more months. Reports, winding down. I've had offers. Personnel development for DCIA, executive vice president for U and P, but I said no. Publisher wants me to do memoirs of the war. I don't know."

They sat on a bench and watched leaves shivering in the breeze. Children on the monkey bars were laughing and yelling, but the wind and the distance swallowed their words. "Look," Graff said, pointing. A little boy jumped from the bars and ran near the bench where the two men sat. Another boy followed him, and holding his hands like a gun he made an explosive sound. The child he was shooting at didn't stop. He fired again.

"I got you! Come back here!"

The other little boy ran on out of sight.

"Don't you know when you're dead?" The boy shoved his hands in his pockets and kicked a rock back to the monkey bars. Anderson smiled and shook his head. "Kids," he said. Then he and Graff stood up and walked on out of the park.

INTRODUCTION TO "THE EMERSON EFFECT"

by Jack McDevitt

Science fiction became my passion at the age of five, largely as a result of seeing the 1940 serial *Flash Gordon Conquers the Universe*. I loved the rocket ships and the uearthly landscapes and Ming's soldiers with their knights' helmets. My early childhood became a long trek across Mars, hanging out at canals with Bradbury, and camping along the dead sea bottoms with Burroughs. One thing led to another, and writing science fiction looked like the only way to live. I wrote my first story as a college freshman at LaSalle in 1954 and was ecstatic when it was published in the school's literary magazine, *Four Quarters*. I thought I was on my way.

But life got busy. And when, as an aspiring writer, I looked at the work being done by Heinlein and Clarke and the others, the level seemed so far out of reach that I put my ambitions aside and found other things to do.

A quarter-century later I was training inspectors at the U. S. Customs Service Academy in Brunswick, Georgia. It was a job that had become routine, and I took to grumbling around the house that I regretted not having become a globe-trotting archaeologist, or a gunrunner, or a stock car driver. Something with movement.

My wife Maureen pointed out that I'd been threatening to commit science fiction for at least the fifteen years she'd known me. Why not take the plunge?

It seemed like a wacky idea. But I decided to give it a chance. More or less to satisfy her. And maybe because I was beginning to suspect the day would come that I'd look back and discover I'd never realized the one professional ambition that meant something to me. Worse, that I wouldn't know whether I might have succeeded because I hadn't tried.

Ralph Waldo Emerson seemed like a propitious subject for the effort. Emerson, after all, tells us that we're far more talented than we realize, that most of us go through our lives listening to people explain to us what our limits are. And that eventually we come to accept those limits. If we want to make things happen, he says, we need only learn to believe in ourselves, and act as though we expect to succeed.

That seemed encouraging.

So I created a postal employee with dreams but no drive and no confidence and I arranged for Emerson to send him a letter.

"The Emerson Effect" went out twice and came back with the standard reply thanking me but pointing out that it did not fit their editorial needs, etc. I don't take rejection well so I was ready to quit. But Maureen brought in a friend to look at it and make suggestions. She did, I made some changes, and a few weeks later T. E. D. Klein bought it for *The Twilight Zone Magazine*. December 1981 issue.

I had a difficult time accepting the fact that I'd made a professional sale. That my name was going to show up in print. Absurd notion. I was sure something would step in, that the publishing company would go out of business before that December issue appeared. That nuclear war would break out.

But it showed up on schedule, and I never looked back. Once you break the barrier and make the first sale, the confidence rolls in.

And the correspondence with Emerson? I suspect he sent me a letter, too.

THE EMERSON EFFECT

by Jack McDevitt

THE package looked as if it had been kicked into a bathtub. The brown wrapping paper was brittle and wrinkled, the address a blue smear. A long piece of twine hung from the parcel. It was stamped *Books Only—Second Class Matter*. There didn't seem to be a postmark.

Hank sipped his coffee and held the package up to the window. The only thing legible in the return address was the single word "Braintree." No zip codes had been used. Further, the abbreviation for Massachusetts (he knew where Braintree was) was clearly not the two-letter designate sanctioned by the Post Office. Hank vaguely disapproved of the package.

Outside, a truck backed into the loading dock. He looked up at the sound and glanced across the workroom at Jenny McIntyre, the new clerk. Jenny stood at the counter, her back to him, writing a money order for a woman in a threadbare coat who looked tired and bored. Hank wondered how anyone could stand in front of Jenny looking tired and bored.

He reached for his scissors and, carefully opening the tattered package, removed the contents, a heavy leather-bound book. He looked for some clue to the sender or recipient. There was none. Why did people neglect the simple precaution of enclosing an address?

He balanced the volume in his hand. It had a heft and texture that suggested walnut paneling and oak furniture.

He had assumed it was a Bible, and was surprised to discover that it was not. Sharp gold letters across the front spelled out *Emerson*. He recalled the name from school: something about hobgoblins.

Four colored ribbons served as bookmarks. The pages appeared to be India rice paper and were gold-trimmed. The book was old, worn, but well cared for.

He opened it and glanced at the publication data: "Boston, 1878." On the inside cover, in ink faded almost to gray-green, he read *For Henry, with Confidence and Best Wishes.* Below this was the single initial *E*.

Hank looked again at the wrapper. It wasn't even insured!

Jenny McIntyre disposed of her last customer and started over toward the Midwest case, where she had been working on several piles of mail. It was not a route that would take her close to Hank's desk, so he bit his lip, took a deep breath, and walked halfway across the workroom to intercept her, trying to look unobtrusive. He took the book with him.

She turned at the sound of her name and smiled. Hank's resolve melted in that moment, and his heart began to quicken. It was, he thought desperately, the sort of smile that melts men into their socks. Her alert brown eyes, vaguely amused, watched him. She was bright, friendly, and well-pressed; her uniform had clearly been designed by a man who grasped both trigonometry and nuance. Hank, however, was afflicted with a middle-aged soul.

Perhaps later things would fall into place. For now, he was content simply to speak with her. He showed her the book and complained of human carelessness in an uncomfortably husky voice.

"Hank," she said, immediately becoming interested, "do you think that's really his writing?"

"Whose?"

"Emerson's."

He shrugged. "If it is, they might have found a better way to ship it . . . Do you know anything about him?"

Her lips crinkled in good humor. " 'Here once the embattled farmers stood, And fired the shot heard round the world.' He was required reading. He's remembered because he always said you should stand on your own feet, and that you can do anything you really want to." She returned the book. "You better put it somewhere safe. If that's actually his signature, it's worth a lot of money." She smiled again, self-consciously this time. "I've always intended to go back and read him on my own."

Slightly breathless, Hank carried his find the rest of the way across the workroom and into Wade's office. Wade Schreiber, the postmaster, was younger than Hank by several years. He was gregarious, liked to tip a few with the boys now and then, and probably ate too much. His frame was sliding down into his belly, but he was still young enough to carry the excess weight.

Schreiber was also clearly competent, and would no doubt be moving on in a year or so. Hank didn't like Schreiber very much, but he would have been hard-pressed to find a reason.

"What have you got, Hank?" he asked, tossing some documents into his pending tray.

"This came in from Boston today, Wade. No address, forward or back. Looks as if it might have originated in Braintree." He handed the book across. The postmaster riffled the pages, gave it back.

"Okay. Put it with the other stuff." He squinted at Hank. "Is there some reason to give it special attention?"

"Well, it might be a rare edition, and it looks like it was signed by the author. Probably pretty valuable, Wade."

"Where signed?" Wade frowned and grinned simultaneously. "Isn't that a Bible? No? All right. Save the wrapper and anything else that pertains. Log it, and we'll put it in the safe for the time being. Notify Boston that they can have it if they want it. If they do, we want a receipt." He examined the book a second time and read the inscription. "I'll be damned," he said. "Who's Henry?"

Hank shrugged. "You know anything about him, Wade? Emerson, that is?"

"Sure. He wrote about New England a lot. I saw his grave once."

The Winona Post Office, a branch of the Philadelphia, emptied promptly at five. Old Jake Hobson and Don Tebbetts, both nearing retirement, pulled on jackets and left together as they had almost every afternoon for the ten years that Hank had been there. Then half a dozen of the younger men, all carriers except Golden, a driver, crowded noisily out the door with newspapers and lunch buckets, waving to Hank, joking with Jenny.

It had begun to rain lightly.

Jenny pulled a light brown coat gracefully about her shoulders. She shook her long chestnut hair free over the collar and was gone. Hank felt an easing of tension. *Too young for me*, he thought. Anyhow, not a good idea to get involved at work.

Wade locked his office, rattled the knob, stopped for an inconsequential remark or two with Hank, buttoned his jacket tight (it was early October, and there was still a chill in the air), and then Hank was alone.

Wade made him nervous. Hank smiled too much when he

talked to his boss, and he was always slightly out of breath. Irritating. But it was good to be last man out. He looked around at the empty canvas mail sacks piled near the rear exit, at the sorting cases, and at the old battered tables. All his life he had liked being in public places when they were deserted: churches in the late afternoon, schoolrooms at night.

He strolled across to Jenny's section and picked up some mail that had come in late. One letter in pink was going to Riverside. Another, in a white, hand-addressed business envelope, was bound for Needles. He'd always been fascinated by the names of towns in far-off places: Mountain Home and Tarzana and Pueblo and Cando and Truth or Consequences. Once, years ago, in the most courageous undertaking of his life, he had driven to California, stopping along the way at towns he had come to know. It had been exhilarating to leave Winona behind, to roll past the farms and villages where he'd spent his entire life, and to burst into Ohio in his dusty Toyota. That first night on the road he had spent in Steubenville. He'd checked into a motel, eaten dinner, and then wandered aimlessly around town, reflecting on how utterly alone he was. Lights were on in the high school, and its parking lot was full. Through open doors he could see clusters of people. It all looked warm and friendly, something he would have liked to have been part of.

He had not really enjoyed his trip much. Mostly he had driven aimlessly around various towns, strange places with familiar names, stretched dinner hours as long as he could, gone to the movies. He'd found Needles breathlessly hot and Loveland brutally cold. He hit a couple of bad restaurants in Salt Lake and endless construction outside San Diego. But that was trivial. Or would have been, had he not recognized that any relationship between these towns and the neat little pigeonholes into which he shoved their mail was strictly administrative.

In the end he had been glad to get home, back to the sorting cases, where the "real" towns appeared again on the crisp white envelopes.

He folded the postal form notifying Boston of the undeliverable package, slid it into an envelope, and dropped it on his desk to go out tomorrow. Then he locked the book away in the safe, reflecting sadly that, when he finally got up the nerve to approach Jenny, he would undoubtedly make a stuttering hash of it. Then he turned out the lights and went home.

*   *   *

He had trouble sleeping. He lived just off the main bed of the Penn Central, and trains whistled and rumbled in the night. Rain hummed steadily against the windows, and soundless lightning glimmered in the curtains.

It was uncomfortable to watch younger men move past him. Wade had come in about a year ago when John Myers retired. Wade was openly affable and self-confident, and Hank, hoping somehow to improve his situation, or just to make friends in high places, had gone out of his way with the man. Not fawning. Not like that. But not himself either. And he was certain that Wade sensed it.

And then there was Jenny. All the lovely women he had pursued with varying degrees of failure over the years smiled at him through Jenny's eyes. Gentle, compelling, almost shy, she seemed unreachable. Not that he wasn't successful with women. He'd had a few romances, but they had been things of mutual convenience. And occasionally, when someone like Jenny drifted into his life, his personality went into its paperweight phase.

He turned over and listened to the rain.

He had begun, but not finished, two books on self-assertiveness. Both had demanded a dynamic, self-confident psyche to perform exercises guaranteed to bring advancement, women, money. He didn't much care for all that. But he would have liked . . . what? He had never really known, never tried to put a name to it. But it was beginning to look as if he would divide his life between this small apartment and the post office.

Finally, as the two-twenty freight to Philadelphia rumbled by, darkness closed in. His last thought was of the man who said you could do anything. Vaguely he wondered how Emerson had done with women.

Next day he had lunch with Jenny. It was more or less an accident. The weather was still wet and cold, and Norman's Delicatessen was just across the street. Hank sat at the corner table, sipping hot tomato soup in an effort to keep his weight down, when Jenny entered. The place was full, but Jenny spied Hank from the doorway, nodded, smiled, and pushed her way to his table.

"Nasty day," she said, folding her raincoat over a chair. "Did you find the owner of your book yet?"

"It'll take a while," he said. "Probably a few weeks, unless the consignee comes in and complains. Even then we'll have to establish ownership." He dipped a piece of bread into his soup. "I read a little of it yesterday before I went home." This was a lie, uttered without thought and immediately regretted.

"Oh? Do you like him?"

"Well, I really didn't have time to do much more than look through it . . . Yes," he said, realizing that she was expecting an answer. "Very much."

"What did you read?" She was studying the menu but, to Hank's dismay, she seemed much more interested in the direction the conversation was taking.

"Not much, actually." He tried to look as if he were sorting things out in his mind. "A little bit about how important it is to have confidence in yourself." That seemed safe enough. "No limit to what a single determined mind can do," he went on. Suddenly he laughed.

"What's funny, Hank?"

"Oh, Edgar Rice Burroughs once said much the same thing about two well-armed friends."

She ordered a hamburger and coffee, and smiled brightly at him. "They may both have been right. Did you come across any of the stuff about oversouls and circles and whatnot? No? Well, I have to admit I never understood any of that. And I never knew anybody else who did either, except an English teacher once, who really might have, but he couldn't explain it to anybody."

Feeling adventurous, Hank wondered whether the people with the most confidence in themselves didn't cause most of the problems in the world.

"Hank," Jenny said quietly, fixing him with a shrewd look that seemed beyond her years, "I'm not sure I've ever known anyone who had much self-confidence . . . Have you?"

Hank could think of all sorts of people who seemed to qualify: Clay, his milkman, most of the women he had known, Jenny herself. But he said, "No, not really," not entirely sure where he was being led.

The conversation shifted gears, glanced off the food, the weather, and an absurd remark made the previous day by the President. Jenny mentioned a few more books in which she was interested, but it quickly became apparent that Hank had neglected the literary side of his development. He grew restive, sensing that she was losing interest in him. He was a one-hamburger man . . .

Through it all Hank ached to suggest that they have dinner together. And he might have done it, had she not begun glancing around the interior of the deli, anxious to be off, to think of other things. And he watched, discouraged, like some third person, as they finished their meal.

Maybe tomorrow.

Hank stayed late that night, rattling around the drab little building, inspecting odd pieces of mail, clearing off tables, arranging things. Eventually he stopped before the safe and pulled open the heavy slate-gray doors. The tattered package lay alongside three rolls of masking tape.

He took it out and returned with it to his desk. The flyleaf bore a line silhouette of the author, highly suggestive of dignity and capacity. It didn't occur to Hank then that a line silhouette of anyone in such a book could not fail to carry weight. He lifted the green ribbon; the book fell open about midway through, and he began to read.

Emerson had gone to England. He'd sat on a rock at Stonehenge and talked about time, but Hank couldn't really follow it. He flipped some pages, caught Jesus's name, and tried again. It was more interesting this time. Emerson seemed to be upset by some Church rituals. Pretended he couldn't understand why the washing of the feet had never become a sacrament. Hank was amused: the old guy had a sense of humor.

The rain had stopped about three o'clock, but the sky continued gray. Now, finally, it darkened. The security lights out back in the Manley Building came on.

Hank read about New England snows, and the value of integrity, and an odd handyman named Henry. (The Henry of the inscription?) Emerson talked about Nature a lot, but he didn't seem to mean forests and squirrels. He suggested that the physical world was an illusion.

No, that was not right. The physical world was real. But something unseen, of more substance, was behind it. A greater reality, into which a man's mind was a direct conduit.

The sovereignty of this nature whereof we speak is made known by its independency of those limitations which circumscribe us on every hand. The soul circumscribeth all things. As I have said, it contradicts all experience. In like manner it abol-

ishes time and space. The influence of the senses has in most men overpowered the mind to that degree that the walls of time and space have come to look solid, real, and insurmountable; and to speak with levity of these limits is, in the world, the sign of insanity. Yet time and space are but inverse measures of the force of the soul. A man is capable of abolishing them both.

Hank kept his eyes on the printed words, but the fingers of his right hand pressed lightly against the hard wooden desktop.

He went to a movie, a slapstick comedy with truck drivers and Southern sheriffs. He'd thought it might lift his spirits, but somehow the chases and the pranks fell flat. He got home at eleven-thirty, had some cheese and milk, and went to bed.

Tomorrow was Thursday. With a mild sense of relief, he decided it was too late in the week to ask Jenny out anyhow. She would certainly have plans by now. Maybe he'd make a more serious effort next week.

He read awhile, a political thriller about a missing Vice President. But like the film, it seemed dull, and he found himself unable to extract sense from the lines. Over the weekend he would look for a bookstore and pick up a paperback copy of Emerson.

That night he dreamed.

His car had broken down. In fact, in the disjointed manner of dreams, wheels, motor, and chassis had dropped off, until only his seat and the steering wheel were left. Now he sat on a hard green bench on a brick street, waiting for a bus. It was dark, and the street was empty. He looked behind him and was surprised to find that he was sitting in front of the post office. But the familiar parking lot was gone.

The usual lights in the lobby and the workroom were on. He tried the door; it was open. Stepping inside, he went directly to Wade's office. (Peculiar: he had never known that door existed.) And now, with no sense of transition, the semistupor in which one walks through most dreams, blandly accepting incredible events, was replaced by a crystal clarity. The details of the office—the desk and chairs, a letter opener and a stapler, some paper clips—solidified.

He was standing in his pajamas, barefoot, in Wade's office. Behind him—and he knew it without looking—the door through which he had entered was gone, replaced by the bleak plaster wall with its array of diplomas and awards, certificates of merit, special recognitions and special achievement, of attendance at the gunnery school somewhere. (That one was from his Army days.)

It was very quiet. The only sound was the soft hum of power in the walls. Hank exhaled slowly — and suddenly realized what was happening.

This was no dream. He was really here. And he was very frightened. He stood for a long time, not moving, sweat running down his arms. The face of the Thompson wall clock out in the workroom was in shadow, but he could make out the time: twenty minutes after three.

Hank eased himself into Wade's chair. He was shivering.

Sleepwalking! My God, he had walked six blocks through a cool October evening to get here. (Or had he driven?) How had he gotten in? He had no key, either to the lobby or to Wade's office. He locked the building regularly, but he needed no key for that. Had he somehow broken in?

He surveyed the office: there was no damage.

He *had* gone to bed. No question about that. What then? Nothing other than his usual routine. Was he missing something? He sat, trying desperately to keep calm, to answer the questions, to find some piece of reality to hold on to. And it really was the middle of the night. And here he was.

He looked again at the wall, covered with its framed awards. An elaborate joke?

Whatever, it was going to be a cold walk home. Unless he wanted to stay here until they all came in. He tried to force himself to grin at the idea, but he was too shaken.

Worse: he was locked in. The door couldn't be opened from either side without a key. He fought down a panicky urge to throw a chair through the window and run.

It might have been possible to get a plastic credit card under the latch. If he'd had one.

He was almost grateful for the problem, and pushed everything else out of his mind. The obvious tool was the letter opener. He tried to work it under the latch, but gave up after a few minutes and used it instead to remove the hinges.

There was an old service raincoat in back. He wrapped himself in it and, after a short search, found a pair of rubbers. Then he let himself out into the street. (Wade's door leaned awkwardly against the jamb.) The rubbers tripped him twice, and he kicked them off, pulling the raincoat tight about him.

*   *   *

They blamed it on Mrs. Simpson.

Adele Simpson was a widow, intense, worn down by thirty years of unpaid bills, difficult kids, and wandering husbands. She came in three times a week as the Government's house-keeper. She had keys to everything and, except for Wade himself, was the only one who did. Since Hank had been the only employee left in the building when the postmaster went home, Wade had questioned him closely. Hank had done what he always did; the building had been secured behind him.

Certainly true, as far as it went.

Hank was amazed at Wade's failure to detect his guilty manner. Waves of heat had rushed into his face; his voice had dropped two octaves. But Hank was an unlikely suspect, unless Wade had left his own door open. The hinges, after all, were on the inside.

"Why the hell," said Wade for the sixth or seventh time that morning, "would the woman go into my office and take the hinges off the door?" He put his coffee cup down on Hank's desk and rolled his sleeves halfway up his forearms. "Hank," he said, shaking his head, "she must be starting to hit the juice."

"Are you sure nothing's missing?"

"Have *you* found anything missing?" Hank hadn't. (He hadn't looked very hard.) "Damn lucky, too. If we had to report this, I'd have to explain why the burglar alarm never got fixed."

"How long's it been out?"

"Since I got here."

Hank felt guilty about Mrs. Simpson, but what story could he invent to explain why *he* had removed the hinges? They'd think *he* had gone alcoholic. Or worse. No, this was clearly every man for himself. At least Mrs. Simpson could deny everything.

She did, of course. In fact, she told Wade coolly on the phone, she hadn't been to the post office at all last night. And considering his attitude, she might not come tonight either.

"I just don't understand that," Wade said later to Hank. "Maybe I forgot to lock the office, but that still doesn't explain why anyone would take the door off the hinges."

Hank's next emotional jolt came late in the afternoon. He was talking with Hal Crawford, whose prime responsibility was making certain that outgoing mail was presorted and ready for pickup. Hank, with his mind on Jenny, mentioned that she was learning her job quickly. Crawford leaned forward, his lean features almost obscured in a screen of cigar smoke. "Yes," he leered. "Got a good head, that one. Good tail, too. I hear the boss has been biting off a piece."

He played pinochle that night. It was a game he relished not only because it blocked out the solitary meals and the silent apartment, but because he excelled at it. He had a natural intuition for the potential of a hand, always seemed able to pinpoint the missing ace or construct an opponent's suit distribution. He seldom lost money. This night, however, he was brilliant. He pushed the conversation with Crawford out of his mind and concentrated on the game. It was as if they were playing with their hands exposed, aces and kings reflected in a glance, a long heart suit in the tone of a bid. He made narrow bids all night, consistently hit his partner's strength, and set everything within reach. Only a terrible run of cards near the end of the evening restored a semblance of competition to the game.

Afterwards, at the Downtowner, he bought a round of beers.

On the way home, retracing part of the route he had taken the night before in his bare feet, he realized that his dismay over Crawford's remark had swallowed even that eerie experience.

The thing to do was to call her. Stop fooling around and make his move. But how could he compete with Wade Schreiber?

It took him until three the next day to dial Jenny's number. He had planned it carefully. He would fall back on his recent reading, ask her a few questions about Emerson. He had become involved with the book: that would be his approach. And then he'd suggest dinner. Maybe next Friday, at Delia's Courtyard.

She didn't answer, and he didn't call again.

The nightmare came Sunday night.

He had fallen asleep with the tv on, and dreamed himself back at work, outside, at the base of the loading dock. Hal Crawford lounged on a mailbag, lunch bucket open beside him, laughing silently while devouring a large sandwich.

Hank stumbled away from Crawford, seething, miserable,

up the concrete steps, onto the dock, and through the loading door into the workroom.

The lights were out. As he groped his way inside, a cool blast of air hit him. Overhead, stars blazed. He found himself walking across a metal grid that bit into his feet.

The wind, the metal, and the stars became very real. And with the sudden knowledge that he was again out of his bed, fear took hold. Far below him, headlights moved slowly. Dark in the distance was the Philadelphia skyline.

Somewhere nearby a red light was blinking. He stepped off the grid onto a concrete platform, flat, rectangular, and raised to about the height of a man at each of its corners. Walking toward the edge, he dropped to his knees and peered over. The sides of the structure fell away into the darkness. The lights below were pin-sized. Lower still, water glittered.

A chill raced out of the depths of his soul, and left him weak and trembling in its wake.

He had no doubt that it was the Delaware beneath him, cold and polished between the glow of Philadelphia and South Jersey, curving north past the wharves, between the massive piles of the Benjamin Franklin Bridge.

There could be no question where he was: on the companion bridge, the Walt Whitman! He was sitting atop the western tower, perhaps not a thousand feet in the air, but feeling very much like it.

My God, Hank, you really went for a walk this time!

One by one, he examined the four structures at the corners, keeping well away from the edge. They were the steel anchors of the suspension cables. Three were identical; the fourth held a surprise: a pair of elevator doors and a red button. He pushed the button.

There was no sound in the shaft, no vibration, no indication of power in the red button. He tried to force the doors open.

After almost an hour he gave up on the elevator and wondered about his other options. He could wait until daylight and try to attract someone's attention. Not likely at this height. He'd have pneumonia before anyone spotted him. Maybe a traffic chopper. If they took him seriously and didn't just wave back.

He was beginning to realize that he would have to climb down. There might be a ladder built onto the side of this thing, but he wasn't certain he could summon the nerve to step out over the edge.

Carefully, flat on his belly, he examined the side of the tower. It was smooth, smooth everywhere he looked. Oddly, he felt relieved. It appeared he had no choice but to sit there, well away from the edge, and wait for rescue.

There was one other possibility, and he tried to turn his thoughts from it: the suspension cables, a precarious, swaying escape route with all too good a view of the roadway and the river. But they were a big enough to walk on, the descent to street level appeared to be gradual, and there was even a pair of guide wires to serve as handrails.

The wind, chill and damp, blew against him. It was a factor that cut both ways. It virtually forced him to make the attempt, but cold temperatures and fear would combine to stiffen his fingers, dull his reflexes. If he were going to do it, he had best get to it.

A lone car pulled into the toll booths on the Philadelphia side. The bell rang, and the car rolled on. Hank envied its occupants.

He looked down at the juncture of the cable, possibly three feet below, and past it. He felt dizzy, and terribly afraid.

He lay for a long time, clamped to the edge. The most difficult part would come in the first moments, lowering himself onto the cable. After that, if he could forget where he was, not panic, he could get down. Even without the guide wires he could walk it easily, *if it were on the ground.*

He lined himself up with the cable, turned over on his belly, and pushed himself toward the precipice. He summoned images of Jenny, bare throat framed by her chestnut hair, eyes closed, lips parted, breathing deeply. She reached for him, but he lay paralyzed. Nothing like sitting on the edge of this goddam tower to give you a sense of what really counts in this world.

He squeezed his eyes shut, barely breathing, pushed out, and reached down with his feet. Nothing. He lowered himself farther, wishing he had something to hold onto. The edge of the structure was sharp against his belly. Where was the damned cable? But his feet only dangled. In a supreme act of courage, he let go and dropped!

Inches.

He fell onto the center of the cable, grabbed wildly for the

guide wires, and threw himself off-balance. One hand closed
on a flange. He was looking straight down, watching a wisp of
mist far below ripple in the bridge lights. But he hung on,
counting the rivets that secured the cable housing to the tower.
After a while, he stood up, took a last look back across the platform, not quite chest high, turned carefully round, and started
down.

The cable swayed gently.

Hank smiled.

> *I am the owner of the sphere,*
> *Of the seven stars and the solar year,*
> *Of Caesar's hand, and Plato's brain . . .*

When he stepped off the cable onto the concrete walk at
street level, he was exultant.

He deliberated turning himself in at the toll booths; but what
sort of explanation could he give? They'd think he was a mental basket case, a man who'd tried to commit suicide in his pajamas.

He got off the bridge without being seen, made his way
down an embankment, crossed to Delaware Avenue, and
emerged forty minutes later on Oregon, where he caught a cab.
The driver had clearly been doubtful at first, but he stopped,
rolled down a window, and inspected Hank.

"My girl friend threw me out," he said.

"You're kiddin." Hank grinned. "Hey, you don't look so
good, buddy. How long you been out here?"

"Awhile."

"Get in the cab. You wanta go to the hospital?"

"Home," Hank said. "Just take me home."

"Where's that?"

Hank told him.

"Hell, that's out past Valley Forge. You got money?"

"I will have when we get home."

"Okay," said the driver, laughing suddenly, and shaking his
head. "I'll have to call in for the fare. We can't do Winona on
the meter."

"Fine," said Hank. Which also described how he was feeling. He looked back at the western tower, dark against the stars,
and resisted an urge to tell the driver thta he had just jumped off
that son of a bitch.

*   *   *

Monday was a good day. He was down with a cold, and everything ached, arms and legs, ribs and back. But he felt good nonetheless. By God, he had learned a few things about himself last night. But he was going to have to take steps to prevent these early morning excursions. Where might he go next? Chicago? Accessibility didn't seem to be a problem. The Moon?

Several people, including Wade, asked him if he were feeling okay. He wondered whether they referred to his obvious physical condition, or to the smug attitude which he was unable to cast aside. Hank recognized that there was indeed a sense throughout the office that he was not himself today.

Jenny stopped to talk with him. She seemed puzzled, unsure of herself.

"I fell off the porch roof," he said; and, in answer to her silent inquiry, "I'm fine."

Later, bent over the ledgers, he became suddenly aware of her presence behind him. He felt her heartbeat; her pulse quickened in his veins; she inhaled and he felt the gentle tug of silk against breast. Then it was gone.

He was surprised to turn and find her across the room at her desk. For a long time he did not move.

At five o'clock Wade and Jenny went out the door together, in animated conversation. Moments later they appeared in the parking lot, visible through the window in the postmaster's office, and drove off in Schreiber's Monte Carlo.

Hank slumped at his desk and watched the daylight fade.

When he woke, it was after seven and quite dark outside. He looked across the empty workroom at Wade's office. The door was back on its hinges, and it had acquired a new lock. He thought about breaking in to remove it again and lean the door once more against the jamb, in a final act of defiance before Wade claimed Jenny.

Damn.

He got up, and the book drew him, a black lodestone with its treasure. "You're doing this," he said aloud. "I don't know how, but it's you." And he settled down with it again.

No, the thought came, *not the book. The man.* The incredible being locked by time and space into snowbound Concord,

1850, who refused to acknowledge his limitations, who looked across the years to him, beyond him . . .

As there is no screen or ceiling between our heads and the infinite heavens, so is there no bar or wall in the soul.

The mind is open on one side to the power that fuels the universe. But we are so blinded by the senses, so certain the tree is solid, that we are trapped by Einstein. But at night, as the conscious world sinks into moonlight and rumbling freights, the shackles loosen . . .

At eleven he went home, stopping at McDonald's for a hamburger. When he went to bed that night, he stayed dressed. And he kept his wallet with him. Three feet of clothesline fastened his right foot to the bed.

It was dark. He stood quietly, his hand on the back of an armchair, listening to someone breathing softly across the room. As his eyes adjusted, he could make out a bed against the far wall, a small table, a dressing stand. Curtains whispered against the windows. As he watched, thinking *It's happening again*, the room grew silent.

"Who's there?" The voice was thin, edged with fear, familiar. The figure on the bed was on its side, her side, looking at him.

He froze. The thing to do was to find the door and get out. Hank, the burglar. What next?

"Who is it, please?"

Well, it's sure better than last night.

"Who are you?" Her voice rose to a near-shriek.

Hank realized he was back in his pajamas! Where was the door.

"Ma'am," he said, "I'm sorry. I know this looks bad. All I want is out . . ."

"Hank, is that you?"

Jenny!

"Hank, what are you doing here? How'd you get in?"

"Oh, Jenny," he said, holding out his hands, overwhelmed with a sudden desperate need to tell her the whole story.

"Hank, this is not funny." Her voice was cold and even. But unexpectedly, in the dark, she giggled. "I'm serious now. What's going on?"

Relief flooded through him. Whatever else, he wouldn't wind up in jail. Nor turned over to Wade. He watched her roll slowly onto her back. One knee rose slightly. "Hank," she said soothingly, "you didn't break any of my windows, did you?"

Her brown hair was fanned across the pillow. While he could not see her face, he felt her eyes on him. An alarm clock ticked. He had finally located the door, and stood now, indecisive, when a portion of sheet fell away, apparently of its own volition, revealing a cool white arc of shoulder.

Hank's chemical flows shifted abruptly. He crossed the room, and slid in beside her. She pulled his pajamas away, and flung them into the dark. He started, inanely, to protest, but she held a finger softly to his lips, and then replaced it with her mouth. Hank took her into his arms, and the moment dissolved in a rhythm of wet kisses, of nipples and navel, and Jenny breathing against his throat. He buried himself in her hair, in her breasts, and she quivered in his hands. He closed his eyes while her fingers explored him, gasped as she seized him. They withdrew, and he waited.

There was a tug at his ankle.

Not her: clothesline.

He was still in bed. In fatigues. And alone.

Frustration washed over him. This time it *had* been a dream. He sat up. A long line of freight cars was clicking slowly by.

A man is a god in ruins.

The passion did not subside. Rather it was changing, shading into something else, blending with his will. This time it had been only a dream. But his dreams were acquiring a peculiar substance of late.

He could have her.

And with that knowledge, he felt a surge of power, as if someone had touched a release. He looked out, through the walls of his bedroom; across the empty streets, sensing Jenny asleep in her third-floor apartment less than a mile away, and Wade, several blocks east, tossing fitfully.

Hank lingered over Wade momentarily: the postmaster didn't like his job, considered himself a failure after a promising start. He worried about his weight, and about the passing years. He was divorced, had a son he seldom saw, and badly needed the fling with Jenny, which he had not yet succeeded in engineering.

And Jenny: good-hearted, anxious to please, defensive. (Why had he not seen all this before?) If she did not commit herself too soon, could gain a couple more years' experience, she would do well with her life.

Ultimately, she could be neither his nor Wade's. But for now, they could help each other, and he would leave it that way.

He lay back, eyes wide but unseeing. He touched Hal Crawford in his mindless sleep, and moved on. The taxi driver who had rescued him was turning off Sixth Street into Oregon; he immediately thought of Hank, in his pajamas, and laughed. Hank laughed with him.

The stars were brilliant, looking much as they had from atop the tower. But not so distant. Without thinking, he reached for Sirius.

Slowly, like snow falling from a New England sky, he came to understand the meaning behind the book . . . Who had sent it . . . And who Henry was.

Eventually, when no one stepped forward, he would acquire the volume. Somehow. And forge another link by sending it forward to someone else.

No: that was not the way. Hank would construct his own message, insert it into a cosmic bottle, and lob it in the general direction of anyone who could read.

He wondered who had communicated with Emerson.

Smiling, he reached down and unfastened the tether.

THE WRITING OF
"MUCH ADO ABOUT NOTHING"

by Jerry Oltion

I still remember the afternoon when I came up with the idea for "Much Ado About Nothing." It was a blustery autumn day and I was looking for story ideas. I went out for a walk and saw all these dry leaves falling out of the trees, and since I wanted to write a science fiction story, I started to think about what that same scene would look like to someone from another planet. Boom! Story idea.

It had to marinate for another three or four months in the back of my mind before the plot came together. In the meantime, I sold another story called "The Sense of Discovery" to *Analog*. That was my first sale, and I assumed it would be my first publication, but when I sent this story to *Analog* a few months later, Stan Schmidt said he would like to buy it, and since it was an autumn story he could put it in the November issue—in the slot he'd been holding for "The Sense of Discovery."

So I bumped my own story from the lineup, and my second sale wound up being my first publication.

I couldn't decide on a title when I first wrote the story, so I squeezed a couple of my favorite candidates together and called it "Axial Tilt, or Much Ado About Nothing." Fortunately, when Stan bought it, he suggested we drop the "Axial Tilt" part, and by then I had enough distance on it that I could see he was right. It became simply "Much Ado About Nothing," and when it was published, I was as proud as a new father.

I'm still proud of it. Some writers belittle their early

work, perhaps as a way to convince themselves that they're improving with age, but I am happily uncritical of my freshman stories. I still read them from time to time just for the fun of it. I was pleased a few years ago when Hypatia Press put together a collector's edition of my early work, and I'm pleased now to see my first story come out again in the twenty-first century. May everyone who missed it the first time enjoy it now, and may those of you who didn't miss it the first time enjoy it again.

MUCH ADO ABOUT NOTHING

by Jerry Oltion

QUIFFIK stood at attention. He held his three manipulating tentacles respectfully below and to either side of his lowermost eye, his eating tendrils even and still, and his two uppermost eyes directed straight ahead at a point just over Captain Trovven's head. In deference to the captain's rank he kept all three ears turned forward, and he tried not to let them twitch at the shouting.

Trovven's eating tendrils were bright green at the ends with rage. They radiated out in all directions from his mouth, like ejecta from a supernova explosion. "I don't want excuses!" he shouted, nearly rising out of his chair with the effort. "I want those krem out the air lock! This is an exploratory vessel, not a zoo, and I won't have krem running around on board, do you understand?"

Quiffik blinked his lowermost eye, shifted weight momentarily to his rear leg, and said, "I have them in cages, sir. They're not—"

Trovven's exhalation fluttered his eating tendrils like flags. "I don't care if they're embedded in plastic! I want them off this ship! Now! We'll be landing in a couple of hours, and I want every last krem dead before we do. Do you have any idea what could happen if they got loose down there?" Trovven answered his own question. "They could destroy every living thing on the planet, that's what! And I'm not going to take chances just because some idiot engineer can't leave his pets at home. Out the air lock, Quiffik; that's an order!"

"Yes sir," Quiffik said, then, hesitating, he went on. "But, sir, I don't understand. Krem are harmless herbivores. How could they kill anything?"

Trovven took a deep breath, during which he contemplated how someone could get to be an engineer on a starship without knowing a thing about biology. He counted to a high imaginary number, stilled his quivering tentacles, and said, "They could reproduce, that's what they could do. Krem are very good at that. Small as they are, they could wreck the whole planet simply by reproducing. They don't have to kill directly; they can do it just as effectively by eating another animal's food supply. You see, the life-forms down there have never met up with our kind before, and they wouldn't have any defense against something we introduce from home. We've got to be careful about everything, even microbes, but *krem!* You know how hard krem are to exterminate. Well, imagine what would happen if a breeding triplet got loose where they had no natural enemies. They could overrun the planet in a year!"

Trovven leaned forward and fixed all three eyes on Quiffik. "I don't like killing things any more than you do," he said, "but we can't afford to take any chances. Those krem have got to go. Do you understand?"

"Yes, sir."

"Do it then. And Quiffik . . ."

"Yes, sir?"

"Keep out of trouble."

"Yes, sir."

Quiffik swiveled around and moved swiftly out the door. As soon as he was out of the captain's sight, his ears fell limp and his eyes threatened to cross. Space his krem! They'd been his only friends on the long voyage between stars. To just stuff them out the air lock now—what a way to repay them for their companionship. He knew that Trovven was right, but that made it no easier.

He sometimes wished he'd never signed on for the expedition. Sure, there would be fame and recognition for being on the first voyage to the stars, and when he got home he could give up engineering to become the poet he'd always wanted to be, but in the meantime it was all monotonous drudgery, made even more so by Trovven's militaristic rule. Quiffik didn't fit into that kind of a mold. Only his krem and the thought of actually setting foot on another planet kept him going from day to day. And now he would no longer have the krem.

He couldn't look into the cages as he put them in the air lock. He set them close together near the outer door and turned back into the ship, closing the inner door behind him. He didn't pump the air out of the lock, but instead pulled the eject handle as soon as the inner door had sealed. There was a thump as if something had brushed by the side of the ship. When he closed the outer door and opened the inner one, the cages were gone. He tried not to think about it.

For the next few hours, it wasn't hard. They were taking the ship down, and Quiffik was too busy monitoring the engines to think about krem. Blood rushed green in his veins with excitement at the thought of landing on an alien planet. At last! And what a strange planet it was! It was nothing like Quelch. This planet, the third one out from its star, was smaller, had less air, and spun faster on an axis that was tilted at an astonishing angle to the plane of its orbit. It had a single gigantic moon that no doubt produced catastrophic tides on the surface. Yet despite all that it held life! The planet was covered with it, and at least one species was intelligent. Well, Quiffik thought, maybe that was stretching it a bit, but they did build cities.

Trovven had deliberated a long time before deciding to land. The Quelchie had never encountered another sentient race before, and it made sense to be cautious. They couldn't know what kind of strange creatures might inhabit such a hostile planet. They might be friendly, but then again they might not. Whatever the case, the Quelchie couldn't very well study the planet from orbit without being seen and possibly causing a disturbance among the natives, and they wouldn't get much useful information from farther out, so that left no choice but to land. There were quite a few uninhabited areas where they might safely hide until they learned more about the planet and its occupants, and though they would have to be careful about contamination, they would be able to learn much more this way.

They took the ship in fast, dropping low to the ground and zigzagging for a few hundred miles before heading for the hiding place that Trovven had picked out. It was a small lake in the middle of a low mountain range, far from any major population centers. They dived in over the last ridge and landed with a splash in the middle of the lake, then slowly sank to the bottom.

Nervously, engines ready to lift at a moment's notice, they waited. High in the sky an air vehicle left a white wake as it continued on toward the east, but it showed no sign of seeing them. They waited longer.

Finally, after a full day at alert, Trovven relaxed and let the scientists out to collect samples of the planet. He made them wear pressure suits even though the thin air checked out to be breathable, and they had to disinfect themselves both coming and going with a blast of full spectrum radiation before they could leave the air lock. Trovven was taking no chances.

The scientists were already developing theories and arguing among themselves about the strange conditions on the planet. The most puzzling feature was the axial tilt, and that had them all stumped. How could anything live in the varying conditions that must bring about? Temperatures must change drastically as the planet swung around the sun in its orbit, exposing first one pole to the light and then the other. No known organism could survive under those extremes, yet the biologists cheerfully brought in hundreds of samples that were doing just that. Quiffik looked at them through the glass walls of their airtight environment boxes and marveled at the diversity of life. They were like nothing he had ever seen before.

Some of the animals bore a certain resemblance to those of the Quelchie home world—some even reminded him vaguely of krem—but the plants were totally different. The ones that would fit into the environment boxes were flat, slender, blood-colored things, but the biologists brought back tales of some that were taller than ten Quelchie and as stiff as hullmetal. The mountains were covered with them. Quiffik wished he could go out and see for himself, but Trovven wasn't letting anybody but the scientists off the ship.

Three days after the landing he was down in the engine room, running static tests on the gravity polarizers, when Raffid, the ecologist, stuck his head through the doorway.

"Ah, there you are!" he said. "I've been looking all over the ship for you. Could I get you to lend me a tentacle with the flier? I finally talked Trovven into letting me take it out."

"Really?" Quiffik said as he closed the access panel and levered his way out from between two thrust rings. "I'm surprised.

He's really paranoid about even being here, much less flying around."

"He's the captain; he's supposed to be paranoid. But I convinced him we need to look at some other areas of the planet, too, so he's letting me out to scout around. He won't let me get out of the flier, but I can at least take pictures."

"Yeah? That's still a better deal than I get. I could be the only Quelch on board to go home without setting trod-pad off the ship."

"Oh, you'll get out eventually. We'll be here a long time just studying the life-forms, and then there's the native race to contact, too. You'll have lots of opportunity."

"I hope so. Has Mottik had any luck with their language yet?"

Raffid waggled his ears. "None at all. He's still trying to detect meaningful patterns in their video broadcasts, but so far he's found nothing."

"Hmmm. They must be more complex than we thought."

Quiffik led the way into the hangar bay, where the flier was still fastened to the floor with a set of wide straps. It was small, simply a gravity polarizer with a bubble on top; barely twice the height of a Quelch and double that in circumference, Quiffik released the straps and threw them over the top, then opened the bubble and climbed in.

"Stand back," he said, and turned on the power. There was a soft hum, and the control board lit up. Quiffik watched as various systems indicators evened out. When the last light blinked off, he fed power gently to the polarizer. The flier lifted up, but the phase light came back on and he could feel a faint vibration in the controls. He set it back down, climbed out, and opened an access panel in the side.

"What's wrong?" Raffid asked.

"Nothing major. Phasing's a bit out from sitting idle for so long." Quiffik adjusted a setting in the engine, climbed back up and tried it again. The light stayed out.

"There. I can't test it under heavy load without taking it outside, but this ought to do for just flying around. Don't feed it more than ten gees or so and you ought to be okay. Keep an eye on that phase light, though."

"Right." Raffid climbed up and settled himself in the seat. He pulled the bubble down over himself and fastened it, then edged the flier over to the big cargo air lock. Quiffik opened the door for him and closed it behind, then ran the sterilizing cycle and then the air lock cycle. He watched through the port as water rushed into the lock, then the outer door opened and the flier floated out and up.

"Lucky Quelch," he muttered as it disappeared from view.

He was just finishing up on the engines a few hours later when the whole ship rang with Trovven's voice on the intercom. "First Engineer Quiffik, report to the captain immediately!"

Quiffik nearly dropped a heavy piece of test equipment on his trod pad. He managed to get it onto a bench, then, smoothing his tendrils out along the way, he ran up the corridor to Trovven's cabin.

He took a couple of deep breaths outside the door, then knocked and announced, "First Engineer Quiffik, sir."

"Don't just stand there; come in! You've just volunteered for a rescue mission."

Quiffik stopped just inside the door. "A rescue mission, sir?"

"That's right. That fool of an ecologist Raffid has got himself stranded with a phased-out polarizer, and I need somebody to go fix it before the natives spot him. That's you. You do know how to rephase a polarizer, don't you?"

"Yes, sir." Quiffik screwed up his courage and said, "In fact, sir, I think I could talk Raffid through it over the radio. It's quite simple, sir."

"No doubt," Trovven rumbled, "but Raffid hasn't got a suit, and even if he did I don't want him opening up the bubble. I'm still not convinced we're safe from cross infection. You'll just have to suit up and go fix it first tentacle."

"Yes, sir!" Quiffik couldn't keep the excitement out of his voice. A chance to go outside! But then he had another thought. "Uh, captain? We've only got one flier, sir. How am I going to—?"

"You'll have to walk. It's not far, and the gravity is less than you're used to. Raffid managed to nurse it almost home before the polarizer went out for good. He estimates about half a day's walk in this terrain. If you shake it, you can get there by dark and ride back on the flier."

Quiffik nodded. He was stricken dumb with astonishment. Walk! Alone, through unexplored territory, on an alien planet!

For half a day! It was everything he'd hoped for. It was too much to believe all at once.

It seemed like only moments later when he stuck his head up through the surface of the lake and took his first cautious look around. His pressure suit helmet was a clear bubble, affording him a full panoramic view of his surroundings. The tall, blood-green plants the biologists had described grew all around the lake, hemming it in completely with their thick foliage. Quiffik looked for movement within the forest, but all was still. With a last glance into the deeper water that concealed the ship, he leaned forward and thrashed his way toward shore, pulling himself up onto the bank with one space-suited tentacle.

It took him a moment to get used to standing under plants many times his own height, but Quiffik had never been claustrophobic, and besides, the plants looked solid enough. He could see where a few had fallen over, but that seemed to have been a long time ago, judging by the undergrowth that surrounded them. It was unlikely that the big plants posed any threat no matter how awesome they seemed. In fact, combined with the undergrowth, they looked like they should provide excellent cover.

Quiffik turned his suit radio to the flier's channel with a flick of an eating tendril and said, "Calling Raffid. This is First Engineer Quiffik, calling Raffid."

"Raffid here," Raffid's voice answered in his helmet. "Where are you?"

"I just left the ship. Let me get a fix on you here. Send the homing signal."

"Homing signal," Raffid acknowledged, and a soft monotone sounded in Quiffik's ears. A holographic meter at the base of his helmet swung around to point off to his left.

"Okay, I've got you." The tone stopped. Quiffik turned until the pointer aimed directly in front of him, then, with his lowermost eye on the direction finder and his upper two on the forest, he headed off into the trees.

He was so used to wearing his pressure suit that it hardly hindered his movement at all. It fit snugly, and though the higher pressure of Quelch normal air kept it inflated a bit, it was still easier to move here than in space. And with air on both sides of his helmet, he could hear almost as well as if he wasn't wearing the suit at all.

He said into the radio, "So how did you lose the polarizer?"

Raffid sounded apologetic. "Oh, it was my own stupid fault. You told me not to push it too hard. I was taking pictures of one of the native cities when a couple of their fliers spotted me. One of them fired some kind of missile and I panicked, jammed the power on full lift without thinking. It about shook my eyeballs off before I could shut it down again, and all I could get out of it after that was about half a gee. I lost the other fliers. but I could only glide until I came down. Even in this low gravity half a gee won't hold you up for long. I had to feed it power again to make a soft landing, and now I can barely get any lift at all."

Quiffik nodded to himself. "Sounds like the polarizer all right."

"You think you can fix it?"

"Oh, sure. It's only a phase problem. If it had burned out completely, you would have fallen like a rock. All you've got to do is tune it up to resonance again and it'll be as good as new. If Trovven wasn't so worried about starting a plague you could do it yourself, but the tuner's in the engine compartment."

"Might as well be on Quelch, then. Trovven's mad enough already without me opening up the bubble, too. I think if that missile had hit me, he'd have been madder about the possible contamination of the air than about the attack."

Quiffik snorted. "Probably. You don't think there's much chance that those fliers will spot you again, do you?"

"Hardly. I'm buried in a bunch of vegetation taller than the ship. They'd have to be straight overhead to even catch a glimpse of me. But it might be a good idea if we didn't use the radio. They could pick up on our signals."

"Right. I'll see you when I get there, then. Quiffik out."

"Enjoy your walk. Raffid out."

Quiffik began to concentrate on doing just that. He looked at the vegetation around him. He was no biologist, but he could see that it all seemed to be based on some sort of rigid tentacle system, with two major variations. On most of the larger plants the tentacles ended in thousands of flat things that rustled in the breeze, but some had tentacles that ended in an equal number of sharp points. The ones with the flat things greatly outnumbered the others, though. As he watched, an animal of some sort launched itself from the top of one of them and flew away. Quiffik began to notice other animals high above him too.

There was room there for a whole ecosystem above the ground! He walked onward, fascinated.

Eventually he came to another lake; much smaller than the one that hid the ship, but still large enough that he had to detour around it. When he was about halfway around, he noticed the sun glinting off something shiny just ahead of him. He stepped back into the forest and advanced cautiously until he came to the source: a dwelling of some sort, facing out over the lake.

He watched it from behind a thick plant stem until he was certain that none of the sentient aliens were near, then circled around it once, staying hidden as much as he could by the forest. The place looked deserted. He finally decided to risk a look inside, so he sidled up to the building and stuck a cautious eye up over the edge of one of the windows. He had to stretch to reach that high.

Inside was all one room. The wall facing the lake was all glass; it let in plenty of light to see clearly. There were no aliens inside, either. Quiffik recognized some of the furnishings: a bed in one corner, a table surrounded by what had to be chairs for creatures with no hind leg, and softer looking chairs of similar design facing a stone hole in one wall. Other objects made less sense, but were no doubt useful to an alien. Quiffik maneuvered around for a better look.

He found the door easy enough, though it was twice as tall as a Quelch and the latch was much trickier than it needed to be. He stepped inside, his sense of wonder edged with the spice of fear.

He looked around him, not sure what he was looking for. He noticed a group of photographs on the wall opposite the door, and went to investigate them. Most of them were of the aliens, either standing in front of the house or floating in a small boat on the lake, or holding some sort of aquatic animal at the end of a cord. Quiffik tried to quell his revulsion at the alien forms and study them carefully.

Beside those was a group of four pictures in a row that obviously belonged together, though what they signified wasn't at all obvious to Quiffik. They were all taken from inside the house, out through the glass wall toward the lake, but each one was different from the others. The photographer had evidently been using color filters, or maybe the aliens' eyes were sensitive to a wider spectrum than Quiffik's, but the color balance on the plants was off in one photo, and another looked like it was taken with K rays. Quiffik looked at them for a moment, shrugged, and moved on.

He spent a few more minutes searching through the house, identifying eating utensils and clothing and various other household items common to both Quelch and alien, but eventually his apprehension at the thought of the aliens returning home became too much for him and he went back outside, relatching the door behind him. Rescuing Raffid was first priority anyway; perhaps later when they had both returned to the ship he could come back and look at things more thoroughly.

He checked his direction finder and strode off into the forest again, confident that his discovery would cause a stir back on the ship. He began to recite one of his own poems as he walked, one that he had written when he was first considering going on the expedition.

The ground began to slope downward after a while, and Quiffik followed his direction finder into a long, wide canyon. He was letting himself be overwhelmed by all that he saw, filling his mind with sensations to carry back to Quelch in verse. He tried to store every detail, knowing that everything he remembered now would be priceless when he got home. The others on the expedition would carry back technical reports, but he, Quiffik, would bring back the *flavor* of this place. He could feel his whole life coming into focus in this moment, this afternoon trek on a planet light-years away from home. Everything he did for the rest of his life would be affected by this day. He would become famous. Even Trovven would—

He froze. Something moved in the brush ahead of him. He stood perfectly still as two small, black, fur-covered creatures bounded into view, one chasing the other, obviously in play. The one in front nearly crashed into Quiffik before it spotted him. It skidded to a stop, the other one ran into it from behind, and they both wound up in a heap at Quiffik's trod pads.

They scrambled up and ran back the way they had come, making a kind of surprised yelping sound as they ran. Quiffik chased after them, delighted. They were the very essence of humor. Playful little fat creatures knocking one another about—he had to see more of it.

He burst through a patch of foliage into a clearing just as they disappeared behind a big—uh-oh. He should have guessed that they were younglings of some sort. And if this was what they would grow up to be, then Quiffik didn't want anything more to do with them. Or it. He backed up slowly, reaching for his reaction pistol with one tentacle while he searched for something to hide behind, but he was too late. The creature raised up on its hind appendages, emitted a deep roar, and charged.

It hit him straight on, smashing him to the ground and ripping at his suit with enormous claws. For a moment they were a snarling, screaming, writhing ball of action, then suddenly Quiffik felt the air puff out through a rip in his suit and a flash of pain tore through his side. They both stopped thrashing, the creature evidently startled by the rush of air, Quiffik expecting death at any moment. He heard the suit's emergency beacon begin to wail.

Raffid was shouting something over the radio, but Quiffik missed it in his struggle to pull his pistol out from under him and fire. It was only a reaction pistol, used for maneuvering in space, but it generated a hot flame, and it was the only weapon he had. Quiffik sprayed it across the creature's face. In an atmosphere the pistol gave off a roar almost as loud as the creature's cry of pain and rage.

The noise and the heat were too much for it; the creature turned and fled, followed by its two little ones. Quiffik tried to get up, but something felt broken inside. He saw the rip in his suit and the blood beginning to ooze out onto the ground. His last thought before he fainted was that Trovven was going to be very mad about that.

He woke up in the ship's infirmary, a tube stuck in one tentacle and bandages wrapped completely around him. As soon as he moved, Raffid appeared at his side.

"Don't try to get up," he said. "How do you feel?"

"Uh . . . alive," Quiffik said, surprised. "How did I get here?"

Raffid looked embarrassed. "I—uh—I brought you back."

"You? But the flier—how did you—?"

"I defied orders and opened the bubble. I'm afraid I didn't do the polarizer any good. I didn't know what to adjust, so I twisted everything I could find until it flew." He stopped, then went on. "I'm sorry about this. The whole thing was my fault."

"Nonsense," Quiffik said. "It was my own stupidity." He changed the subject before Raffid could protest. "How did Trovven take it? I bet he was pretty upset."

"A little, " Raffid understated. "We're both in quarantine until he's sure we didn't catch anything from out there."

Quiffik said, "I expected as much. What about outside? Did we—?"

"No telling yet. But I wouldn't worry. We've had test animals living in our air since we got here and it hasn't hurt them yet. I don't think what few organisms we let out can hurt anything. The alien organisms seem to be tougher than ours anyway."

The following weeks seemed to prove Raffid right. Searchers found and watched the animal that had attacked Quiffik, and aside from the burns on its face it had suffered no ill effects from its meeting with a Quelch. The burns eventually healed. The creature grew fatter. Its two cubs continued to be playful.

Quiffik healed quickly also. Neither he nor Raffid caught any alien diseases, but Trovven kept them in quarantine anyway, possibly out of spite. Raffid nearly tore out his eating tendrils in frustration; all the scientific discoveries were going on without him.

The planet swung on in its orbit. Outside the days were getting shorter as the rotational axis began to tilt away from the sun. The average temperature began to drop as the meteorologists had predicted it would, and the moisture began to precipitate out of the atmosphere in a few brief but heavy storms.

Then the plants began to die.

It happened slowly at first, just a few of the smaller ones shriveling up and growing brittle, but within a week of the first observed case it had become an epidemic. It wasn't confined to the areas Quiffik and Raffid had contaminated, but seemed equally severe everywhere. Long-range surveys discovered that the disease was spreading southward over the entire planet, evidently carried by global winds. It was affecting only the plants, and only one of the two major types of plants at that, but the biologists were having little luck in isolating the responsible pathogen. They had never really understood what kept the alien plants alive in the first place, so trying to determine what killed them was doubly difficult. They were certain that some Quelchie organism was involved, but all of the cultures came up negative. Specimens from Quiffik and Raffid grew only the most ordinary flora, and healthy alien plants exposed to them refused to die.

And much to Quiffik's dismay, neither did he. It looked like he was going to survive to become the greatest villain in Quelchie history, and have to go home to tell about it himself. His only consolation was that not everything was dying. A few of the small animals had begun to hoard food, and some of the winged ones were flying to unaffected areas, but other than that the animals hardly seemed affected yet at all. Perhaps they might still find a way to survive.

Raffid destroyed that hope, though. Ironically, he was trying to cheer Quiffik up at the time. He was talking about his own ecological studies.

"Well," he said, "at least I'll be able to trace the food chain throughout the whole ecosystem now."

"How's that?" Quiffik asked.

"Simple. I just watch for starvation. The animals who starve first will be herbivores, and the next ones will be primary carnivores, and then secondary, and so forth."

"You mean everything's going to die anyway? It's not just the plants?"

"Of course not," Raffid said, surprised that Quiffik hadn't seen that for himself. "Everything's interconnected. When you upset a food chain as badly as we've upset this one, there's no hope for it. We've killed the food supply, so of course everything it supports will die too. Even the decomposers will go eventually, I suppose."

"But the plants that aren't dying—won't they support some kind of life?"

"Oh, it's possible, but hardly likely. I imagine any that *can* be eaten *will* be eaten long before they can reproduce. There may be a few inedible ones left, but I think all the animals are doomed."

Quiffik writhed his tentacles in agony at the thought. "Isn't there something we can do? Shouldn't we try to warn the sentient race—try to help them? If they knew what was causing all this, maybe they could stop it. Don't you think?"

Raffid nodded. "Trovven has talked about it, but he doesn't want to contact them until we understand their language better. There are still a lot of concepts that we just don't understand, and he thinks there might be some danger if we go about things wrong. From what we've seen, these creatures are a pretty vindictive sort, and they might conceivably try to take revenge on Quelch."

"So we're just going to sit here and watch the planet die?"

"We're doing everything we can. The disease hasn't reached the other hemisphere of the planet yet, so we've been able to get a few uncontaminated specimens. We might yet discover what's causing this in time to prevent complete annihilation."

But even then, Quiffik thought, millions of innocent creatures will die. He thought of his krem, also killed because of his own stupidity. Trovven had been right all along. But he should have thrown Quiffik out the air lock as well.

He thought of the poems he had meant to write. They were a hollow mockery now. What good were words when a planet was dying? What could they possibly do but add to the sorrow? He had not only killed a planet; he had killed his own reason for being.

Quiffik thought about it way into the night. When he could no longer think, he got up and found some pills to help him sleep. It took a long time to wash down the entire bottle.

He knew he hadn't taken enough when he began to dream. He was back in the alien house by the lake, only this time he was hiding from Trovven, who was rushing the barricaded door from outside and screaming in rage. Quiffik was trying to hold shut a gigantic rip in his pressure suit, all the while searching for some kind of weapon, anything to defend himself with, but everything was incomprehensibly alien to him. He *knew* that what he searched for was somewhere in the house, but he couldn't tell one thing from another.

"Murderer!" Trovven screamed from beyond the door, his cries blending with the ominous hiss of breathing air from Quiffik's suit. "Open the air lock. That's an *order*, Quiffik!"

Quiffik stumbled backward away from the door until he was up against the far wall. One of the pictures fell off onto his helmet and clattered to the floor. It showed himself holding a dead krem by one tentacle, grinning stupidly into the camera. He leaped up to dash the others from the walls, but stopped when he saw the four photos of the lake. They were unchanged. The first still showed the lake ringed with the blood-green trees, much as it had looked when Quiffik first found the house. The second was still mottled with strange colors, but Quiffik recognized them now. The third one was a familiar sight now too—

all the plants dead. But the fourth showed the same plants beginning to grow again. Quiffik turned to look out the windows. They were growing now. He looked back at the photographs. Growing, dying, dead, and growing again. In that order. But the photos were taken before any of them had died. Unless . . .

Could an alien die twice?

Quiffik reached up and cautiously removed the photo mural from the wall. Holding it before him like a shield, he went to open the door.

INTRODUCTION TO
"BARTER"

by Lois McMaster Bujold

The year was 1983. I was thirty-four years old, and living with two preschool children and "no job", i.e., no paid employment, in the middle of the Reagan Recession in small town Marion, Ohio. My physical and intellectual world had shrunk to one block long, seemingly peopled by no more than my kids, a handful of mothers of the other preschoolers on the street, my parents, and my erratically-employed spouse. Out of the middle of this life-devolution, inspired by my own early passion for reading and by a friend from my youth, Lillian Stewart Carl, who had begun writing and selling, I began trying to bootstrap a career as a science fiction writer.

I count the beginning of this effort as Thanksgiving Day, 1982, when, visiting my parents, I wrote a paragraph or two on my dad's new Kay Pro II to try out the toy. I dimly recall that the fragment of description actually had its genesis from a writing exercise done for a couple of visits to a local Marion writers' group. (They were mostly middle-aged and elderly women who met in a church basement and wrote domestic and religious poetry; after a hiatus, I found them again the following year when they'd moved to a bank basement, and inflicted much early SF on them. They were a very patient, if wildly inappropriate, audience.) The fragment generated, the following month, my first story, a novelette eventually titled "Dreamweaver's Dilemma," although the actual paragraphs were cut from the final version.

Over the course of the following nine months, I finished my very first novel, then titled *Mirrors*, and began on the second, *The Warrior's Apprentice*. I also started trying to circulate short work to the magazine markets. In addition to the novelette, I sent out a recycled short story from a college writing class, a really lame short-short, and a brief new piece titled "Garage Sale" based in content on the friction between a couple of my neighbors, and in style on having read Garrison Keillor's Lake Woebegone tales from the library.

Somewhere about the middle of chapter five of the second novel, in the late fall of 1983, I stopped to pop out "Barter." It took only two or three writing sessions, no more than ten hours. I'd jotted the opening line in a notebook earlier that summer, based on personal observation at assorted breakfasts, without anything to attach it to at the time. (Along with, " 'Did you know that red ants explode when you put them in the microwave?' her nephew inquired.'—a hook I've still not used, having given up short work in favor of long.)

It was easy work. The setting of Putnam, Ohio, had been developed in seed form for the earlier tale, "Garage Sale." (Marion was a revolutionary war general, so was Putnam, hence the transference.) The cats, the kids, the house, the Smurfs, the desperation, and the Christopher Parkening record, if not the peanut butter on it, thank God, were all lifted nearly verbatim from my life at the time.

I still have in my files my rejection letters and a piece of lined notebook paper with the hand-jotted log of my short story submissions for the year 1984. For "Barter" it goes:

Rejection letter from *Amazing Stories* dated Dec. 11, 1983.

Form rejection from *Redbook* received 2/9/84. (Hey, the writer's guide said they had a high word rate.)

2/10/84, sent to *Asimov's*, returned 3/26.

3/27, mailed out to *Women's World*, another completely inappropriate market with a high word rate, returned 5/2.

5/3, mailed out to *F&SF*, returned 6/29.

6/30, off to T.E.D. Klein at *Twilight Zone Magazine*.

9/28/1984—big block letters—SOLD!!!

The news came on a little teeny personally-typed TZ letterhead postcard, almost lost in the bottom my mailbox, which I still have. I was ecstatic. The meager money was soon spent, but the morale boost was critical to power me through the following year and third novel until my final vindication, when I sold the three completed manuscripts to Baen Books. *Mirrors* was retitled *Shards of Honor*, and is still in print to this day, including a recent and very beautiful hardcover reprint from NESFA Press.

Looking back through my files to jog my memory for this essay, I note several points of interest to aspiring writers. Those personal editorial rejections I received in that period were actually a lot more encouraging than I realized, now that I know how to decode editorialese. (Alas, at the time, I didn't, and neither did my relatives.) The turnaround times, that is, the amount of time a manuscript languishes on the editor's desk waiting to be looked at, were agonizing; today, unfortunately for new writers, they're even longer. But in turning the story around and sending it out again the very next day, I was doing exactly the right thing. Three times may be a charm, but it took me six.

The sales saga of "Barter" had a sequel, a success story—not to mention a cautionary tale—in miniature. The story was seen in its *Twilight Zone Magazine* appearance in the spring of 1985 by a producer from the TV series *Tales From The Darkside*, who threw me into total confusion, in my pre-agent days, by calling and offering to buy the story rights for scripting for the show. The episode that resulted bore almost no relation to the original. Their scripter not only eliminated almost every element I'd invented and reversed the outcome, but used it as a hook to hang an *I Love Lucy* pastiche upon, a sitcom I'd loathed utterly even back in the 50s when I'd first seen it. Since *Tales From The Darkside* didn't play in my viewing area, I've never seen the episode broadcast, a nonevent I do not regret. But I was very grateful for the money.

BARTER

by Lois McMaster Bujold

HER pancakes were all running together in the center of the griddle, like conjugating amoebas. Too much milk in the batter, Mary Alice thought. She should have measured it. She poked dubiously at the fault line with a spatula, trying to chivvy the congealing paste back to its original assigned quarters. The spatula, cracked down the middle from metal fatigue, hooked some of the half-cooked goo on its ragged edge and drew it out of the pan as she was setting the tool down. It dripped on the burner, and smoked. She batted at it hastily with a kitchen towel, which scorched and sparked.

The television blared suddenly from the next room at triple volume. "Turn it down!" Mary Alice screamed. *The Space Kidettes* at any audible level was bad enough, but this . . . She glanced at the digital clock, which read 3:16 A.M. in glowing red numerals. Since the sun was shining outside, she deduced the kids had been messing with the reset button again. No matter—if it was *The Space Kidettes*, it had to be nine thirty AM Saturday. I have measured out my life not in coffee spoons, she thought bitterly, but in TV schedules. She bounded into the living room, hands pressed to her ears.

"Down!" she screamed again, and blasted the button herself. "You let your baby brother mess with those controls again, and I'm going to turn it off!" The Ultimate Threat . . .

"Aw, Mom . . ."

"You're out there, I'm not—you're supposed to be keeping an eye on him."

"I didn't see him."

"How could you not see him—he had to be standing in front of you to turn the knob!"

Baby brother deedled to himself in loud delight, and emerged around a corner dragging a cat by its hind leg. "Let the cat *go*, Bryan . . ."

Janie huddled, miffed, closer to her electronic panderer of injection-molded delights, eyes widening lustfully at Malibu

Barbie with Swimming Pool, fifteen cents worth of assorted petroplastics bloated to a week's grocery budget. "Mom, I want one of *those* for Christmas . . ."

"It's August, for God's sakes," snapped Mary Alice, retreating to her kitchen. The pancakes were burning and the other cat was up on the counter top, lapping out of the batter bowl.

"Aargh!" gritted Mary Alice. She scooped up the cat and flung it back into the living room, hoping the baby would get it, too. She stared into the bowl, wondering how much the cat had eaten, and where. It wasn't like margarine, where the rough tongue left little telltale swirly grooves, that helped you figure out which side to cut off. She carried the bowl to the sink and skimmed off a token ladleful or two, dropping them into the disposal side with a white splat. Well, it was all going to be cooked anyway . . .

Her eldest son swaggered through. General Teddy Han Solo Moore, Jr., age seven. On his way to battle, evidently; massing his troops.

"Mom, have you seen Luke Skywalker?"

"I think your baby brother had him. He's probably bitten his head off by now, the little geek . . ."

"What kind of pancakes are those?"

"Banana."

"I don't like banana."

"So, pick out the banana pieces—out, out, you little ingrate," she snarled. "I'll call you all when it's ready."

Her husband slinked past, toward the kitchen door.

"Where are you going? Breakfast is almost ready."

"Coffee's all I want. I'm going to start my diet again today."

"I fixed for five."

"I can't help that."

"You could've *told* me."

"You didn't ask me. Anyway, I'm going down to Lawson's with Harold Krieger to get some out-of-town papers. Gonna help him look through the help wanteds."

Going to the video arcade, she thought in numb resentment, *to blow another five bucks on Pac-Man with ol' buddy Unemployed Harold. And I didn't buy a shower cap last week, for the fourth month in a row, because two dollars and sixty-nine cents was too much to spend and I can tie my hair out of my face with that old scarf which hasn't quite rotted through . . .*

"All right, kids, come eat."

"Mom, can I have mine in the living room?"

"I don't *like* banana!"

"Deedle-deedle . . ."

"Mrwowrrr . . ."

She hurtled through the living room on a fast roundup, using the flat of her hand like a cowboy's bullwhip. Keep those dawgies movin', Rawhiiide . . . Janie refused the already-poured orange juice and demanded ice water, two cubes. General Solo picked out banana pieces with elaborate scorn. Deedle-deedle, with high shrieks of "Die, die!" threw all his to the cats, who swirled like sharks beneath his high chair. Mary Alice was not sure if the cries were directed to his breakfast or the bombees.

Mary Alice, grimly, ate her way through two adult portions, thinking of the starving children in China, and wishing there were some way to teleport them all her leftovers. A silence fell, briefly, and she took her first slurp of coffee of the morning. It had been poured some time back, and was now cold. In the quiet, from the living room, floated a liquid choking sound, rich, rhythmic, and resonant; one of the cats was throwing up. On the carpet, of course. They never did it on the linoleum.

The morning was all downhill from there. Janie walked through the cat barf before Mary Alice could get to it, because she was pulling Bryan off the counter top where he had just field-stripped the Mr. Coffee filter basket into its six constituent components. It was simple enough to snap back together— Mary Alice was becoming quite practiced—but it had been full of wet coffee grounds, which were now poured down the stove burners. Malibu Janie and General Solo had a screaming argument over Which Channel; Mary Alice flatly refused to referee on the grounds that any way you looked at it, she lost, caught between the Scylla and Charybdis of Strawberry Shortcake and Smurfs. The dishes, refusing to do themselves, remained piled on the countertop, an obstacle course for foraging cats. Cats, contrary to rumor, are not graceful beasts at all, but klutzes. They knocked Mary Alice's last remaining large platter on the floor, where it shattered.

Mary Alice stood in the kitchen doorway and vibrated miserably, torn between the cat vomit and the sharp slivers of crockery lying ready to slice bare feet. She just could not keep slippers on those kids. She had a vision of a morning spent in the emergency room, waiting for stitches to be taken in wounds festering with Cat Germs.

It was then that the doorbell buzzed.

Mary Alice, muttering words that should not be said out loud in front of children, clawed the door open, ripping a fingernail. "Whatever it is, we don't want . . ." she began, and paused.

What an odd little man. Not an inch over five feet, he had a pale, loose complexion, and breathed asthmatically. He was dressed in a shimmering, silken material that seemed to move through all colors, no colors, unnameable colors, as he moved. A suitcase of a sort, like a salesman's sample case but covered with a similar material, hung by his side—floated, Mary Alice realized; he wasn't holding on to it. Mary Alice, alone with three children and two cats, might have been alarmed, but she made it a rule never to be afraid of men shorter than herself. Besides, he looked ill.

"Give me," he gasped, in an odd, guttural accent, "all your ammonia."

"I beg your pardon?" She sucked on her bleeding finger, gone wide-eyed.

"Ammonia—must have ammonia. Have no money—will trade. What price ammonia?"

As it happened, Mary Alice was in very good shape with respect to ammonia. There had been a coupon special that week at the supermarket, two for the price of one. Mary Alice loathed coupons. They made her feel like a rat in a paper maze, jerked through a lot of meaningless motions, cut and save, fold and paste, push the lever and ring the bell, for a reward of a few pennies. But they were like money, and you couldn't throw money away.

She eyed the little man in awed fascination. "Uh . . . what have you got to trade?"

His answer was drowned in a sudden blare of noise from behind her, its content, if any, obliterated in its volume. She fled out the door and slammed it behind her, like dropping a portcullis against massed shock troops. It helped some. He was opening his—sample case? Candy store? Engineering department? Odd-shaped objects glittered and gleamed in the case, and Mary Alice blinked, dizzied.

"Look, uh, Klaatu, Beelzebub, whoever you are—you're welcome to my ammonia, if you really need it. The only thing

I need is an off-switch for my kids, and I'm sure you don't have *that* . . ." She smiled, an artificial rictus, at her own old joke.

The little man brightened. "Ah!" he said. "Biostasis field. Very easy, nice lady. Have lots of spares."

Mary Alice froze, then thawed, trembling slightly. His words, devoid of clear denotation to her whirling mind but fairly pulsing with implicit promise, conjured ecstatic visions. She almost grasped his sleeve, but drew her hand back, a little afraid he might pop out of existence like the soap bubble he rather resembled, without even a drip to mark his passing.

"Come in," she breathed, "come in to my kitchen. Watch your step . . ."

The three kids, glued to the tube—it was a commercial—didn't even look up as they passed. Mary Alice wished she'd bought stock in Kenner in 1976. She tiptoed through the shards on the kitchen floor and dragged back a sticky chair for her visitor. He sat, heavily, with a grateful smile. His wheezing was becoming quite noticeable. "Nice lady," he gasped. "Ammonia—now?"

"Uh, sure." She bolted down to the basement, where the ammonia and other cleaning compounds were stored on a high shelf, theoretically out of the reach of deedle-deedles. Although since the incident with the bag of powdered sugar and the bottle of Palmolive Green from the top pantry shelf, she had lost faith in height alone as a safety measure. She tramped back up the stairs with a half-gallon plastic jug anchoring each arm. She heaved one into his lap with an anxious smile. "Bo-Peep Cloudy all right with you?"

He nodded, wheezing, and fumbled the cap off. He blinked and smiled as the fumes rose. "Yes . . ." he aspirated, and attempted to raise the bottle to his mouth with weak and trembling arms. It slipped, sloshing ammonia onto his shimmering clothing. It did not soak in, neither did it bead, but sheeted off into a messy puddle on the floor, leaving not a track behind. "Help . . . me . . ." he whispered.

Hoping sickly that she wasn't helping him to commit suicide, she popped to the Dixie cup dispenser. Empty. She tried the cupboard—also empty; the glasses were all stacked with the rest of the dishes, encrusted with food, stale milk rings, and greasy fingerprints. Wait, there was one—Janie's McDonald's Going Places cup. Mary Alice glanced nervously over her shoulder—Janie usually had screaming fits when anyone else

dared to use her private cup. But her middle child was still en-
sconced in the living room. Mary Alice grabbed a jug and
glugged in ammonia level with the top of Birdie's green airplane, nerved herself, and held it hastily to her guest's lips. He
drank greedily, thanking her with grateful golden eyes. The
pupils, she noticed, were diamond-shaped, not round.

He finished the cupful and sat a little straighter, breathing
more quietly and steadily. He rested a few minutes in the chair,
not speaking, apparently regaining his strength. He took another glassful of Bo-Peep Cloudy, and recapped the jug. Mary
Alice had set the second jug on the floor. Now she pushed it
shyly toward him with her foot. "You were saying something
about a stasis field?" she reminded him hopefully.

"Biostasis field," he corrected. "Yes. Use all the time for
traveling. Very easy. You want remote switch?"

"Uh . . . I guess."

"All right. I fix." He knelt, reopened his case, and rummaged within. He paused a moment, picked up the second jug
and tightened its cap securely, and set it within the case. The
bottle shrank, melting and curling away from Mary Alice—but
not toward any other part of the kitchen. It curled away from all
sides at once. When it was reduced to the size of a straight pin,
her guest placed it carefully in a holder displaying a long row
of other tiny, ambiguous shapes, and sighed satisfaction.

"How many you want?" he inquired. "You call in children,
I fix."

"Well, there's Teddy, and Janie, and Bryan . . ." Her eye fell
on one of the cats, sleeping stretched out in the middle of a sun-
beam on the kitchen table, its tail resting across a plate pooled
with pancake syrup and floating banana bits. Teddy always
poured too much syrup. She felt a slight maternal qualm at the
thought of subjecting her firstborn to an unknown operation.
"Can you do cats, too?" she asked.

"Can do anything," he stated confidently.

"All right—let's start with that one," she pointed.

The cat was placed on her guest's lap, where it settled, pout-
ing at having its nap disturbed. The little man stroked it, then
held a curious device the size of a cigarette lighter above the
back of the beast's neck. A strange blue light, at once transpar-
ent and material, descended into the thick black fur and vanished.

"Okay, see." He handed her the device. "Press here."

The cat jumped down, stretching disdainfully. Mary Alice pressed. The cat froze in a blink, as though strobed. Unbalanced, it fell over and lay stiffly.

"Wow," Mary Alice breathed. "How do you start it up again?"

"Press there."

The cat flipped indignantly to its feet and scampered off.

"I'll call the other one," said Mary Alice happily, pressing the electric can opener. At its quiet whir, both cats appeared as though conjured. The operation was repeated in a moment. Mary Alice experimented for a few minutes, turning the cats on and off.

"How long does this thing keep working?" she asked. "I mean, do the batteries run down or anything?"

"Not run forever," the little man said. "Takes big power, you bet. Power cell only good for—your time . . ." He lost himself in a mental calculation, lips moving. "One hundred ten years."

"That'll be okay," she reassured him. "That'll be just fine." She moved to the doorway of the living room. "Oh, Teddy . . ."

She lined them up on the couch, one, two, three, like the Chinese monkeys, with the cats on either side like bookends. Last of all she turned off the television set. Silence, blessed silence, fell, broken only by the drip, drip of the refrigerator defrosting itself.

"Must you go so soon?" Mary Alice asked the little man. "You only just got here. Shouldn't you rest?"

"Must go," he shrugged.

"But my husband isn't home yet. He could roll in any time now. Just a few more minutes? Please?"

The little man shook his head apologetically. "Must go."

"Wait." An idea tugged at Mary Alice's brain. It was worth a try, anyway. "Just one second—" She galloped back down the basement stairs, and returned in a flash with another white plastic jug with a red and blue label. "Can you use any of this?" It was only three-quarters full, but still . . .

He uncapped it, and sniffed. His face lit up. "Ah!" he cried. "Hooch!"

He tilted the Clorox jug up on his arm, hillbilly style, and took a swallow. "Ahhh!" He smiled, then belched hugely. Mary Alice, remembering what had happened in her toilet the time she had mixed ammonia and chlorine bleach, thinking to clean and disinfect at the same time, was not surprised. "Nice lady. Maybe I got one, two more minutes . . ."

They waited, Mary Alice popping up every few minutes when a car was heard passing, or a car door slammed in the neighborhood. With a few moments' quiet, she began to think.

"You know," she said after a while, "my husband doesn't really need an off-switch."

"Oh?" said the little man. "I go, then."

"No, wait—what I mean is, do you have anything like an, uh—an *on*-switch, in the bag of tricks?"

The little man rubbed his lips thoughtfully, and took another slug of Clorox. "Sounds like a focal stimulator."

"What's that?"

"We use instead of toxic caffeine-laden beverage. To work."

"Work, eh? That sounds about right," Mary Alice mused. "Can I trade you that gallon of Clorox for one?"

The little man looked at the jug respectfully and grinned. "Nice lady, you got deal."

Mary Alice sat back down and prayed for a power outage at the video arcade. At last came the familiar engine noise in the driveway, the crunch of gears and the squeal of brakes.

"What's this, company?" asked Teddy, Sr., entering the kitchen.

"Uh, hello, dear. Mr., uh, Klaatu is a Jehovah's Witness. We've been having the most fascinating conversation . . ."

"Oh," he said, his eyes glazing over. "Well, I'll leave you to it, then." He turned on the water, and rummaged in the cupboard for a suitable vessel. He finally chose a sherbet dish, and drew a drink of water. The little man, from his chair, sighted upon the back of her husband's neck. The glowing red blur sang quietly as a mosquito through the air and vanished into the skin of the nape.

"Do you want anything to eat, dear, after skipping breakfast?"

"Oh no. Harold and I stopped at McDonald's. I had two Big Macs, fries, and a shake, so I guess I don't want anything till lunch . . ." He yawned. "See if you can keep the kids quiet, huh? I'm going to try to get a nap and—"

Mary Alice pressed her button.

Her husband blinked. "—clean out those gutters. Should have done them last fall, y'know. There's no time like the present . . ." He bounded energetically back out the kitchen door, heading for the garage and a ladder.

The little man shouldered his Clorox bottle and bowed his way out.

"Do stop by again, any time you're in the neighborhood," Mary Alice invited cordially. "Just let me know you're coming, and I'll lay in plenty of ammonia and bleach. Bye!"

She turned back to her house with a sigh. She had much to do herself, but at least it wouldn't be undone four times faster. One could not keep the kids switched off all the time, of course—thirty years down the line, applying for Social Security, she might still have a preschooler in the house if she were too self-indulgent. But there was no rush. First she would clean the kitchen, then the rest of the downstairs. Then, perhaps, she might sit down with a glass of fresh iced tea, and listen to a record. Not the high, piping voices of Chipmunks or Smurfs, hiccuping over the peanut butter jammed in the grooves, but a record of her own, maybe *Parkening Plays Bach*. The television would remain off. The silence was not total; scraping noises from the eaves intruded gently through the summer-open windows, but that was all right. She began to sweep the kitchen, planning her day. *Her* day.

INTRODUCTION TO
"THE XEELEE FLOWER"

by Stephen Baxter

"The Xeelee Flower" was first published in 1987.

By then I'd been writing stories for around 15 years, without success in placing anything for publication; I'd even tried out a novel. I'd tried to study the craft—notably, in those days, Larry Niven. I was a great fan of stories like *The Hole Man*, which was written in such a lucid style that studying it helped me figure out how such pieces work.

The core of "Xeelee Flower" was the central jeopardy situation: I had an image of an astronaut, stranded in orbit around a sun about to go nova, sheltering behind an energy-soaking "umbrella." To develop the idea I did some technical research, to figure out just how much each square meter of the umbrella would have to absorb.

But I also figured out the background: Who was this guy? How had he got stranded there? Where did the "umbrella" come from? I came up with the notion of powerful offstage aliens called the Xeelee (I can't remember where I got the name), whose purloined artifact, the Xeelee Flower itself, would save my hero's life. Accompanying this was the vague idea of a galaxy full of minor species, including ourselves, living in the shadow of the Xeelee.

All this was very playful; I wanted the tone to be light and fast-paced, and writing was just a hobby for me in those days. I worked on the story in the early summer of 1986. I remember sitting up late to watch soccer matches in that year's World Cup; when the action was dull, I would progress the story a little more.

I actually had the story completed before I found *Interzone*, its eventual market. I was lucky in a sense that the magazine had an upcoming new writers' issue, with a slot just big enough for "Flower." But I'd been pushing on a lot of closed doors for a long time; one of them was eventually going to open for me.

The Xeelee, of course, continue to be very important for me. In my next story I posited humans in a four-dimensional cage, put there by more powerful offstage aliens. Eventually I realized that if I made the aliens the Xeelee, I had the beginning and the end of a future history, which grew, organically, from that point. I suspect for much of my career I'll be referring back to elements of this story.

THE XEELEE FLOWER

by Stephen Baxter

I still get tourists out here, you know. Even though it's been so long since I was a hero. But then, I'm told, these days the reopened Poole wormholes will get you from Earth to Miranda in hours.

Hours. What a miracle. Not that these tourist types appreciate it. Don't get me wrong, I don't mind the company. It just bugs me that every last one, after he's finished looking over my villa built into the five-mile cliffs of Miranda, turns his face up to the ghostly blue depths of Uranus, and asks the same dumb question:

"Say, buddy, how come you use a fish tank for a toilet?"

But I'm a good host, and I merely smile and snap my fingers. After a while, my battered old buttlebot limps in with a bottle of valley bottom wine, and I settle back and begin:

"Well, my friend, I use the fish tank for a toilet for the same reason you would. Because my boss used to live in it."

And that's how I got where I am today.

*   *   *

By working for a bunch of fish, I mean, not pissing in the tank. Although I don't know what stopped me from doing just that by the time we reached Goober's Star eight months out from Earth.

"The resolution, Jones, the resolution!" The shoal of Squeem darted anxiously around their tank, griping at me from the translator box taped to one glass wall.

I put down the spare tank I'd been busy scraping out, and blinked across the cluttered little cabin. The buttlebot—yes, the same one, squeaky-clean in those days—scuttled past, humming happily in its chores. I picked my way to the control panel. I got out my adjustable spanner and gingerly tweaked the fiddly little enhancement vernier. Like most Xeelee-based technology it was too fine for human fingers. The secretive Xeelee evidently have great brains but tiny hands. Then again, some people haven't managed to evolve hands at all, I reflected, as the Squeem flipped around in their greenish murk.

"Ah," enthused the Squeem as the monitors sharpened up. "Our timing is perfect."

I gloomily considered a myriad beautiful images of two things I didn't want much to be close to: Goober's Star—about G-type, about two Earth orbits away, and about to nova; and a planet full of nervous Xeelee.

And the most remarkable feature of the whole situation was that we weren't running for our lives. In fact, we were going to get closer—a lot closer—drawn mothlike by the greed of the Squeem for stolen Xeelee treasure.

The buttlebot squeezed past my leg, extended a few pseudopodia, and began pushing buttons with depressing enthusiasm. I sighed and turned back to my fish tank. At least I had one up on the 'bot, I reflected; at least I was getting paid. Although, like most of the rest of humanity at that time, I hadn't exactly had a free choice in the nature of my employment—

The Squeem's rasp broke into my thoughts. "Jones, our planetfall is imminent. Please prepare the flitter for your descent."

Your descent. Had they said "your" descent? I nearly dropped the fish tank.

Carefully, I got up from my knees. "Into Lethe's waters with that." I defiantly straightened my rubber gloves. "No way. The Xeelee wouldn't let me past the orbit of the moons—"

"The Xeelee will be fully occupied with their flight from the imminent nova. And your descent will be timed to minimize your risk."

"That's a lot of 'you' and 'your,'" I observed witheringly. "Show me where my contract says I've got to do this."

Can fish be said to be dry? The Squeem said dryly, "That will be difficult as you haven't got a contract at all."

They had a point. I reluctantly took off my pinafore and began to tug at the fingers of my rubber gloves. The buttlebot smugly opened up the suit locker. "You ought to send that little tin cretin," I said; and the Squeem replied, "We are."

I swear to this day that buttlebot jumped.

And so the buttlebot and I found ourselves drifting through a low orbit over the spectacular Xeelee landscape. We watched morosely as the main ship pulled away from the tiny, human-design flitter, and wafted our employer off to the comparative safety of the farside of one of the planet's two moons.

My work for the Squeem, roughly speaking, was to do any fiddly, dirty, dangerous jobs the buttlebot wasn't equipped for, such as to clean out fish tanks and land on hostile alien planets. And me, a college graduate. Of course, the role of humanity at that time was roughly equivalent.

It isn't that the Squeem—or any of the other races out there—were any brighter than we were or better or even much older. But they had something we didn't, and had—then—no way of getting our hands on.

And that was stolen Xeelee technology. For instance the hyperdrive, scavenged by the Squeem from a derelict Xeelee ship centuries earlier, had been making that fishy race's fortune ever since. Tools and gadgets of all kinds, on which a Galactic civilization had been based. And all pilfered, over millions of years, from the Xeelee.

I use the word civilization loosely, of course. Can it be used to describe what exists out there—a ramshackle construct based on avarice, theft, and the subjugation of junior races like ourselves?

We began our descent. The dark side of the Xeelee world grew into a diamond-studded carpet: fantastic cities glittered on the horizon. *The Xeelee*—so far ahead, they make the rest of us look like tree-dwellers. Secretive, xenophobic. Not truly hostile to the rest of us; merely indifferent. Get in their way and you would be rubbed aside like a mote in the eye of a god.

And I was as close to them as any sentient being had ever got, probably. Nice thought.

Yes, like gods. But very occasionally careless. And that was the basis of the Squeem's plan that day.

We dropped slowly. The conversation left a lot to be desired. And the surface of the planet blew off.

I recoiled from the sudden light at the port, and the buttlebot jerked us down through the incredible traffic. It looked as if whole cities had detached from the ground and were fleeing upwards, light as bubbles. The flitter was swept with shifting color; we were in the down elevator from Heaven.

Abruptly as it had risen, the Xeelee fleet was past. Immense, night-dark wings spread over the doomed planet for a moment, as if in farewell; and then the fleet squirted without fuss into infinity. Evidently, we hadn't been noticed.

The flitter moved in looser arcs now toward the surface. I took over from the buttlebot and began to seek out a likely landing place. We skimmed over a scoured landscape.

From behind the darkened planet's twin moons, the valiant Squeem poked their collective nose. "The nova is imminent; please make haste with your planetfall."

"Thanks. Now get back in your tin and let me concentrate." I wrestled with the flitter's awkward controls; we lurched toward the ground. I cursed the Xeelee under my breath; I thought of fish pie; I didn't even much like the buttlebot. The last thing I needed at a time like that was a reminder that what I was doing was about as clever as looting a house on fire. Get in after the owners have fled; get out before the roof caves in. The schedule was kind of tight.

Finally, we thumped down. Reproachfully, the buttlebot uncoiled its pseudopodia from around a chair leg, let down the hatch, and scuttled out. Already suited up, I grabbed a data desk and flashlight laser, and staggered after it. That descent hadn't done me a lot of good either, but in the circumstances I preferred not to hang around.

I emerged into a bonelike landscape. The noise of my breath jarred in the complete absence of life. I imagined the planet trembling as its bloated sun prepared to burst. It wasn't a happy place to be.

I'd put us down in the middle of a village-sized clump of buildings, evidently too small or remote to lift with the rest of the cities. In a place like this we had our best chance of coming across something overlooked by the Xeelee in their haste, some toy that could revolutionize the economies of a dozen worlds.

Listen, I'm serious. It had happened before. Although any piece of junk that would satisfy the Squeem and let me get out of there would do for me.

The low buildings gaped in the double shadows of the moonlight. The buttlebot scurried into dark places. I ran my hand over the edge of a doorway, and came away with a fine groove in a glove finger. The famous Xeelee construction material: a proton's width thick, about as dense as glass wool, and as strong as Life itself. And no one had a clue how to make or cut it. Nothing new; a familiar miracle.

The buttlebot buzzed past excitedly, empty-handed. The vacant place was soulless; there was nothing to evoke the people who had so recently lived here. The thorough Xeelee had even evacuated their ghosts.

"Squeem, this is a waste of time."

"I estimate some minutes before you should ascend. Please proceed; I am monitoring the star."

"I feel so secure knowing that." I tried a few more doorways. The flashlight laser probed emptiness. —Until, in the fourth or fifth building, I found something.

The artifact, dropped in a corner, was a little like a flower. Six angular petals, which looked as if they were made of Xeelee sheeting, were fixed to a small cylindrical base; the whole thing was about the size of my open hand. An ornament? The readings from my data desk—physical dimensions, internal structure—didn't change as I played with the toy in the light of the flashlight laser. Half the base clicked off in my hand. Nothing exciting happened. Well, whatever it was, maybe it would make the Squeem happy and I could get out.

I took it out into the moonlight. "Squeem, are you copying?" I held it in the laser beam, and twisted the base on and off.

The Squeem jabbered excitedly. "Jones! Please repeat the actions performed by your opposable thumb, and observe the data desk. This may be significant."

"Really." I clicked the base on and off, and inspected the exposed underside in the laser light. No features. But a readout trembled on the data desk; the mass was changing.

I experimented. I took away the torch: the change in mass, a slow rise, stopped. Shine the torch, and the mass crept up. And when I replaced the base, no change with or without the torch.

"Hey, Squeem," I said slowly, "are you thinking what I'm thinking?"

"Jones, this may be a major find."

I watched the mass of the little flower creep up in the light of the torch. It wasn't much—about ten to the minus twelve of an ounce per second, to be exact—but it was there. "Energy to mass, right? Direct conversion of the radiant energy of the beam." And the damn thing wasn't even warm in my hand.

I clicked the base back into place; the flower's growth stopped. Evidently, the base was a key; remove it to make the flower work. The Squeem didn't remark on this; for some reason, I didn't point it out. Well, I wasn't asked.

"Jones, return to the flitter at once. Take no further risks in the return of the artifact."

That was what I wanted to hear. I ran through the skull-like town, clutching the flower. The buttlebot scurried ahead. I gasped out, "Hey, this must be what they use to manufacture their construction material. Just stick it out in the sunlight, and let it grow." Presumably the petals, as well as being the end product, were the main receptors of the radiant energy. In which case, the area growth would be exponential. The more area you grow, the more energy you receive; and the more energy you receive, the more area you grow, and . . .

I thought of experiments to check this out. Listen, I had in my hand a genuine piece of Xeelee magic; it caught my imagination. Of course, the Squeem would be taking the profits. I considered ways to steal the flower . . .

My feet itched; they were too close to a nova. I had other priorities at that point. I stopped thinking and ran.

We bundled into the flitter; I let the buttlebot lift us off, and stored the Xeelee flower carefully in a locker.

The lift was bumpy: high winds in the stratosphere. A spectacular aurora shivered over us. "Squeem, are you sure you've done your sums right?"

"There is an inherent uncertainty in the behavior of novae," the Squeem replied reassuringly. We reached orbit; the main ship swam toward us. "After all," the Squeem lectured on, "a nova is by definition an instability. However I am confident we have at least five minutes before—"

At once, three events.

The moons blazed with light.

The Squeem shut up.

The main ship turned from a nearby cylinder into an arrow of light, pointing at the safety of the stars.

"Five minutes? You dumb fish."

The buttlebot worked the controls frantically, unable to comprehend the abrupt departure of the Squeem. The nova had come ahead of schedule; the twin moons reflected its sick glory. We were still over the dark side of the planet, over which screamed a wind that came straight from the furnaces of a medieval hell. On the day side, half the atmosphere must already have been blasted away.

The flitter was a flimsy toy. I estimated we had about ten minutes to sunrise.

My recollection of the first five of those minutes is not clear. I do not pretend to be a strong man. I remember an image of the walls of the flitter peeling back like burned flesh, the soft interior scoured out . . .

Leaving one object, one remnant, spinning in a cloud of metal droplets.

I realized I had an idea.

I grabbed the Xeelee flower from its locker, and wasted a few more seconds staring at it. The only substance within a million miles capable—maybe—of resisting the nova, and it was the size of my palm. I had to grow it, and fast. But how?

My brain chugged on. Right. One way. But would there be time? The flower's activating base came off, and went into a suit pocket.

The buttlebot was still at the controls, trying to complete its rendezvous with a vanished ship. If there'd been time, I might have found this touching; as things were, I knocked it aside and began entering an emergency sequence. My thinking was fuzzy, my gloved fingers clumsy, and it took three tries to get it right. You can imagine the effect on my composure.

Now I had about a minute to get to the back of the vessel. I snapped closed my visor and de-cycled the air lock. I failed to observe the mandatory safety routines, thus voiding the manufacturer's guarantees. The buttlebot clucked nervously about the cabin.

Clutching the Xeelee flower, I pulled into space and set off one-handed.

I couldn't help looking down at the stricken planet. Around the curve of the world, the air rushing from the day side was gathering into a cyclone to end all cyclones; clouds swarmed like maggots, fleeing the boiling oceans. A vicious light spread over the horizon.

Followed by the confused buttlebot, I made it to the reactor dump hatch. In about thirty seconds, the safety procedure I had set up should funnel all the flitter's residual fusion energy out through the hatch into space, in one mighty squirt. Except, the energy pulse wasn't going to reach free space; it would all hit the Xeelee flower, which I was going to fix into place over the hatch.

Right. Fix it. With what? I fumbled in my suit pockets for tape. A piece of string. Chewing gum. My mind emptied. The buttlebot scuttled past, intent on some vital task.

I grabbed it, and wrapped the flower in one of its pseudopodia. "Listen," I screamed at it, "stay right here. Got it? Hold it for five seconds, please, that's all I ask."

No more time. I scrambled to the far side of the flitter.

Five seconds isn't long. But that five seconds was long enough for me to notice the brightening of the encroaching horizon. Long enough to note that I was gambling my life on a few more or less unfounded assumptions about the Xeelee flower.

It had to be a hundred percent efficient; if it couldn't absorb all that was about to be thrown at it, then it would evaporate like dew. It had to grow exponentially, with the rate of growth area increasing with the area grown already. Otherwise it couldn't grow fast enough to save me as planned.

I also had plenty of time to wonder if the buttlebot had got bored—

There was a flash. I peered around the flitter's flank.

It had worked. The flower had blossomed in the fusion light into an umbrella-sized dish, maybe just big enough for the hard rain that was going to fall.

The flower tumbled slowly away from the now-derelict flitter, as did the buttlebot, sadly waving the melted stump of one pseudopod. I kicked it out of the way, and pushed into space. The heat at my back was knife-sharp.

I reached the flower and curled into a ball behind it. The light flooded closer, beading the edge of my improvised shield. I imagined the nova's lethal energy thudding into the material, condensing into harmless sheets of Xeelee construction material. My suit ought to protect me from the nasty heavy particles which would follow. It was well made, based on Xeelee material, naturally . . . I began to think I might live through this.

I waited for dawn. The buttlebot tumbled by, head over heels. It squirmed helplessly, highlights dazzling in the nova rise.

At the last moment I reached out and pulled it in with me. It was the stupidest thing I have ever done.

The nova blazed.

The flitter burst into a shower of metal rain. The skin of the planet below wrinkled, like a tomato in steam.

And that buttlebot and I rode our Xeelee flower, like surfers on a wave.

It took about twelve hours. At the end of that time, I found I could relax without dying.

I slept.

I woke briefly, dry-mouthed, muscles like wood. The buttlebot clung to my leg like a child to a doll.

We drifted through space. The flower rotated slowly, half-filling my field of view. Its petaled shadow swept over the wasted planet. It must already have been a mile across, and still growing.

What a spectacle. I slept some more.

The recycling system of my suit was designed for a couple of eight-hour EVA shifts. The Squeem did not return from their haven, light-years distant, for four days.

I did a lot of thinking in that time. For instance, about the interesting bodily functions I could perform into the Squeem's tank. And also about the flower.

It grew almost visibly, drinking in the sunlight. Its growth was exponential; the more it grew, the more capacity it had for further growth—I did some woolly arithmetic. How big could it grow?

Start with, say, a square mile of construction material. I made educated guesses about its surface density. Suppose it gets from the nova and surrounding stars about what the Earth receives from the Sun—something over a thousand watts a square yard. Assume total efficiency of conversion: mass equals energy over cee squared.

That gave it a doubling time of fifteen years. I dreamed of numbers: one, two, four, eight, sixteen . . . It was already too big to handle. It would be the size of the Earth after a couple of centuries, the size of Sol a little later.

Give it a thousand years and you could wrap up the Galaxy like a birthday present. Doubling series grow fast. And no one knew how to cut Xeelee construction material.

The Universe waltzed around me; I stroked the placid buttlebot. My tongue was like leather; the failing recycling system of my suit left a taste I didn't want to think about.

I went over my figures. Of course, the growing flower's power supply would actually be patchy, and before long the edge would be spreading at something close to the speed of light. But it would still reach an immense size. And the Xeelee hadn't shown much interest in natural laws in the past. We drifted into its already monstrous eclipse; the buttlebot snuggled closer.

This was the sort of reason the Xeelee didn't leave their toys lying around, I supposed. The flower would be a hazard to shipping, to say the least. The rest of the Galaxy weren't going to be too pleased with the Squeem . . .

These thoughts sifted to the bottom of my mind, and after a while began to coalesce.

The secret of the hyperdrive: yes, that would be a fitting ransom. I imagined presenting it to a grateful humanity. Things would be different for us from now on.

And a little something for myself, of course. Well, I'd be a hero. Perhaps a villa, overlooking the cliffs of Miranda. I'd always liked that bust-up little moon. I thought about the interior design.

It was a sweet taste, the heady flavor of power. The Squeem would have to find a way to turn off the Xeelee flower. But there was only one way. And that was in my suit pocket.

Oh, how they'd pay. I smiled through cracked lips.

Well, you know the rest. I even got to keep the buttlebot. We drifted through space, dreaming of Uranian vineyards, waiting for the Squeem to return.

INTRODUCTION TO "DANCE IN BLUE"

by Catherine Asaro

I wrote "Dance In Blue" on invitation from David Hartwell for the anthology CHRISTMAS FOREVER. Some months earlier, I had sent David a book titled *Lucifer's Legacy* (which later became *Primary Inversion*, my first novel). When I met him at Philcon in the early 1990s, he expressed interest in *Primary Inversion* and extended the anthology invite. It was a plum opportunity for an unpublished, unknown author, and I jumped at the chance.

I wrote "Dance in Blue" fast, a sort of retelling of "The Gift of the Magi." A few weeks later I received a response: David liked aspects of the story, but he didn't think the Magi theme worked in its original form, and he felt the characterization needed retooling. I found our phone conversation exhilarating; for the first time, I was receiving editorial feedback, and from one of the best. On the basis of David's comments, I rewrote "Dance in Blue," and he accepted the second version for publication.

The story is about holography, both in a literal and symbolic sense. It reflects some of my thoughts on illusions in how we perceive ourselves and others. It isn't co-incidence that my first published story concerns a ballet dancer. I studied and performed for thirty years, not only ballet, but also jazz, modern, and flamenco, and when I was earning my doctorate in Chemical Physics at Harvard, I founded the Mainly Jazz Dance program and Harvard University Ballet.

In writing "Dance in Blue," I thought a great deal about characters and plot, in particular how the dancer would respond to her odd situation. If I had it to do over, I would try to integrate the holography more smoothly into the story.

When I first started out in science fiction, I tended to avoid the "hard science fiction" label, because of stereotypes associated with it. My works also often include a love story, and I was initially advised to avoid the romance label as well. After much thought, I decided I had no reason to be embarrassed by either. "Dance in Blue" has aspects of both, but it is first and foremost a tale about how people come to see past surface impressions.

DANCE IN BLUE

by Catherine Asaro

THE hovercar hummed on its cushion of air as I drove through the Rocky Mountains, following a narrow road between the snow-covered fir trees. I came around a curve—and saw the house.

It stood on a plateau across the valley I was just entering. Mountains sheered up behind it, on its north side, the peaks scantily dressed in scraps of cloud. On the east and west sides, cliffs dropped down until they disappeared into the lower range. The house was three stories high, with arched windows on its upper levels. At first I thought the slanted roof was blue, but as I drew nearer I realized it was covered with panels of glass that reflected the sky and the drifting clouds.

I smiled. Soon I would see Sadji again. *Come to the mountains*, he had said. *Come spend Christmas with me*. It would be my first visit to his private retreat. I wasn't performing in the New York Ballet Theater's production of the *Nutcracker* this year, so they let me have the holiday.

Sadji Parker had been a multimedia magnate when I was in kindergarten. When we first met last year, I had been so intimidated I could hardly talk to him. But I soon relaxed. He was like me. He also had grown up on a farm, also loved walks in the country and quiet nights in front of a fire. He too had found unexpected success in an unexpected talent. For him it was holography; he built his fascination with lasers and computers into a financial empire, earning with it an unwanted fame that he sought refuge from in the privacy of his holidays.

There was only one difficult part. Sadji had invited his son to spend Christmas with us, and I had a feeling if the son didn't approve of me, I would lose the father.

As I pulled into a courtyard in front of the house, the wall of a small building on my right rolled up into its roof. I looked inside and saw an unfamiliar hovercar parked there, a black Ferrari that made my rental car look like a junk heap.

I drove into the garage and pulled in next to the Ferrari. When I turned off the ignition, my car settled into the parking pad so gently I hardly felt it touch down. Then I slung my ballet bag over my shoulder, got out, and headed for the house.

It would be good to see Sadji. I had missed him these past weeks. He had been traveling, something to do with his business rival Victor Marck, the man who owned the Marcksman Corporation. Sadji's preoccupation with the war he and Marck were fighting had spilled past the usually inviolate barrier between his private and professional lives. Before he left on his trip he had told me how much he needed the respite of our holiday together.

I stopped in front of the house, faced by two imposing doors made from mahogany. The mirrors of a solar collector were set discreetly into the wall above the doorframe, their surfaces tilted to catch the sun. When I rang the doorbell, chimes inside played a Mozart sonata.

No one answered. After a while I knocked. Still no answer. I looked around, but there was no other entrance. Nor was there any way around the house. A rough stone wall bordered both the east and west sides of the courtyard, and on the other side of each wall, cliffs dropped down in sheer faces. Beyond that, the spectacular panorama of the Rocky Mountains spread out for miles.

"Hello?" My breath came out in white puffs. I rang the bell again, then pulled on the door handles.

"Bridget Fjelstad?" the doors asked.

I jumped back. "Yes?"

They swung open. "Please come in."

I blinked at them. Then I walked into a wonderland.

Tiles covered the walls, the floor, even the ceiling of the entrance foyer. Shimmering globes hung in the air in front of each square. The spheres weren't solid; when I stretched out my hand, it passed right through them. If I moved my head from side to side, they shifted relative to each other as if they were solid. When I moved my head up and down, their relative positions stayed fixed but they changed color. Rainbows also filled the foyer, probably made from sunlight caught by the solar collector and refracted through prisms. It was like being in a sea of sparkling light.

I smiled. "Sadji? Are you here? This is beautiful."

No one answered. Across the foyer, a doorway showed like a magical portal. I walked through it, coming out into an empty room shaped like a ten-pointed star. The doorway made one side of a point on the star, with the hinges of the door in the tip of the point. The three points on the east side of the room were windows, six floor-to-ceiling panes of glass. Pine tiles covered the other walls, each a palm-sized square of wood enameled with delicate birds and flowers in colors of the sunrise. Light from the foyer spilled out here, giving the air a sparkling quality. It made faint rainbows on the wood and the white carpet.

But there was no Sadji. I felt strange, alone in his oddly beautiful house. I went to the windows and stood in a point of the star. Outside, the wall of the house fell away from my feet, dropping down into clouds. All that stood between me and the sky was a pane of glass.

Something about the window bothered me. Looking closer, I realized a faint glimmer of rainbows showed around its edges. Was it spillover from the foyer? Or was that breathtaking view only a holo? It wouldn't surprise me if this place had the best holographic equipment the twenty-first century had to offer. If anyone had the resources to create a mountain-sized holo it was my absent host, Sadji Parker. Why he would do it, I had no idea.

Then I had an unwelcome thought: what if the view was real but not the glass? Although there were no sounds to make me think I stood in front of an open window, there wasn't really anything to hear out in that chasm of sky. And I had been in stores with exits protected by moving screens of air that kept heat in and wind out better than a door. The newer ones were so sophisticated you couldn't detect them even if you were right next to them.

But if this was a holo, where was the hologram? My only knowledge of holography came from a class I had taken in school. This much I remembered, though, to make a holo you needed a hologram, a recording of how light bouncing off an object interfered with laser light.

I shook my head and my reflection in the glass did the same, showing me a slender woman with yellow hair spilling over her wool coat down to her hips.

Then I smiled. Of course. This couldn't be a holo. There was no way my reflection could show up in it unless I had been there when the hologram was made.

I reached out and pressed glass on both sides. It wasn't until my shoulders relaxed that I realized how much I had tensed.

There's no reason to get rattled, I thought. Then I went to look for Sadji.

Footsteps. I was sure of it.

I peered through the glittering shadows. Coming in here had been a mistake. I couldn't see anything. It was dark except for sparkles from a chandelier on the ceiling. The chandelier itself wasn't lit, but its crystals spun around and around, throwing out sparks of light. There had to be laser beams hitting them, but the scintillating lights made it impossible to see anything clearly.

More footsteps.

"Who's there?" I asked. "Who is that?"

The footsteps stopped.

"Sadji?" So far I had found no trace of my host in the entire house. But I had made other, much less welcome discoveries. The front doors had locked themselves. There was no way out of the mansion, no food, no usable holophones, not even a working faucet.

A man's accusing voice came through the glittering darkness. "You're Bridget Fjelstad, aren't you? The ballet dancer."

I tensed. "Who are you?"

He walked out of the shadows, a tall man with dark hair and big eyes who was a few years my junior. I recognized him immediately. Sadji kept his picture on the mantel in the New York penthouse.

"Allen?" I exhaled. "Thank goodness. I thought I was trapped in here."

"You are," Sadji's son said. "I've searched the house twice

since I got here this morning. There's no way out. Nothing even works except these damn crazy lights."

"You don't have a key?"

"Don't you?" The shifting light made his face hard to read, but there was no mistaking the hostility in his voice. "You are his girlfriend, aren't you?"

The last hour had made me wonder. I couldn't figure out what was going on. "I don't know." I regarded him. "Did you turn on these lights?"

"Don't flatter yourself." Although he spoke curtly, he almost sounded hurt rather than angry. "I have better things to do than make light shows for my father's money-grubbing mistress."

I stared at him. If anything, Sadji's intimidating wealth had almost scared me off. I stepped back, as if distance could soften Allen's words, and bumped into a horizontal bar at waist level. It felt like a ballet bar, what we held on to during exercises.

I ran my hand along the wood. Brackets fastened it to the wall. But how could a wall be here? More sparkles glittered beyond the surface than on this side. The glitters went back a long way. A *long* way.

It was a mirror. Of course. When I looked closer, I could make out my reflection. I knelt and laid my palms on the floor. It felt like wood too.

"What are you doing?" Allen asked.

I stood up. "We're in a dance studio."

He stared at me. "So Dad built his new love a new dance studio in his new house." He swallowed. "Nothing like throwing away the old and replacing it with the new."

I would have had to be a cement block not to hear the pain in his voice. I doubted it was easy being Sadji's son, the child of a woman who had divorced Sadji over ten years ago.

I spoke gently. "Allen, let's try again, okay? I don't want to be your enemy."

He regarded me. "And I don't want to be your son." Then he turned and walked away into the glittering shadows.

I was afraid to call him back, sure that my clumsiness with words would only make it worse.

Blue. Blue tights, blue leotard, blue skirt. Dance in blue, dance to heal. *Chassé, pas de bourrée, chaînés*, whirling through the glitters that sparkled even now, after I had found the regular lights. In defiance of being trapped here, I had left my hair free instead of winding it on top of my head. It flew in swirls around my body.

When I first joined the Ballet Theater ten years ago, I dieted obsessively, terrified they would decide they had made a mistake and throw me out. I ended up in a hospital. Anorexia nervosa; by giving my fear a name, the doctors showed me how to fight it. Three months later my hair started to fall out. A dermatologist told me that when I quit eating, my body let the hair die to conserve protein. There was no logic in my reaction, yet when I started to lose my hair I felt like I was losing my womanhood.

But hair grows back. It danced now as I danced, full and thick, whirling, whirling—

"Hey," Allen said. "You found the light."

I stopped in mid-spin, the stiff boxes of my pointe shoes letting me stand on my toes. Allen stood watching from the doorway.

"Doesn't that hurt your feet?" he asked.

I came down and walked over to him. "Not really. The shoes are reinforced to support my toes."

"Where did you get the dance clothes?"

I motioned to my ballet bag in the corner. "I carry that instead of a purse." Sadji had once asked me the same question in the same perplexed voice. I think he understood better when he realized that with performances, rehearsals, and technique classes, I often spent more time dancing even than sleeping.

Allen spoke awkwardly. "You . . . dance well."

The unexpected compliment made me blush. "Thanks." After a moment I added, "It helps me relax when I'm worried."

He grimaced. "Then you better get ready to do it again."

"What do you mean?"

"I'll show you."

We followed wide halls with blue rugs, climbed a marble stairway that curved up from the living room to the second story, and went down another hall. He finally stopped in a circular room. There was a computer console in one corner and hologram screens curving around the walls.

"Dad left a message here." Allen turned to the wall. "Replay six."

The holoscreens glowed, speckled swirls moving on their surfaces as the room lights dimmed.

Then, in the middle of the room, Sadji appeared.

The holo was perfect. From every angle it showed Sadji walking toward us, a handsome man in gray slacks and a white sweater, tall and muscular, his dark curls streaked with gray. If I hadn't known better, I would have sworn he was real.

And that was what had made Sadji Parker rich. He didn't invent the holomovie, he did the inventors one better. Twenty years ago, using genius, hard work, and luck, he had figured out who would first find practical ways to make holomovies that could be seen by a lot of people at once. Then he bought huge amounts of stock in certain companies at a time when they were barely surviving. In some he became the major shareholder. People said he was an idiot.

Now, two decades later, when those same companies dominated the trillion-dollar entertainment industry, no one called Sadji Parker an idiot.

Sadji stopped in front of us. "Hello. There is a holophone in the garage. Call me when you get there."

Then the image faded.

I stared at Allen. "That's it?"

"That's it."

"We can't get to the garage. We're locked in here."

He gritted his teeth. "I know that."

There had to be an explanation. "His business must have held him up."

Allen shook his head. "I talked to him yesterday. He was just getting ready to come up here."

I voiced the fear that had been building in me since I realized Sadji wasn't here. "Maybe he had a car accident."

Allen regarded me uneasily. "We should have seen something—broken trees, marks in the snow. That road is the only way here. If it happened off the mountain, *someone* would have seen. There's always traffic down there. We would know by now.

"The phones don't work."

"A helicopter would come for us."

I exhaled. Of course. If Sadji had been hurt, people would swarm all over this place looking for Allen. He was the heir, prince to the kingdom. Actually, glue and tape was a better description. His father was training him to run Parker Industries, protection against a stockholder panic if anything ever happened to Sadji.

But if Sadji hadn't been in an accident, where was he? I

couldn't believe he had locked us up on purpose. Yes, he could be ruthless. But that was in business. I had also seen what he hid under that hardened facade, the gentle inventor who wanted to curl up with his girlfriend and drink mulled wine.

"None of this makes sense," I said.

Allen pushed his hand through his hair. "It's like one of his holoscapes, but gone crazy."

"Holoscapes?"

"They're role-playing games." He smiled, and for the first time I realized how much he looked like his father. "It's fun. He makes up whole worlds, life-sized puzzles. Last week he sent me a mysterious note about how I should be prepared for adventure and intrigue on New Year's Eve." His smile faded. "But it's all haywire. He never messes with people's minds like this."

I motioned toward the door. "Let's try to get to the garage."

We went back to the rainbow foyer, but the front doors still refused to open. I clenched my teeth and threw my body against them, my ballet skirt whirling around my thighs as I thudded into the unyielding portals. Allen rammed them with me, again and again.

I wasn't sure how long we pounded the doors, but finally we gave up and sagged against them, looking at each other. I didn't know whether to be frightened for Sadji or angry. Was he in trouble? Or was this some perverse game he was playing at our expense?

We went back to the star room and stood looking out at the mountains. Our reflections watched us from the glass, breathing as we breathed. I sighed, leaned against the window—

And fell.

No! I felt a jet of air and heard Allen lunge. My skirt jerked as he grabbed it, but then it yanked out of his grip. My thoughts froze, refusing to believe I fell and fell—and hit a padded surface. A weight slammed into me. Struggling to breathe, I looked out at a blue void. Blue. Everywhere. I closed my eyes but the sky stayed like an afterimage on my inner lids.

The weight shifted off of me. "You okay?"

Allen? He must have fallen when he tried to catch me. I opened my eyes again, looking to where I knew, or fervently hoped, I would find the cliff.

It was still there. Emboldened, I looked around. We had landed on a ledge several yards below the window. Allen sat watching me with a face as pale as the clouds. Behind him the sky vibrated like a chasm of blue ready to swallow us if we so much as slipped in the wrong direction.

Then the ledge jerked, the sound of rock grating against rock shattering the dreamlike silence.

I sat bolt upright. "It's breaking."

Allen grabbed my arm. "Don't move.

Breathe, I told myself. Again. The ledge was holding. All we had to do was climb up to the window. Except that the wall was sheer rock. There was no way we could climb it.

Allen looked up at the window. "If you stand on my shoulders, I think you can reach it."

I nodded, knowing we had to try now. It was freezing out here. Soon we would be too stiff to climb anywhere. "If— when I get up there, I'll get a rope. So you can get up."

He pulled a medallion out of his pocket, a gold disk on a chain. "My Dad sent this with his note about New Year's Eve. It must do something. If I don't make it and you do, you might need it."

I stared at him, absorbing the horrible realization that he would die if the ledge broke before I got him help. Then I took the medallion and put the chain around my neck.

Suddenly the ledge lurched again, groaning as if it were in pain. I held my breath while it shifted. Finally, mercifully, it stopped.

Allen took a deep breath, then turned to the wall and braced himself on one knee like a runner ready to sprint. "Okay. Go."

Struggling not to think of what would happen if I fell, I got up and put my hands on his shoulders. But when I knelt on his back, I couldn't keep my balance well enough to stand up. I finally found a tiny fingerhold on the wall. It wasn't much to hang on to, but it let me hold myself steady while I maneuvered my feet on his shoulders. Then I stood slowly, my cheek and palms sliding against the wall.

"Ready," I said.

Allen grunted, and began to stand. The wall slid by, slid by—and then I was at the window. When he reached his full height, my chest was level with the opening. I could see the glass retracted inside the wall like a car window rolled down into its door.

I clutched a handful of carpet and tried to climb in. My feet slipped off his shoulders, leaving me balanced on my abdomen with only the top third of my torso inside the tower. My legs kicked wildly in the air outside as I started to slide out the window. Clenching my hands in the carpet, I heaved as hard as I could—and scrambled into the room. Then I jumped up and *ran*.

The only place I had seen a rope was in the kitchen. Running there seemed to take forever. What was Allen doing? What if he died because I didn't move fast enough?

Finally I reached the kitchen. I yanked the rope off its hook on the wall and took off again, running through the house. Halls, stairs, rooms. I reached the star room and skidded to a stop at the window.

Allen was still there.

I lowered an end of the rope out to him. As soon as he grabbed it, I sped to the doorway to the foyer. I looped the rope around both knobs on the door that opened into a point of the star—

The screech of breaking stone shrieked through the room, and the rope jerked through my hands so fast it burned off my skin. I clenched it tighter and it yanked me forward, slamming me into the door and slamming the door against the wall. Braced against the door, I struggled to keep my hold while the rope strained to snap out the window.

Then it went limp.

"Allen, *NO*. Don't let go!" I spun around—and saw him sprawled on the floor. I ran over and dropped down next to him. "Are you alive?"

He actually smiled. "I think so."

I laughed, then started to shake. He sat up and laid his hand on my arm. "It's okay, Bridget. I'm fine."

I took a breath. "The ledge broke?"

He nodded. "Come on. Let's get out of this whacked-out room."

We headed for the dance studio, the nearest place with no windows. I wanted to believe that open window had been an accident, some computer glitch. But then why had there been a holo of it? I hadn't even known you could create an instantaneous holomovie of reflections. It couldn't have happened by accident any more than the air jets had "accidentally" kept us from feeling the cold.

When we walked into the dance studio, an army of reflections faced us. Most studios had mirrors on one wall, so dancers could see to correct their steps. But this one had them on all four. The Bridget and Allen watching us in the front mirror also reflected in the one behind us, and that image reflected to the front again, and on and on.

The image of our backs also reflected back and forth, so looking in the mirror was like peering down an infinite hall of alternatively forward and backward-facing Bridgets and Allens. It was strange, especially with the chandelier's light show reflecting everywhere too.

Allen stood staring at the images. "He's gone nuts."

I knew he meant Sadji. "Maybe he's angry. Maybe he thinks what you said before, that I just want his money."

Allen glanced at me. "Do you?"

"Of course not."

"Everyone wants his money."

"Including you?"

"No." He hesitated. "There's only one thing I've ever wanted from my father. But it's a lot harder for him to give than money."

I touched his arm. "You mean everything to Sadji."

Allen regarded me warily. "A part of me still wants to believe he feels that way about Mother too." After a moment he exhaled. "I don't think she ever believed it, though. He was so absorbed in his work, day and night. It made her feel like she didn't exist for him."

That hit home. More than one man had said the same to me. It wasn't only that dance demanded such a huge part of my life. I also felt awkward and stupid with men, lost without the social education most people absorbed as they grew up. Ballet was all I had ever known. But as much as I loved dancing, I couldn't bear the loneliness. It was the only thing that had ever made me consider quitting. My success felt empty without someone to share it with.

Then I had met Sadji, who understood.

Allen was watching me. "Dad never used to much like Tchaikovsky's ballets. But after he saw you dance Aurora in *Sleeping Beauty* it was all he could talk about."

I had only done the part of Aurora once, as a stand-in for a dancer who was sick. "That was months before I met him."

He smirked. "It took him that long to get up the guts to introduce himself."

Sadji, afraid of me? I still remembered the night he sent me flowers backstage and then showed up at my dressing room, tall and broad-shouldered, his tousled hair curling on his forehead. He was about the sexiest man I had ever seen. "But he's always so sure of himself."

"Are you kidding? You scared the hell out of him. Bridget Fjelstad, the living work of art. What was it *Time* said about you? 'A phenomenon of grace and beauty.'"

I reddened. "They got carried away." I looked around the room, trying to find a less personal subject. "I guess Sadji didn't understand about dance studios. There shouldn't be mirrors on all four walls."

Allen shrugged. "My father never makes mistakes. Those other rooms had a purpose."

Something about his reflections bothered me. I pulled my attention back to him. "Purpose?"

"The display in the foyer distracted us when we came in so we didn't notice the doors locking." He thought for a moment. "The light it spilled into the star room must have hidden the lasers making holomovies of our reflections in the window."

"I didn't think it was possible to make realtime movies like that."

"The hard part would be the holograms." Suddenly he snapped his fingers. "The window, the one next to where we fell. I'll bet it's a thermoplastic."

His reflections kept distracting me. "Thermowhat?"

He grinned. "You can make holograms with it. The stuff deforms when you heat it up. And it erases! All you have to do is heat it up again. Last year Dad showed me a holomovie he made by hooking a sheet of it up to a thermal unit and a computer."

His enthusiasm reminded me of Sadji. "But wouldn't it have to change millions of times a second to make a movie?"

Allen laughed. "Not millions. Just thirty or so. The newer thermoplastics can do it easy."

I nodded, still trying to ignore his reflections. But they were driving me nuts.

"What's wrong?" Allen asked.

"I'm not sure. The mirrors." I gave him back the medallion, then tucked my hair down the back of my leotard. Then I did a series of *pirouettes*, turns where I lifted one foot to my knee and spun on my toe. I spotted my reflection, looking at it as long as possible for each turn, then whipping my head around at the end. It was how I kept my balance. Normally I could easily do double, even triple turns. But today I stumbled on almost every one.

Spin. Again. Something was wrong, something at the end of the turn. Spin. Again. Again—

"It's delayed!" I turned to Allen. "That's what's throwing me off. The reflection of my eyes comes back an instant later than my real eyes."

He whistled. "Another holomovie? Maybe whatever is making it can't keep up with you."

"Then where's the holoscreen?"

"It must be the mirror itself." He pulled me over to the doorway. But at the edge where it met the mirror, we could see the silvered glass.

"This looks normal," I said.

He motioned at the far wall. "Maybe the screen is behind that. A holo there would reflect here just like a real object."

We went over to the other mirror. I reached out—and my hand went through the "glass," vanishing into its own image. "Hah! You're right."

Then I walked through the holo.

I had one instant to register the screen across the room before I heard the whirring noise. Spinning around, I saw a metal wall shooting up from the floor. It hit the ceiling with a thud.

"Hey!" I pounded on the metal. "Allen? Can you hear me?"

A faint voice answered. "Just barely. Hang on. I'll find a way to get you out."

I looked around, wondering how many other traps Sadji had set for us. The room was small, with pine walls and a parquetry floor. Light came from two fluorescent bulbs covered by glass panels on the ceiling. A table and a chair stood in the center of the room. Actually, "table" was the wrong word. It was really a large metal box.

I scowled. If this was Sadji's idea of a "warm holiday" I hoped I never saw his vision of a cold one. Lights glittering like demented fireflies in an otherwise darkened room, mirrors to make the studio look huge—it was an ingeniously weird way to trick us into this prison. And when I had found the studio's normal lights instead of stumbling in here, the chandelier's display gave perfect cover for the laser beams that had to be crisscrossing the studio.

I went and sat in the chair, too disheartened to stand anymore.

"Hello," the table said. "I am Marley."

I blinked. Marley? "Can you let Allen and me out of the house?"

"Yes."

That sounded too easy. "Okay, do it."

"You must use your key."

"I don't have a key."

"Then I can't let you out."

That wasn't much of a surprise. "So why are you here?"

A panel slid open on top of the table, revealing a hole the shape of Allen's medallion. "I am the lock."

I put my thumb in the lock. "Here's the key."

A red laser beam swept over my hand. "No it's not."

Oh well. I hadn't really expected it to work. "How do you know what the key looks like?"

"I have a digitized hologram of it. By using lasers to create an interference pattern for whatever appears in the lock, I correlate how well it matches my internal record."

Could it really be this easy? A holo made from Marley's own hologram would correlate one hundred percent with its record. I grinned. "Good. Make a holo of the key inside the lock."

"I can't do that."

"Why not?"

"I have nothing to print a hologram on."

I motioned at the ceiling. "What about the light panels?"

"I have no way to print or etch glass."

"Oh." So much for my bright idea. "I don't suppose there's anything else here you could use."

Marley's laser scanned the walls, floor, ceiling, and me, avoiding my eyes. "Appropriate materials are available."

"You're kidding."

"I am incapable of kidding."

"What materials?"

"Your hair."

I tensed. "What do you mean, my hair?"

"It is of an appropriate thickness and flexibility to use in making a diffraction grating that can serve as a hologram."

"You want me to cut my hair?"

"This would be necessary."

"No." I couldn't.

Why not? I could almost hear the voice of the therapist who had treated my anorexia. *You're the same person with or with-*

out your hair. She had also said a lot of things I hadn't wanted to hear: *You've spent your life looking in mirrors to find flaws with yourself, striving for an impossible ideal of perfection. It's no wonder you've come to fear you're nothing without the beauty of form, of motion, of body that your profession demands.*

"Pah," I muttered. Then I got up and hefted the chair onto the table. By clambering up onto it I was able to reach the light panels. Both came off easily. I climbed down, put one panel on Marley, and smashed the other against the table.

Just do it, I thought.

So I did it. I used a glass shard and my hair fell on the floor in huge gold swirls. While I mucked up my hair, Marley's laser played over me. When I finished, a panel slid open on the table to reveal a cavity full of optical gizmos.

"Put the materials inside," Marley said.

As soon as I had stuffed the hair inside with the glass, Marley closed up the cavity again. Then I waited.

Alter what felt like forever Marley spoke. "The hologram is complete."

"Use it to make a holo inside the lock."

The glass slid up out of the table, looking like it had been melted and re-formed with my hair inside. The glassy gold swirls were so intricate it was hard to believe they came from hair. Marley shone its laser on it, using a wide beam, and a red medallion appeared in the lock. I moved my head and saw a reversed image of the medallion floating on the other side of the glass.

"Will you let us go now?" I asked.

"Yes. Mr. Parker is in the hallway north of this room. He appears to be looking for an entrance into here."

So Marley could see the rest of the mansion. It had probably monitored our actions all day. "Can you talk to him?"

"Yes."

"Good. Tell him I'm free, that I'll meet him in the garage. Then let me out of here and unlock the front door to the house."

Marley paused. "Done."

I heard the wall behind me move, and I turned in time to see it vanish into the floor. When I walked into the studio an infinity of shorn Bridgets stared back at me from the mirrors. I looked like I had stuck my finger in a light socket.

I surprised myself and laughed. Then I set off running.

The front door was wide open. I sped out into a freezing night, heading for the garage. It was also open, spilling light out into the darkness. I could see Allen inside seated in front of a computer console on the garage's north wall. There was a holophone next to the console, a dais about six inches high and three yards in diameter. Fiber optic cables connected it to the console and a holoscreen about ten feet high curved around the back of it.

Allen looked up as I ran over to him. "How did you—God, what happened to your hair?"

"I'll tell you about it later." I motioned at the holophone. "Did you reach your father?"

He shook his head. "There's no answer at his house. I'm trying his office."

A dour-sounding computer interrupted. "I have a connection." Then the booth lit up and Sadji appeared on the dais, sitting at the desk in his office. The curtains were open on the window behind him, showing a starlit sky.

"Allen." He smiled. "Hello."

Allen stared at him. "What are you doing there?"

"Some business came up." Sadji looked apologetic. "I'm afraid I can't make it until tomorrow afternoon."

Allen scowled. "Dad, what's going on?"

"Nothing. I just got held up."

"Nothing? What the hell do you mean, 'nothing'?"

Sadji frowned. "Allen, I've talked to you before about your language." He drummed his fingers on the desk. "I'm sorry I'm late. But matters needed attending to. I'll see you tomorrow." Then he cut the connection, the holo blinking out of existence as if he had dematerialized.

I stared at Allen. "That's *it*? After everything he put us through?"

"If you think that's bad, look at what else I found." He touched a button and light flooded into the garage from behind me. I turned around and saw lamps bathing the mansion with light. They showed the cliffs plunging down on the west side of the house in sharp relief. But instead of a sheer drop on the east, there was a snowy hill only a few feet below the level of the ledge where we had fallen: no holocliff, no holoclouds, just a nice, innocuous hill with pieces of the broken ledge lying half buried in the snow there.

I turned back to Allen. "I can't believe this."

"Well, I know one thing. I'm not going to stay here." He stood up. "He can spend Christmas with himself."

"This just doesn't seem like Sadji."

After a moment Allen's frown faded. "He's been late before. A lot, in fact. But he's always made sure we knew right away. And I've never known him to run a holoscape when he wasn't around to monitor it."

None of it made sense to me. "Do you know why this business trip had him so worried?"

He scowled. "Victor Marck went after Parker Industries again."

"Again?"

Allen nodded. "A few years ago he tried to take us over. Almost did it too. But Dad stopped him. He stopped him this time too." He grimaced. "Marck can't stand to lose. That's why he hates my father so much. Not only has Dad plastered him twice now, but both times he really whacked Marcksman Corporation in the process. Already this morning the Marcksman stock has dropped by a point. It's going to get a lot worse before it recovers."

I tried to catch my elusive sense of unease. "If we hadn't been caught in that holoscape, would you have thought anything was odd about our holocall to your father?"

"I doubt it. Why?"

"Maybe someone tampered with the computer."

For a moment Allen just looked at me. Then he said, "There's a way to find out." He turned back to the console and opened a panel, revealing a small prong. He pushed up his shirt sleeve and snapped the prong into a socket on the inside of his wrist.

I drew in a sharp breath. It was the first time I had seen someone make a cyber link with a computer. It meant Allen had a cybnet in his body, a network of fibers grown in the lab using tissue from his own neurons and then implanted in his body. Sadji had wanted to have it done, but he couldn't find any surgeon willing to perform so many high-risk operations on a man who had more power than some of the world's heads of state.

Allen had an odd look, as if he were listening to a distant conversation. Then I realized his "conversation" was with the computer.

"There's a virus," he suddenly said. "No, not a virus. A sleeper, a hidden program. It has an interactive AI code that emulates my father's personality." His forehead furrowed. "It also predicts how he'll move down to the smallest gesture, then works out the hologram each rendered figure of him would make if it were real. And it's *fast*. It can calculate over sixty interference patterns per second." He whistled. "It's making holo-movies of him."

I stared at him. "You mean that holocall was fake?"

"You got it." Allen swore. "The sleeper is also set up to record arrivals and departures. After you and I go it will destroy itself, leaving a record of our presence disguised to look like the operating system made it." He paused. "But whoever set it up didn't know about Dad's holoscape. When the sleeper identified me, it set off a part of the holoscape that was supposed to identify us on New Year's Eve."

This sounded stranger and stranger. "So those holos in the house weren't supposed to be going when we came?"

Allen nodded. "We weren't meant to fall out that window either, at least not how it happened. There are safety nets, but the routines that control their release aren't running." He regarded me. "According to Dad's calendar, he meant to be here when we arrived. And it's obvious he never meant for us to be imprisoned in the holoscape. It's just a game he had set up for New Years Eve."

I frowned. "Then he couldn't have written the sleeper."

Allen pulled the prong out of his wrist. "I know only two other people who have both the ability and the resources to do it: Victor Marck and me. And I sure didn't."

"Why would Marck want evidence to prove we were here?"

Allen paled. "Can you imagine what it would do to Parker Industries if both my father and I were suddenly, drastically, out of the picture? It would be a disaster." He gritted his teeth. "And I can guess whose vultures would be ready to come in and strip the remains clean."

I spoke slowly, dreading his answers. "How could he get both you and Sadji so thoroughly out of the picture?"

His voice shook. "Implicating me in my father's murder would do just fine."

"No. Allen, no." Sadji *dead*? I couldn't believe it.

"We've been fighting Marck for years. I've seen how his mind works." Allen took hold of my shoulder. "How do you think it would look: you and I come here, spend the night, then leave. A few days later my father's body is found on the grounds, time of death placed when we were here or not long after we left."

I swallowed. "No one would believe we did it."

"Why not? Who has a better motive than me? I stand to inherit everything he owns. The greedy son and beautiful seductress murder the holomovie king for Christmas. It would splash across every news report in the country."

"Sadji's alive. *Alive*." I put up my hands, wanting to push away his words. "No one would dare hurt him while we were here. The computer would record their presence just like ours."

Allen had a terrible look, as if he had just learned he lost someone so important to him that he couldn't yet absorb it. "Not if they left him to die before we came. They could have used a remote to turn on the system after they were gone."

"But Sadji's not *here*. We've been through the entire house."

Sweat ran down Allen's temples. "The damn computer keeps telling me he's in his office."

"Marley!"

"What?"

"It's a sensor Sadji set up for the holoscape. It knew exactly where you and I were."

Allen grabbed my arm. "Show me."

We ran back to the holoscreen room in the dance studio. My holo of the medallion was still in the lock, keeping the room open.

"Marley." I struggled to keep my voice calm. "Can you locate Sadji Parker?"

"Yes," Marley said.

I almost gasped in relief. "Where is he?"

"I can't tell you."

"This isn't a game. You have to tell us!"

"I can't do that."

Allen slammed his fist against the wall. "Damn it, tell us!"

"You must supply me with the proper sequence of words," Marley said.

"Words?" I looked around frantically. "What words?"

"The ones printed on the key." Marley sounded smug, like a game player who had just pulled a particularly clever move. Then it closed a panel over the holo medallion, hiding it from our sight.

I whirled to Allen. "The medallion! What's written on it?"

He had already pulled it out of his pocket. " 'Proverbs 10:1,' " he read. " 'A wise son makes a father glad.' "

"That is the correct sequence," Marley said. "Sadji Parker is located in storage bin four under the floor in the northeast corner of the garage."

Allen grabbed my arm, yanking me along as we ran back to the garage. He hurled away the rug in the corner and heaved on the handle of a trapdoor in the ground there. When it didn't open, he ran across the room and grabbed an axe off a hook on the wall. Then he sped back and smashed the axe into the trapdoor, raising it high and slamming it down again and again, its blade glittering in the light.

The door splintered, disintegrating under Allen's attack. He dropped the axe and scrambled down a ladder into the dark below. As I hurried after him, I heard him jump to the floor. An instant later, light flared around us. I jumped down and whirled to see Allen standing under a bare light bulb, his arm still outstretched toward its chain as he looked around the bin, a small, dusty room with a few crates—

"There!" I broke into a run, heading for the crumpled form behind a crate.

He lay naked and motionless, his eyes closed, his mouth gagged, his wrists and ankles bound to a pipe that ran along the seam where the floor met the wall. Ugly bruises showed all over his body. Dried blood covered his wrists and ankles, as if he had struggled violently against the leather thongs that bound him.

I dropped on my knees next to his head. "Sadji?" In the same instant, Allen said, "Dad?"

No response.

I undid his gag and pulled wads of cloth out of his mouth, trying desperately to remember the CPR class I had taken. "Please be alive," I whispered, tears running down my face.

Slowly, so slowly, his lashes lifted.

I heard a choked sob from Allen. Sadji looked up at us, bleary-eyed. As Allen untied him, I drew Sadji's head into my lap and stroked the matted hair off his forehead. He tried to speak, but nothing came out.

"It's all right," I murmured. "We'll take care of you now."

It seemed like forever before they all left, the police and the doctors and the nurses and the multitude of Parker minions

buzzing around the mansion. But finally Allen and I were alone
with Sadji. No, not alone; the bodyguards hulking discreetly in
the background would never again be gone, neither for Sadji
nor for Allen.

Sadji sat back in the cushions next to me on the couch,
dressed in jeans and a pullover. He had refused to go to the hospital, but at least he was resting now, his furiously delirious attempts to go after Victor Marck calmed by food, water, and
medicine. His face was pale, his wrists and ankles bandaged,
his voice hoarse. But he was alive, wonderfully alive.

He watched Allen and me. "You two are a welcome sight."

I took his hand. "Do you think they'll be able to convict
Marck?"

Sadji's face hardened. "I don't know. That hired thug he had
waiting up here for me will be out of the country by now." He
spoke quietly. "But no matter what happens, Marck will pay a
price far worse, to him, than any conviction."

Allen regarded him. "The only thing that could be worse to
Marck than the electric chair would be losing Marcksman Corporation."

Although Sadji smiled, it was a harsh expression far different than the gentleness he usually showed me. "He'll lose a lot
more than Marcksman. The publicity from his arrest will finish
him even if he's not convicted."

I didn't ask who would be the driving force behind the public hell Victor Marck was about to experience, or who would be
there to scavenge the remains of his empire. All I could see was
Sadji lying beaten and bound, dying of exposure and thirst.

Sadji looked at me, his expression softening. "When I
opened my eyes and saw you, it was . . . appreciated."

Allen snorted. "An angel rescues the man from a horrible
death and the best he can come up with is that he 'appreciated'
it." He leaned toward his father. "I'm going to the kitchen to get
some of that pizza your Parker people brought us. I'll be gone
for a while."

Sadji scowled at him. But after Allen left, he laughed. "My
son has the subtlety of a sledgehammer." He paused, clearing
his throat with an awkwardness incongruous to the self-assured
man I knew. "I was going to wait until Christmas. But perhaps
now is appropriate."

I regarded him curiously. "For what?"

"I know the prospect of having Allen for a stepson may look daunting. But he really can be pleasant when he wants."

I smiled. "That sounds like a marriage proposal."

He spoke quietly. "It is."

I tried to imagine marrying Sadji. I loved him, and he understood about my dancing. But was I ready for the life he led? "I have to think about it."

For a moment he looked excruciatingly self-conscious. Then he covered it with a glower. "Why," he growled, "do women always feel compelled to say that?"

I slid closer and put my arms around his neck, more grateful than I knew how to say that he was alive, growls and all. "Merry Christmas, Sadji."

"It's not Christmas."

"It's close. Two more days."

"Are you going to marry me?"

I kissed him. "Yes."

His face relaxed into a smile. We were still kissing each other when Allen came back with the pizza.

INTRODUCTION TO "TELEABSENCE"

by Michael A. Burstein

"TeleAbsence" had its genesis in a panel I was on at the Arisia science fiction convention in January 1994. At the time, I was trying to sell stories to the science fiction magazines, and not succeeding. But I had received my first personal rejection letter, a short note from Stanley Schmidt at *Analog*, which inspired me to keep sending him stories until he bought one.

I was in graduate school studying physics, and thus had managed to convince the Arisia committee to put me on their science program. So at noon on January 22, 1994, I found myself discussing "2001: Image and Reality" with Hal Clement, Jeff Hecht, Toni Lay, James Turner, and Victoria Warren. The premise of the panel was to make predictions of what the world would really be like in the year 2001, and I believe it was James Turner who triggered the first idea behind my story.

"By the year 2001," he said, "everyone will have an e-mail address." He went on to say that everyone would also have free access to the so-called Information Superhighway.

The other panelists tended to agree, with two exceptions: Toni Lay and me. She pointed out that the "free" information out there was *not* free—at the very least, you needed to be able to afford a computer, a modem, a telephone line, and an Internet provider. I echoed the sentiment, but James disagreed with us, saying that such things would be cheap by 2001. In the end, convinced of my position, I decided to make my point in a science fiction story.

Of course, the Internet wasn't science fiction anymore, so I had to extrapolate a little. I created the idea of a disadvantaged boy (named Tony in honor of Toni Lay) who lacked access to the school of the future, a Virtual Reality (VR) classroom in which students from all over the country could interact with each other and with their teacher. I decided that the VR school had been developed in order to solve the problem of violence in schools; if the children aren't actually in physical proximity, they can't harm each other. The boy, who I made a black student living in Harlem, New York City, hates his decrepit home school, and one day finds a pair of spex and sneaks into a private Telepresence School. After enjoying a morning of learning and fun, he is found out . . .

I wrote a version of this story and sent it to Stan Schmidt. By happy coincidence, I got the story back from him on the same weekend as the Lunacon convention in March 1994, when I had a chance to have lunch with Stan and a few other people. Stan hadn't quite rejected the story; he had typed up a one-page note explaining the problems in the story and had enclosed a few newspaper clippings about kids sneaking into schools in better districts. But nowhere in the note did he explicitly ask me to revise the story. So I asked him at Lunacon if he wanted to see another version, and he laughed and said yes.

I took a few weeks to expand the story a bit, involving the character of the teacher more, a woman sympathetic to my protagonist's plight. But I got the story back from Stan again, with a note that it was not quite there yet and still needed work.

By this point, I had been accepted to the 1994 Clarion Science Fiction and Fantasy Writer's Workshop in East Lansing, Michigan. I wrote back to Stan, saying that I was going to Clarion and that I'd have the story for him in publishable form by the time I returned.

By an interesting twist of fate, the instructor for the first week, John Kessel, chose my story as one of the two the class critiqued on the first day. Since they ended up critiquing the older version, I also made a point of getting feedback on the newer version from Howard Waldrop, who was the instructor during the fourth week of the workshop. For over an hour, we discussed the problems in my story and improvements I could make. By the time we finished our session, I had two pages of notes on how to rewrite the story.

Clarion ended on July 30. I finished a third version of the story in late August and mailed it to *Analog*. In October, Ian Randal Strock, who was the magazine's Associate Editor, called me to congratulate me on my first acceptance. "TeleAbsence" appeared in the July 1995 issue, published right around the time of my wedding. A second sale to *Analog*, inspired by the circumstances of my first sale, occurred almost right afterward, and "Sentimental Value" appeared in the October 1995 issue.

And then "TeleAbsence" won the Analytical Laboratory Award, got nominated for a Hugo Award, and eventually won me the 1997 John Campbell Award for Best New Writer.

It's been interesting to see how different the world has become since the story was published. For a brief time in the late 1990s, with the "dot com" boom, it appeared as if my predictions of a poorer world were off base. Now, as I write this essay in 2001, the idea of everyone having an e-mail address seems much more realistic—but so does my 1995 prediction of a slower economy. And, despite the fact that the idea of distance learning has made many inroads, we're still dealing with the issues of violence in schools—as the students of Columbine High School in Littleton, Colorado, can attest.

Occasionally, people have asked me what happened to Tony and have suggested that I revisit him, find out what he's up to and expand "TeleAbsence" into a novel. I've considered it, but not yet. Maybe someday.

TELEABSENCE

by Michael A. Burstein

TONY put on the spex and scrunched his hands into the tight datagloves. He pushed a button on the right earpiece, and the world around him changed.

He had been sitting in his little room, with torn clothes scattered about, a broken dresser, and a dirty window that looked out onto a brick wall. Now he found himself in a classroom. The floor was clean and the walls were a bright yellow. Tony counted fifteen desks arranged in a roomy and orderly fashion, fewer desks than he had ever seen in a classroom before.

Tony had jacked in at a few minutes before nine so he'd have a chance to explore before anyone else showed up, and he started with the windows. These windows weren't broken, like those at his own school, and it looked as if morning sunlight actually streamed in from a clear blue sky. He opened one and stuck his head out to see an incredibly large playground a few stories down; nothing like the old broken-down one in his neighborhood, where Mom never let him go, even in the middle of the day. Not that Tony was about to do so, ever; he was just as scared of the gunfire as his mom was.

Tony pulled his head back into the room and continued exploring. Walking around felt strange, since he could feel his legs not moving as he sat in his room. And yet, in this classroom he was standing, and moving his hands around caused the rest of his body to follow. He traced the edge of the room, sliding along the screenboard at the front with the alphabet printed above it, and along the walls on the side, which were decorated with the artwork of the school's students. There was a calendar, set to this month, September. He also noticed a seating chart, with each student's name in different handwriting.

He came to a mirror in the back corner of the room, and stopped short. Staring back at him wasn't his deep brown face and curly black hair that was all too familiar, but an image of a white kid with blond hair, dressed in a button-down shirt and slacks. The spex and gloves didn't appear in the mirror either, just sparkling brown eyes and smooth pink hands. Tony moved his arms and face around, and noticed that the mirror image did so, too. *No wonder the gloves are so small*, Tony thought, *this kid has got to be at least a year younger than me. Maybe this isn't a sixth grade class—*

A sharp buzz startled Tony and he jumped. At the front of the room appeared a pretty white woman who looked as old as Tony's teachers, but she wasn't scowling the way Tony's teachers always did. Instead, she was smiling. Despite that, Tony felt scared.

"Good morning, Andrew," she said. "I'm surprised to see

you here early." Her voice was soothing to Tony's ears, and he calmed down. There was no way she would figure out that he wasn't Andrew; the mirror had shown him exactly as he appeared in this virtual classroom.

"Hello, Miss . . ." Tony trailed off. He knew that he had taken Andrew's place, but he had no idea what the teacher's name was.

"Why *are* you here early? You're usually one of the last to jack in."

"Ummm . . . well . . ." Tony looked around as he stalled, and spotted a nameplate on the desk. Fortunately, it was facing toward him.

"Miss Ellis, I just felt like taking a look around before we started." Tony's voice sounded like his own to his ears, which worried him. Would Miss Ellis be able to hear that he wasn't Andrew?

Apparently not. "Okay, Andrew, though you won't have much time." She looked at her watch. "In just a minute—"

Another buzz, and this time a cute girl popped in, already seated at a desk. "Good morning, Miss Ellis."

"Good morning, Sheryl."

"Hi, Andrew!"

Tony wasn't sure how to respond, but it seemed safest to say little. "Hi, Sheryl."

Sheryl opened her mouth to speak, but was interrupted by another buzz. The ritual repeated itself over the next few minutes; another kid popped in each time, some already sitting, some at the door, and one or two in the corners, until there were fourteen other students. Most were white, although he saw two who were black and three who he thought were Chinese. Tony noticed how happy they all looked, as they milled about talking to each other. Tony wanted to mingle, but was afraid, and so he stayed off to the side, studying the seating chart. Andrew was assigned to the front row, second seat. At least he would know where to sit when class began.

He traced the name of the student he was replacing, Andrew Drummond. Now he had a full name to attach to the spex.

Another buzz, deeper and longer, startled Tony, and a chill went through him. What if that was Andrew jacking in? He would ruin everything, and everyone would know that Tony was a fake! Tony looked around, scared, but didn't see anyone that resembled the kid in the mirror.

"Okay, class," said Miss Ellis, "it's nine o'clock. Time to begin." So that's what that different buzz meant. Tony relaxed into his—into Andrew's—seat. As long as he had Andrew's spex, he realized, he *was* Andrew, and there was no way that the real Andrew could pop in and prove otherwise. Tony wished he could be Andrew all the time, but at least he could be Andrew for the school day. Then he'd have to return to his own life. For the first time, he dreaded the final bell that would go off at three o'clock.

Miss Ellis began the class by taking attendance. Tony remembered to respond when he heard Andrew's name, which was second, right after Melissa Connor, who sat to his left. Once Miss Ellis noted that all were present, she told the class to take out their homework from last night.

At first, Tony didn't know what to do. He felt a lump in his throat as he realized that he couldn't take out last night's homework since he wasn't really Andrew. He knew the punishment he could suffer for not having his homework with him, and he started to tremble.

Then he noticed what Melissa was doing. She pushed some button on her desk and her computer screen flashed, and now she was waiting patiently. *Maybe the homework is also done in virtual space,* Tony thought, and he looked at the buttons on his desk. Sure enough, among all the letters and numbers of the keyboard there was a button labeled "HOMEWORK." Tony pushed it with relief.

His screen blinked, and a message came up: "Please enter your homework password."

Oh no! I don't know Andrew's password! Tony thought. Now what? Maybe Miss Ellis wouldn't notice if he just sat there looking intently at the screen. If he kept his head down, perhaps she wouldn't call on him. Then he wouldn't be found out.

"Melissa? Please tell us how you did the first problem."

The first problem was an easy math problem, but Melissa got it wrong. Tony braced himself for the explosion, but it didn't come.

"That's okay," said Miss Ellis instead. She worked out the problem on the screenboard in front and showed Melissa where her mistake had been. Tony was shocked. She hadn't yelled at Melissa for being wrong, and Melissa hadn't made any rude comments back or started crying.

"Andrew? Would you please explain the next problem?"

Bad luck. It looked as if Miss Ellis went through the class alphabetically when going over homework, and naturally that meant Andrew was next. But Tony knew he couldn't go over the next problem. What could he do?

"Andrew? Is there a problem?"

Tony looked up. Miss Ellis wasn't frowning, and she didn't seem upset at all. She hadn't yelled at Melissa for being wrong; maybe Tony could pretend to be having a problem as Andrew and not get yelled at.

"Yes, Miss Ellis. Ummm . . . I forgot my password."

"Oh, is that all? You should have said something." Miss Ellis came over to his desk, pushed a few keys, and accessed the assignment for him. It made sense, he realized, that she would be able to do that.

The homework that Andrew had done came up on the screen. Feeling relieved, Tony puzzled out the solution to the second problem, which fortunately Andrew had done correctly. Tony treasured the "Very good" that Miss Ellis said in his direction, even if it was followed by "Andrew."

The class continued throughout the morning, with Miss Ellis going from subject to subject. A little math, some English, a bit of art. Tony especially enjoyed the art, as being in a virtual classroom enabled him to create beautiful pictures almost by just thinking of them. He could paint pictures in three dimensions, and he even created a collage using video images that moved and sound effects that came from a classroom library of such things. It almost got him discovered, because apparently Andrew was not too keen on this subject, and Miss Ellis became suspicious of "Andrew's" newfound enthusiasm for light sculpting. But it turned out all right; Miss Ellis was actually more pleased than suspicious to see Andrew taking an interest.

A little after eleven o'clock the buzz sounded, announcing the lunch period. Miss Ellis and the students jacked out one by one. Tony envied the other students; he imagined them in comfortable homes, sitting at tables with steaming hot plates piled up with food.

Tony himself didn't jack out. He spent the entire forty minutes in the virtual classroom, relishing every minute he was there. He played with his desk computer, using it to create more works of art and to read history textbooks that changed the

words they used when Tony punched in that he didn't understand something. He didn't mind the stomach rumbles he felt
near the end of the period; he was used to them.

"Now, class, we're going to learn a little geography. Who
can tell me what this is?" Miss Ellis pushed a button at the top
of the blackboard, and a holographic map appeared, floating
halfway between her desk and the class. Tony recognized it and
raised his hand. So did most of the class.

Miss Ellis called on Tony. "Yes, Andrew?"

"It's the United States." Tony thought it was the most beautiful map he had ever seen. It shimmered in the air, floating in
and out of insubstantiality. The features—states, cities, mountains, and rivers, just to name a few—were displayed in many
different intense colors. There was a vibrancy to this map
which made it more real than any flat map Tony had seen in his
own classroom.

"Very good, Andrew. Well, class, today I want to introduce
you to the various parts of our country, and I think the best way
of doing that is to have you do it for us. Who wants to be first
to tell us where they're from?"

The girl sitting to Tony's right raised her hand. "Janice?"

"I live in Florida, Miss Ellis, in Neptune Beach, near Jack-
sonville. But I just moved there from San Francisco."

"Can you point out both places on the map?"

Janice punched a few keys on her desk computer, and a
small spot in northeastern Florida lit up in green. A second
later, so did a spot in northern California.

"Very good! Someone else?"

One of the Asian girls raised her hand. "Sandra?"

Sandra hit a few keys and a spot near Washington, D.C.,
turned green. "I live in Silver Spring, Maryland."

Miss Ellis continued going through the class, and the students became very enthusiastic about it. "I'm in East Lansing,
Michigan!" shouted a kid named Brian, who had just moved
from Los Alamos, New Mexico. "I live near Boston!" shouted
another. Each student's hometown was lit up, either by Miss
Ellis or by the student.

Tony felt scared. He lived in Harlem, in New York City, and
desperately wanted to volunteer that information, but he
couldn't. He was supposed to be Andrew, and he didn't know
exactly where Andrew lived. He knew it was out on Long Is-

land, because the car with the spex had displayed Long Island license plates. But where on Long Island?

And how did the other students use the computer to light up the map?

The next one to go was Sheryl, who had been the first student to pop in after Tony. She used her computer to light up Suffolk County, on Long Island. "I live in Port Jefferson," she said, "right near Andrew."

"Andrew, would you like to locate your hometown as well?" asked Miss Ellis. "You could come up to the map since it's already lit up."

Feeling trapped, Tony ran up to the map, stabbed at Suffolk County with his—Andrew's—finger, and sprinted back to his seat.

Miss Ellis went through the rest of the class. All over the map, the hometowns were lit up in green. "Who would like to talk about their hometown first?"

Tony felt Miss Ellis' eyes staring right at him, and worried that she might call on him. Her eyes passed over him, though, and she called on Brian. Tony exhaled a breath that he didn't realize he had been holding.

Since he knew Los Alamos better than East Lansing, Brian chose to talk about his original hometown instead of where he was now. Tony barely paid attention as Brian talked about the joys of small-town life and then displayed some pictures from a family photo album that he was able to pull up using his computer. Miss Ellis then discussed the arid mountainous area where the town was located, and how there had been a scientific laboratory there until the year 2010.

Janice went next, and again Tony was too scared to pay attention. Janice described San Francisco, and, possibly still thinking about lunch, mentioned the delicious seafood and sourdough bread. Miss Ellis talked about other things, such as the earthquakes that San Francisco had experienced, and the Golden Gate Bridge, which she said had been one of the longest suspension bridges in the country until the earthquake just last year that destroyed it. She showed three-dimensional video images of the earthquake, and even made the classroom shake up a bit, so the students could experience a bit of what an earthquake was like.

Janice continued, "But now I live in Florida, and it's really nice, except it gets awful hot in the summer. But let me show you!" With that, Janice hit a few keys, and on the screenboard appeared a picture of a large white house. "See! There's my front yard!"

"Oh, yeah?" said Brian. Using his computer, he erased the picture of Janice's house. A few seconds later, a picture of Brian appeared, wearing spex and sitting in some sort of large black chair with arms that closed in front. Tony felt uneasy, looking at that picture.

Brian waved his hand in class, and so did the Brian in the picture. "See!" he said. "That's me in real time!"

"Oh, yeah?" said Janice. "Well, watch—"

"Janice! Brian!" Miss Ellis interrupted. *Oh no*, thought Tony, *now they're going to get it*. He braced himself for the shouting. Instead, the two students each mumbled an apology.

"It's okay," Miss Ellis said. "I understand why you're excited, I just didn't want you to get out of hand. You see, class, one of the nice things about being here is that we all jack in from different places. Each of you can learn from one another about the great diversity we have in this country. Here you are, telling each other about your hometowns, even though you may live thousands of miles away from your classmates. I figure it will also give you a chance to find out more about each other, since it is so early in the school year."

Sheryl raised her hand, which worried Tony. "Couldn't people do that before?"

"Well, yes," Miss Ellis replied, "but it wasn't so immediate. In fact, you're experiencing something now that in the past only college students could usually experience. And they had to travel physically to one common location to share their backgrounds, which was much more expensive and time-consuming. You don't need to do that at all."

Miss Ellis turned to Tony. "Andrew, since Sheryl asked a question, why don't you tell us about your common hometown of Port Jefferson?"

Tony looked down at his desk. His stomach felt queasy. If only Sheryl hadn't brought attention to herself, and then to him as well. Or if only Sheryl hadn't been here in the first place. Then he could make up anything he wanted about Port Jefferson, and Miss Ellis would never know. But Sheryl would see right through any lies he might tell, and anyway, Tony didn't like to lie.

But wasn't that what he was doing right now, pretending to be Andrew?

"Andrew? Are you okay?"

"Yes, Miss Ellis. I—"

Tony was interrupted by a sharp buzz, and he looked up. At the front of the classroom appeared an older man with thick gray hair. He headed straight for Tony, a scowl on his face, and Tony looked down again, in fear.

He heard Miss Ellis speak. "Mr. Drummond, what are you doing here?"

The man didn't answer Miss Ellis. He went right up to Tony and said, "Give them back! They're mine!"

Tony shivered. It had been too good to last; now he was going to be found out. This man was obviously Andrew's father, come to get the spex back.

"Mr. Drummond!" said Miss Ellis, with an angry tone that was familiar to Tony. "I would appreciate it if you would not interrupt my class to talk with your son! Can't this wait until later?"

"This is not me—I mean, this is not my son!" Mr. Drummond shouted.

There was silence for a moment. Tony felt Miss Ellis move next to him and Mr. Drummond. "What's going on?" she asked.

"This kid stole my—I mean, my son's spex!"

Tony looked up at Miss Ellis, and saw her smile. Facing Mr. Drummond, she said, "That's you, isn't it, Andrew?"

For the first time since he appeared, "Mr. Drummond" looked uncomfortable. "Ummm, yeah, Miss Ellis. I had to use Dad's spex to jack in. Whoever this is—" he pointed at Tony— "stole my own spex."

"Ah-ha. Andrew, go home. I'll take care of this."

"Ummm. You won't tell my dad, will you? I don't want him to know that I've been careless."

"No, I won't tell him. Now go. I'll contact you later."

The image of Andrew's father vanished, and Miss Ellis turned to Tony. He was on the verge of tears.

"Well, young man, who are you?"

He sniffled, and whispered, "My name's Tony."

"Tony? Did you steal Andrew's spex?"

"Yes." He could barely hear himself.

Miss Ellis sighed. "Why?"

Tony looked up into Miss Ellis' eyes, and it all started pouring out of him. "I just wanted to go to a good school, one where I wouldn't be afraid, where the teachers and kids are nice, where I don't have to worry about guns or drugs or being beaten up or—" Tony stopped. He felt as if everyone was staring at him. They probably were, but it was too late to take back anything he had said.

"I found the spex in Manhattan, Miss Ellis. I know it was wrong, but I didn't care. I just wanted to go to school somewhere *nice*. I'm sorry." He started to sob.

"Class, I'll be back in a moment. No one jack out."

Miss Ellis tapped at the air to the side of her face, and the classroom around Tony vanished.

Tony found himself alone with Miss Ellis in a much smaller room furnished with a desk, chair, and sofa. He had been sitting at a desk; now he was standing. He was still crying, though. He wasn't worried that Miss Ellis would beat him, since she really couldn't hurt him through the spex. She might yell at him instead, but when she spoke her voice was calm.

"Tony, I've brought us here so we could talk alone for a few minutes, away from the rest of the class. I hope you don't mind, but I didn't think you'd want to continue talking about this in front of everyone."

Tony nodded, and wiped away the tears on his face using his sleeve. He didn't want to get the datagloves wet. "Thanks."

Miss Ellis sat on the chair, and motioned Tony to the sofa. As he sat down, he spotted his image in a mirror he hadn't seen before. He still looked like Andrew.

"Tony, why don't we start with you telling me about yourself, like where you live and what your full name is."

"I'm not going to get into trouble, am I?" he asked.

Miss Ellis smiled. "No, you're not, Tony. I want to help you."

Tony told Miss Ellis about his life; in particular, about the horrors of his awful school. He was surprised to discover that Miss Ellis also lived in Manhattan, but downtown, below the fence. When Miss Ellis found out that Tony was black, she made some adjustments and asked Tony to check his appearance in the mirror. Tony was surprised to see a black kid facing back. It still didn't look like him, so he told Miss Ellis more about his real appearance. He watched as Miss Ellis changed the image again, until it more closely resembled his true appearance.

When Tony was satisfied, Miss Ellis gave him a long hard look. "Tony, I'm not going to tell you how wrong you were to steal the spex, because I can see how bad you already feel." She paused. "And, frankly, I agree with what you did."

Tony was surprised. The teacher thought it was okay that he stole something?

"I guess it's because I remember when those spex you're wearing were first developed. They were praised as being the first step to solving the problem of violence in schools — if the students weren't physically in one real place, they wouldn't be able to hurt each other."

"Do you mean that I was supposed to have the spex in the first place? Is that why you approve?"

"Well, I don't really approve of the stealing. But I understand. After all, Tony, you and kids like you were the main reason they were invented in the first place. But I guess people forgot that it's not enough to develop the proper technology. You've got to fund it too."

Miss Ellis stood up and walked across the room, her back to Tony. She took a deep breath, and then turned around to face him.

"Tony? Would you like to stay in telepresence school? Not have to go back to your old school ever again?"

Tony's eyes opened wide and he let out a breath he hadn't realized he had been holding. "You mean I can stay?" He tried to keep the eagerness out of his voice.

"Well, not as Andrew. This is going to be difficult to arrange. Technically, you can't come to telepresence school unless you can afford it, and obviously you can't. But we might be able to sneak you in."

Tony couldn't believe what he had just heard. "Sneak me in? Isn't that as bad as my taking a pair of spex?"

"Yes and no. I might be able to work it out so that you have your own set of spex, and can attend my class on a regular basis. We'd have to get you a full simulator too, if you want to participate in outdoor games. But you won't be able to attend as yourself."

"You just said I can't be Andrew. I don't understand."

Miss Ellis sighed. "Tony, I believe you have a right to be here, as much right as any other student. But I personally can't afford to pay for you. And I suspect that your parents can't either."

"My mom. We don't know where Dad is."

"Your mother, then. The problem, Tony, is that the computer that runs telepresence school keeps track of every student through the spex, and so it knows how to charge you. Your little visit today cost Andrew's family some money."

This made Tony feel worse. "Then maybe I shouldn't be here at all."

"No, Tony, you can be here. I have a — a friend who can do something to a pair of spex so you won't be charged, but the cost of attending will be spread out onto all the other students. That way, no one student will be charged too much for you, and you'll be able to attend the school."

"Isn't that stealing?"

Miss Ellis thought a moment. "Technically, yes, but the theft is so small and spread out that no one would notice. Besides, it's the only way I can arrange it.

"So, Tony, would you like to attend telepresence school?"

"Yes, Miss Ellis, very much," he whispered. After all, he told himself, it couldn't be completely wrong if the teacher was willing to do it.

"Okay, but we can't let you enroll as Tony, because the other students know who you are."

"Does that mean I have to be white?"

"No, Tony, of course not. No one else has seen your real appearance but me, so you can look like yourself if you wish. That's no problem. But we'll have to call you by a different name, and probably pretend that you live somewhere other than Manhattan. Will that be okay?"

"Fine. Ummm . . . Miss Ellis?"

"Yes?"

"Why are you doing this?"

Miss Ellis frowned, and for a moment Tony worried that he had just said the wrong thing. But then she smiled. "Never mind, Tony, it isn't something you need to worry about. In the meantime, you'd better give me your phone number and go home. Tell your mother I'll call her tonight."

"Excellent work, Howard."

"Thank you, Miss Ellis," Tony said. For three months now he had been enrolled at the telepresence school, in the same class that he had visited using Andrew's spex. Tony now had spex of his own, along with a full simulator, and had begun to strike up a few friendships with the other students, including, oddly enough, Andrew.

Of course, they didn't think of him as Tony. He was "Howard," from a middle-class family living in Forest Hills on Long Island. Forest Hills had once been a part of the city, but was now a neighborhood in one of the three independent boroughs, a place where it was reasonable to assume that a family had the money to send a child to telepresence school.

At first, Tony felt strange pretending to be from someplace where he was not. But Miss Ellis had brought him through a virtual representation of the neighborhood before bringing him into the school, and fortunately, none of the other students had tried to trip him up with questions about his hometown.

Which was good, because Tony was happy here. He couldn't remember ever having been happier.

"Howard? Are you with us?"

"Oh, sorry, Miss Ellis, I was just thinking." Tony felt his cheeks flush as the rest of the students turned around to stare at him in his back row seat. Fortunately, no one could see his embarrassment in the virtual classroom.

"As I was saying, it's time for playground recess, so everyone get ready." With that, Miss Ellis tapped at the air next to her ear, and the class was virtually transported to the playground "outside." They did this every day of school, but it never stopped amazing Tony. He always felt a warm sun and cool breeze playing against his face, which seemed perfectly real, even though he knew it had to be an illusion.

He closed his eyes and took in a deep breath; the stale air reminded him that he was really in the simulator back in his apartment. As he was about to breathe out, he felt someone tap him on the hand.

"You're it!" He opened his eyes; it was Andrew who had tagged him, and who was now running as fast as he could go. Tony usually played with Andrew and Janice anyway, so he smiled and raced toward Andrew as fast as he could go, on virtual legs.

They played tag and ran around for most of the recess period, and near the end, the three friends sat down on a bench to rest up. It would soon be time to return to the classroom. Janice took a minute to catch her breath, then jacked out to get a glass of water, leaving Tony and Andrew alone.

"Boy, that was fun!" Andrew said.

"Yeah, it sure was."

"Listen, Howard, I've been thinking. You live in Forest Hills, right?"

"Ummm . . . yeah. I do."

"Well, that's practically next door to me! Why can't we get together in the real world?"

Uh-oh. Tony was afraid that Andrew would suggest something like this. "Wouldn't it be too difficult? I mean, you don't *really* live next door."

"So?"

"So it would be a problem for me to come out to Port Jefferson."

"Hey, is that all? My Dad can drive me to your house, then, no problem. He usually has business to do in Manhattan anyway, and sometimes lets me come along with him. I think I can get him to drop me off at your place for a day."

That was the last thing Tony wanted to hear. "I don't know," he replied, speaking slowly. "I don't think my mom wants me to have friends over."

"Can't we just go hang out in Forest Park or something? We wouldn't have to spend the day at your house. My dad could just drop me off there."

"Well . . ."

"Besides, we can invite someone else along too."

"Who?" Who lived close enough to join them?

"Sheryl." Andrew smiled. "I've seen the way you look at her. You like her, don't you?"

"No," Tony lied. He felt pained.

"I know! Let me go ask her now! We can try to get together this weekend!" Andrew jumped up and started shouting Sheryl's name.

"No! Andrew, please don't!" Tony started to cry.

Andrew sat back down. "Howard, what's wrong? I'm just suggesting a little friendly get-together."

"We can't get together at my house. We *can't*."

"Why not?"

Tony thought hard. He liked Andrew, and he knew that Andrew liked him. They hung out together almost every recess, and usually worked together when Miss Ellis made everyone find partners for school projects. Surely Tony could trust him, couldn't he?

Besides, he still felt very bad about lying. No matter how much he wanted to be here, no matter how much Miss Ellis said he had a right to be here, it still bothered him. Perhaps if someone else knew, someone like Andrew, it would make him feel better. After all, Andrew liked him. Surely Andrew would keep the secret.

And, come to think of it, there was no way Andrew would tell anyone. If he did, his father would find out about the time Andrew was careless about his spex.

"Howard? Why not?"

A deep breath, then: "Because my name's not Howard. It's Tony."

Two days later, on Friday afternoon, Miss Ellis asked Tony to stay after school so they could have a private talk. After all the other students jacked out, she asked, "Tony? I notice that you and Andrew don't seem to be getting along as well as you used to. Is there a reason for this?"

Tony squirmed in his seat. Miss Ellis wasn't smiling. "Uh, no, Miss Ellis."

"Are you sure?"

He remained silent for what seemed like a minute.

"Tony, did you tell Andrew about our little arrangement?"

He didn't say a word. He couldn't; his throat was choked with fear.

"Tony? Did you tell Andrew?"

He croaked out a whisper. "Yes, Miss Ellis. I *had* to."

She sighed. "Tony, I was afraid of this. You shouldn't have told him."

"But Miss Ellis, he wanted to come over and visit me. I couldn't let him. I had to tell him why; I wasn't about to lie to him."

She smiled bitterly. "No, I guess not. Tony, I applaud your honesty, but this afternoon you and I are going to have to face Mr. Drummond."

"Mr. Drummond? Do you mean Andrew actually told his father?"

"Yes, and it gets worse. Mr. Drummond is a lawyer, and he's on the board of trustees of the telepresence school program. Do you know what that means?"

"No, I don't."

"It means that he's one of the people who makes policies for the school. He makes decisions on how money is spent to keep the school operating. And I don't think he wants to see us because he agrees with how we're spending the school's money."

"I'm sorry, Miss Ellis. I didn't mean to get you into trouble."

"It's all right, Tony. In a way, your honesty makes me proud. But—" she pushed a button and a clock appeared on the screen, "—we have only half an hour until Mr. Drummond jacks in to talk with us. I suggest you jack out for that time and talk to your mother; let her know what's going on. Then come back."

"Can Mom come too?"

Miss Ellis looked at Tony sadly. "I'm afraid not, Tony. You only have one set of spex at home, and Mr. Drummond wants to see you, not your mother. But don't worry. I'll be here too."

Tony had a hard time telling his mother about what had happened. He was worried that she would be very angry at him for ruining his chances of attending a good school. Fortunately, her attitude had been similar to his teacher's.

"We'll figure something out, Tony, we always have," she said while hugging him tightly. "You just go back and talk to Mr. Drummond. Maybe you can make him change his mind about you. Show him what a good boy you are."

Tony jacked in, for what he thought might be the last time, and was back in the classroom with Miss Ellis. She was talking to Mr. Drummond.

At the sound of the buzz signaling Tony's arrival, the two adults turned to face him.

"So here's the young man," said Mr. Drummond gruffly. Tony took a good, long look at Mr. Drummond, and tried not to seem afraid. Mr. Drummond towered over Tony impressively. His hair was thick and gray, and he wore an elaborate suit with a vest and chain. Tony also noticed that Mr. Drummond was sporting a pair of metal frame glasses, which didn't make sense to him. In real life, after all, Mr. Drummond had to be wearing a pair of spex, so having his image wear glasses had to be a personal choice.

Tony almost laughed at that—*how silly of Andrew's father to have his image wear glasses!*—but he bit off the laugh quickly. *Mr. Drummond's glasses probably mean as much to him as my skin color means to me.*

Tony greeted him solemnly. Mr. Drummond returned the greeting with an embarrassed smile and turned back to Miss Ellis.

"As much as you may like the boy, it's unfair to the rest of us to keep him enrolled at this school. Your little billing stunt is grounds for dismissal, you know."

"Yes, I know. But, Mr. Drummond, if you knew what Tony had to face each day in a regular school—"

"That is not the issue here. I understand what Tony has to deal with at his local school. But look at what his presence does to our own resources." He tapped at the air and a sheet of figures appeared on the screenboard.

"The fact that you tried to spread the expense out to everyone is commendable, Miss Ellis, but it's still patently unfair to those families who are just barely able to send their children to telepresence school. If you look at these records, you can clearly see that some families are about to receive bills that may only be slightly higher than expected—but still higher. Did you honestly expect that no one would take notice?"

Miss Ellis turned to look at Tony. "I hoped," she said.

"Well, I'm afraid it's not possible. The money simply doesn't exist. The school cannot afford to keep him here."

"He's one of the best students in the school. Is there nothing we can do for him?"

Mr. Drummond sighed. "What about all the other Tonys out there? We'd be unfair to all of *them* if we favored just one particular student. This is a private institution, not a public one. It's completely supported by the families, and quite a few of us are stretched to the limit. I'm sorry."

"I knew you had to be rich to attend," Tony heard himself say.

Mr. Drummond frowned at Tony. "Tony, to you we may seem rich, but believe me, we're just getting by. Perhaps we don't find it as difficult to live as you do, but we honestly can't afford to keep you here."

He turned back to Miss Ellis. "We'll have to make arrangements to retrieve the simulator and the spex. I have to go now; I have a trustees meeting to attend." He tapped his earpiece and disappeared, leaving Tony and Miss Ellis alone in the classroom.

"I guess I won't be able to stay, then." Tony said. "But I don't want to go back to my old school." He started to cry.

"Tony, don't cry. Listen to me. There is a way out."

The following Monday afternoon, Tony took the subway down to Greenwich Village. He had to show a pass at 96th Street in order to continue under the fence, but Miss Ellis had arranged everything.

He went to the address Miss Ellis had given him, a brownstone on West 10th Street, and rang the doorbell. A black woman opened the door. She had a thick red scar seared across her right cheek.

Tony stammered. "I'm sorry, I'm looking for Miss Ellis. I must have the wrong place." He started to back down the steps.

"It's okay, Tony, this is my house."

Tony stared at her, afraid to enter. The voice was right, but . . .

She laughed. "It's me, Tony. Come on in."

Tony hesitated, then followed her into the house. "I'm sorry, Miss Ellis, it's just that—"

"I understand. I've set up a classroom in back."

They entered a small room with a tiny green blackboard in one corner and two small desks. Written on the board with actual chalk were the words, "Welcome, Tony." Sitting on the desks were notebooks and textbooks. They looked old and worn, but also loved.

Tony looked at Miss Ellis and smiled. She smiled back. Even with the scar, she was the most beautiful sight in the world. "Well, let's get started," she said. "I told you things would be different."

INTRODUCTION TO "FIRST CONTACT INC."

by Julie E. Czerneda

My first published short story came about through a combination of right place, right time, and a stunning amount of innocence. The right place was the World Fantasy convention, where a good friend and I had an appointment to meet the famous Martin H. Greenberg to pitch our anthology idea. The right time? While the anthology didn't go any farther than concept, Marty and Larry (Segriff) were gracious enough to ask me to submit a story to their upcoming anthology, *First Contact*.

By the end of next week.

The innocence? Blissfully unaware of the rarity of being asked, as an unpublished unknown, to submit to one of these anthologies, I went home to Canada, wrote this story, and had it back to them in four days. It wasn't until I announced the sale with delight and people around me gasped "to a GREENBERG??!! anthology," that some hint of the enormity of what I'd done trickled into my consciousness. Fortunately, by then it was too late to panic. Rejoice, yes!

"First Contact Inc." turned out to be not only my first published short story, but my first published fiction. I'd sold my debut novel, *A Thousand Words for Stranger*, to DAW Books the day before I learned I'd sold this story. It confused many of my relatives when I tried to explain the distinction, although the confusion may have had something to do with my jumping up and down with joy at the time. It didn't exactly help matters when the anthology came out several months before the book. Suffice to say there are still a few booksellers scratching their heads over the Czerneda/Starink Store Invasions of 1997.

What do I think about this story now? I'm very happy with it. It was fun to write, while giving my somewhat muddled view—call it optimistic pragmatism—about "first contact." I believe we can't help but react on an individual level, with personal and possibly profound consequences. However, as a species, I suspect we'll be astonished, for about a day, then simply absorb the different as another part of ourselves and go on with life. Human beings are amazing creatures that way.

Look at me. Right place, right time, and a dose of innocence. Thank you, Marty and Larry, for taking that chance on an unknown. Personally, I'm still astonished, but that hasn't stopped me going on to write science fiction ever since.

FIRST CONTACT INC.

by Julie E. Czerneda

FIRST Contact Custom Simulation PC91-Base Borden © First Contact Inc. Licensed for military use only.

Humanity's big moment. And a moment was how long it lasted.

They'd run. Lt. Courtland—the Ironman himself—had been the first to break, flinging from him the state-of-the-art translator they'd brought to this meeting place with such care, his boots driving deep into the mud with each stride so that he lurched from side to side in an agonizing effort to put distance between himself and It.

Lt. Desroches had hesitated a second longer, staring into the writhing mass of filaments as if somehow this would help her find a point of correspondence, a suggestion of a face. Then she shuddered and whirled to follow Courtland.

Lt. Smith, the one who'd barely made the final cut for this mission, the one considered the weakest link, remained the longest. This had more to do with his complete conviction that his legs wouldn't obey him than any desire to stay within reach of that thing. His paralysis left him with the alien's first tentative reach in his direction.

"So I tell the Colonel: You pick the partner; we just do the music."

Nance's pale eyes gleamed through her ragged fringe of bangs. "And what did he say to that?" Her fingers continued to search for a disk among the piles of Post-it-coated pages layered on her desk. The keyboard balanced on her lap shifted with every movement as though trying to save itself from falling to the floor and being lost among even more piles of journals and clippings. For a company listed among the top five software producers, the office of its CEO and resident genius looked a great deal more like a newsroom from the early fifties than the site of executive splendor.

Henry Fergus, graphics whiz and sales rep, when he wasn't fussing over hardware, dropped his voice into a fair imitation of Colonel Dunwithy's growl. "Your so-called music sent three of my best officers into therapy! Why should I pay for that?"

"To which you said . . ."

Henry flopped into the swivel chair that doubled as a printer stand on the odd occasions when they needed hard copy. "You know what I said." Two fingers tugged a folded check from his pocket. "You pay for it, because it worked."

Nance, Dr. Nancy Vzcinza to those who were not her friends, pushed her hair out of her eyes for a moment. "Henry. Driving people crazy is *not* what we do here."

"No?"

"No. They do that all by themselves." She found the disk she was after and dropped it into the drive, fingers now jabbing at keys. Henry glanced around in vain for the mouse. She'd lost it again, he bet, or was using it as a foot pedal. "We just . . ." tap, tap, ". . . illustrate . . ." tap, tap, tap, ". . . the circumstances." Tap.

He kicked off his shoes, thinking nostalgically of the days not long ago when he'd made all his sales calls in sandals. Even better, when most of his business contacts had been over the vidphone. He'd really loved putting on that shirt, tie, and jacket over his bike shorts. Pants and dress shoes. The cost of success.

"So what's up?"

She looked up from the screen as though startled to still find him there. Henry was used to that. He blanked out the world himself when there was a glitch to track down. "Last minute upgrade for the new theme park in Australia."

He whistled. "Way to make those bucks. We can retire soon." Which was a joke. Nance had no clearer concept of how much the company—and they—were worth these days than he did. There were people on the next floor who kept track; annoying people in suits who drove better cars than he did and who routinely forgot to tell new staff that he and Nance paid their salaries. That always messed up the lunch-hour softball games.

And retire? Just when they could at last actually own the best systems for themselves? Just when they could do what they loved doing all day long? Being paid for it was, was—

"Convenient."

"Pardon?"

Nance looked innocent. "Convenient that the park wants this particular upgrade. I've been wanting to play with it a bit more."

Henry winced. Nance's idea of playing usually involved roping him and anyone else still breathing into the VR chamber at ungodly hours. "What did you have in mind?" he sighed, slipping down into a more comfortable slouch—interested despite the likely unpleasant consequence to his own workload.

First Contact Custom Simulation DC101-Smithers © First Contact Inc. Licensed for home experience only.

Dark red blood settled into the star-shaped cracks in the windshield, forming a network of pleasing regularity. Mildred Smithers, grandmother of three and leading voice in the Real Goldies Choir, shut off the still-racing engine of her car with a satisfied nod. "Gotcha again, you bastard," she said primly, glancing around as if to reassure herself that this descent into rough language had been safely unnoticed. But she was alone, of course.

She pushed up her bifocals to better see the face of her watch. Not bad. Shaved at least a minute off her response time. Practice makes perfect, as she always reminded her good-for-nothing son-in-law. For a moment she considered the lifeless form draped over what was left of the hood of her car. Pity you couldn't buy the same experience a little closer to home, she thought. Then again, the whole point of the exercise was to be ready to act—something she knew full well her family would depend on her to do. "When you get here," she promised the tentacled being her driving skill had shattered into two equal halves, "Mildred Smithers will be ready."

The next morning, Henry poked his head into Nance's office. Nothing appeared to have changed, unless you counted the accumulation of dead leaves under the plant cowering on the windowsill. "How's the Aussie upgrade?"

There was an incoherent grumble from behind the monitor. He used his knuckles to sound a drumroll on the doorframe. "Made a coffee run."

Half a face showed, the one eye looking wistful. "Bagels?"

"With blueberry cream cheese."

The eye blinked slowly. "I hope Meaghan appreciates you."

Henry, unable to find a clear surface for his offering, chose the most stable pile of paper and set the tray down with care. "She appreciates me. It's the rest of my family that has doubts."

Nance popped the lid from one of the coffees, blew away the steam, and took a huge swallow, looking as though the caffeine was heading straight to her bloodstream. Henry was convinced her mouth had an asbestos lining. "So how's the sim?" he persisted. "Mustafa said you've been on it all night."

She gave him a condescending look over a mouthful of cheese-drifted bagel. "How would he know? Mustafa's idea of getting in early is anytime after the traffic's died down on the freeway." Another gulp of coffee. "It's weird."

His eyes went to the wall unit behind Nance's chair, loaded with dusty jars of pickled insects and mollusks, interspersed with museum-quality replica skulls of various mammals, and tied bundles of bird feet. Fortunately, the cleaning staff had insisted the eyeball collection go home, despite Nance's protests about the importance of biological reality to her simulations. "Weird how?"

Nance stood up, stretching with a twisting motion that made audible cracks. "They keep adding to the specs." She handed him a set of faxes clipped together with a clothespin Santa her niece had made last year. Nance kept everything.

"Bit late for this many changes. Park opens the day after tomorrow." Henry started leafing through the pages. Each contained one minor requested change. There must have been about twenty, sent at roughly equal intervals over the past day and night. "You've told them modifications on the fly like these are extra, I hope."

Head half inside a sweater, Nance muttered darkly, "I told them to stop it after the first two. I hate being interrupted. But they wouldn't." She pushed her head out and glared fiercely at Henry. "Not to mention that what they're asking for is silly."

"Silly." Henry looked more closely at the top page and read aloud, "The pupil of each eye must be an unreflective black, not luminous orange." The next page, "Four appendages in total, mobile at a sequence of six joints." He tried not to grin. "They are being quite specific. Someone's had a nightmare lately."

Nance dropped back into her seat. "I'll give them nightmares."

First Contact Custom Simulation PC225-Fernandez © First Contact Inc. Licensed for home experience only.

He wasn't sure what had disturbed his sleep. It was an older building; pipes and joists had a tendency to be musical in changing weather. But that wasn't it this time.

Juan sat up, trying to listen more carefully. There. A scraping sound. From outside. He yawned and lay back down. The old elm out front was wide enough to kiss the bricks with an east wind. He'd remind the super about having it trimmed at the next tenants' meeting.

Snick. Skitter, skitter.

That wasn't the tree! Juan had his feet on the cold floor this time, hand racing for the light by his bed. Sounded like a cockroach convention. He hit the switch and found himself facing what he'd never even dreamed of. . . .

Equally startled, his visitor scampered from the now-open patio doors to the top of his bureau in a ripple of reflective scales.

For a seeming eternity, the only sound was a sigh of wind through the doors and Juan's heart hammering in his ears. Then the creature shivered, a motion that made the plates covering its gaunt body touch together with a faint bell-like tinkle. It had eyes, two large and one smaller, centered on a triangular head. Around its neck was a wreath made of autumn leaves.

Juan reached slowly for the phone at his bedside. When he brought it to his ear, there was a soft voice already speaking to him. The creature tilted its head and settled more comfortably on the bureau.

"Juan Fernandez," whispered the soft voice. "I have chosen you to contact first of all of your kind. Your music has touched even the stars. Play for me and let there be peace between us."

Numbly, his eyes never leaving his visitor, Juan put down the phone and reached for the saxophone on its stand beside his bed. He'd always known he'd make it big one day—not necessarily this big—but big.

"What's the original design base?"

"Standard PC30, peaceful contact following initial suspicion, overtones of economic congruence of mutual benefit. Nothing flashy." Nance sent the fifteenth paper airplane of the hour soaring overhead. "Not until they started this last minute nonsense."

Henry caught it before it hit his ear and unfolded the paper to read the request. "Strands of keratin 30 cm long to be attached behind each auditory organ?"

Nance raised her eyebrow. "We are definitely dealing with someone who knows their biology—if not how to stay within a budget. Hair, Henry. They want me to put hair on its head."

First Contact Custom Simulation FC 1301-Grant, R. © First Contact Inc. Licensed for home experience only.

There was no place left to hide, Roger decided grimly, his bike sucking fumes as it coasted off the deserted highway. He could stand and fight here and now—or die without ever seeing the face of his enemy. Funny, he hadn't imagined death would come as a cliché.

Had it only been yesterday? The aliens had been so well prepared, their technology so superior. The only wonder was that crumbs of humanity like himself still existed on the planet. A crumb. What a joke on the world that he had lasted hours after the rest were obliterated.

There was a whistle in the distance, the sound piercing and ominous as though it could summon hell's demons to chase him. And weren't they, despite their appearance of being only machines? He'd watched the trackers demolish a city block of apartments—an economical way of dealing with the vermin inside. He'd known better than to hide in the subways, too, having witnessed yet another set of machines burrowing into the streets, somehow fully aware of every crack that still harbored humankind. Roger no longer remembered how he escaped. There were too many other images in the way.

Another whistle, this time an answer from the direction he'd vaguely hoped might be away from Them. Roger considered his surroundings: the once-blue sky smudged by the smoke from the city, the highway boiled away in places where cars had been targets, the landscape pitted and ruined overnight. He reached into the saddlebag of his bike and pulled out the gun he knew was there. Would he have the courage to end it for himself this time? Or would he have to wait for the mercy of the aliens to make it stop?

"Good morning, fellow geniuses!" The door flew open as if propelled by a hurricane. "Have you started celebrating without me?"

Mustafa, a man who rarely smiled before noon and then required an excuse to make the effort, was beaming from ear to ear. Henry and Nance traded knowing glances. "Cracked the blackjack table?" Nance asked.

"Much better," Mustafa announced. He pointed one pudgy finger at them and shook it. "You didn't check your mail again. When are you going—"

Henry cut short what promised to be the usual diatribe about corporate responsibilities and other nonsense that had invaded their lives since home simulation machines had become the rage—with First Contact Inc. already poised for success with its custom VRs. "Tell us what we need to know, o keeper of the secret."

"Guess who's opening the Aussie theme park."

Nance scowled, which widened Mustafa's smile even farther. "Am I supposed to care?" she growled. "Some rock star or other."

Henry tsk-tsked. "You never think about sales. So who, Mustafa? Must be a good one to make you drool."

"The President."

Nance's head came around from its hiding place behind her monitor. Henry swallowed hard and managed what he hoped was a nonchalant, "Pardon?" that cracked partway through the middle. He tried again. "Which President?"

Mustafa positively glowed. "*The* President. You know. The first one to win a majority from every country."

"President Polemski. *He's* going to open the park."

"Gets better, compadres. The Pres is apparently a fan of your work, Nance. He's going to be the first person to try your latest and greatest First Contact sim."

Henry and Nance dived for the pile of pages in the wastebasket, Henry winning by an arm's length. "No wonder you couldn't track down the source with the Aussies," he gasped, trying to smooth the abused paper into order. "These must be straight from his office."

"Whoa, there," Nance interjected uneasily. "That's a pretty big guess, Henry."

He shook his head, holding up the pages. "What time exactly did the President's office announce this?"

Mustafa looked from one to the other of his bosses, his satisfied look fading into puzzled concern as he saw the expressions on their faces. "At the nine A.M. press conference yesterday. I e'd you guys when I found out. Why?"

Nance took the sheaf of faxes-turned-airplanes from Henry. She found the first one. It was dated yesterday, 9:30 A.M. Their eyes met. "I think I'd better input every one of these after all."

Henry nodded slowly. "And I think we'd better have a look before it goes out."

First Contact Custom Simulation PC 30mod352a-Australia's Down Under Theme Park Corporation © First Contact Inc. Licensed for public on-location viewing only. Test run.

Until today, he'd enjoyed flying; sympathetic but unable to understand why so many of his aides became white-knuckled with every air pocket. This flight was different. He wasn't sure whether his newfound anxiety stemmed from being the only living thing on board or his destination. Likely both. He turned from the window and switched on the recorded briefing from his aides for the third time. The familiar voices were reassuring, edged though they were with unfamiliar tension.

The arrangements had been made using numerical expressions that both sides understood. There was some negotiation required regarding the location of that critical first meeting.

The home world was not as wet as that of the guest. And beauty was important. The meeting would be carried live on both planets. A good first impression would do wonders for the ultimate response from the public.

Yet, despite concern and some honest fear of the unknown, there was goodwill. There was a sense of inevitability, too—that events would unfold regardless of the careful planning of governments. All that remained was the moment when strangers met.

He'd studied the pictures, but nothing truly prepared one for such an encounter. Aides had informed him of what they understood to be appropriate alien protocol. No weapons, at least none in sight, was a reassuring common factor. Gifts might be misconstrued at this earliest point; who knew what values they shared or didn't? What to wear—best to err on the side of formality; no one liked to be slighted. And much of what transpired was meant purely for the viewers. His people had definite expectations of him, if not of the one he met.

They'd chosen a beach on an isolated, uninhabited island, large enough for automated transports to land. He set the controls as the techs had instructed in order to set up the transmission and recording equipment. Each, visitor and host, had a designated half of the landmass for their preparations. The island was blessed with a central lagoon lovely by any standard. Its beach was the designated meeting site. It could be reached by either representative in a short walk.

He drew in a last deep breath of the salt-scented air, took one last look at the technology that was his only link to his own kind, and prepared to make history.

"Stop." Henry hit the kill switch on the simulation and looked at Nance and Mustafa. "This is ordinary. It's dull. Some nice work on the scenery, but face it. First Contact Inc. makes its money on custom sims real enough to make you wet your drawers. Any one of our competitors could do better than this."

Nance stopped him just by raising her eyebrows. "We haven't reached the climax, Henry. And that's where most of the changes were made. Shall we?"

Henry muttered something to himself, but restarted the sim.

*　　　*　　　*

He drew in a last deep breath of the salt-scented air, took one last look at the technology that was his only link to his own kind, and prepared to make history.

The walk was too short. World leader or not, there was something inherently terrifying about this meeting, something that threatened his very grasp upon reality. Before panic could truly overwhelm his intentions, it was too late. There was the Other.

The Other was strangeness given life. The body shape was roughly cylindrical, with appendages located with reasonable symmetry. Clothing covered many of the important details, but he knew from his aides that the appendages had a remarkable range of movement. The body was topped by a short stalk that in turn supported a round cranial mass. Keratin strands attached behind each auditory organ tossed in the wind.

Some sort of exudate coated the rest of the cranial mass. It glistened in the warm sun and the Other used one appendage to spread the exudate over the keratin strands in what looked to be a reflex. Just in case, he mimicked the gesture as best he could. The openings on the front portion of the cranial mass changed position almost at once. Startled, he moved back a bit. The Other spread its appendages in what seemed a peaceful gesture.

His people were watching. He gathered himself, then moved forward slowly. The Other echoed his movement until they were close enough to touch. He held out his—

"Stop!" This time it was Nance's decision.

"Holy Mother of Mainframes," Henry breathed, not surprised to feel himself shaking. "We just made contact with the President." The other two looked just as shocked, then Nance began to chuckle, a deep throaty sound so contagious Henry found himself laughing suddenly, too.

"I don't see what's funny," Mustafa said, his complexion as pale as it could get.

Nance popped the sim's cartridge out of the player and held it up reverently. "Don't you get it? These last changes didn't come from the Australians."

"Of course not, they came from the President. But why would Polemski want to meet—himself?" The words came more and more slowly. Mustafa's eyes glazed over and he sat down on the floor. "Oh, my."

Henry nodded, not too sure on his feet either. He took the cartridge from Nance and stared at it. "Looks like we have a new customer for First Contact Inc."

Nance's expression was the same one she'd had when they'd delivered the quad photon storage system for her computer—a combination of worship and glee. "I'd better make sure this gets sent out immediately. The customer may want to run it a few times to get it right."

They all glanced up at the ceiling. "Shouldn't we tell someone?" Mustafa whispered.

Nance held out her hand and Henry dropped the cartridge into it. "Well, if you can think of someone who'd believe us, I'll give it a shot." She paused and swept her bangs out of her eyes. "You realize we're all out of a job in two days. First Contact Inc. will be definitely redundant once it really happens."

Henry thought happily of shorts and sandals. "I've been telling you we should be doing more historicals. And westerns. I've always wanted to do westerns."

"Westerns," Nance grumbled, leading the way out of the VR chamber. "Pirates, maybe."

As they went down the corridor, Mustafa's voice trailed behind. "What about the new guys? They already like our stuff."

ABOUT THE AUTHORS

Betty Dehardit is the daughter of Murray Leinster.

Murray Leinster (1896-1975) was the pseudonym for William Fitzgerald Jenkins, a consummate professional who wrote for a wide number of venues during his varied career. Although he wrote more than forty novels during his fifty-year career, it is for his short fiction, including stories such as "The Lonely Planet," "First Contact," and "Sidewise in Time" that he is best remembered. Fascinated with the idea of alternatives to reality as we or his protagonists know it, he pioneered the concept of the multiple points along one time continuum, or the simple concept of parallel worlds. Well-regarded in the science fiction community, he was the Guest of Honor at the 21st World Science Fiction convention in 1963.

L. Sprague de Camp (1907-2000) began his writing career in the 1930s, and has more than three dozen novels, dozens of short stories, and many nonfiction works to show for his efforts. Known early on for his space opera novels, he was first critically and popularly recognized for his novel *Lest Darkness Fall*, about one man's attempt to change history during the Roman Empire. In his wide-ranging career he has written everything from fantasy (*The Incompleat Enchanter* series) to Conan pastiches, revising and publishing Robert E. Howard's unfinished works in the collection *Tales of Conan*, to books on writing science fiction (*Science-Fiction Handbook*). He also wrote many excellent nonfiction books on topics that varied from science to the Scopes trial. He married Catherine A. Crook in 1939, and they remained together for more than sixty years, until her death in 2000.

Anne McCaffrey has been writing science fiction for nearly half a century and published her first novel, *Restoree*, in 1967. She won acclaim for her third novel *The Ship Who Sang*, an influential story of human-machine interface written well before the cyberpunk movement, but is renowned for her bestselling

Pern novels, introduced in her Hugo Award-winning story "Weyr Search" and Nebula Award-winning story "Dragon Rider" in 1968. The Pern books, which are the chronicle of an Earth colony that is linked symbiotically to a native race of sentient dragons, number more than a dozen, including *The Dragonriders of Pern* trilogy, *The White Dragon* and *The Dolphins of Pern*. They are complemented by a trio of young adult novels —*Dragonsong, Dragonsinger* and *Dragondrums*— set in the same world, as well as the graphic novel rendering, *Dragonflight*. McCaffrey has been praised for her strong female characters, particularly in the Rowan sequence (*The Rowan, Damia, The Tower and the Hive*). She is also the author of *To Ride Pegasus* and *Pegasus in Flight*, a duo concerned with future psychic sleuths, and the Ireta books set on Dinosaur Planet. Her short fiction has been collected in *Get Off the Unicorn*, and she has edited the anthologies *Alchemy and Academe* and, with Elizabeth Ann Scarborough, *Space Opera*.

Hal Clement's first novel, *Needle* was published in 1950, and he has written carefully extrapolated, fully realized novels of alien worlds and detailed hard science fiction ever since. Through such novels as *Mission of Gravity, Ocean on Top*, and *The Nitrogen Fix*, his humans, and more importantly his aliens, remain true to their desires and wants, and their evolution as well. Ever since his first story, he has also written excellent shorter fiction, the best of which has been collected in *The Best of Hal Clement*.

Sir Arthur C. Clarke's lengthy publishing credentials include articles in mid-century scientific journals that laid the groundwork for development of the telecommunications satellite. Among his many influential works of science fiction are the visionary novel of man's future in the universe, *Childhood's End*, and the now legendary film and fiction that grew out of its concepts: *2001: A Space Odyssey, 2010: Odyssey Two, 2061: Odyssey Three*, and *3001: Final Odyssey*. Clarke is regarded as one of the masters of hard science fiction, and his novels *A Prelude to Space, A Fall of Moondust*, and *The Fountains of Paradise* have all been praised for their meticulous scientific accuracy. At the same time, he has explored the metaphysical and cosmological implications of science and space exploration in such works as the Hugo and Nebula award-winning novel *A Rendezvous with Rama*, and the oft-reprinted title story of *The Nine Billion Names of God*, one of the many collections of his short fiction which include *Reach for Tomorrow, Tales from the White Hart, The Other Side of the Sky, Earthlight*, and *Tales of Ten Worlds*.

As a small boy, Gene Wolfe says he used to hide behind the candy case in the Richmond Pharmacy to read the pulps — and in a sense, he says, he has never come out. He's written "No Planets Strike," which was nominated for a Hugo, plus a couple of hundred other stories. Also some books, he says with grand understatement, including *Operation Ares, The Fifth Head of Cerberus* and *Shadow & Claw*. The most recent is *Exodus From The Long Sun* . . . part of *The Book Of The Long Sun*, a tetrology.

Barry N. Malzberg is a seminal figure in contemporary fiction, and not just because he's written so much of it. In addition to his fiction, he's also written some of the most perceptive and engaging commentary on the craft of fiction and how it's practiced in these turbulent times. Though known primarily as a science fiction author, Malzberg's best novel is a powerful, unforgettable book about a hack writer's mental and spiritual breakdown titled *Herovit's World*. It proves that commercial fiction can also be true art. *Night Screams, Acts of Mercy, The Running of Beasts* (all with Bill Pronzini) are just a few of his other titles. He has been honored with the John Campbell Memorial award (1973) and the Locus award (1983).

George R. R. Martin's varied output includes horror, fantasy, and science fiction and has earned him both multiple Hugo and Nebula awards as well as a Bram Stoker award from the Horror Writers' Association. His science fiction novels include *Dying of Light* and, with Lisa Tuttle, *Windhaven*. Martin has written some of the best novella-length science fiction in the past two decades, including the award-winning "Sandkings," and "Nightflyers," which was adapted for the screen in 1987.

Much of his best writing is collected in *A Song for Lya and Other Stories, Songs of Stars and Shadows, Sandkings, Songs the Dead Men Sing. Tuf Voyaging,* and *Portraits of His Children.* His horror novels include the period vampire masterpiece *Fevre Dream* and *The Armageddon Rag,* an evocative glimpse at the dark side of the '60s counterculture considered one of the top rock-and-roll novels of all time. Martin has written for a number of television series, including the new *Twilight Zone* series, and edited fifteen volumes of the *Wild Cards* series of shared-world anthologies.

Howard Waldrop fuses such diverse elements as alternate history, UFOs, and rock and roll into finely researched and detailed stories unlike anything else being written today. He primarily writes short stories, which have been collected in anthologies such as *Howard Who?: Twelve Outstanding Stories of Speculative Fiction.* His novels include *A Dozen Tough Jobs,* in which the Twelve Labors of Hercules is recast in Mississippi in the 1920s. A winner of the Nebula and World Fantasy awards, he lives in Washington.

Although best known for his Nebula and Hugo award-winning science fiction novels *Ender's Game* and *Speaker for the Dead,* Orson Scott Card is also an accomplished fantasy and horror writer. Among his other achievements are two Locus awards, a Hugo award for nonfiction, and a World Fantasy award. Currently he is working on the *Tales of Alvin Maker* series, which chronicles the history of an alternate nineteenth century America where magic works. The *Alvin Maker* series, like the majority of his work, deals with messianic characters and their influence on the world around them. His short fiction has been collected in the anthology *Maps in a Mirror.*

Jack McDevitt has been a Philadelphia cabbie, a naval officer, an English teacher, a customs officer, and a motivational trainer. During his years as a teacher, McDevitt also directed high school theater groups, appearing (like Hitchcock) in cameos. He was a native in *South Pacific* and a Nazi bodyguard in *The Sound of Music,* but his proudest moment came when he played the corpse in *Arsenic and Old Lace*. His first novel, *The Hercules Text*, was published in the celebrated Ace Specials series under the editorship of Terry Carr. It won the Locus award for best first novel, and the Philip K. Dick Special award. In 1991, his "Ships in the Night" won the $10,000 international novella competition sponsored by the Polytechnical University of Caltalunya. His novel *The Engines of God* was a finalist for the Arthur C. Clarke Award. *Ancient Shores, Moonfall* and *Infinity Beach*, all from HarperCollins, have been on the final Nebula ballot. His most recent novels are *Deepsix* and *Live From Babylon*.

Jerry Oltion has been a gardener, stone mason, carpenter, oil-field worker, forester, land surveyor, rock 'n' roll deejay, printer, proofreader, editor, publisher, computer consultant, movie extra, corporate secretary, and garbage truck driver. For the last twenty years, he has also been a writer. Since the publication of "Much Ado About Nothing," Jerry has had over a hundred short stories published in *Analog, The Magazine of Fantasy & Science Fiction*, and various other magazines and anthologies. He has also published twelve novels (three under the name "Ryan Hughes"). He won the Nebula Award for best novella of 1997, and has been nominated for the Hugo. He lives in Eugene, Oregon, with his wife, Kathy, and the obligatory writer's cat, Ginger.

Lois McMaster Bujold was born in Columbus, Ohio, in 1949. She now resides in Minneapolis. Her first three novels were published by Baen Books in 1986; her fourth, *Falling Free*, won her first Nebula in 1989. The Vorkosigan series includes the Hugo award-winning novel *The Vor Game* (1990), the Hugo and Locus award-winning novels *Barrayar* (1991), and *Mirror Dance* (1994), and the Hugo-and-Nebula winning novella "The Mountains of Mourning" (1989). Her books have been translated into sixteen languages. Her most recent novel is a new fantasy, *The Curse of Chalion*. A fan-run web site, The Bujold Nexus, may be found at *www.dendarii.com*.

Stephen Baxter is the author of twenty science fiction novels and collections and over a hundred published short stories, and his work has won awards in Britain, the U.S., Japan, Germany and elsewhere. His most recent books are *Origin*, the third novel in the Manifold series; a collection in the same series and a novel called *Evolution*.

A challenger of rules since childhood, Catherine Asaro regards those which constrict literary genres with a why-not gleam in her eyes and a multitalented hand. That's why the stories from this Harvard Ph.D. in chemical physics, classical ballet dancer, and owner of Molecudyne draw praise from reviewers and readers of science fiction, romance, action adventure, suspense, and from men and women alike. Her first novel, *Primary Inversion*, created a stir in the science fiction community because she combined romance with hard science fiction. Rather than turning off fans of either genre, the novel earned her readers and high praise in both communities. Among the many awards earned by the Columbia, MD, author of nine novels are the 2002 Nebula Award for Best Novel for *The Quantum Rose*, the National Readers' Choice Award for Best Futuristic Fiction and the Homer Award for Best Novel for *The Veiled Web*; and Romantic Times magazine's Reviewers' Choice Award for Best Science Fiction Novel for *The Radiant Seas*. "Dance in Blue," her first published story, presented here, demonstrates why Catherine was destined to be a favorite among readers everywhere.

Michael A. Burstein was born in New York City in 1970, and attended Hunter College High School in Manhattan. In 1991 he graduated from Harvard College with a degree in physics, and in 1993 he earned a Master's in Physics from Boston University. A graduate of the Clarion Science Fiction and Fantasy Writers' Workshop, in 1997 he won the John W. Campbell Award for Best New Writer. He has since been nominated for several other awards, including the Nebula and Sturgeon awards. From 1998 to 2000, he served as Secretary of Science Fiction and Fantasy Writers of America. He lives with his wife Nomi in the town of Brookline, Massachusetts. When not writing, he is the Science Coordinator K-8 and Middle School Science Teacher at the Rashi School in Newton, Massachusetts.

More information on him and his work can be found on his webpage, www.mabfan.com, or via his electronic newsletter, MABFAN.

Canadian author and John W. Campbell Award finalist Julie E. Czerneda lives in a country cottage with her family. Her novels include *A Thousand Words for Stranger, Beholder's Eye, Ties of Power, Changing Vision, In the Company of Others* and *To Trade the Stars*. She is currently working on *Hidden in Sight*, the next in her Web Shifters series. A former biologist, she has written and edited several textbooks, including *No Limits: Developing Scientific Literacy Using Science Fiction*. Julie recently edited *Space Inc.* with Martin H. Greenberg and is series editor of "Tales from the Wonder Zone," original SF for young readers. Julie is only the second person to win an Aurora Award for both long and short fiction (English) in the same year, for her novel *In the Company of Others* and short story "Left Foot on a Blind Man." More information about Julie and her work may be found at www.czerneda.com.

OTHERLAND

TAD WILLIAMS

"The Otherland books are a major accomplishment."
–Publishers Weekly

"It will captivate you."
–Cinescape

In many ways it is humankind's most stunning achievement. This most exclusive of places is also one of the world's best-kept secrets, but somehow, bit by bit, it is claiming Earth's most valuable resource: its children.

CITY OF GOLDEN SHADOW (Vol. One)
0-88677-763-1

RIVER OF BLUE FIRE (Vol. Two)
0-88677-844-1

MOUNTAIN OF BLACK GLASS (Vol. Three)
0-88677-906-5

SEA OF SILVER LIGHT (Vol. Four)
0-75640-030-9

To Order Call: 1-800-788-6262

DAW 44

CJ Cherryh

EXPLORER

0-7564-0086-4

The *Foreigner* novels introduced readers to the epic story of a lost human colony struggling to survive on the hostile world of the alien atevi. In the final installment to this sequence of this series, can diplomat Bren Cameron, trapped in a distant start system, facing a potentially bellicose alien ship, help prevent interspecies war, when the secretive Pilot's Guild won't even cooperate with their own ship?

Be sure to read the first five books in this action-packed series:

FOREIGNER	*0-88677-637-6*
INVADER	*0-88677-687-2*
INHERITOR	*0-88677-728-3*
PRECURSOR	*0-88677-910-3*
DEFENDER	*0-7564-0020-1*

To Order Call: 1-800-788-6262

Julie E. Czerneda

Web Shifters

"A great adventure following an engaging character across a divertingly varied series of worlds."—*Locus*

Esen is a shapeshifter, one of the last of an ancient race. Only one Human knows her true nature—but those who suspect are determined to destroy her!

BEHOLDER'S EYE
0-88677-818-2
CHANGING VISION
0-88677-815-8

Also by Julie E. Czerneda:

IN THE COMPANY OF OTHERS
0-88677-999-7
"An exhilarating science fiction thriller"—
Romantic Times

To Order Call: 1-800-788-6262

Julie E. Czerneda

THE TRADE PACT UNIVERSE

"Space adventure mixes with romance...a heck of a lot of fun." —*Locus*

Sira holds the answer to the survival of her species, the Clan, within the multi-species Trade Pact. But it will take a Human's courage to show her the way.

A THOUSAND WORDS FOR STRANGER
0- 88677-769-0

TIES OF POWER
0-88677-850-6

TO TRADE THE STARS
0-7564-0075-9

To Order Call: 1-800-788-6262